BY ROBYN CARR

CHELYNNE
THE BLUE FALCON

THE
BLUE FALCON

THE

LUE

FALCON

Robyn Carr

Little, Brown and Company
Boston / Toronto

COPYRIGHT © 1981 BY ROBYN CARR

ALL RIGHTS RESERVED. NO PART OF THIS BOOK MAY BE REPRODUCED IN ANY FORM OR BY ANY ELECTRONIC OR MECHANICAL MEANS IN-CLUDING INFORMATION STORAGE AND RETRIEVAL SYSTEMS WITHOUT PERMISSION IN WRITING FROM THE PUBLISHER, EXCEPT BY A RE-VIEWER WHO MAY QUOTE BRIEF PASSAGES IN A REVIEW.

FIRST EDITION

The translation of Der von Kürenberc's poem "I Trained Myself a Falcon" is by R. W. Barber and appeared in *The Knight and Chivalry* by R. W. Barber. It is reprinted by permission of the translator.

LIBRARY OF CONGRESS CATALOGING IN PUBLICATION DATA
Carr, Robyn.
  The blue falcon.
  I. Title.
PS3553.A76334Q4   813'.54   80-24878
ISBN 0-316-12972-0

RRD

Designed by Susan Windheim

Published simultaneously in Canada
by Little, Brown & Company (Canada) Limited

PRINTED IN THE UNITED STATES OF AMERICA

7008153

For Jim, with love

The author wishes to thank Neva Hoofnagle and
Lowell Stokes for their interest in this work.

FALCONS AND LOVE

I trained myself a falcon through a year's long days.
When he was safely tamed to follow my ways
And his plumage shone golden, painted by my hand,
With powerful wingbeats rising, he sought another land.

Since then I've often seen him, soaring in fair flight,
For on his feet my silken jesses still shine bright
And his plumage gleams with scarlet and with gold.
May God grace lovers and reunite them as of old.

Der von Kürenberc

THE
BLUE FALCON

Prologue

EFORE the sun rose over the tall walls of Anselm Keep, a small figure concealed within the folds of a heavy cloak crept through the streets. The woman kept her hands clutched inside of her wrap, and a basket dangled from her arm. Her head was shrouded, and she glided through the mists more like a spirit than a mortal.

The tinkling of the vespers bell alerted her to slow her pace, and she sank to her knees and crossed herself as the priest passed. She did not glance up at him and he did not look in her direction, but each was profoundly aware of the other. Once he had passed, she was again moving quickly, her head bent and obvious determination guiding her step.

She stopped before a humble shop and tapped impatiently at the door. It opened immediately. A woman of perhaps fifty years and of robust health stood in the portal. "My lady," she greeted her. "Please, come within and sit by the fire."

She entered eagerly, almost before the woman completed the invitation. Once inside, she pushed back the hood of her cloak and her exquisite beauty was revealed. She shook out her thick, dark hair, not yet properly bound for the day, giving away the fact that she had not partaken of her morning grooming rituals, but had come on her errand quickly upon rising. "You knew I was coming," she said. It was not a question.

The room was crowded with spools of fine threads and sewing trivia. Lace hung as if on display, and articles not yet completed were stacked about the simple shop. Near the door that led to the shopkeeper's living quarters there sat a table covered with a rich cloth of scarlet. Upon the cloth rested a stone of crystal, which seemed to twinkle of its own. The lacemaker, Giselle, looked toward it and said, "Your footsteps in your chamber early this morn roused me from my sleep. I knew you were bound here."

Lady Udele turned her attention to the fire to hide the light of impatience that glittered in her emerald-green eyes. She stretched her hands toward the fire, though in truth she was not cold. Indeed, the high flush on her cheeks indicated that she was filled with the warmth of great energy. "Then would you also know why I have come?" she asked without looking at the woman.

Giselle did not answer at once. She let her mind go back over the past. Twenty years ago, Lady Udele had been the youthful bride of Lord Alaric de Corbney. She was directed to Giselle by one of the serving women in the castle. Then her belly was swollen with babe and her eyes had that same excited, almost desperate, light. She was only fourteen years old.

"It must be a son," she had said passionately. "Strong and powerful. He will be a great success and the master of my house when my husband is gone. He will be devoted to me."

Reading in Udele's future that she would bear a son who would be a powerful figure was an easy thing. This son would be all that his father was; Lord Alaric was a high and mighty man. Giselle could see, also, that this son would be skilled in the knightly arts, and his devotion to his parents would be beyond question.

The prediction did not satisfy the lady. Udele insisted on potions and incantations to ensure such a future for the unborn child. Giselle gave her heavily herbed wine and mumbled words that had no meaning, for she was terribly opposed to attempts to alter the future. When the child was born, he was handsome and healthy.

Udele felt great joy and elation in the birth, but she did not see that Conan was the image of his father. To Udele, Alaric was already an old man — thirty-seven — when his first child was born. The young noblewoman had little passion for her aging groom.

Udele turned from the fire and stared at Giselle. "I have heard Sir Conan is home. Is that why you've come?" Giselle asked.

"My lord husband has sent word far and wide that Conan is come. There will be a tournament today. And the knight will no doubt prove himself worthy of his father's boasting."

"You do not fear for Sir Conan's well-being, lady? He is by far the best to ride through the gates of Anselm in many years."

"I do not fear!" Udele snapped. Her face fell. In this humble cottage there was no need for pretense. Although Udele's beauty and vitality were sung throughout this land, here, in the company of only Giselle, she could relax her features and let the lines of years of unhappiness show. Alaric was envied by his peers, for Udele was possibly the most beautiful woman in England, but only Giselle knew that Udele scorned her husband. "If I fear, it is only because my son loves fighting better than anything," she said more calmly.

Giselle felt pity for the great lady. "Come," she bade her. "Sit with me here and give me your hands. I see a proud day ahead for the mother of a great knight."

"I will manage the day," Udele replied. "You must tell me what is ahead for Conan."

"But, madam —"

"I've brought you something," Udele interrupted. She reached into the basket and pulled out a soiled and torn shirt, the type a man would wear under his tunic and mail. Giselle fingered the garment. The many hours of wear, the odor of a man's perspiration and the smell of leather and horses aided her in feeling a closeness with the owner. She knew at once that it belonged to Sir Conan.

Giselle went to sit at the table. With one hand she fondled the linen shirt, and with the other hand resting on the crystal stone, she closed her eyes lightly. He was there then, his image burned into her mind. She smiled, feeling a special fondness for him. She had, after all, predicted his birth and much of his life. Giselle had been the one to suggest the boy be given a merlin, and the child immediately proved his natural ability to handle the bird. Next, he was given a falcon and soon after, many falcons. Even now his shield bore the blue falcon, and one beautiful bird of a deep midnight blue rested more often on Conan's forearm than anyplace else.

It had pleased Udele to see this child excel. She had seen him leave his home at the age of only six to serve as a page to a skilled and seasoned knight, Sir Theodoric. While Lord Alaric certainly approved of the teacher, he would not have sent his son at such an early age. But Udele prodded and pushed, for she had great ambitions for the lad.

Conan learned quickly. He served as a squire and was knighted ahead of his peers. Now, at the age of twenty, Conan's gift for fighting was well known in this part of England. All those qualities — strength, power, loyalty — that Udele had yearned for her firstborn to have were certainly his. Still, she did not see that he was his father's son.

Giselle could see him in her mind's eye, a handsome young man standing taller than his father. His deep blue eyes and full beard drew a sigh from many a maid; the cold glint those same eyes could possess when he took up his sword caused his opponents to shudder. Giselle was one of the few to remember that Lord Alaric's eyes had once held that same powerful and hypnotic quality, for now they were faded and tired, and only in moments of great passion or anger did they light as Conan's did now.

"I can tell you of his greatest moment in the day," Giselle offered without opening her eyes.

"He will fare the tourney well?"

"Certainly," Giselle replied.

"I will rest easy. There is another matter that plagues me," Udele announced. Giselle frowned. She could feel the tension radiating from Lady Udele. "My lord husband insists it is time for Conan to take a bride."

Giselle nodded. Of course Alaric would feel strongly about Conan's marriage. Conan could take some of the burden from his father by managing at least the farthest corners of his lands. He would have time to sire at least one child before King Henry found some battle to fight.

At the moment the prospect of his marriage seemed bright, but Giselle felt the presence of a cloud on this otherwise sunny image.

"Has he brought you a bride?" Giselle asked.

"No. He dallies with his chore."

Giselle smiled faintly as she let the vision of Conan come clearly to mind. "There will be many maidens turning their heads to the Blue Falcon on this day, madam. But none of these, I pray you. Today is not the day for him to choose a bride. I fear he would choose poorly."

"Whom does he love?" Udele asked sharply.

Giselle was not perturbed. She was accustomed to Udele's restlessness. "So many will bid the knight take their colors to the contest, and in the garden of his mind many blossoms abide." She laughed lightly. "Sir Conan has the flesh of woman much upon his mind, but not of one woman. He loves no one so well as his horse and his blade."

"But the time is now! If we are to wait upon his pleasure, I must at least know why —" Udele stopped and saw that Giselle's kind gray eyes were open and locked with her own. "Whom will he choose? The name."

"I dare not give you a name, lady," Giselle said firmly. "I seldom — almost never — see a name. And Conan's life is no longer in your charge."

"You can tell me what I wish to know," Udele said.

"Madam, I must warn you again of dangerous matters."

"But there has never been any danger." She laughed nervously. "You fret too much, Giselle."

"You ask too much, madam," Giselle said, knowing the harm was not so much in the asking. It was the touch of Udele's interference in an otherwise perfect picture in her mind. Left alone, Conan would have his share of problems, but would manage them well, and the overall image showed a content and prosperous man. "You take these gifts of the spirits too lightly."

Udele's expression was closed. Her voice dropped to a lower pitch. "You've played your witch's games with me and you've done as I bade you before. Now you will say me nay?"

"For your own life or for the future of a child in your charge, I can freely tell you what you want to know. But, madam, Conan is a man fully grown. I cannot say too much to another."

Udele looked at the lacemaker closely. "You've given me potions and said witch's words. You would be killed were it known."

The two stared at each other. Giselle's eyes showed wisdom and compassion, not the ability to play games with spirits or impose hexes and curses. Udele's eyes, on the other hand, sparked with life, the green shining like emeralds in her determination to be satisfied.

The history of these two was long and unchanging. Giselle was a woman of gentle manners, helping those in need whenever she could, but using caution and discretion with her special gift. And fearing somewhat this special sight. For twenty years, Udele had intimidated and threatened her when she would balk from her desires.

Giselle many times regretted that first meeting when she had taken pity on the frightened lass wed to Lord Alaric. Unsure and afraid, with the awesome duties of being lady of Anselm, Udele begged aid from the sighted lacemaker. From the time Udele was aware of the potential of this gift, she was intent on securing her future beyond doubt, and always seeing her own will met. If Giselle predicted a lean year for crops, Udele would store more provender than usual. If a heavy tax or tithe lay ahead, Udele would quickly make many purchases for herself.

"Though you would make this difficult for me, I would know. You will be soundly beaten if you do not."

"I will tell you what I can," Giselle said wearily.

Giselle placed her hand again on the crystal and closed her eyes. Her fingertips gently caressed the linen shirt, and through them she let her mind lead her into the future. Again the handsome young knight was in her sight. She searched for a woman in his life, for already she could see there would be one. It was as if she held Conan in the palm of her hand. Alternating between the world as others knew it and the world as she saw it, she spoke to the knight. "So — you will love as passionately as you fight — holding your love with a fierce strength — yielding so much — Ah! Not a portion of your heart — but the whole of yourself. But then nothing else would befit the Falcon — the loyalty and commitment of your love will match your dedication in knighthood. And so you shall be bound — through all eternity."

Udele leaned forward in her chair. Alert, she listened for more.

"She will be his lady fair. Her hair is flaxen and her cheeks flushed with youth. Young — yea, she is young and has not seen full womanhood, but she nears that threshold. I see beauty and courage — forsooth, her courage matches the knight's! A worthy match. But — Sir Conan does not see her yet. Yea, she is there, available to him. When he is ready for her, when his eyes choose to see, she will be under his hand and he will take her. For now, the knight's spirit is moved by other things, but he will have his lady."

Udele's hands were together just under her chin as if in prayer. "And her family?" she questioned softly.

"I see a strong family bond," Giselle said, straining for a vision. "And a strong family. Strong and respected."

Udele nodded. "And wealthy?" she asked.

Giselle's brow was creased. "Beauty and abundance," she said softly. "There is wealth to be had, but what belongs to the lass is modest. Nay, she is not rich, but in her many strengths she is wealthy."

Udele sat back, her mouth slightly open, yet silent. Finally Giselle opened her eyes and looked at her.

"She has no fortune?" Udele questioned with discomfort.

Giselle smiled tolerantly. "Fear not, lady. Conan will never be poor. And what he will attain through marriage to this lass will be modest, true, but not to be ignored. Her dowry will please —"

"Please a poor knight perhaps," Udele said tartly. "My son is among England's finest knights. These lands his father holds, rich and wide! He could easily have a princess!"

"Nay, I think not, madam. Sir Conan does not seek —"

"Ah! And what does he seek?"

Giselle let her gaze drop. "I cannot say, madam, but that the knight proves himself to be honest and chivalrous. I can tell you that he will surely have the respect of his countrymen."

Udele shook her head in obvious discontent. "Respect will not clothe and feed us," she said. "And do you warn me that Conan will choose a simple bride, without regard for our family?"

"I do not see a simple lass, but one nobly bred. And though her family is not as rich as yours, she is not without coin. She will bring Sir Conan much, managing his house with care and —"

"*His* house. It is not his house yet, nor will it be *her* house. And I will not easily stand aside to watch a young lass barely ripe dole out my possessions."

"Madam, if she is his choice —"

"You must tell me how to prevent this. My son must not be so bent to a woman of little means. Not now."

"There is no way to prevent this," Giselle said slowly.

"There must be a way."

Giselle shook her head. "You must not interfere. It would be your ruin and his. Let it be, madam, and rejoice that your son has a future so bright. Forget —"

"Forget," she barked. "Forget my only hope? Forget that at the tender age of three and ten I was given to a man older than my own father and used freely and without tenderness? Forget that I was a child myself when I labored with my son?" Udele shook her head and her eyes burned bright with a rage that almost overwhelmed her. "I cannot forget that I have been chained to serve my lord husband for twenty years! When Conan prospers, I can live as I will and not bend to the whims of a stubborn and foolish old man. I have had to plot and pray for a few extra coins!"

"Lord Alaric has given you much —"

"Alaric throws his gold to an army that does naught but decorate yon wall!" she fairly snarled. "And I have not worked and waited all these years for more of the same from my son!"

"Madam —"

"If you will not help me, I will help myself. But I warn you, one day you will regret your reluctance."

Giselle shook her head sadly. "You will find no success,

my lady, for there is a plan and it is not yours to decide. Conan is bound to her already, the stars in the heavens know this. He will seek her, even in death."

Udele sprang to her feet, knocking over the chair in her haste and anger. Her cloak swirled wide as she spun and reached for the basket on the bench. "I would have some lace," she said coolly. A few coins were dropped onto the table where Giselle sat.

Wearily, the woman rose and carefully drew out some lengths of lace that had been many tedious hours in the making. She spread a half dozen samples across a bench and stood back so that Lady Udele could make her choice.

Udele looked at them blandly, not interested in the lace at all. She let her eyes rise to meet Giselle's and saw that the woman had not changed her mind. Udele would have no help in changing the course of Conan's life. With a furious hiss she snatched up a length of lace and stuffed it into her basket. She whirled and was gone.

Giselle stared for a moment at the door left ajar by the most powerful woman in Anselm. She suddenly felt very tired. Her energy was drained, and it took great effort to walk to the door and close it. She leaned against it and mused aloud, "I could not have known that to entwine my life with yours would create havoc."

In the beginning, Giselle understood the difficulty of Udele's situation. While Alaric was a good and generous man, always fair and just, he was settled into a role of master. He worshiped Udele's beauty and youth, but he also commanded her. She did not easily see the good fortune in having been given to a man such as Alaric. Giselle had expected Udele to mature and in time come to appreciate her incredible good fortune, but that did not come to pass. While Udele served her husband dutifully and played the devoted wife skillfully, it was plain she had never come to love him.

All the years of visits had meshed their minds so completely that when Udele was troubled, Giselle woke from a sound sleep. When Udele was gay, Giselle would feel the energy. And when Udele was enraged, Giselle could not work the intricate patterns of her laces because her hands would shake so severely. Now, without the need of the precious crystal, Giselle could feel the disaster Udele would weave into her son's life.

Giselle moved slowly to the one-room addition to the shop that served as her home. Behind a curtain on a shelf she found the earthen bowls she sought. She reached into one and pulled out some black, brittle twigs. From another she withdrew a pungent-smelling orange powder and from yet another bowl she took a silver, flaky substance. In the palm of one hand she combined the things and moved to the fire. She sprinkled some of the mixture over the embers and the flame sparked. A purple smoke seemed to fill the room. Her eyes closed and she was entranced. She sprinkled more of the mixture over the flame. More smoke filled the room, though the opening in the roof of her small cottage should have allowed the purple cloud easy escape.

"Bring the woman to Sir Conan's eyes with haste," she muttered. Again her fixings were sprinkled into the fire. "Let his eyes fall on her this very day. Move his spirit before his head this once. Put the maid of his choice before his eyes before it is too late."

Within a few moments the room cleared of the colorful smoke, and the lacemaker's eyes opened. She had beseeched some power greater than her own without much confidence. Though her ability to see things to come was clearly recognized in her youth, her ability to alter or hasten the events was never proved to her satisfaction.

Giselle brushed the powder off her hands and moved to a humble pallet. She let her head rest on the fresh straw and fell into a deep and badly needed sleep.

At the tower stairs, the lady of Anselm turned as if by some outside force and looked in the direction of the lace-maker's cottage. In the predawn light, she could see a strange cloud moving through the mists.

"If she has betrayed me," she mumbled, "I will kill her."

PART

I

CHAPTER

1

THE banners flew high over Anselm Keep, as high as the expectations surrounding the tournament. Streamers decorated the lists and pavilions housing knight's armor. Within the great manor all was quiet, for the hour was early.

Chandra Ellard sat upright on her pallet and looked around the dim room. Her sisters slept on, but would be rising soon to the call for the first mass. With great care to be quiet, she stood on the cold stone floor and moved to the window. A slight pull did not open the crude covering, but she fought the stubborn wood, for she was so eager to know the sun had finally risen on this day. She won the battle, and the wooden slats creaked and flew open.

Chandra looked guiltily over her shoulder to see if she had disturbed anyone's sleep. Edwina, her oldest sister, rolled over and pulled the covers more tightly about her. Laine did not stir, but lay flat on her back the way she imagined a nun would sleep. Chandra made a face at her sisters and turned back to the window.

The banners and streamers upon the wall made her heart leap. The soft glow of the sun just creeping over the land was the sight she had longed for. At last! She stretched her arms out the small window, and a smile to make the land shine brighter broke over her face. Her first tournament!

Chandra, the youngest of Sir Medwin's three daughters, had looked forward to such a day for years. King Henry's ban on tournaments had lessened the likelihood that she would ever see one, but Lord Alaric was not so easily discouraged. He said that the fees the knights were paying to participate in this contest would surely cover any fine the king could levy, but it was not likely Henry would bother: his problems in France kept him too busy. And if not for the fact that her father was a close friend to Lord Alaric, they might not be here even now.

The tournament would be grand! Invitations were sent far and near to bring knights and their families, landholders and vassals, barons great and small, priests both pious and unscrupulous, Jewish usurers looking for nobles in dire need of credit, and every interested spectator for miles.

And Sir Conan!

Chandra leaned on her forearms and peered dreamily out the window. It had been a few years at least since she had seen him, but it had not been very long since she had thought about him. Since as early as she could remember, she had looked to him as the one special boy in her life — but he was a boy no more. Now he was a man, and a recently dubbed knight. She sighed deeply, as she hoped he would find her more woman than child.

Her breath caught in her throat as she noticed something over the wall in the direction of the lists. The falcon split his wings and soared into the clear morning air. Down he tumbled, through the mists of early day and then up again, up into the sky, straining his wings and pushing himself farther and farther into the soft satin of blue. With precision he circled, watching the ground below. A whistle, sharp and shrill, caused the bird to break his pattern and disappear behind the wall.

He is there, she thought wildly. There, near the lists, working with his bird.

Chandra turned and scurried toward her pallet, pulling off her shift as she went. She shivered in the crispness of the morning air as it invaded the room through the open window. She thought to shut it before the others were awakened, but too late. Laine was stirring and looking in confusion at Chandra's nakedness.

"Chandra? What are you doing?"

Chandra shrugged and knelt on her pallet to grasp her fresh new shift to pull it on. "It is nearly time for the first mass," she said as casually as she could.

"I have never known you to hurry to mass," Laine grumbled, beginning to rise herself.

Chandra kept her face turned from her older sister so that her sly smile would not show. She moved to a stool in the corner of the small room where her favorite gown had been so carefully laid the night before. Trying not to appear rushed, she pulled the precious gown over her head and smoothed it over her middle and thighs. It was the softest cream, topsewn with green. On the breast a fish had been carefully embroidered. The sleeves were full and flowing, and she pulled the green ribbon tightly under her breasts.

She reached within the deep pocket to be certain the article she treasured was there, and feeling the soft fabric strip within, she patted it confidently. She sat on the stool to fit the small slippers onto her feet and then grabbed up the wimple she would wear on her head.

When her hand touched the door to the small bedchamber, Edwina was just coming awake.

"The window," she moaned. "Who opened the window?"

"Good morningtide, Edwina," Chandra sang cheerily.

"Where are you going? The sun is barely up."

"It is almost time for mass," Chandra said brightly, moving out the door as quickly as she could.

The air was cool and the ground moist. Chandra lifted her skirts and walked briskly, smiling and nodding good morning to those men-at-arms she passed. The smile was quickly returned and with a slight bow, for her manner was gay and her face as bright as a morning star. She saw the falcon again as she neared the lists, and then finally she saw him and her pace slowed abruptly.

She stopped and looked at his back as he stroked his bird. His robes of red and blue accentuated his broadness, and her heart jumped again. The bird suddenly spread his wings and Conan's gauntleted hand responded by moving with the bird. "That will do," he said. The bird moved again and seemed to communicate something to him, for he threw back his head and laughed. With that action she could see the bright smile break the darkness of his beard. "Not now, Mars," he said. "Other things command my attention this morn."

Sir Conan fitted a hood over his bird's head, and Chandra felt sharp disappointment, for she had longed to see him perform. When travelers would pass through her father's hall, they often had heard of or seen Sir Conan. They painted a picture for her with their words, a vision of a man taller than his peers and dark as the night, with bright, sparkling blue eyes and a trained falcon that seemed to respond to his very thoughts.

The bird made no further argument and was put to rest on a perch outside the blue and red pavilion. Conan surveyed the equipment of his profession, stacked neatly against the sides of the tent. Mail, armor, shield and sword shone as they had not shone in years.

Conan picked up a bag of oats to attach to his horse's snout, but Orion seemed to refuse the nourishment and pawed at the turf. Conan whirled to look behind him as if he expected an assassin. The quick action caused Chandra to jump in surprise.

Chandra recovered herself and moved closer, smiling at the frown he wore as he studied her. She dropped into a low curtsy, then rose to meet his suspicious eyes. "Good morningtide, sir knight," she said softly.

Conan's eyes roved over her, devouring the petite form and fresh little face. He looked to her hand and saw her wimple still held there, not covering the long, golden locks that trailed down her back. When his eyes fell upon the fish embroidered on the breast of her gunna, the suspicion vanished from his eyes and he smiled with amusement.

"Damsel, you took me by surprise."

She laughed lightly. "I would have known you anywhere, Conan. I bring you good tidings."

"And early tidings," he chuckled.

"I saw the falcon and I knew it must be you," she told him.

"You have not changed so much after all, my fair Chandra. Still chasing birds in the wood and courting mischief." He raised one dark brow. "Though your appearance has greatly changed, I vow."

Her eyes lit up with happiness that he would even notice the changes in her. "Then, sir knight, am I now a maiden of enough years to give you a token to carry to the contest? I have a small thing."

She pulled a sheer strip of cloth the same color as her gown from her pocket. It had been carefully topsewn with the same green, and a small fish to identify the piece adorned one end of the strip. "I would be honored."

Conan frowned slightly as he took it from her. "It's unseemly for a maid to bring her token to a knight. You are uncommonly bold, Chandra."

Chandra was not insulted by the remark, for she knew she was an unconventional maid and more determined than most. Still, her brows drew together as if in thought. "In truth, I was prepared to offer my token at the tourney, but I was awakened this morn with a great start and knew I must hasten to you with my colors." She shrugged off the uneasy feeling and smiled, mischief sparkling in her eyes. "There will be so many maids waiting with tokens in hand, you would likely have passed me by."

His blue eyes warmed as he looked at her. "Not likely, fair lady," he said, reaching for her hand and placing a courtly kiss on its back.

"You will be too weighted down with gifts to do justice in the lists."

"You overstate my importance here," he said.

Chandra grimaced and then laughed outright. The cocky devil! "In any event," she said quite happily, "I will be the first."

"Do you wish to name yourself as the first then?" he laughed.

"For the moment," she replied. "But never will it be enough." She curtsied briefly and turned to leave him.

"Chandra," he called. When she turned back to him, he simply looked at her. She did not flush or fidget, but stood poised, at ease during his leisurely appraisal. It gave her a feeling of great importance and brought a lightness to her head. The expression on his face went from curiously entranced to pleased and contented. Finally his eyes met hers again, and he held the token up as if presenting it. "I will carry your token and hope to defend it with honor."

"I have no doubts, Conan," she said softly.

She raised a hand briefly, and he imitated the parting gesture. She turned to leave him.

Conan had often felt a sudden rush of excitement when a beautiful maiden was near. He had not, however, experienced much disappointment as they walked away from him. He stood rooted to the ground as Chandra walked away, and though no one could see, the blue of his eyes had warmed in appreciation.

The last time he had seen her, she was a prancing and quite unladylike little girl, a giggling, energetic package of trouble. That glimmer of trouble was still in her eyes, but the rest of her had changed. He could not help noticing the absence of chubby cheeks and the appearance of breasts. And the gentle swing of her skirts as she moved away from him sparked his imagination. He chuckled and shook his head as he noticed that she still carried her headpiece and had a vision of her hastily plopping it upon her head as she entered the hall. Child? he asked himself casually. Nay, he decided. But neither woman.

When she was out of sight, he turned and finished the task of feeding his horse. With a brush he began working over the steed's coat, bringing the lustrous black to a fine sheen. Since early in his youth he had taken responsibility for his horse. This he had learned from Sir Theodoric. His steed was his greatest possession. He would trust this animal to carry him into battle and respond to his command, indeed, his touch, with the utmost precision. Orion was a fine horse, and should he lose him it would take months, possibly years, to train another. For this reason Conan kept all the care of his beast as his own burden.

Conan looked over his shoulder in the direction Chandra had taken, remembering the sight of her quite well.

"Another secret he has kept from us."

Conan turned and smiled at the speaker. Sir Mallory stood in the opening of the tent, holding back the flap so that Thurwell might also see. Conan laughed and went back to brushing his horse, ignoring the jibe. "I didn't know you had arrived," he said.

"You were occupied. We saw the maid and came around the back of your pavilion so as not to disturb you."

"You were spying," Conan said flatly.

"That, too," Thurwell laughed. "You didn't tell us about the maid."

Conan looked at them now. They both wore the tunics he had ordered put out for them, the colors of Sir Conan. How it inflated his pride to have his own livery, and to have knights such as these ride at his sides! "I didn't know of her, to tell you truly. She is Chandra, daughter to Medwin of Phalen. When last I saw her she was a sprite of Galen's years. She rode as fast as any lad. And now, it seems, she's growing up."

"Indeed," Mallory sighed. "Would she meet with Lord Alaric's approval?"

"She would, should that meet my fancy. He and Medwin are old friends." He shrugged. "She is barely a woman. That does not meet my mood at the moment."

"A man of moods," said Thurwell. "How suits your

mood for the joust? Does any maid's hand rest on the outcome?"

"None," Conan said.

"And do any old enemies challenge you?"

"There are a few," he returned confidently. "No one of
great importance."

"There is Tedric," Mallory said.

"Tedric?" Conan's head shot up and he stared at the
two, though he shouldn't have been very surprised. Tedric
was the son of Sir Theodoric. They had been together for
many years, and the relationship had been a tense one.
Conan's early achievements had galled Tedric.

"He is a fool," Conan finally said.

"He has only lately issued the challenge," Mallory informed him.

"What could he hope to gain? He knows he cannot best
me."

"His hopes are great," Thurwell said, walking closer to
Conan and giving an easy brush to Mars's dark feathers.
The bird did not flinch, for it was a touch he knew. "He
spends too much time hoping to best you. Put him down
well and finally."

Conan turned back to his horse, brushing the mane.
"Perhaps if he could beat me once he would forget this
foolery."

"That is folly, Conan," Mallory insisted. "His head
would swell with thoughts of power and he would seek a
higher advantage."

"He will lose his horse without much effort from me, but
what more can I do? While my beloved Theodoric watches,
shall I break his son's bones?"

Thurwell shook his head and moved closer. "Nay,

Conan. But listen well: Tedric is a weasel, and soon he will
see he cannot beat you in fair trials. One day he will learn
the way to make you pay for the years you have excelled in
Theodoric's house. Be sure he reckons well that you are the
stronger."

" 'Tis truth, Conan," Mallory agreed. "Guard your back
from him in the future. He is a weak knight, but his hunger for power is evident even now. He is not slow-witted —
and he is restless for your hide."

Conan laughed off these warnings. "Why should I fear?
Two of the most skilled and well-known knights of this
land ride at my sides!" He clapped a hand on Mallory's
arm. "Could the strongest man take me with my advantage?"

Neither knight laughed at Conan's lazy assessment.
"Your house yields us comfort, true, and we abide with you
pleasurably," Mallory said. "You know where our loyalties
lie, but we're not to be bound, Conan.

"Three years past, you were the young squire to pull us
out of a slimy marsh that would have been a grave, and
from that time we've ridden only in your company. Your
own purse bought a new set of clothes, and horses for us to
ride," Mallory said. "And you know we are grateful and
would repay you with our lives."

"Your company has not hindered my way, but helped,"
Conan insisted. It was true that while Theodoric was his
teacher and the best he could have had, Mallory and Thurwell were not only skilled but worldly wise. They had been
his closest friends. "You repaid the price of a horse and set
of clothes in your first year with me. You saved my hide
more times than I care to remember. I am indebted to
you."

"There is no debt, Sir Conan," Thurwell said. "Nor shall there ever be. You gave us aid when our luck was low indeed, and that score has been settled. Hence, any act is an act of friendship and there is no tally. Now we'll leave you for a time, but we'll return."

Conan did not show his disappointment. "I won't hinder your passing, but you will send word of your whereabouts?"

"In blood, if it pleases ye," Mallory laughed.

"We go first to Canterbury and from there to whatever tournament boasts great prizes. We will send word."

"By your call we are here," Mallory assured him.

Conan snorted. "I rue the day I pulled you from that mire. Had I left you I would not be plagued with your womanish concern."

"Womanish!" Thurwell croaked.

Mallory ignored the jesting. "On this very day, Conan, show Tedric his master. Do not take his challenge lightly. I've seen his likes before. Tedric will throw down his sword early and find his power in cunning."

"Your worry outpaces your wit, Mallory."

"Nay, Conan. Tedric is the youngest of many and his inheritance is bleak indeed. Your success and your wealth leave him bitter. I heard him speak to his brother last eventide. He hates you, Conan. It is not a boyish fancy. It burns in him."

"I grieve for Theodoric," Conan said. He had long found it an aggravation that Tedric disliked him and often sought to make him look the fool, but in respect for Theodoric he had not complained or badly bruised his childhood rival. "Be assured I will keep a watchful eye turned to Tedric."

"A watchful eye and more, Conan," Mallory said. "And all loyalty to Theodoric aside, if Tedric threatens your life, you must kill him."

The thought of it made Conan's blood run cold. "These are fine parting words," he told his friends.

Mallory shrugged. "The young knight has come home, and the lists are his plaything. The maids bring him ribbons and roses to carry close to his breast, and his lordly father waits impatiently to fit him with a castle to tend. Aye, Conan, it will be hard for you to think ill thoughts today when all your future looks so bright, but much of what is ahead is unpleasant. And mark me, one day you will have to deal with Tedric as a man would, not with the ease of a contest of arms."

The three stood silently for a moment, contemplating Mallory's words. Finally Thurwell broke the silence. "Lord Alaric puts out his best to break the fast. The hall is crowded with men, none so hungry as I."

"I'll be along," Conan told them, turning again to Orion. He looked over his shoulder to watch his friends depart for the hall. He could not imagine the years ahead without them ever at hand. They had promised they would ride off one day when some adventure called them, but he had not really foreseen this parting of ways. They would return, he assured himself.

A squire ran up, bowed briefly and took up Conan's mail. Without giving much thought to his actions, Conan allowed the lad to help him don the burdensome garment. A coat of bright blue was held up for him to shrug into, and his gauntlets were handed to him.

Conan removed the hood from Mars's head and fed the bird a piece of meat. Like his falcon, Mallory and Thurwell hungered for freedom. And Conan, so like his father,

THE BLUE FALCON , 31

needed the thick walls of some manor to give him ease. To ride out to some adventure made his heart pound and his blood race, but only because he knew he could ride home to the secure walls of his father's house — his house. Thurwell and Mallory would spend their life's blood to escape such ties. Conan would willingly spend his life to secure them.

"Would that I could make them a hood like yours, my friend," Conan said to his bird. "I would hide the thought of wandering from their eyes and keep them ever near me."

The great bird flapped his wings and turned his head in full circle as if in protest. "Yea, you are wise, Mars. They would not serve me so tethered." The hood was replaced on the falcon's head, and with Mars riding his arm, Conan walked toward the hall to join his friends.

CHAPTER
2

THE blue and red of Anselm took on a new meaning now that Sir Conan was home. Conan's victories in contests of arms had become as well known as his love for birds, Mars in particular. His shield was blazoned with the blue falcon's image, and he was often called the Blue Falcon. And the deep midnight blue of the huge falcon that rode his arm or shoulder cast an eerie shadow when Sir Conan entered a crowded hall.

Much of what belonged to Lord Alaric de Corbney could be seen from the six outer bastions of Anselm's great outer wall. Of course there was other land, smaller keeps and farming villages, but Anselm was the largest and strongest possession of this respected family.

This harvest in the year 1187 was to be celebrated with food, drink and frivolity. Masses had been paid for and sung with copious devotion, and those squires to be knighted had confessed, prayed and fasted. Now the harvest would reach an unusual culmination: Lord Alaric would host a contest of arms.

Anselm housed every patron of mentionable birth or honorable station, but word of the tournament had spread even throughout the common folk in neighboring towns. In the hamlet, the villagers leased any vacant corner to travelers. Crude tents and meager shelters crowded the land beyond the outer bailey for those unable to find housing within and for serfs eager to see the contests but unable to pay the price for the humblest lodging.

Banners of many colors and repute crossed the drawbridge to enter Anselm and take part. Knights whose prowess in battle was well known but who lacked wealth in lands and influential family traveled in search of tournaments, when they weren't hiring out their battle skills as mercenaries. If they were successful in the joust, they could demand ransom for the horse and armor of the knight beaten. Should the landless knight lose himself, he would forfeit the articles of his profession — his horse and armor — unless perchance the victor or some visiting dignitary offered the sum of his ransom in exchange for the knight's service.

On this day, Conan de Corbney would show his battle skills in the joust and melee. Lord Alaric was not worried about paying ransom for his eldest son. Rather, Conan would add monies of his own to his father's purse. And, if the day was well spent, some damsel in the gallery would catch his eye.

This son had been the life and breath of Alaric. At the age of fifty-seven years, Alaric would witness his son's skill on the field of battle. His manhood had fully arrived, and the time had come for him to live by his oath: service to God and his king, and the promise to uphold the chivalric code, living by the virtues of piety, honor, valor, courtesy, chastity and loyalty.

Alaric smiled to himself as he noticed the young boy beside Conan's pavilion. It was Galen, his youngest, a son who promised one day to be as powerful as Conan.

"What is your business here?" Alaric asked Galen as he approached.

"I was only looking at his things, my lord," Galen answered, blushing slightly as if he had been caught doing something wrong.

"Conan prizes his possessions. He would be grateful for help in guarding and caring for them."

Galen's grin was quick and bright. "Yea, my lord," he replied. And from that moment on, Galen stayed near Conan's tent, serving him in any possible way.

Red and blue pennants and streamers flew over the center gallery. The fair and beautiful Lady Udele sat before all others as the Queen of Beauty. Deep rose was the color of her woolen gunna, and a soft pink kirtle showed beneath, matching the length of sheer pink cloth that fell from her headpiece to cover her hair. When the tournament was over, she would be the one to present the prizes to the victors.

Beside her was Lord Alaric, his hulking frame erect and proud as he waited for the opening ceremonies. His thick hair was white and his beard full and snowy, but one look at the powerful lord's eyes would quell any thoughts that he was weakening with age.

To the left of Alaric's pavilion flew a pennant bearing the fish. Medwin sat there with his daughters. Medwin had no sons, but he was not lacking in strength. Many knights in service to him were present, and Medwin had the funds to back them. His strongest holding was Phalen Castle and its surrounding lands. That alone made him a rich man indeed, but he also held the picturesque hamlet of Cordell and its modest castle on the sea, which had been dearly loved by his late wife. In dedication to her, his banner flew the fish.

A man with so much should have sired only sons, but to Medwin came three daughters. Edwina, the eldest, would one day bring Phalen to her marriage. Laine, the middle child, was promised to the convent at an early age. And Chandra, the youngest, would take Cordell.

On Alaric's other side, the banner flew the fox. Sir Theodoric sat there proudly. This was a man of wealth and wisdom, Conan's master for many years. He sired seven sons, all grown and knighted. That a man would bring so many successfully through boyhood was a tribute, for of all children born alive, nearly three fourths died in their youth.

In this contest, Tedric, the youngest of the seven, would show his skills. Other sons' successes were highly sung, but for this youngest, Theodoric had no great ambitions. Tedric had never shown a great love for battle and had proven himself poorly. In this contest, he could have ridden at the right hand of Conan in the melee, but Tedric would not. Instead he insisted on challenging the obviously stronger knight. The outcome was inevitable, and Tedric's action raised Theodoric's ire no small bit. There was no valor in foolishness, and Tedric would draw the ransom from his own purse.

Among all the prestigious families present, with their banners rippling in the wind against the clear blue sky, these three men were considered to be the most powerful, if not in wealth, at least in arms and influence. They brought their best, and the money to back them.

Scattered below the gallery on the grass were hundreds of peasants eager to see the matches. The contest promised more than good sport and victories; there would be a feast of colossal proportions. Inside the great keep, special delicacies were being prepared for the gentry, while outside, the spits were turning to roast venison and boar. Huge quantities of cider, mead and ale stood ready to be consumed.

The trumpets sounded and the crowd cheered. From opposite ends of the field the knights rode together, their helms still held in their hands or resting on the pommels of their saddles. They met in the center of the field and rode toward Lord Alaric and Lady Udele. Their shields told their identity, and spectators craned their necks to have a good look at the procession.

Garrett the bastard bore his shield proudly. The bent sinister and black rose that once suggested his lack of belonging was now his symbol of success, for he was one of the mightiest. In the midst of this throng was the scarlet dove, the shield of Sir Byron, another brave knight of seasoned experience. And the wolf on a pelt of green. The serpent mounted on an arrow. The black hawk against the blue sky.

Quarrels broke out among the common folk as they pointed to their favorites and predicted the winners. Occasionally Lord Alaric's men-at-arms, who patrolled the lists to keep order, would have to drive a lance between those who were wont to take their differences too seriously. But none placed such credence in their choices as the young maids who leaned over the palisade to wave a length of sheer cloth or a flower at the powerful knights, crying out the names of their favorites.

Alaric smiled every time he heard a soft, feminine voice praise the Blue Falcon.

Order fell over the crowd when the knights had returned to opposite ends of the fields. A squire in colorful chausses and tunic approached the palisade and announced the first combatants in the tilt. At the sound of the trumpet, two huge war horses tore up the field as they charged toward each other. Their lances were braced and ready to reach across the tilt, each knight hoping to jar the other from his horse. A crash of metal sounded at the impact, but the crowd moaned as both knights escaped still horsed. They passed, returning to the ends of the fields, and charged again, the thumping of heavy hooves preceding the sound of smashing metal. Both knights were thrown and took up the battle on foot with heavy broadswords. The crowd delighted with each powerful clash of metal.

"Perhaps our choice will be made easy, lady," Alaric whispered in Udele's ear.

Udele followed her husband's eyes and watched as Conan approached the gallery, his great steed picking its way through the peasants almost daintily. She began to smile, thinking him proceeding toward her, but she stopped short when he paused before Medwin's box. His helm still in his hand, he pulled the cream-colored fabric from around his neck and showed Chandra that he wore her token. Chandra leaned over the rail and touched his arm. Her golden hair tumbled from beneath her veil, and her cheeks glowed with a rose flush as she laughed with him.

"I could not have chosen better," Alaric remarked.

Giselle's words slashed through Udele's mind and ripped her composure to ribbons: *And so he shall have the young beauty with flaxen hair . . . though her fortune is meager, in her many strengths she knows wealth. . . .*

"She is too young," Udele said.

"Nay, lady, I think not. And I have wished for him to take one of Medwin's daughters. I have long treasured his friendship."

Udele's mind spun recklessly as her fears suddenly became very real. So, she was there, under his hand, available to him when he would see. There were other women present, many fine potential brides spotting his travels, but he had found none he desired. Giselle's prediction had promised a woman-child whose means were not impressive. Udele knew quite well what Medwin would be leaving his daughters. To the oldest, Edwina, there would be Phalen Castle, a piece of property that was not poor, but neither did it compare to Anselm. And for Chandra? The simple farming and fishing village of Cordell.

The sound of another trumpet brought Udele out of her musings, and she noticed Conan braced and ready for the contest. Opposing him was Tedric, and she relaxed with easy confidence: Tedric was simply no match.

The great destriers bore their riders toward each other with astonishing speed. Lances ready and heads down, Tedric and Conan smashed together with powerful force. The crowd seemed to rise as one in mute horror as Conan's lance splintered and broke, and he fell roughly to the ground.

Conan's breath left him in one great whoosh as he hit the turf. He lay stunned for a moment, but instinctively he rolled and gained his footing, showing his foe he was still able and determined to fight. He drew his broadsword, sheathed to protect his opponent in the games, and stood ready to meet Tedric on foot.

Orion moved quickly away from his master. Conan was not at ease as he waited for Tedric to dismount and meet him on the ground. As Tedric drew out his mace, Conan nearly chuckled, but his amusement at Tedric's move vanished as he watched the lesser knight. Tedric had maneuvered his horse to the opposite side of the tilt as if meeting Conan astride for a second time. In spite of the roar from the knights and the crowd, Tedric spurred his horse and charged the fallen knight.

To dive and miss the weapon never occurred to Conan, for so strong was the fury at being unfairly attacked that his better judgment failed him. Instead he threw down his sword and braced himself. When Tedric drew near, Conan stepped toward the swinging mace, ducking slightly, and grabbed the offending weapon just behind the spiked ball. He felt the bones in his hand crack and yield, but he did not. With one tug, he brought Tedric to the ground with a crash of metal and a surprised yelp from the victim.

For a moment Conan's vision failed him, the pain in his hand was so severe. It took as long for Tedric to begin to regain his senses and find himself looking up into the victor's blue eyes, which seemed to glitter like the wrath of God. Dimly, Tedric saw the great spreading wings of Mars as the bird glided low over his head and came to rest on Conan's shoulder.

"You are bedeviled," Tedric gasped.

"I should have killed you for what you would have done," Conan said through gritted teeth. "But better you should bear your shame alive. You have dishonored yourself — and your father."

"I could not see you were down! I knew your lance was destroyed, but I did not reckon you'd lost your horse. There is a splinter here, in my eye! I would have met you astride even with my injury!"

"You lie!" Conan's voice dropped low, barely above a whisper as he heard Alaric's mounted men coming to the field. "Would you have chosen a mace instead of a sword thinking me astride? You may stay your father with your winsome tale, for he is too tolerant with you, but I am the one to know. Your aim was far too accurate. It belies your blindness."

As the men came closer to take a look at the situation, they heard Tedric's words. "I humble myself to you, Conan! Even now I cannot see you clearly!"

Conan shook with rage as the men-at-arms helped Tedric to his feet. "Sir Theodoric has ordered you from the contest," one guard reported.

"But I have broken no tournament rule," Tedric argued.

"By the eye of God!" Conan roared. "I will kill you the next time you dare so much!" And with that he turned and walked toward his pavilion. It did not occur to him to stride valiantly toward Medwin's box and collect a kiss from the fair Chandra in reward for his success. Outside his tent his squires were bent over the splintered remains of his lance, with Thurwell and Mallory looking on.

"See here, Conan," Mallory said. "This could be the mark of an injustice. Someone has tampered with your lances. There are small holes bored into the wood to weaken them. I would swear that it was Tedric."

Conan looked sharply over his shoulder to see the beaten knight leaving the lists.

"You can bring charges against him," Mallory suggested. "It looks bad for Tedric."

"Is there any point?" Conan asked sharply. "Tedric has done me a great service. I have no doubt those marks were made by him or someone in his service, yet no one saw the act. I have other opponents on this day. Why not one of them? Charges would be difficult to prove, but even without proof I have come to see Tedric's methods clearly. There is little chance he will find me so disadvantaged again."

Galen approached Conan, his eyes downcast and a bright flush on his cheeks.

"Sir Conan, 'twas I who was set to guard your things. Though I did not leave or look away, the fault must be mine."

Conan turned and looked at his young brother. "If this is trickery, Galen, there is no blame. You did your job well."

Galen looked up to Conan. "Someday, Conan, I will prove my worth. Someday I will be as skilled as I am faithful. It is my promise."

Conan smiled at him. "I have no doubts, brother. And the day is not so far away, I vow."

When Conan turned back to his friends, he was met with Mallory's grave and determined stare.

"Push him, Conan," Mallory urged. "If you do not, you will find yourself faced with his treachery again."

Conan smiled slyly and tried to bend his painful hand. "Yea, he will make another attempt one day. And I relish the opportunity."

Udele looked to Medwin's box and saw Chandra sitting on the edge of her seat. Her hands were folded in her lap and her back was straight, but the maid chewed her bottom lip nervously. She did not seem interested in the new knights making ready for the next contest. Rather, she intently watched the men gathered about Conan's pavilion. Udele could nearly feel the upset churning in Chandra's stomach. "Ah," she thought angrily. "She loves him! It is plain!"

Lady Udele sent a page off to find out the extent of Conan's injury, but her mind was not occupied with that. She bit her finger in concentration as she studied Chandra. It was clear that Chandra had set her sights on Conan.

Udele knew Chandra to be a willful lass, and to further the burden, she was lovely and would become more beautiful with the passage of time. Already many young swains were looking in her direction.

The page returned and knelt at her feet. "Sir Conan's hand is badly broken, lady, but he says 'tis yet good enough to see the day well met. He wraps it tightly for the next match."

"My lord, you must stop him," Udele said. "He will do some further injury, and at the very least will lose because of it." Udele touched the sleeve of Alaric's great robe, for he did not move a muscle, but looked straight ahead to the lists. "Alaric? Stop him, I pray you."

"Nay. His life is his own. I gave him his last command when I told him to live by his oath."

"He will do as you order!"

"Aye, he will," Alaric replied, looking at his wife and setting his jaw.

"We will be humiliated should he —"

"Madam, I will not have a son whose only strength comes from his father's order. He will do as he will — and live with the result."

Udele gritted her teeth, for she had never succeeded in moving Alaric to her will and the frustration grew greater as the years passed. "He may well live with a stump at the end of his arm. And that would please you well."

"Silence yourself, madam! Give credit to Conan's good judgment. It was years in the making."

It seemed an eternity before Conan was ready to ride again. Udele held her breath as she noticed his opponent bore the crest of the black rose. Given the best circumstances, Conan would find it difficult to best Sir Garrett.

Udele cast a glance toward Chandra to find the maid

giving all her attention to the contest while the other young women all around her chattered and flirted. Why would one so young give anything such serious attention? Udele wondered. To think that Chandra was ready for marriage was unsettling.

Conan and Garrett rode toward each other. Conan's lance was braced under his right arm, but he used his left hand to steady it. Garrett's blunted lance struck Conan's shoulder, but glanced off. Conan's lance did not reach his opponent. They passed, came around the tilt to change sides, and made ready to charge again. Conan shifted his lance and moved it to his left side. It was an impossible position, giving Garrett every advantage.

"See," Udele said, tugging at Alaric's sleeve. "Conan uses his left hand and the weapon is heavy. He will lose. He may be badly injured."

Alaric grunted. "He may indeed, madam."

"Give thought to the future, my lord," she beseeched him. "What good can Conan do if he is maimed?"

"I cannot stop the contest," Alaric said.

Conan and Garrett came together with a great smashing of armor, both knights falling to the ground. Conan threw down his lance and shield. The crowd became quiet and intent. Conan could not hold both his shield and his broadsword: he had but one good hand. Sir Garrett stood momentarily confused, not wishing to take unfair advantage of an opponent so beset. Garrett was a proud knight — beating Conan when his hand was crippled would mean little.

Conan did not wait for Garrett's approval of the conditions of the contest. He crossed the tilt and came to stand on Garrett's side, sword drawn and ready. Garrett hesitated, but Conan struck the first blow, removing any further doubt that he was ready to carry on the fight on foot.

Conan fought mightily, Garrett's sword glancing off his armor and Conan's weapon meeting most often with the shield. A blow to the shoulder caused Conan to lose his footing and hit the turf, but he rolled with an agility that belied the weight of his armor and was upright again, ready for the fight. He braced himself for Garrett's next blow, but the opposing knight seemed stunned. The crowd stood.

Sir Garrett threw down his shield and faced Conan. It was a thing so rare that the spectators did not know how to react. Winning was so important that never did a knight give any advantage to an opponent.

"Alaric, what has he done?" Udele asked.

"It is plain, madam, that Sir Garrett will find little joy in besting an injured knight. He will meet Conan with the same advantage."

The two came together again, void of shields, their heavy swords bouncing off each other. The sheath covering Garrett's broadsword so that he would not do severe injury to his opponent was lost, and neither knight seemed to notice. The crowd gasped and cried out, and the men-at-arms made ready to ride onto the field.

"God above!" Udele cried. "Alaric, stop the contest!"

But Alaric was as still as stone. The men-at-arms would put a halt to the fighting before any real damage could be done, and the two combatants would not be allowed to resume until Garrett's broadsword was fixed with the protective covering. But before the men could reach them, Conan's sword struck home and Garrett fell to the ground, stunned and immobile.

Conan stood over him and waited for him to rise. The men-at-arms stopped where they were and waited. Conan dropped to one knee and removed his helm. He reached out a hand to shake Garrett and then threw down his sword. He helped the beaten knight to his feet and the two stood in the center of the field, Garrett slumping slightly.

Sir Garrett's squires came running to aid their master to his pavilion, and Conan raised his hand high above his head, looking in the direction of his parents.

"It is a miracle," Udele breathed.

"It is years of training," Alaric corrected.

"You take this so easily," she accused.

Alaric's jaw tensed. "You take this easily, madam, not I. Do you imagine he would be excused from war because his hand pained him?" Udele sat back in her chair, prepared to hear her husband's lecture. "It is the grandness of this tourney that befuddles your brain. It may surprise you to think of it as more than a pretty party for maids and their swains. It is a contest of arms! Whether Conan wins or loses, what he learns out there today may one day save his life."

Udele pursed her lips and refused to look at Alaric. She despised his patronizing perception of her as a giddy and foolish woman. She understood the tourney, but she had not thought it worth sacrificing her son before he had even begun to make his way in the world.

Udele stood and brushed her skirts down to smooth them. "You must excuse me, my lord. I find watching this contest too taxing."

"You should not leave, lady. You must be here when the tourney is over."

"I will return before very long, my lord. Permit me a slight rest from the trials, at least while my son competes with an injury?"

"Very well, lady. Excuse yourself if you must."

Udele was trailed back to the hall by some of her ladies, her daughter Edythe among them. As she passed Medwin's box she glanced at Chandra. The lass stood and waved toward Conan as he left the field. Her cheeks were flushed bright and her smile was wildly enthusiastic. Chandra yearned for Sir Conan publicly, proudly.

Udele heard her women behind her as they laughed and talked. When she neared the hall she paused and turned to them. "Make yourselves at ease here, ladies, and allow me some moments of quiet. I will return anon."

Those attending Udele remained in the courtyard and allowed her to enter the hall alone. Her step was quick and her head low as she contemplated her situation. She nearly fell over a knight sitting near the stair.

"Pardon, lady, I —"

Udele straightened herself and saw that it was Tedric. For a moment her expression was all surprise, for she had not expected to see him, then her features molded into a sneer.

"So, Sir Tedric, you are waiting out the tourney here?"

Tedric flinched with the insult. "I have been excused, lady, but my father has not heard my explanations. All will be well when I have had some time to clear my name."

"I should think it would take much more than a few words, Tedric. There were many witnesses to your unfair assault."

Tedric's lips formed an insincere smile. "All will assume that Sir Conan is the just and I, the unjust. It has always been thus, in his family and in my own."

"And you will deny it?" Udele questioned tartly. She could not help but notice the swelling of one eye and wondered, briefly, if Tedric had indeed been blinded.

"I have long sought to show my father that I can equal Conan's strength in arms, but once again Conan shines in the wake of my misfortune."

Udele threw her arm wide. "Go yonder, sir knight, and look at the shine of my son! He is sore injured and will not cease in the games. But they will not allow your entry, will they?"

Tedric's mouth formed a thin, furious line and his rage was intense. "My lowly state in my father's house leaves all to praise the Falcon and scorn my every effort to show my worth. But I vow, lady, my wealth and influence will one day match his, and even you will treat me kindly."

Udele laughed outright. "I heartily doubt that, Tedric," she said easily. "But the best to you in your efforts." She turned from him and went toward the stair.

"When my betrothal to Lady Edwina is announced, you will hearken to me, lady. And one day I will hold Phalen and be your friend and neighbor." He bowed elaborately. "If I so choose."

"You will marry Edwina?" Udele questioned.

Tedric smiled. He lazily seemed to judge the great lady's surprise. "My family does not yield me much in money and land, but my father and brothers promise much in their support of arms. Sir Medwin must leave his holdings to a knight capable of preserving them. Yea, he will give me Edwina."

Udele recovered herself and tried to smile. "Then we shall have to learn to become better friends, Tedric," she said politely. Then, turning, she left him alone and climbed to her chamber.

Was it not enough, she thought, for Giselle to predict Conan's marriage to a woman of slim financial means, without learning also that Tedric would gain a sizable holding and become a neighbor? The possibility that Conan and Tedric would eventually come to blows crossed her mind. While a battle between the two of them would certainly leave Conan victorious, she could not relax with that prospect, for Theodoric's strength was not to be taken lightly. And in any battle, Theodoric would have to support his son.

Within moments the dawning came to her: Medwin had not yet approved the betrothal. Alaric wished for Conan to take one of Medwin's daughters. Phalen was not so great, but far greater than the simple Cordell that Chandra would inherit. And the land did lie close to Anselm. If Conan could be persuaded to speak for Edwina, Medwin would immediately agree.

She made up her mind quickly. She feared Giselle's prediction would be accurate and that the young beauty Conan was destined toward was Chandra. There was no time to begin a search for wealthier maidens, and no circumstance could more permanently remove Chandra from his reach than to have him marry her sister. She must find a way to move her son to ask for the hand of Lady Edwina. Tonight. He must ask her tonight!

The tournament came to an exciting finish, with many victorious knights ready to collect their prizes, but in the eyes of the people who had gathered to watch, Sir Conan's victories had been the grandest. And in the eyes of the young lady Chandra, he was clearly the hero of the day.

When Chandra and her sisters returned to the hall, Edythe was waiting for them. "My lady mother wishes our presence," she said anxiously. She gestured toward the stair. "She waits in her chamber."

Chandra and Edwina quickly followed, but Laine had

long since disappeared. The middle sister yearned more for the devotion of prayers than the excitement of tournaments and feasting.

They entered the lady's chamber to find her sitting in her rather regal chair. "Edythe," she called. "Come sit here by me." Happily the girl perched on a stool at her mother's right hand. Chandra and Edwina curtsied before her.

"Please forgive our sister, Laine," Edwina said, her manner quiet and reserved. "She has grown ill from the long day and the hot sun. She begs to be excused."

"Of course," Udele replied. She reached for Chandra's hand. "Dear Chandra, you are not so wearied," she smiled. "You look as though the day is just beginning for you."

"Truly, madam, I feel as though it is! Given the chance, I would spend another day thusly."

Udele laughed softly. "Then you would not mind another chore? Could you serve me now?"

"I would be honored, madam." Chandra bowed.

"Would you go to the hall with Edythe and see the needs of the men served? I would have Edythe act as mistress in my stead and I know she would welcome your company."

Edythe perked up at this, for until today she was kept far from the tasks of a lady and kept mostly with the children. Though she had reached the age that her mother had been when she married, she had never been allowed to do anything of significance within the great hall.

Chandra was likewise pleased, for there was no place she would rather be than in the hall when Conan arrived. "Thank you, my lady," she said politely, trying to conceal her great joy.

Edwina remained and Udele turned to her. "You must

rest for a time before the feast so you will be at your best.
Have you a rich gown to wear?"

"I have one, madam. It was made especially for this
day."

"And a fine wimple? You must let much of your hair
show. You have such pretty hair."

Edwina was confused. She touched her hair in wonder,
for since Chandra had matured, and especially since the
last summer, she had not received many compliments from
her elders.

Udele laughed at the confusion in Edwina's eyes. "You
don't know why I've called you, do you, dear heart? My
son will take a bride soon. I think you should make yourself known to him."

"But madam, he has not noticed me at all. Truly, my
sister seems to be more his desire."

"Chandra is far too young. No doubt she will one day
capture a fine husband, but Sir Conan is ready for a bride
now, and he needs a woman full grown." She reached for
Edwina's hand and drew her near. "You are lovely, dear,
and prosperous as well."

"And you would have me, lady?"

"I would be honored. And I will speak strongly in your
favor."

"But my sister —"

"Chandra must not take Conan's kindness to heart. He
is chivalrous and courtly and would not dismiss her rudely,
but in selecting a bride — ah! He must have a woman!"
She patted Edwina's hand. "Now promise me you'll be
bold."

"I'm not a bold person, madam. I don't know how
to be."

"Worry not, darling. Go. Make yourself beautiful. I think perhaps your knight will come to you."

Edwina smiled shyly, intrigued by the prospect. She had not aspired to so much. Conan had never paid any attention to her and therefore she had not considered him a possibility. But Medwin would be pleased. Her reluctance to speak her preference had made her father irritable.

"But lady," she said suddenly, "Tedric has made his honest proposal to my father —"

Udele's laugh cut her off. "Do you think Tedric will challenge Sir Conan? Go, and smile prettily at your knight. That will be enough."

Udele watched her leave and sat for a long while in the carved oaken chair in her chamber. With deliberate slowness, she allowed her maids to array her in a gown of great beauty: the same rose color, embellished with a gold filigree girdle and long, elaborate train. Gold bracelets and anklets adorned her, and small cloth slippers graced her feet. When she was readied, she made her way to the party below, intent on facing her son.

Chandra flitted about the hall, delighted to be greeting the gathering warriors. Along with Conan's younger sister, Edythe, she kept the serving maids in check and saw that everyone's hand held a filled mug. The chore was anything but burdensome.

She watched Conan from a safe distance, studying his mannerisms and even taking a close look at those he chose to have around him. His closest companions, Mallory and Thurwell, stayed near to him, though they joked and recounted details of the tourney with other knights. Tedric seemed to stay much with his own family, keeping a fair distance from Conan and his men. From what Chandra could judge, Thurwell was not terribly far from the amount of ale needed to goad him into a scene. This older, surly knight grew more boisterous and looked more and more distastefully toward Theodoric's family with every long pull from his cup.

Chandra marveled at Conan's strength. He lifted his mug to his mouth with his left hand, his right bound and hanging loosely at his side. She knew he would not grimace with pain any more than he would actually cry over the injury. More probably, she thought with a smile, he would fall headlong into drink and not remember until morning's light that he had been injured at all.

The crowd around Conan had thinned. Thurwell was drawing a bit too near to Tedric; there was a danger that a battle of words would soon ensue. It would please the masses well to see yet another battle. Mallory, the one most often plagued with a quick temper, dallied not far away with Edythe, a most unlikely pair in Chandra's mind. Mallory neared thirty years and Edythe, a bit younger than Chandra, was barely flushed with womanhood.

Chandra made her move quickly, aware that her chance for a few words with Conan had arrived.

"How might I ease the pain of your wound, sir knight?" she asked softly.

Conan smiled. "Let me look on your lovely face, damsel. That will ease the worst pain."

"You treat me too kindly, Conan. There are so many here who seek your attention."

"None so lovely as you, fair Chandra."

"What will you do now, Conan?"

"Now? Do you mean until the call to ride to the king comes again?"

"But you have only just returned! Surely you will not have to leave again so soon!"

"I think not too soon. I ride to Stoddard Keep soon to see how matters fare there. My father expects trouble from the castellan and his family. Now that I am able, I will likely manage that small manor, and house my men within the Stoddard walls. I suppose that will be my home when I do not ride with Henry."

"You will be so far away —" she began.

A hush seemed to fall over the room and Chandra turned to see Lady Udele enter the packed hall. Close behind her was Edwina and serving women whose position was to trail behind the great beauty. Alaric was the first to rise to greet her, placing a kiss on her hand. Udele smiled toward the many appreciative male glances and the crowd seemed to part magically to allow her passage. She finally came to pause before Conan and Chandra.

"You have made me so proud today, Conan," Udele said to her son.

Chandra almost sighed. Many a young maid hoped one day to have the beauty and grace of Lady Udele. Conan took his mother's hand and brushed a kiss on its back.

Udele turned her attention to Chandra. "I have a gift for you, and for Edythe. Where is she? Ah, fetch her for me, and you will find your gifts in my chamber. And hurry, for soon we begin the feast."

Chandra curtsied and fled to find Edythe. Udele turned to her son. "You've carried the day well, Conan. A word with you, I pray. I will not keep you from your friends long."

Conan presented his arm to his mother, leading her toward the stair where others would not linger to listen.

"Do my eyes deceive me, or are you smitten with young Chandra?" Udele asked with a raised brow.

"Smitten? Madam, I assure you, I would not take advantage of —"

"Conan, do not misunderstand me! Of course you would not hurt the maid. But when you look fondly on any lass our breaths all stop, for we are eager for you to accept your bride. I thought perhaps you had chosen."

"I've pledged nothing, madam, but —"

"Good, for there is another I would have you look to. Edwina is lovely and rich. Phalen will be hers and our lands could be joined to form one mighty holding."

"Edwina . . ." he mused.

"Edwina, of course. The dear child confessed she holds the hope that you will notice her, and the thought of it made my heart sail! To think of our family joined with Medwin's! Mon dieu! I should not try to persuade you."

Conan laughed and reached for his mother's hand. "And when, madam, have you fought that temptation?"

"Do not laugh at me, Conan. I think only of your best interests. And I am concerned for the land Medwin holds."

"Why are you concerned?"

"It lies close to our own, and Medwin is eager to have his oldest daughter married. Edwina is sweet and lovely and I fear he will not choose carefully for her."

"Medwin is not a fool. He will —"

"He considers Tedric even now. If you are tempted by the maid and her dowry, you must speak soon: on this very day."

Conan gave little thought to the bride, but the prospect of having Tedric as a landholder so close to Anselm brought a frown to his brow. Phalen was not as rich as

Anselm, but in time Tedric could be nearly as powerful in wealth and arms as Conan.

"I hardly know Edwina," Conan said, his frown deepening.

"You've known her all your life! And what need a man know of his future wife? Her wealth, family and willingness to give you heirs. Above that, if she is comely, virginal and willing, you have every measure of a man's desire."

As Udele spoke, Conan listened with half an ear. She judged his faraway expression and smiled inwardly. The seed had been planted. Now, if Edwina looked lovely tonight and put forth her best behavior . . .

Udele looked past her son to see Edwina with some other maids. She wore a gunna of the softest blue, and her flaxen hair trailed down her back to fall in ringlets to her thighs. As she laughed with the other maids her face seemed to shine. She was a frail, petite beauty, one who would make Conan seem stronger and larger.

"Should you choose to look further for a suitable mate, Conan, be certain that you will not regret giving her to Tedric," Udele said softly to her son. Conan looked over his shoulder to where Edwina stood. "And be prepared to live with Tedric as your neighbor."

Conan looked back to his mother and frowned. "I had not expected to make this decision so soon," he said.

"Ah, love, you will soon find that the world does not wait on your preference." She laughed softly. "Go, speak with Edwina. You may find that Tedric's proposal to Medwin is your gift and not your curse. Mayhaps you would not have noticed the maid if Tedric were no threat."

Conan smiled at his mother, appreciative of the fact that she had warned him. He squeezed her hand and went off in the direction of Edwina. Udele leaned against the wall, and from a distance she watched Conan react to Edwina's lovely smile. Udele sighed with contentment. She was confident that she had turned around a prophecy.

Edythe pulled Chandra's arm as they rushed back to the hall, each wearing the shining gold bracelet that Lady Udele had set out for them. Many of the delicacies were being brought out for the feasting. Within the hamlet, the common folk dined upon the ground, torches lighting the night while they filled their bellies with meat, bread and mead. But here, in the hall, the food was much more impressive. Chandra had seen feasting before, but nothing to compare to this. Lord Alaric had planned to spare nothing in making this an incredible feast. Chandra turned full circle more than once as the grand dishes were being carried into the hall.

She found herself looking toward the head table where Lord Alaric and Lady Udele would be seated. Some of the best knights and most prestigious guests would be joining them there, along with Sir Conan, of course. But she saw something she never expected to witness. On Conan's arm was Edwina. Chandra's jaw dropped and her throat felt constricted as she noticed her father raising one graying brow toward Alaric, and saw Alaric return the gesture with a brief nod.

Chandra shook herself and began looking for her place, hoping that it would not be terribly far from where Conan was seated. But in this, too, she was to be disappointed. After looking about the hall for a few moments, she found Edythe. There was an empty seat beside her and Chandra knew she was meant to sit there. The two maids were not placed with knights of good reputation but with the more youthful members of the household. Young squires, pages and maidens were to be their meal mates.

"This is not where I had hoped to be this eve," Chandra said softly, her voice catching slightly.

Edythe did not respond, but looked across the crowded hall with tears filling her eyes. Chandra followed her gaze and saw where she looked. Sir Mallory was there, near to Conan, and he looked in Edythe's direction. Then Mallory turned his attention to a knight beside him and Edythe sat down, the disappointment draining her.

"I see that you had other plans for the feasting too," Chandra said sympathetically.

"I had thought to have finally reached a station above child," she said sadly, turning her eyes to Chandra. "When I could easily do my lady mother's bidding, I thought I would at least dine with the women."

"There, do not be hurt," Chandra said with more cheer than she was feeling. "The feasting cannot last forever. And there is much more to the banquet than eating."

Chandra also tried to find the knight of her choice in the packed hall. She had to stand and look over the many heads that blocked her vision to find him, but unlike Mallory, he did not bend his gaze toward her. Instead he spoke to Edwina, leaning close to her and touching her hand as they talked. A rush of fear invaded her heart and she tried to abate it.

The meal was served with great pageantry. Squires and servants brought trays and trenchers filled with grand dishes, first to the lord and then to the other guests. A buffet of grand birds, cooked and then adorned with their jackets of colorful feathers, was displayed. A swan stuffed with a duck and finally stuffed with a quail was served with great flourish. A huge roast of boar dripping with gravy was yet another, and also stag and hens aplenty to go around.

Squires with their carving knives in hand stood ready to serve their lords. For these lads it was more than a night of celebrating, for they were again in training. They must not only carve the meat to perfection but have the proper terminology memorized in the event they would be asked. Chandra listened to the words passing between a squire and his master at the next long trestle table. The lad would "disfigure" the peacock, "lift" the swan, "despoil" the hen and "unbrace" the duck. And an error here was a serious offense.

Edythe touched Chandra's arm. "Chandra," she said solemnly. "Do you see who sits beside my brother? Does Edwina desire Conan?"

Chandra felt herself shudder. "Nay, my sister is soon to be betrothed to Sir Tedric. She has discussed it with my father many times."

"And Edwina wants Tedric?" Edythe asked.

"She wishes to please our father," Chandra replied.

"When the meal is done you must put yourself in my brother's company again, if you wish him to notice you."

Chandra was taken aback by Edythe's advice. She had not thought anyone paid much attention to her preference. She thought herself too young to be considered a choice mate for Conan, but she had not thought it too soon to give him something to think about.

"I suppose I must," she heard herself reply.

The best mead and the finest wines and ales were brought to the nobles. Songs were sung by troubadors while all ate and drank for hours. The feasting would continue until early morning and few would feel the comfort of a soft pallet this night. Even when the women had wearied of the noise and left the hall to retire, the men would carry on until the first streaks of dawn could be seen.

Conversation would not be confined to one's immediate dinner partners, nor even just one table. Knights and lords broke from their seating to meander about the hall and chat with a damsel or argue with another knight. When this moving about the hall once again crowded the room, Chandra rose and began to find friends and new acquaintances to chat with, hoping eventually to find herself near Conan once again. But as she viewed the table where he had been seated, she found Udele in deep conversation with Edwina, and Conan gone. She searched the room with her eyes but he was nowhere to be found.

When he returns, Chandra promised herself, I must at least see that he notices me.

Conan and his father walked away from the hall and into the courtyard. It was a quiet and clear night, the sounds of celebrating in the hamlet and in the hall becoming more distant with their every step. It was a welcome relief from revelry for both of them.

"If it would please you, my lord," Conan started, confident in his every word, "I would ask for the hand of Lady Edwina."

"Please me? Nothing could please me more, and Medwin would in like be pleased. I did not know the maid interested you."

"I have only lately come to see the good wifely qualities in Edwina. And I have just become aware that if I want her, I must speak quickly or await another as appealing."

Alaric's eyes searched his son's, and though the night

was dark, he focused on them. "Is Edwina whom you truly desire?"

"Yes, Father. And she would have me, though she is shy and cannot say so easily. It was a trial to coax her to speak her mind."

"How will she serve your needs, Conan? Will she gladly breed up a small clan, bearing your children with joy? Will she endure with grace the many months you are away?"

"Father," Conan laughed. "How can I know if she is fertile unless I bed her now and wed her when she is ripe with babe? And to endure the months alone — she is Medwin's daughter and there is no better teacher in the ways of knights and lords. Above that, she has land I want and is pleasant and comely. She has not the substance to be shrewish and" — he shrugged and kicked a pebble on the ground — "it will not pain me to give her a place in my bed."

Alaric looked up and took a breath. "Do you love her?"

Conan cleared his throat in embarrassment. "She is shapely and well kept. I have felt a passing fancy for those maids who would play their favors for a knight, and it turned quick to passion. You need not fear that I am ignorant. This I feel for Edwina: I tell you true, I am anxious to have her. But what is love, my lord? Is it something more? I love my horse and my bird and I serve them as faithfully as they serve me. By my oath I would honor and protect her to my death. I know of nothing more to be pledged."

Alaric smiled with satisfaction. Conan's word was his life.

"Medwin grows impatient with Edwina," Conan continued. "He would have her married. I dare not tarry any longer over the prospect or I will find her gone. She has told me that Medwin strongly considers Tedric. I will speak to Medwin tonight if you permit it."

"Medwin will not stay you, but I fear you will anger Sir Tedric beyond your ken. Be certain, son, that you seek Edwina for herself and not as a means to best Tedric yet again."

"It is not in my mind to have another battle with Tedric. I do not think he will challenge me. It is Edwina I want. I will not lose the lady and her lands to Tedric."

Alaric placed his hand on his son's shoulder. "Conan, be sure of what you do. If Tedric had not requested Edwina's hand in marriage, would you ask for her now?"

"Yea, Father. Perhaps I would not seek out Medwin this very night — Tedric's threat to what I want urges me on. Yea, Edwina is a choice mate for a man. She is a timid creature, but I am not an oaf and know the ways to court a maid."

"Then see the matter done, Conan," Alaric said. "And I wish you the very best."

When the hour was late and the feasting finished and empty platters laden with bones and scraps either thrown to the dogs or carried away, Lord Alaric rose and called those in the room to his attention. When some order fell over the crowd of men and maidens, Alaric raised his cup high.

"On this night of good cheer, what could be more fitting than to herald more good news. My own son, Sir Conan de Corbney, will pledge himself in marriage to the daughter of my friend and neighbor, Sir Medwin." Medwin rose and held his cup high, looking with brotherly affection toward Alaric. "Sir Conan will wed the fair lady Edwina some months hence and gives his promise to honor this betrothal. To Sir Conan!" he shouted, drinking deep. The crowd within the hall echoed his salutation. "To the lady Edwina!" he shouted, again raising the horn and drinking deeply of the heady wine. Again the hall echoed its approval.

With glad tears in her eyes, Udele rose with dignity and made her way to the young couple, embracing and kissing them both. Knights approached to congratulate Conan, and many a maid rushed to Edwina to enfold her in their arms and wish her well.

Across the hall where Tedric sat with his father and two of his brothers, he grabbed Theodoric's arm and said between gritted teeth, "I had made my offer of marriage to Medwin for his daughter."

Theodoric snatched his arm rudely from his son and looked at him closely. "On this day you will not interfere," he ground out with threatening slowness. "You will wish Conan well and shame this family no more if you will be called my son!"

Theodoric rose and held his horn high, drinking to the celebrated couple.

In the throng of well-wishers came Chandra, making her way gingerly to her sister and Conan. By the time she reached them, tears were staining her cheeks. She embraced Edwina and they held each other close, both shedding tears that were born of emotions alien to the occasion.

Chandra faced Conan and her glistening eyes struck him oddly. He thought perhaps the torchlight had some strange effect on him, for she looked older and more beautiful.

"I wish you happiness, Conan," she said very softly.

A slight frown creased his brow as he looked at her. A feeling he did not recognize betrayed him then, and to cover his confusion he reached for her and placed a brotherly kiss on her cheek. Her nearness and the sensation of his lips touching her tear-moistened cheek caused his heart to plummet, and his chest was filled with the pain of doubt. Though he could not quell the feeling, he was careful not to let it show. He smiled at her tenderly. He whispered his response. "Thank you, sister."

Dawn's first light had barely touched the land and many a worthy knight lay still upon the rushes, the night's gaiety taking a heavy toll on those who had celebrated in earnest. In the courtyard, two horses were being loaded with bags holding feed and some small amount of provender to carry them and their riders through their journeys.

Mallory stood near his steed in wait of Thurwell who was, of the two, the slower to rise this morn. Although the festivities had ended just a brace of hours before, they supported their plan to ride with the first dawning. Mallory was the more alert and somewhat melancholy of the two. He looked around the courtyard for what seemed the hundredth time.

He secured the saddle again, shifted in his heavy mail and chafed in general at Thurwell's tardiness.

"You leave early, as you promised, Sir Mallory," Edythe said from behind him.

Mallory turned and looked at the maiden. Her hair was unbound and she had quickly donned a gown for this early morning vigil. Her bare feet showed her hasty dressing.

"You would have left without a word," she accused.

"It seemed best, my lady."

"You thought it perhaps less painful, but it would not

have been for the best. I would not send you away without a kind word."

Mallory seemed to shrink from her every word. "There have been too many words between us already, Edythe. Your father would be ill pleased."

"Nay, he loves you."

"Nay! He loves me for a true knight and a good friend to his son, but I tell you again: 'twould set his temper to a fit to think of me courting his daughter."

Edythe hung her head in disappointment. Without looking at him she asked, "Will you find some bride upon the road, sir knight?"

Mallory turned away and gave his attention to his horse. "I have told you, I will wed no one. And no one will have me. I am without land and my money is hard earned."

"You will return. And I will be here."

He turned sharply toward her. "Edythe, stop this foolishness. I have pledged no love, no promise. You are foolish to take such stock in a poor knight. There is nothing I can —"

Thurwell stumbled out of the hall, tripping on the first stone that crossed his path. Mallory turned from Edythe again and the two stood watching while Thurwell went about the complicated business of getting astride. When Mallory turned to look at Edythe again, the pain was clear in his eyes.

"I have something for you to carry with you," she told him. She pulled a medal attached to a bright blue ribbon from her belt and handed it to him. "It was blessed by the friar and will keep you safe."

He took it and looked closely at the cross of Christ. He seemed at a loss for words and Thurwell cleared his throat as if impatient.

"Thank you, my lady," he said softly, starting to mount his horse.

"Will you leave me with no token?" she asked.

Reluctantly he turned to face her. He looked around the courtyard and could detect no eavesdropper present. He looked to Thurwell and saw him staring straight ahead as if he would be invisible. He faltered for a moment and then finally pulled her gently near and placed a light kiss on her lips.

Edythe let her arms rest lightly on his and moved her mouth over his, warming with the touch, and feeling the passion in her tender young body. He would not let her do more; he set her from him.

"You are a young and gentle maid and I would not have you hurt," Mallory told her. "Take the choice of your father, and in good faith give your love to another. Do not linger for a fruitless fate."

"Nay," she said stubbornly. "I will wait."

"Edythe, you must not! There is no hope I will change my mind."

She had the green eyes of her mother and they mirrored Udele's determined nature, though tears sparkled in them now. "You may not, sir knight, but neither will I. My heart cannot countenance another, and I will not make you a false promise now. Go with God. I will pray for your safety."

Exasperated, Mallory shook his head and wearily mounted his horse. The huge oaken doors opened for their departure, and just before they closed behind them, Edythe saw him turn to look at her again. Quickly she raised a hand in farewell, but she was not sure he saw.

With a tear tracing a slow path down her cheek, she turned and left the courtyard.

CHAPTER
3

Servant and noble alike made their stores of grain and sheared the sheep for their coats of wool: all thoughts seemed centered on enduring a long, cold winter. Sir Conan de Corbney installed himself firmly in the house of his father. The men who had lately chosen to ride with him were well received in Anselm and took their pallets with Alaric's men-at-arms. And as fall pressed on to the land, Conan and his father mulled over plans for the future.

To the northeast of Anselm was Stoddard, a keep and hamlet very small by comparison, but one of Alaric's prize possessions. It was there that he bred and raised horses, trained specifically to carry the knight in heavy battle raiment and to respond to the rider's command and touch. The quality of his horses was well known in England. Many were pledged to the king's service, and those that could be sold brought a fine price from nobles who would travel far to select one of these destriers.

It was in Alaric's mind that Galen would one day have Stoddard, and a large portion of the undeveloped land surrounding the keep would go to Edythe for her dowry. Stoddard could be thusly divided, for little space was needed for the small amount of farming the peasants did there for their own subsistence. The glory of Stoddard was its horses, and the land needed for the breeding, grazing and running of the beasts was near the keep and well protected.

Many years before, Alaric had placed the hall in the capable hands of Sir Rolfe, a Saxon with a good reputation among the Normans. The castellan had managed that holding well over the years, following Alaric's orders when they were given and, when necessary, improvising and relying on his instincts. Alaric provided Rolfe and his family with a rich home and a fair percentage of the yearly income, and Rolfe held the keep against would-be raiders.

Now word came that Rolfe had secured the keep with a great number of soldiers. Sir Rolfe had not left Stoddard in nearly two years, and had sent no revenues to Alaric in six months, giving away his intentions to claim the keep and protect it as his own, against even his liege lord: Alaric.

These pretensions on the part of this once-loyal vassal caused Alaric much concern and frustration, the hurt of being betrayed having long since given way to anger. If there had been no son such as Conan, Alaric would have ridden with his men to storm Stoddard. Now, Alaric would make use of his son's strong arm.

Conan's energy soared in anticipation of doing battle on his father's behalf. Many nights wore thin as he and a combination of his and Alaric's men discussed the various means of attacking the barricaded walls.

"I say send bowmen ahead of the horsed knights to absorb their first and early strength of the attack. Later, if the gates do not open, let us move in while foot soldiers try their luck with ropes over the walls," said one.

"Nay, hear me, my lord," said another. "Meet their early attack with like strength, a full army great in num-

bers. Let the bowmen take those on the parapet holding
the keep. The crossbow will make their work a simple
matter if their aim is good and can strike through the em-
brasures. Then scaling the wall will be an easy task."

"Aye, Sir Conan," said a third. "While the bowmen
holding the keep for Rolfe are kept busy with flying arrows
from foot and horsed warriors alike, they will find themselves also occupied with keeping the ropes from the walls
and a battering ram from the gates. Their doom may likely
come as much from confusion at your force as from their
weakness of arms."

Conan took in every word, listening carefully to pro-
posed battle plans, but never did he show agreement or
argument. Those riding with him would not know until
just prior to the attack what plan would be used. Though
it seemed unlikely from this loyal group, there could be a
Judas to forewarn Rolfe of the method of attack devised.
Conan had no great desire to break down the stout walls
of the keep with a battering ram, for the time and cost to
rebuild would lighten the purse he had barely started to
fill. He would choose a craftier course of action.

Though he had informed his men of very little, he had
made one decision: he would attack Stoddard before
Christmastide. The castellan had not earned the right to
be left in peace through the celebration of the birth of
Christ.

One day in late November, the young lord rose and
donned chain mail and armor and was having a squire
carry other battle gear to the courtyard. The barbican was
bolted and no one was allowed to enter or leave. The men
were roused before the cock crowed and found a steaming
brewis ready on the hearth, but they were warned not to
partake in the absence of their leader. All were advised

to don battle gear and have pages and squires make ready their instruments of war.

In the hall were quickly gathered men of many stations: knights, bowmen, foot soldiers, pages, squires and servants. Father Ambert, the village priest, with two presbyters, stood behind a hastily constructed altar in the main hall. All looked at each other in question until Sir Conan, garbed in his chain mail and surcoat of blue and red, with Mars riding his favorite perch, strode into the room. He knelt before the priest shriven for battle. In a moment he rose and faced his men.

"For those of you who have fasted, Father Ambert and his aides are prepared to hear your confession and offer you communion. For those of you who cannot partake, accept the good priest's prayers in no fear of your souls. Today we depart for Stoddard and I promise you, the gates of heaven will not be crowded with my men."

Sir Conan stepped away and watched as the men in the room fell to their knees in the rushes. For the better part of an hour there were light mutterings of prayer and confession in Latin, French and English. The sun was just beginning to rise when the priest, blessing the men and giving them absolution, bade them go with God and spare what lives they could in their venture.

Now all sat before their bowls while servants ran amongst them to deliver food to break the fast. But not one touched the food, for Sir Conan stood and spoke. "Today we ride, and Stoddard is but a day's journey from us. From the time our troop departs until daybreak on the morrow, no man, woman or child shall leave Anselm. If there sits among us a traitor, I give him this advice: cast your lot quickly with the victor, for before we mount, I will tell you the battle is already won."

Cheers went up at the sound of this prediction and it looked as though none among them would even lightly consider betraying this youthful warrior-commander. From Conan's vantage point there was no one suspect, but neither was he fool enough to take a chance. Their ride north would be secret to all. Even Alaric had not known on which morning they would depart.

The meal was swift and silent. Conan was the first to finish, though he did not slight his appetite. As a warrior, his body was his most precious tool, and he did not foolishly test his endurance. Food was fuel for him now, for they would travel through no hamlet or town, partake of no landholder's hospitality, and sleep in no sheltered hall or even a barn. They would take the swiftest route through path and passage without laying open the secret of an approaching conqueror. The next filling hot meal would come when the battle was won and Stoddard was in his possession.

Alaric walked to the courtyard with his son, his hand upon the shoulder of the knight.

"I will not return until I have quelled any disturbance in the town, but I will send you word when there is some quiet within Stoddard walls."

"I would know the details of the fight, if there is one."

"There will be one, rest assured. Rolfe has ignored your orders to yield revenues from Stoddard, and he pays the church in his own name and not in the name of his liege lord."

" 'Tis my hope that when he sees the size of your forces, he will find wisdom in surrender, but I fear he has planned this action for too long."

"And values his possession highly, for only if he yields before the first arrow is cast will he live."

Alaric nodded. He hated the thought of this once-valued friend and vassal's death. He stood before the gibbet that displayed the justice brought to thief or murderer so that his people would not think him weak of mind or will, but the distaste in having to end a life, even a criminal one, was bitter in his mouth. And he confessed and did penance for his obligation in ruling.

Those riding with Sir Conan began to enter the court-yard to mount, and to their surprise, horses were saddled and standing ready. While no one in the hall had been aware, provisions had been prepared for this excursion. Even those carrying out the orders of Sir Conan did not realize that they made ready for his attack on Stoddard. It was only early this morn that Conan personally woke several of those castle folk he wished to have accompany him and set them to the task of gathering equipment to be taken along.

Many a knight stood gaping at the courtyard crowded with heavily loaded carts and horses awaiting riders. While they were often prepared enough to ride out at the first inkling of trouble, and more often alert to defend their walls, a journey such as this would usually take long days of planning. Several smiled as they passed Sir Conan on their way to mount up, for it suddenly was clear that in losing Alaric, as they one day would, they would not lose the wisdom that brought them their successes. Conan's cunning would bring them even more. At this moment he was in complete control, and not a detail had been for-gotten. More than a skilled combatant; he was in com-mand.

When most of the men were ready and awaiting Conan's word, Udele stepped out into the courtyard. Behind her, Edythe trailed along.

"The word is that you are bound for Stoddard, Conan," Udele said a bit brittlely. "I am here to wish you well, though I was not forewarned of your leaving."

"I gave no clue to my departure so as to deter any betrayal."

"And did you suspect your family would betray you to your own cause?" she asked with eyes flashing.

"Nay, madam, but a maid or huntsman might, and for that reason I made no announcement until the gate was bolted and the bridge drawn."

"No word was sent to me," she said, looking at her husband with jealousy in her eyes. "I heard it from the lips of one servant who was set to the task of preparing the morning fare for two score soldiers and — "

"Madam, I saw no need to have word delivered to your chamber. The lord of this hall and the men who will fight are those who needed the word."

"I am the lady of this hall!" she cried.

"Aye!" he shouted, still louder than she. "Lady," he said with more control, stressing the word, "I could not spend my time delivering messages to every member of this family if I was to prepare an army for travel."

Edythe, who had lingered behind her parents, boldly pushed her way forward and briefly curtsied before Conan. Raising green eyes to his, she said shyly, "I shall pray for your safety, my brother."

Conan was lately seeing the gentle beauty and gracious manner of his young sister. He touched her cheek and smiled. "Then I shall rest assured, knowing you pray for me."

He bowed briefly to his parents and moved to the head of his troop. Orion danced in anticipation of a hard ride. A hand raised high to the man atop the wall and the sounds of the bridge crashing down and the huge oaken doors opening signaled their departure. Mars, occupying Conan's shoulder, let his wings flap, and his neck craned and beak opened as if to issue a war cry. Orion reared in lustful eagerness to stretch his flanks. The sense that Conan had a oneness with his animals cast an even more powerful light to his already envied status among his peers.

Alaric watched them ride out and felt his chest expand with pride. He did not notice that Edythe stole away to the chapel, for he stood rooted until the gate was closed and the doors bolted. He then turned to his wife.

"You should not question him now, madam. He will prosper if his masters are few and his servants many. Remember that."

"Yea, my lord."

It had taken great cunning to live with a man as stubborn as Alaric. Udele could enslave him by playing the part he adored: the beautiful and submissive wife. She could pacify him now, and later, when Conan ruled over Anselm and Phalen, she could seek a finer station.

"Serve him as well as you have served me," Alaric said softly.

Udele's eyes twinkled and she stroked her husband's arm. "Of a certain, my lord."

As Sir Conan led his troop toward Stoddard, he thought heavily on his mission. Stoddard was not great and mighty, but it was terribly important. His father held much wealth and the arms were strong. All this would be his in any event. But Conan's goals were different from most ambitious knights': it was not his goal to be the wealthiest knight in all Christendom, but the finest among his peers.

Much of what Conan lived by had come from the heritage of his family lands, a story told and retold many times over the years. The first de Corbney to establish himself in England was Sir Bayard, a knight of simple means, who fought by the side of William the Conqueror. When the Saxons were sufficiently brought to heel, Bayard built a hall on the spot where Anselm now stood and brought his wife and children from Normandy. Under Bayard's firm hand and with his support, the Saxons rebuilt their village. A town and hall called Corbney flourished under his hand.

The only son to survive Bayard was Sir Eldon, who inherited the land. His father had put thirty years of hard work into seeing the small hamlet grow into a substantial little town. But Eldon was more ambitious than his father, and he sought greater kingdoms. To that end, he pressed the people hard, forcing them to labor to provide him with more, but the serfs broke under his pressure and failed him in his quest.

The course Eldon took next left destruction and cruelty in its wake. He attacked neighboring barons and collected himself an army. As his forces grew it seemed he would take the entire kingdom, and after a decade naught but chaos and murder surrounded Eldon.

It was King Henry I Beauclerc who summoned Eldon's cousin, Alaric's grandfather, to gather an army and put an end to the barbaric rule of Sir Eldon.

This was no easy task, for Eldon had accumulated an army whose battle skills were sharp and ready. Cunning was needed more than strength, and after days of attack and counterattack, when forces were low and worn and food was all but depleted, Alaric's grandfather thought the battle lost. It was then that a priest from a neighboring burgh brought a cart holding food and drink to the weary soldiers. He offered more supplies and even men, if need be.

When asked why he would do this, the priest kindly answered that he was opposed to violence, but he had long been at prayer for an answer to the plight of these poor serfs. "The Church has long since abandoned Sir Eldon," he said sadly. "And it would seem that even God has fled, for no church stands in Corbney. Even that Holy Shrine has been fired."

Alaric's grandfather knew that he was at a disadvantage and close to the time he would have to return to his king with a handful of men and admit failure. He sent the priest back to the neighboring towns to ask if simple folk would lend food, supplies or even themselves to the battle. Without much confidence that the priest could help him, Alaric's grandfather held his forces in wait of some miracle.

In about ten days, the priest returned with two score carts bearing supplies of all kinds, followed by more than two hundred young men, none of them seasoned knights, but serf, farmer, mason, viner and the like. Although their weapons were crude, they were prepared to risk their lives in hopes that their villages would not be the next to be crushed by Sir Eldon while the local barons refused to raise arms against the wicked knight.

One day of battle saw Sir Eldon conquered, and many bodies littered the ground.

Alaric's grandfather's first order was to bury the dead: those defending justice in one place, and those wicked men supporting Eldon's greed and cruelty in another. "Let the good who fought and died come to rest on this spot where the shade from a new church will protect their souls. And let those who would not yield to justice find their final repose in the marshes, and if they yet seed evil, even in their deaths, it will be contained in the slime and murk."

He learned that the priest was called Father Ansel. When some semblance of order fell over the land, he called together all those who had fought. "This place can no longer be called Corbney, for my cousin has soured the worth of that name. This town and hall will be rebuilt and will house all of you who would serve a just master. And those widows and children of serfs who died here for this cause will have a place on this land for as long as they desire, with my protection and sustenance. Any mason, farmer, leather worker or smith who would stay here and lend his back to rebuilding is welcome, and this place will grow as large as loyal serfs will build it, be as strong as its people and endure as long as it has the grace of God."

He asked the priest to prepare a blessing for a new beginning. When this was done he remarked, "This town and all its trappings shall be called Anselm after the man who had naught but his goodwill to give and turned his hope for justice into justice served. Before the church, a statue will be modeled to pay homage to the man who turned a handful of serfs into an army of avengers against evil."

The statue of a priest in simple robes still stood before the church in Anselm.

The lesson had been well taught, and the descendants of de Corbney inherited the legacy and the land. In its turn it had come to Conan. Power swelled in the heads of many a knight and lord, but Conan believed that greed and injustice would be rewarded with death, whereas honor and justice would be rewarded with the good life.

It was that ideal that gave him strength at Stoddard. The castellan had betrayed and cheated his liege lord. He needed to be brought to heel, and his rule at Stoddard was over. Conan would give Rolfe one opportunity to yield with his life.

They had come along paths through trees to make a camp within the wood surrounding Stoddard. Conan allowed his men a meal, but would not allow a fire. At sunrise, Conan sat on Orion's back in the midst of his assembled forces and shouted up to Stoddard's wall. There was no quick response. The town around the small keep lay quiet in the dawn. Little by little, the people of the village noticed the gathered army and struggled quickly and quietly to get their animals into their humble shacks to wait out the battle.

Conan's men began to grumble and chafe at the delay in attacking the keep. They might have had the advantage of surprise had they struck early and without warning, but Conan would not budge. He was well aware that he had given Sir Rolfe an opportunity to view the gathered force.

The morning sun was bright in the sky when a guard shouted from the wall, "What army is this and what do you seek?"

Conan edged Orion forward and answered for himself. "I am Sir Conan, lately of Anselm, and I have come to relieve Sir Rolfe of my father's keep."

There was silence for a moment, and Conan noticed many more men from within the Stoddard walls lining the wall and parapets.

"Where is your lord?" he called, but received no response. "Tell Sir Rolfe if he will open the door to my men, he may yet escape this day with his life."

Conan expected no answer. He raised his arm, and a force of bowmen moved ahead of him and, kneeling, began to pepper the top of the wall with arrows. From behind them came twenty men bearing a battering ram. With the first blow against the oaken doors, another group moved to the wall with ropes and ladders. The horsed knights kept their places behind Conan, shields up and broadswords ready.

Flaming pitch was heaved from the wall to destroy the battering ram and the men holding it. Rolfe had been ready. Shouts from the bowmen had alerted most of the men holding the ram, but there were screams from those who could not escape in time. Conan's raised arm brought another ram and another twenty men from behind the horsed knights to continue the siege against the oaken doors.

Less than an hour of heavy assault on the wall and door was needed. The bolts began to creak and split, and finally the doors crashed open. Conan let go with a cry of battle, and twenty horsed knights stormed the keep. Rolfe had a greater number of men, but when Conan's force was within the wall, Rolfe's men seemed to lose all spirit in the fight. Several were quickly killed and the remainder seemed to hang back in submission, dropping bows and making themselves easy captives.

"Rolfe!" Conan shouted. "Where is Sir Rolfe?"

A quick survey told Conan he was not there fighting beside his men. Conan made a circular motion with his hand. His men darted off in all directions, and two followed Conan's lead as he dismounted and, with broadsword in hand, went into the hall.

Conan found only frightened servants there and was on his way to the upper chambers when he heard a great commotion in the courtyard. He turned and descended the stair and saw that two of his men held Sir Rolfe, a hulking Saxon with a graying beard, his robes covered with blood.

Conan stared at the man in some wonder, his first reaction being that the aging knight was badly injured and yet struggled wildly in his men's grasp. Then his eyes narrowed in suspicion as he wondered at the presence of so much blood. He walked closer, his eyes blazing the more with every step.

Sir Rolfe spat on the ground just before Conan's foot. "And you are the young upstart lord who will take my home!" the man growled.

"I am Sir Conan," he replied with a serenity that belied his true feelings.

"A babe!" Rolfe said with disgust. "This is my thanks after a score of years tending this stable! How many fine men have you killed on this day for one simple farm?"

Conan felt his pulse quicken and his muscles tense, but he gave no outward sign. "There need not have been blood spilled on this day, Rolfe," Conan replied. "You have proven yourself an unwise lord, for you would allow little to be preserved. The stain is clearly on you — you are a vassal here, not landholder."

From somewhere near the door one of Conan's men shouted, "They plead for mercy, Sir Conan!" The two men who had entered the hall with him returned to the courtyard with Rolfe's wife, Lady Vinna, and two small children. Conan glanced over his shoulder in time to see Vinna fall to her knees and cling to her offspring, a look of terror etched on her gentle features.

Conan eyed Rolfe coldly. "You have risked so much," he said as calmly as he could. "And for what? Was your life not worth more than this simple hall?"

"Twenty years," Rolfe blustered. "After twenty years and two wives, to have all I could call my own given to some upstart knight!"

"You are a fool!" Conan snapped, his eyes flashing. "Stoddard is part and parcel of what my father owns, but Lord Alaric has never put a faithful vassal from his home! You were assured your place here for ten score years to come in exchange for your loyal service!"

"And my family when I am gone? Do sons of a castellan inherit the demesne? Nay! They would be cast out to —"

"To prove their worth! As all sons, rich and poor, are meant to do! You have driven yourself to foolish ends if you thought to wrest this property from a lord as mighty as Alaric! Now you have lost all, for your sons, babes still, will have no home and no father!"

"Mercy, sir knight," Vinna whimpered.

Conan did not turn but studied again Rolfe's bloodstained robes. He looked to one of the knights holding Rolfe with a questioning frown. "In yon stable, Sir Conan, he has slain ten of Lord Alaric's finest destriers."

Conan's eyes glittered with rage and disgust. Without turning, he instructed the knights behind him. "Take the woman and her children to her chamber and keep them there." He looked into Rolfe's eyes, searching for some reason that this man would take leave of his senses. For these little boys? His action could not serve them; they were too young to benefit. For power? Greed?

He heard the oaken doors to the hall ease closed.

"What means did you use to kill the steeds?" he asked.

"A blade," Rolfe said indignantly. "With my own hand. I have bred up these horses for Alaric — with little reward."

"He cut their throats, Sir Conan," one of the men said.

Conan could hear the teachings of his father: *When you are lord of men and property, let those you lead see the strength of your own hand. If they fear and respect you, they will serve you well. When you deal out punishment to others, your people will not only fear your authority, they will fear every man loyal to you. And those loyal to you will attain your equal in power.*

"My father loved you well," Conan said grimly. "I would have liked to spare you. I would have liked to return to my father with the revenues due and your promise to remain faithful to your oath to serve him. You have sealed your own fate. You will suffer the same as you have dealt."

Rolfe threw back his head and laughed, his teeth gleaming and his eyes almost wild. When he ceased, he looked at Conan with venom. "Are you so mighty? You are but a boy!"

Conan heard his father's words ringing clear: *By your own hand that no lesser man need take your sin. Ruling is not all glory, but ofttimes a burden only the truly mighty can bear. . . .*

Vinna's sins were few, Conan reasoned. He doubted she had anything to do with Rolfe's treachery. And the lads were too small to fear. There seemed no need to display the castellan's death.

Conan put away his broadsword and drew out a finely honed knife. He looked at his blade for a moment, and then took two long strides toward Rolfe. One of the knights grasped a handful of Rolfe's thick, graying mane and yanked back his head to expose his throat. Without flinching or grimacing, Conan slit his throat, the blood from that wound quickly staining his hand.

Within seconds Conan's men held the limp, bleeding

form of Sir Rolfe. He motioned the men to take him away and turned to clean off his blade and return it to his sheath. He consciously made his actions smooth and unhurried.

"What would you have us do, Sir Conan?" a young knight asked.

"Bury the dead and burn the carcasses in the stable. Shackle Rolfe's men; I will deal with them later."

Conan walked into the hall where wide-eyed servants seemed to try to shrink into the walls. "Is there a chamber I could use for myself?" he asked a woman in the hall.

The woman approached him gingerly. "The lord's chamber, sir?"

"Nay. Another will do. One not spoken for."

"Aye, m'lord," she replied, going ahead of him up the stair.

Conan did not look about the room the woman offered. He nodded once and closed himself inside. He leaned against the door and looked at the blood on his hand. He had killed at least once before, but it had been in defense of his life. This was very different.

He fought the rising gorge, his eyes closed tightly. The bloodied hand formed a fist, and he pressed it against his stomach. He breathed deeply once; twice. He let his eyes open slowly, looking around and willing himself to be strong — to manage his deeds as a man would. There could be no more boyish ways.

I will ready this place for my wife, he thought. I will in time have a son — sons. Will I come to understand Rolfe's madness?

He moved to the window and looked into the court-yard below. His men were doing their work well, escorting Rolfe's men away and carrying bodies out of the courtyard for burial. He could not think of this place as a home, a place to bring a wife. He could not envision his life as it would be when a warm, feminine voice would greet him in his chamber. He closed his eyes and sought a vision of Edwina — but nothing came.

CHAPTER
4

OR a long time the leaves had been gone from the many fruit trees that surrounded Phalen Castle. The gardens were now barren and brown. In the court-yard, beyond the gardens, was a small lot set apart and guarded by a fence. Within lay the graves of those who had lived in the castle. There was a grave for the fair lady of Phalen, Medwin's wife.

In the spring and summer, Chandra brought flowers to her mother's grave. In the winter she could only bring her thoughts. Often she visited this place to be near her mother's spirit.

Millicent had been a delicate beauty, much as Edwina was. She was never strong of body, not bringing a baby to full term until she was over thirty years old. And after three girls, her body was exhausted of its use for bearing children. With Chandra's birth, Millicent nearly lost her life. After that her bedchamber was set apart from Med-win's and, much to the disapproval of the local priest, she did not prove with child again.

The devotion between husband and wife bloomed more beautiful than before as Medwin sacrificed his own desires for the sake of his wife's health. Chandra was grateful, for had her father been more selfish, she might not have had her mother for the twelve years longer that she lived.

Though Millicent was not robust, she was wise and learned. She managed the financial and the writing chores for Medwin through all the years they were together and was his counsel in the management of his lands. Medwin often admitted that Millicent's good advice had made Phalen the strong holding that it was.

Medwin's assets were clearly his strength and stamina, his battle skills and his qualities as a leader of men. His gifts, combined with his lady's wisdom ruling ever at his side, made Medwin an esteemed lord among his peers.

Edwina had been born with her mother's weak constitution. Millicent did not pamper Edwina as a child, possibly hoping that will alone would make the child hardy. But it had been useless, for Edwina was often beset with illness.

Laine had been born with Medwin's sturdy strength and, since early in her childhood, had a strong devotion to the church. Millicent had not discouraged this, and Laine had been allowed to spend weeks at a time with the Benedictine nuns. Even now Laine spent more time praying than doing anything else.

Chandra had not pondered which qualities she might have inherited from her parents. She knew she had not the frail, petite beauty of her mother. Already, at three and ten, she was as tall as Edwina and could easily bear twice the burden. She could not consider herself as wise as her mother, though she had done well at learning to write and count. She could ride as well as any lad her age, but she had less time for riding now. Since her sisters were not overly conscious of managing the keep, Chandra was her father's right hand. When Millicent died, it was Chandra who had tried to take her place.

Although her work in the manor usually kept her mind

off her problems, she often found the need to escape to the gardens, even in the cold of winter. There was a bench of stone near Millicent's grave that had become her favorite perch. She brushed the snow away and sat, pulling her fur-lined mantle tightly about her. Tears were near to spilling. Every day was more of a trial and she cursed her own womanhood.

The small pubescent mounds on her chest ached and itched, pressed tightly into clothing sewn for a younger maid. The hem of her woolen skirts had risen since the winter before, and her ankles were exposed. Just this morning some of the castle women had taken the task of altering her clothing to fit her more mature frame. And in the same morning she had found her shift stained bright red by her first flow. Her back and belly ached.

Chandra straightened her back and bore the discomfort in silence. She protected her clothing as she had seen her sisters do and spoke not a word to any of the women.

It was the custom in this time for a maid to marry at this early age, by thirteen or fourteen, certainly by fifteen. Edwina, now six and ten, was older than her most mar-riageable age. Medwin's friends and neighbors had snick-ered. He was too protective of his daughters, holding fast to them until a late age. Medwin gloated now. His patience had secured for his daughter a fine husband.

It very often happened that a lass barely blooming, her young body physically prepared for childbirth, or nearly so, was given in wedlock to a man. Not a gangling youth who had never tasted womanflesh, but more often an older man, one well advised. The lack of emotional readiness for such a union usually left the maid at a disadvantage, and that first coupling was anything but delightful.

Such could not be the case with Chandra. Within her heart there was a base yearning for a man, for his caress and his kiss. She cursed herself for the fantasies she indulged in just prior to sleep, when the curtain of reality was just beginning to blend into the dream world; when her own arms wrapped around her could become the arms of her knight. She could imagine perfectly every muscle and curve of his body, and she knew instinctively how his tall form would fit against her smaller body.

But in these blissful moments, he was as hungry for her as she for him. In reality this was not the case.

As Christmastide drew nearer, more and more rich gifts arrived for Edwina. Conan courted her well. Edwina's spirits were high and she seemed much in love — or at least in love with the attention.

To watch him from afar and try as I might to still my longing, Chandra thought in near despair. That is all I can do.

Chandra sighed, her thoughts never changing and her disposition never improving. She abandoned the biting cold for the warmth of the hall, thinking as she went, Would that I could have been the firstborn, then there would be no choice. And then . . .

She warmed a cup of milk with a hot poker from the fire and sat near the hearth, absorbing the heat. Locked in her heart was a love so strong it burned brighter every day. And every day the inevitable marriage of her sister to the man she longed for drew nearer.

"You seem not even a part of this world," came the voice of Medwin.

Chandra jumped in surprise and looked up at her father. She smiled at him fondly.

"Do you think I have not noticed your low spirits, lass? Are your troubles so many?"

"Oh, nay," she replied, smiling and reaching for his hand. "I always miss Mother most when the cold is here. I remember when we'd sit before the fire and do our sewing — all of us — and we would talk of so many things. Women's things. It seems the winters are colder now." Her voice became softer and drifted off. When no response came from Medwin, she looked up to see the old gray eyes looking off into some distant place.

"I'm sorry, Father. I know you miss her too."

"Aye, the winters were not so cold then."

"Spring will be here soon. The flowers will bloom and —"

The old gray eyes took light. "And Edwina will be wed. Ah, it will be a glad day when I welcome Alaric's son into my family. A glad day!"

Chandra looked into her lap and nodded.

"Have you seen what new gift he has sent? A mare of fine lineage came for her just this morn, a gift from Stoddard. All the finest horses are raised there, and the one for his lady is among the finest."

Chandra frowned. "Edwina has never been much for horses," she said quietly.

"Perhaps that will change when she is married to Conan. She must learn to keep pace with her husband. Conan is a man of great energy."

"Do you think it possible, Father?"

"Aye, I think she will manage. Since these many gifts have been arriving she seems brighter, livelier. Yea, marriage to a man as fine and strong as Conan may serve as a healing balm for Edwina."

"She will be well cared for —" Chandra started.

"I had hoped for a match for Conan from my house. In truth, I had not thought of Edwina and knew not Laine —"

Chandra stared at her father with her mouth slightly agape and her eyes wide. She was half afraid of what he might say. He chucked her under the chin.

"I thought in one more summer I would speak to Alaric about you. Your temperament and hardy fitness seemed a like match for Conan. But the lad surprised me with his choice and —"

"By the heel of Satan!" she cursed. One more summer!

"What say you, lass?" He frowned.

"Nothing, Father. Only that I wish the star-struck knight could have given me one more summer. I would not have argued against you."

He raised one brow. "I had not thought you ready to take a husband. Do you tell me now that you wish to be wed?"

"Nay, but that I could have been ready for that one," she said, pouting. "And I will tell you that I think I would have been a far better choice than the one made!"

Medwin's frown deepened. "Do you covet what is your sister's?" he asked slowly and sternly.

Chandra dropped her head. "Nay, Father. I am pleased for Edwina."

"We do not speak of a frock or bauble, Chandra. We speak of a man and woman in marriage. 'Tis a serious sin to find your heart cast to a man thus committed."

"Yea," she murmured, her guilt and frustration wrenching her insides.

"I am indebted to Lady Udele for bringing our children together. I had not aspired to so much. Conan's reputation

is firm in England and France, and I half expected him to
bring a duke's daughter home to wed. Surely he could have
had more —"

Chandra looked at Medwin in awe. "Udele?" Chandra
questioned softly.

"Aye, Lady Udele was quick to see that joined together
our lands would make a greater power." Medwin shrugged.
"It is a thing I've known for a very long time, but Conan
expressed no interest in my oldest daughter. All he needed
was a word from his mother and a soft smile from Edwina.
Where is the need for faraway lands, however rich? Now
he will rule over a large holding in his own England."

Chandra's throat ached and tears welled under clenched
lids. She could not pretend that it didn't matter, for her
whole dream seemed crushed. However important the consideration of lands and wealth, Edwina was not strong
enough or wise enough. She could never love him enough!

Medwin lifted her chin and gave a rather perplexed
look at his daughter's tears. He questioned her with his
eyes.

"Conan needs a woman of strength and spirit to help
him prosper," she heard herself say. "A woman with as
much strength and spirit as he has! Father, how *can* you
think this a good match when I —"

"Chandra!" Medwin snarled.

The door to the keep burst open, and, with a gust of
wind that sent his dark blue mantle billowing, the intruder stepped inside. Soft leather boots were strapped
tightly to his legs, covering to the knee his blue chausses.
A red tunic covered chain mail, and his helm was still
resting in one gauntleted hand. He gave the door a lusty
kick to close it, and there he stood, feet braced apart and

his hand on his hip. His white teeth gleamed from behind his dark beard.

Chandra's mouth formed his name, though silently. "Conan."

Medwin was more verbal, and his smile nearly matched Sir Conan's. "Conan! Here! We could not have known you would come! We would have set a boar to roast had we known."

"I could not send word ahead, my lord," he apologized. "I did not think I could be spared from my duties, but I have wrestled away a few days and thought to spend them here, with my bride and her family."

"She will be delighted! Honored! You have ridden so far and through this hateful weather — for Edwina! A fine son you will make!"

Chandra's hand flew to her mouth to still an outraged cry. Her feet took her quickly to the stair, and with tears flowing in spite of her efforts to stop them, she fled the room.

Conan looked aghast as she flew past him, her pretty face streaked with tears and her glorious hair bouncing down her back as she ran up the stairs. He cast a confused look toward Medwin. "My lord?"

" 'Twas not of your doing, lad," Medwin said, shaking his head in disappointment.

"She seems heartbroken," Conan said.

"Aye, it would seem. You should be aware, since you will have to deal with this. The lass had her own ideas for a bride for you."

"Chandra?" he questioned.

"Ah, she plays at this now. She is young." He laughed suddenly. "And what lass doesn't set her sights on you?

You are young, strong, rich! And a fine figure of a man. Many, I am sure, will have to give their hearts time to mend when you have spoken your vows to Edwina. 'Tis the way of life.''

Conan looked at the memory of Chandra fleeing up the stair, and with a somewhat melancholy voice he said, "The way of life."

" 'Tis not like her to begrudge her sister's happiness. In truth she is often the one to take extra chores upon herself so that Edwina can be lesser burdened. She has often given up something she loves to satisfy another's craving. Aye, a generous lass. I am sorry you had to see her selfish jealousy this once.''

Conan looked up the stair, a strained expression on his face. He had barely had a moment to notice Chandra, but she had seemed even more beautiful than before, if that was possible. Suddenly, the moments she stood before him at his pavilion months earlier were quite clear in his mind — her glowing eyes, her lustrous hair and her captivating smile. Aye, little more than a child then, but blossoming into womanhood in a most alluring way. He cursed himself then for looking at one so young with such carnal thoughts, but he remembered well the dip his heart had taken. It was the same little lurch he felt just now when Medwin confessed that Chandra desired him. He had not felt that for his betrothed. He thought her fine and good and lovely, but there had been no passion stirring in his blood.

"She is young and lovely," he heard himself say. "She will make a man a good bride.''

"Aye, and I will see that matter done after you and Edwina are wed. A horn of good ale, lad, and a toast to the spring and your wedding.''

"Aye," Conan said with a smile, taking the proffered cup and imitating Medwin, though a little less enthusiastically. "To the spring — and the wedding."

With the bloom of the roses and lilies, the blossoms of the pear and apple trees, Phalen saw the arrival of many guests: the prestigious lords and ladies who would witness the wedding of Sir Conan and Lady Edwina.

Though Medwin's hall was not small and could accommodate many for meals and revelry, trestle tables were set in the gardens, for Phalen would flaunt the flowers and blooming fruit trees that filled the air with a soft romantic scent.

About the village, seeds were sown for lettuce, melons, cresses, beets and onions. The humble folk no longer hid within the walls of their huts, but came out to hang the wash and weed their gardens, lingering for long periods over these tasks to converse with their neighbors. Bakers pulled their carts about the streets, and washwomen hummed as they hefted their heavy baskets from tub to line.

Within the hamlet the people chattered about the upcoming wedding, for the simple serfs were as enchanted by this union as the lordly guests were. Tales of Sir Conan's feats in battle were well known, and his most recent occupation of Stoddard was one of the favorite stories. His choice of bride, the frail and genteel lady of Phalen, pleased one and all. Gossip surrounding the clothes sewn for Edwina and the gems the family would gift her with were as important as Conan's technique in wresting Stoddard Keep from the usurper's hands. Everywhere, from castle to town, there was buzzing over this noble couple. Many times Chandra wanted to cover her ears with her hands and run screaming from their voices.

Chandra's birthday was over and she had passed four and ten. Had there not been so much ado over Edwina's wedding, more notice might have been taken of the fuller breasts and long slender legs that appeared on this young maiden. Some voices broke from the preoccupation with the wedding to remark, as Chandra passed, that she had locked herself away within the keep for the winter and emerged a woman. But Chandra heard none of that. She heard only the praises attesting to Edwina's petite beauty and her likeness to their beloved Millicent.

Within the great walls of a nobleman's castle there is no protection from the realities of life. Chandra had known about the coupling of a man and woman for many years. She had already given assistance to women in childbirth. Most of her childhood companions were already wed to her father's men-at-arms or bowmen or village farmers and apprentices. While she envied them their round bellies, they envied the delicacy of decision over the marriage contract of a nobly born woman.

Cordell was the prize Chandra would dangle before her suitors. It was not nearly as rich as Phalen. It had belonged to Millicent and to Millicent's mother, managed by women for many years. Medwin had given his wife a free hand to manage her dower lands, and when Chandra married, the contract would be the same.

Chandra had been reared to manage Cordell, for it had been decided long ago that Phalen would be Edwina's, Laine would take money as her dowry to the church, and Cordell would belong to Chandra. She knew every detail of the estate by heart. It was not a rich castle or wealthy village and had been maintained more as a retreat than a fortress. There was ample protection, but Cordell did not house a grand army.

Early in her youth when she would see Conan at celebrations during days of feasting and hunting, she had seen herself one day being his bride. He would have rich holdings, his own men-at-arms and stout walls, and Cordell would remain her haven. But now that that dream was crushed, she would attempt the next best possibility. She hoped to persuade her father to allow her Cordell and freedom from matrimony. What difference, after all, did marriage make to her right to manage her own dower lands? She would not bear children, but she would gladly allow the lineage from Conan and Edwina to inherit. A niece, perhaps. She doubted she could be a good wife to any man — now.

Cordell protected fewer than two thousand English commoners. It was mainly a fishing village, but there was fertile land surrounding its other sides. In many ways it was a paradise. The people were well fed and healthy, which was a rarity in most of England's small burghs. It did not lie in a path of destruction when armies traveled through the country. To the east side the keep was built along a high and dangerous section of coastline, perched atop some rugged rocks. It was even too much trouble for the barbarous Vikings, when other ports were more easily conquered.

To the other sides just past the farmland was a forest so dense that to travel south to London one had to venture first north to Colchester to find the passable land routes. Except in the little bit of wood closest to the keep, only those with the king's permission were allowed to hunt. And it was no dandy wood where children ran and played; it was a dense, thick jungle filled with wild game ranging from rabbits to wild boar. If an opposing army chose to attack Cordell, they would have to enter by the only road or spend weeks clearing a path through the wood. Marshes and gullies lay hidden, and the overgrowth was so thick that in many places the sunlight did not touch the ground.

Cordell had a clean, freshly scrubbed look, and the keep was bright and airy. There were large open courtyards, and the flowers seemed to bloom longer, the fruit trees seemed to yield more, and the people were industrious yet unhurried.

Chandra longed for Cordell. In the midst of her sister's wedding, it would have been a blessed solace to be there.

There was no quiet to be found in all of Phalen. The arriving guests had made even the once-quiet gardens a flurry of activity. In the courtyard several men participated in javelin-throwing contests, and others prepared for a hunt. The women filled every corner and cubicle with sewing circles aimed at exchanging gossip.

She knew that with the wedding but a few days away she must press her way into Edwina's crowded bedchamber and make herself available to her sister, or later endure her father's wrath.

As she passed the many fussing women, one of her fears vanished. She needn't face Edwina's happiness, for in the farthest corner of the room, Edwina slumped in a chair. Her hand was resting on her brow and her eyes were closed. One maid passed her a cool cloth to hold to her face while another fanned her.

"Edwina, are you ill?" Chandra asked.

"Nay, dear heart," Edwina replied weakly. "The room has become — so — close . . ."

"A quiet moment will do you well," Chandra advised.

"I will be fine in a moment," Edwina answered.

"Let us send the ladies away, Edwina. They can see your gifts another time. You need rest and quiet."

"I've promised them, dear," Edwina sighed. "They have come so far, and all they ask is to see my gifts and gowns."

"You cannot entertain them if your head aches. Invite them to breakfast with you tomorrow. That will do as well."

Edwina shook her head. "I will be fine in a moment. I have not the heart to disappoint them. They have come so far and bring so many lovely —"

"Edwina, if you press yourself beyond your endurance, you will not see your wedding day. Now, you have no wish to be sick abed when it is time to speak your vows. Never mind. I will do it for you."

Chandra turned and sighed with impatience as she looked around the room. A stronger woman would swoon in the presence of such fussing and tittering. Without further hesitation, she approached some of the ladies in the room. She tactfully begged them to excuse her sister for a brief rest and promised every one she would have a chance to see the many fine things.

Chandra's forthright manner would not accept disfavor or impertinence from any of them, and they did not show her anything less than understanding. With smiles of consideration and a few frowns of concern, the busy ladies departed the chamber and left Edwina and Chandra in peace and quiet.

Edwina did not open her eyes. She sighed, pressing the cool, damp cloth to her brow. Chandra drew a stool near, feeling some sympathy for Edwina and pity for the fact that she could endure very little strain. Chandra shook her head. "I do not know how you will manage," she said so softly that Edwina did not hear.

"Already my head ceases to ache," Edwina sighed, opening her eyes and smiling at her sister.

"I think you must take these wedding parties in smaller drafts," Chandra suggested. "It will do you no good to make yourself ill. Have you eaten?"

"I am not very hungry, dear," Edwina replied. "A short rest will cure all my ills."

Edwina pulled the cloth from her brow and with a half smile handed it to Chandra. "Thank you, Chandra. You are good to think of me."

"You'll have to sleep for a while if you're to be at your best for this evening's entertainment."

Edwina laughed softly and began to rise. "There is far too much to be done —" She stopped abruptly as though she felt a catch somewhere, but then straightened herself purposefully. "I have a few more things to see finished before I rest."

Chandra felt trapped. She could plainly see that Edwina was exhausted and would likely collapse before she neared the altar. It was tempting indeed to allow her older sister to run herself into the ground and never be able to rise from her bed to meet Conan before the priest. Then wouldn't everyone praise the grand match, Chandra thought spitefully.

But she could not abandon Edwina, much as she would have liked to. "What more needs to be done?" she finally asked, though softly.

"A great deal — a great deal indeed. I have not yet selected the birds to be roasted nor the food to be put out for the villagers. There are gifts to be given to the women attending me, a tithe for the priest — an amount not yet settled — and the minstrel I sent for has not arrived. I shall be busy until Conan arrives tonight."

Chandra frowned in disapproval. Many of those chores for the wedding could have been taken care of days earlier, but Edwina was not very good at planning. "It is not so very much," Chandra said. "Will you rest if I promise to see it done?"

"Oh, Chandra, I couldn't let you —"

"I assure you, I shall roust Laine from her prayers and put her to work. A better emissary to Father Michael I cannot imagine."

Edwina laughed at that. "You are so good to me, Chandra dear."

"I would rather be working than sitting to sew with the women," she said with a shrug. "But I will not lift a finger unless you promise to rest until the evening meal."

"That will not be easy, knowing you are working so hard for my wedding day," Edwina said sweetly, embracing Chandra and holding her near.

Chandra was caught off guard by the action and returned her sister's embrace almost fiercely. I love them both! she thought miserably, tears springing to her eyes. While she had hoped they would not be man and wife, neither did she want them to be unhappy.

Edwina was aware of the tears and held Chandra away from her, looking quizzically at her younger sister's face. "Chandra, why do you weep?"

Chandra wiped impatiently at her tears and tried to smile, but it was a lame attempt. "I will miss you so much," she told Edwina, her voice catching as she realized she would, indeed, be very lonely without her sister.

Edwina's long, slender fingers gently brushed Chandra's

cheeks. Chandra looked with fondness at Edwina's face. Her eyes were a pale blue, small and soft, and her complexion was fair, not rosy. But when she smiled and comforted, there was a beauty that was nearly regal. Edwina was good and kind. There was much about her to love, even the weaknesses that could be exasperating made Chandra love her, for it made her feel stronger and more capable. Perhaps Conan would feel the same. Perhaps it would be as it had been with her parents, and they would be devoted to each other.

"Now you must dry your eyes and smile prettily," Edwina said. "You are so beautiful when you smile. You are more beautiful than any — so bright and wonderful. But when you weep, my dearest, your nose is very red!"

Chandra laughed suddenly.

"There! That is what I love best about you! When you laugh you are so very beautiful!"

Chandra kissed Edwina's cheek. "Rest easy," she reassured her. "I will see the chores done."

Each of Medwin's daughters had stirrings that were difficult for the others to understand. Laine's calling to the faith was something that Edwina and Chandra did not share. Edwina's soft, retiring manner was a thing that her more robust and lively sisters were impatient with. And as for Chandra, her obsessiveness over managing a large keep and many people with such an intensive regard for every detail was something that confused and bewildered Laine and Edwina, who did not share that appetite for hard work.

Despite their different interests, a deep and unquestioned devotion for one another sustained them. So while Chandra went about making preparations for the wedding, she did it with a glad heart. She had never been very good at sitting still, and these many tasks made her feel more confident, for she knew no other in her father's house could manage with like perfection.

She judged the stock of available birds and chose four round peacocks to be skinned, cooked and then glided back into their colorful feathered skins with the tail feathers spread to make the main dish. She sent maids to gather roses, violets and primroses to be dried and chopped and stirred into the sweet pastry that would make the dessert. She selected the wines to be served at the wedding feast: vernage, a red wine from Tuscany; capric, a special possession of Medwin's from Cyprus; and a Rhenish wine. She worried over the fact that there were no raw apples to set out in case of a disagreeable wine.

For the common folk a boar would be roasted — or should she make that two? With roast goose and piglet and plenty of bragot, a drink made from ale, honey and spices, one boar should be enough. And spiced cakes and cheese would complete their fare.

She gathered together all those who had been selected to serve the prestigious guests in the hall and gardens. She explained carefully, at least a dozen times, how to serve. The goblets must be held so that no unsightly finger marks showed on the side. Wine must be poured with two hands. The meat must be carved before the master of each table after carefully pulling off the wings. When she was convinced they understood, she inspected the clothes they would wear and sent several off to have their tunics cleaned or stitched, warning them of grave consequences if they entered the hall looking shabby.

The minstrel finally arrived with acrobats to aid in the entertainment, and she hurriedly found them lodging

within the castle, though that was a difficult task, so full
was the keep. Some poor castle woman would have to find
a pallet in the town, for her room was given away.

She then, as an afterthought, had a drink prepared with
diaciminum and sweet wine for Edwina, to ward off possible indigestion. She sent diaprune along to make her
immune to fever. She hoped no other affliction would
catch Edwina unawares — she was so susceptible, it seemed,
to illness.

So that some of the festive colors would adorn the breads
and gravies, saffron, leeks and certain floral buds were
gathered. Strings soaked in honey were ordered hung
about the hall so that the flies would not bother the food.
For this great occasion the silver, brass and pewter were
polished, inspected by Chandra, and polished again.
Wooden mazers and cups made of tin were procured, for
there was never enough of the finer metal, but all must
be given an implement to drink from.

Laine had settled with the priest on a sum for the wedding tithe, and as the evening meal was just beginning,
Chandra went with her father's helpmate to his counting
room to draw out the sum. Though the monk attending
her was older than she, he seemed to be in awe of her. He
couldn't quite accept a woman's handling of sums. And
Chandra, already tired and eager to finish these undone
chores, was quick and decisive, and impatient with the
man's slow and tedious counting. More than once she
jerked the coins from his hand to count them herself and,
claiming possession of the quill, scribbled the amounts on
the parchment for Medwin's records.

When that was done, Chandra assured herself that Edwina would already be in the hall, and in near exhaustion

she leaned her forehead against the cool stone wall just outside the chamber she and Laine shared.

With a sigh she opened the door to her bedroom, only to find that the room was no longer her own. Her presence was stripped from the room she had shared with her sisters since birth. The large oaken frame that would belong to the bridal couple replaced the three smaller beds that previously occupied the room.

The transition had been discussed. It was not a complete surprise to her. At least it should not have been. A special chamber for the bedding of the bridal couple needed to be set aside. And for their business of that first night together it would not do to be without a bed that could accommodate them both. For their short stay at Phalen, Edwina and Conan must have a privileged chamber.

But seeing the women preparing the room, hanging bed curtains, sprinkling herbs on the sheets in a fertility ritual, caused Chandra to lean against the open door in near despair. She was in awe of the business before her. The reality of it left her breathless. Their lives would be intimately entwined. The wedding was a formal exchange that would prepare them for this, and the picture was clear. It was the image in her fantasy — but the woman pressed passionately against Conan's body would be Edwina.

"Knowin' you was so busy, milady, we took your things to —"

"I know which room is to be mine," she replied meekly. Giving a last look about the chamber, she smiled sheepishly at the serving woman and quit the room.

Her things were neatly stacked in a room on the other

side of the keep, thankfully far from where the bridal couple would sleep. She was sticky with perspiration and grimy from supervising the cooking. Her hair was limp and dirty, but there was no time to wash it. There was no servant free to aid her in dressing, and with a numb acceptance she moved through her grooming with a general malaise. When she scrubbed her face with a cold cloth she realized with a start that Conan would be downstairs now. Now! He and his family were due to arrive this afternoon, but her chores had kept her far from the guests.

Her hands began to tremble as she pulled her ivory comb through her hair. She donned her dress hurriedly, a pale gold kirtle and a darker gold gunna to cover it. She fastened an anklet about her slender ankle and slipped on her one good pair of slippers. Her gold girdle was the last thing to be applied, and since there was no one to help her, she left her hair to trail loosely down her back.

She paused only a moment to catch her breath and then hurried to the party below. Medwin was the first to notice her and greeted her warmly, not questioning her on her lateness or her appearance. She had missed the meal, and just looking at the trenchers of bones and gristle from the pork caused her stomach to cry out with a loud gurgle, a sound never heard in this noisy hall. Medwin pulled her into a tight circle of friends, his closest friends: Alaric and Theodoric.

"Each spring she blossoms more beautiful than the spring before," Theodoric attested loudly.

"And she is still free to roam among these swains and set their hearts to flutter," Alaric said. "You are unfair, Medwin, to leave her unbidden for so long."

"She is the youngest born and not easy to give away to

any eager young buck. I grow cranky with the thought. She is a great help to me here."

Chandra looked at her father with a twinkle in her eye. It was such a bright spot in her otherwise bleak day to hear someone attesting to her good qualities. "You are kind, Father, to flatter me so, but speak the truth to your friends. He is often angry with me and complains that I nag him overmuch on household matters. I think he will be glad when I am no longer his burden."

"I pray for such burdens," Theodoric roared.

Sir Tedric joined their circle, bowing elaborately over Chandra's hand, making quite a show of his courtly manners. He, too, made several remarks about how lovely she was and offered his escort for any time during the days of celebrating. Even though she did not much like Tedric, even his compliments were easy to bear.

The next to make their way toward her were two knights she barely knew, but recognized with an eager smile. Sir Mallory and Sir Thurwell she knew to be close friends to Conan, and for that reason alone she smiled more gaily than before.

Following was Lady Udele, smiling brightly and showing her most gracious manners. She embraced Chandra warmly.

"Dear child — nay! Child no more, but woman! You are exquisite, but then I knew you would be. You grow more beautiful every time I see you." She cast Medwin a simpering look. "My lord, you have the most beautiful daughters in the land. Lady Chandra," she sighed, taking Chandra's hand in her own. "You are a vision."

Chandra smiled, thanking the lady rather awkwardly. She could not help but believe that had Udele kept silent,

Conan might not have been persuaded to ask for Edwina's hand. "You are overkind, my lady," Chandra demurred.

"I am not kind!" Udele protested. "I speak only the truth! Sir Medwin, you must catch a fine husband for this lass, and soon. Her face and body beckon a man's touch!" The men laughed loudly at Udele's compliment and Chandra felt her cheeks burn with embarrassment.

"Come, dear," Udele urged. "Come and greet my son and soon-to-be daughter."

Chandra let Lady Udele pull her toward the bridal couple, and all those compliments that only moments earlier made her confidence soar seemed long ago and far away. Now she felt her stomach jump and her heart race at the thought of facing Conan.

Edwina was glowingly lovely at Conan's side, her pale, soft beauty radiating her high spirits. Her gown was the same soft blue that she had worn to the tournament feast, a gold girdle that had belonged to Millicent fitting snugly about her narrow hips. A sheer length of pale blue cloth fell from her circlet, a gold band that was perfectly fitted about her head. The cloth did not hide her beautiful hair, but rather drew attention to it, for the golden locks fell luxuriously down her back to far below the sheer blue.

Chandra had wanted Edwina to look her prettiest for the wedding, but this sight of her only made her feel dowdy. Her composure was teetering on a brittle edge, nearly ready to tumble.

Conan kissed her hand and greeted her warmly, but she did not hear his words. He seemed to have grown taller, his shoulders broader than before — or had her memory failed her? His widely acclaimed victory at Stoddard might cause him to stand taller, more self-assured. He was terribly at ease with being the center of attention.

"I thought by coming early I might be of some help to Edwina, with her blessed mother gone," Udele said, patting the bride's hand with affection. Chandra felt stung. It was her mother, too. "But I've made the rounds and find she has completed all the preparations. The church is decked in the finest of colors and the meals well planned. Even now the cooks work hard to please her. There is not a thing undone."

Chandra looked in some perplexity at Edwina, who smiled shyly at the compliments and never uttered a word that she had done very little of the work herself. Then she looked at Udele and saw the glitter in her green eyes. Chandra was not a fool. Had Udele truly asked, she would have learned that those in service to the castle worked by Chandra's orders. This play was for Conan, making his bride appear industrious and efficient.

"You are so lovely, dear," Udele said to Edwina. "How proud I shall be to call you daughter."

"Thank you, madam," Edwina replied shyly.

"Is she not the most perfect bride, Conan? Ah, you are a lucky man."

Conan's arm slipped around Edwina's delicate waist and he pulled her close, smiling into her eyes. "She is, madam," he agreed. His lips came down slowly and Edwina met him in a kiss.

It did not go unnoticed, for first one man cried out and then many joined in, making jests, crude and otherwise, over the groom's eagerness. Conan seemed to enjoy the attention and Edwina lightly blushed. The one who glowed was Udele, taking a sidelong glance at Chandra, meeting the younger girl's eyes. She seemed to be saying something, announcing that she had the situation well in hand.

Without asking to be excused, Chandra turned and melted into the crowd of knights and ladies. She took the first exit from the stifling hall and fled straightaway to the gardens. She startled a young couple who had escaped to that haven in hopes of having a few private moments, finding their hopes dashed as Chandra breezed through. Her steps were quick and agitated. She walked deep into the roses toward her favorite hiding place, plopping down on the garden bench with a huff, feeling the anger and frustration tighten her every muscle.

It was only moments before the anger fled and she relaxed into a rush of tears. Her tired body simply could not support her wish to be gay and composed. She was not only to stand and watch her every dream blow away like clouds on a windy day, but her labors were to go completely unnoticed as well. She could not stand pleased and poised; it was too much to ask.

Chandra was not disturbed in the garden and her tears became less passionate as the hour grew later. The sounds from within the hall grew dimmer and she knew that many were giving up their horns and seeking their beds. But Chandra did not leave. She would allow enough time for all the guests to retire. She could not enter the hall and let her swollen eyes betray her own weak emotions.

When the hall was completely quiet she rose with a sigh and made her way into the keep, oblivious to how long she had hidden in the garden. Her steps were slow and lazy, her hands plunged deep into the pockets of her gunna and her head down. She kicked at a pebble now and then in her path.

Suddenly she felt as if she'd been hit with a ramming log and before she could fall, strong arms encircled her and righted her.

"My pardon, lady, I—" Conan apologized. "Chandra! I'm sorry, I didn't see you."

"Nor I you," she said breathlessly. " 'Twas my fault. I was watching my feet." She made to pass him to go on her way, but he stopped her.

"Is something amiss? You're about so late — Chandra? Have you been crying?"

"Nay, I am only very tired. Good night, my lord."

"A moment, I pray. I think I should at least give you thanks. I know what you have done."

"I?" she asked, confused.

"I know you labored hard in preparation for the wedding."

"How would you know?"

"Edwina. She is not so selfish as to take credit for your hard work, but I urged her to let the matter rest as it does with my mother. If it brings pride to my mother and her pleasure with Edwina, no harm done."

"No harm done," Chandra murmured.

"Is that your reason for tears?" he asked with sincerity.

"Worry not over my moods, Sir Conan. Maids are often silly and given to foolish giggling or crying."

He smiled faintly and shook his head. A warm feeling possessed him as he looked at her in the moonlight. He felt smitten as a virgin lad on the one hand, and a brotherly pride on the other. "But you are not a silly maid, Chandra. I have known you since you were a little girl and even then you would not cry easily. I think if you have tears, they must be hard earned." His expression changed slightly and he looked at her closely. "Has someone done you harm, Chandra? Has some ill-mannered oaf brought you to this spot and treated you unkindly? Taking advantage —"

"Sir Conan! 'Tis most unseemly of you to be so concerned with my virtue! Nay, there was no one. I wish to heaven there had been."

"I rather assume there will be many, if there are not already," he replied rather sullenly. "You will be sorely set upon, and wandering alone in the gardens late at night will make you easy prey."

"I am not wandering. I wanted to be alone. As to the many men: they will court my father for my dower estate, and no interested man will dare treat me ill with that prize in the balance."

"Still, you should take greater care."

"Strange that you show concern," she threw back at him. The fool, she thought. I want no part of his brotherly affection. "Wouldn't your efforts be better spent seeing to Edwina's virtue?"

He laughed at her and leaned back against the tree. "Her virtue is the most guarded in all Christendom. I dare not steal a kiss lest her women fall on us and whisk her away to her bedchamber."

Chandra could not resist an adolescent pout. "She seemed the eager bride in the hall tonight."

"Did she now?" he replied, looking at the ground and giving a rock a kick with his toe. "Aye, I suppose she did. But her head began to ache and the day proved too tiresome."

"Too tiresome!" she cried. At the very moment the words left her mouth, she felt the hot sting of tears again. She wanted to scream and stomp her feet, but faced with her sister's betrothed she could say nothing.

"I know it must be hard for you to watch Edwina shine in the wake of your hard work," he said consolingly.

She groaned and turned away from him, clenching her fists and grinding her teeth. Oh, that was the least of it!

"But I know there is more that causes you pain," he said from behind her, his hands holding on to her upper arms as if he would not allow her to turn and face him.

"Oh, you are a fool," she sighed.

"Am I a fool, damsel?" he said in a low voice. "Tell me. How am I a fool?"

Tears coursed down her cheeks and she knew the battle lost. She could not contain herself. She was grateful that her back was to him, but he was very near. Too near to give her comfort. "How did you not see that I sought you out, bold though it was, as a proper betrothed? I prayed you would take notice of me as a woman deserving —"

"I noticed," he said, his voice barely a whisper. "But you were so very young." It was more of a sigh than a statement.

She rambled, forgetting herself. "Edwina never made mention that she was interested. She was so very near to a proper betrothal to Tedric, and we all thought it would be only days before my father would give his consent and the matter would be done. Never, never would I have come to your pavilion that day had I known you would take Edwina! Oh, Conan," she sobbed, trying to turn to look at him. He held her fast, keeping her back toward him.

His voice was soft in her ear. "Two beautiful sisters both desire me and I am the last to know." He laughed a bit ruefully. "Do you know, chérie, how many men pray for this problem?"

She hung her head dejectedly. She could not bear to have him pity her, or worse, laugh at her. "I thought it quite sensible," she said, controlling her voice better now and wiping the tears from her cheeks. "I swore a thousand times I would never tell you, but since I was a child I have watched you, learning your habits, understanding your ways. When you chased me and teased me," she said, her voice catching, "I was determined, even then, that someday — Oh! You must think me so foolish!"

"Nay, fair Chandra. I am sorry you are hurt."

" 'Tis no fault of yours," she sighed. "I will not embarrass you again, have no fear."

"You were so young then," he repeated, a melancholy note to his voice. "If only I could have known. If I could have been more patient. I could not have known I would regret this day."

"Jesu!" she gasped. She tried to turn to look at him, but he held her fast.

"Do not turn, lady. Be still."

Startled by his request she stood as still as stone, the pressure where his hands held her upper arms sending shivers through her. He did not want her to face him. What would she see? A pained look in his eyes? A tear? She waited and listened.

"God forgive me," he said. "I feel wretched!"

"Say not another word," she begged.

"And what are we to do, Chandra? Pretend we have not spoken? Pretend these words have not passed between us? Can I look at you now and not see a woman who loves me? Will you be blind to what you see in my eyes?"

A part of her was shamed at her own impetuous tongue and another part swelled with pride. He did not think her a foolish maid. What she felt was real and mirrored his feelings.

"Do you know what binds a man?" he asked. "Not pretty

parties and the number of maids who desire him. It is honor! Oath! The code of chivalry that I have pledged to keep. My promise, my word is my life. If I have erred, I pray God gives me the courage to live with my mistake as a man would and not whimper like a babe in arms."

Chandra's eyes were dry and the pain was gone from her chest. The necessity that she accept this marriage between Conan and Edwina washed over her like a warm bath. Conan did not take these words lightly. He was a leader of men, a lord over lands. The slightest mark against his name would bring him trouble. If his word could not be believed, who would trust him to lead them into battle?

"Yea, my lord," she murmured. "Your promise has been given. I love my sister true and wish her no ill. You shall never again hear complaint from my lips, and your chivalry will not allow you to bring your sorrows to my ears."

His lips, so close to her ear, brought his words in a whisper. "Walk away from me. Quickly." The grip on her arms slackened and she was free of his hold.

The first step took the greatest strength, but with every additional step her resolve became firmer. She prayed he would not so much as speak her name to draw her back.

The night was dark and the stars shone brightly. The scents from the garden were intoxicating, the air cool and comfortable, with the slightest breeze stirring. Conan watched her go. With every step she took away from him, he prayed she would not turn. If she turned to him now he knew his oath would mean nothing.

CHAPTER
5

THE witching hour came and went. The petals of the flowers were closed against the night, and the moon, barely a sliver, did not give much light. The gardens of Phalen Castle lay quiet and still. Not a whisper was heard within the great walls of the keep, for hardly a man could raise his head since the drinking ceased. Only the occasional bark of a hound or the song of the night bird could be heard.

Another knight now leaned against the tree that earlier had supported Sir Conan. Deep in the garden where no one from a castle wall or window could see, Sir Mallory waited. He idly struck a twig against his thigh as his mind turned over in consideration of his deed.

His ears were pricked by a slight stirring on the garden path. He would know every sound alien to the night, and even if he had been sleeping soundly he would have roused to any noise out of place. He turned in the direction of the approaching intruder.

Edythe stopped when she saw him and paused a moment to behold him. That he was there at all caused her heart to jump. With three quick steps she was in his arms.

Mallory had lectured himself long and hard on the inadvisability of touching her or letting her touch him. But as she came through the shrubs, looking so like an angel in her pale white dressing gown, her feet bare and her dark hair trailing loose down her back, his arms received her when he would have willed it otherwise.

Good sense was abandoned as he held her against him, his hands caressing the silky tresses of her hair, his head filling with the heady scent of her. It was with great reluctance that he released her.

"I was afraid you would not come," she breathed.

"Edythe, I should not have come. This is very dangerous."

"I perceive no danger, sir knight. As I see it, the very worst that could come of this is my father could force us into wedlock." She laughed softly. "He would be surprised at my meager reluctance."

"You have seen precious little of the real world in your guarded home. If it did not please your father to see us wed, he could have me banished or even killed, and you sent to the convent. And it would be called justice."

"Do not talk," she pleaded. "Hold me."

He sighed wearily. "That is dangerous as well. Edythe, do you not see? I have lived over thirty years. Had I the inclination or the opportunity, I could have fathered a child of your years. And I have known too many women. I do not have the patience to hold a virgin lass. You cause me great pain with your persistence."

Her smile was sweet and soft. "But you came."

"Yea, but I do not think it wise."

"But you force this upon us. Court me openly and let us see the truth to their reluctance. Would my brother oppose you as a just mate for me? Would my father, your beloved friend, banish you for loving me? Yea, let us see."

He grabbed her by the arms. "You once gave your word

you would confide in no one. I hold you to your word even now. You promised me."

"Aye, Mallory, and yet I keep my word. But you are foolish to force this secrecy upon us. Your efforts would be better spent in finding us a way to marry."

"There is nothing more impossible. Would that it could happen simply and with your family's blessing, but I promise you, it cannot."

He had said the word impossible many times, but this time Edythe smiled and touched his arm. This time he had finally said he desired marriage with her. "Though you would have me believe otherwise, sir knight, I know you love me."

Mallory's face was twisted with his frustration. He turned away and ran a hand through his thick, dark hair. Edythe stood with hands folded in front of her and studied the broad expanse of his back as she had often done in the past. For a long time she had watched this friend of her brother's, studying his mannerisms and examining his frame to the smallest detail. The slightness of her own form made his seem even more powerful.

His lack of lands and power might make him less desirable to another maid, but this in part added to his flavor in her eyes. He was not bound by family ties nor was he a slave to prosperity. His spirit seemed so free and laced with a certain wildness. He had not been raised within the cold and protective confines of a mighty castle but knew the way to live with naught but his knife. He knew not only the ways of lords and princes, but the laws of the land and nature. He could boast that everything he possessed had come of his own hard labors and was never the gift of another man. He had known more of life in his thirty years than many men would know in sixty.

Perhaps too much. Perhaps he had seen the cruel acts of too many nobles. Even though he lived now as a part of their circle, did he still hold them above himself and not dare think of himself as an equal because of his landless state? She knew it was a thing she could not help him with, but a challenge he must meet on his own.

"I said, I know you love me, Mallory."

He turned back to her. He looked at her for a long moment, and with great impatience in his voice he answered her. "Yea, I love thee," he whispered. "More than I allowed I could," he said even more softly.

"Do you not see this as a beginning?"

"I cannot see the beginning, nor can I see the end. 'Twould be a simple matter to deal with your infatuation if I felt nothing, but I see years of futile wanting, ages of hopeless yearnings, and that is not what I wish for you. You should not be cast to secret meetings that come to naught. You should be properly wed to a baron or rich knight, not scampering about bushes late at night for as little as a kiss from a penniless mercenary."

"You are not a heathen mercenary," she breathed. "A knight of Henry!"

"How do you think I began? Not as Sir Conan, son of a fine lord with money to buy my armor and a noble teacher such as Theodoric."

"Matters not to me," she said, lifting her chin. "You are a knight of Henry now."

"Compared to the men who will ask for you, I am nothing. And you are here in the darkness against your parents' will, tempting me with your hopes and dreams of things that can never be!"

"But this is where I want to be," she said softly.

She caressed his chest with her hands, and with a groan

he took her in his arms again, covering her mouth hungrily. He heard her sigh joyously, and he hated himself and her for this emotion that enslaved them. He wished that she would flee from him, declare her hatred for him, so that the agony would end. But if she left him he thought he might die. He ached and trembled with the urge to find a grassy bed and become a part of her, but instead he softened his grasp and tilted her back so that he might look into her eyes.

"Do not turn me away, my love," she pleaded softly. "If you want me, claim me before the world."

"Edythe, sweet maid —"

"Your head turns with worry when you should be working plans and methods. There is yet time, for my father will not press marriage upon me too soon. And if it cannot be, let us make a home in the deepest forest and hide us there forever."

He touched the ivory softness of her cheek, making a line to her fine, strong jaw with fingers that were rough from many toils. He smiled at her loveliness, admiring the bright, determined green eyes. "I am glad for you that you have not seen the many truths that cause pain. I am glad that you are still driven by hope. I will pray earnestly that life does not rob you of your good faith."

"Tell me that you will hope."

"I cannot prevent it."

"Tell me you will try to find the way."

"I will try."

He lifted her chin with a finger and placed a kiss upon her lips. Though he wanted much more of her, he set her from him. "We've taken enough chances for one night. Go back to your bed."

"Will you meet me once more? Once more before you leave?"

He thought better of it, but he nodded his assent. She threw her arms around his neck and hugged him close, trying to keep the sensation of his arms about her to take with her to bed. She would have lingered into the night, but he turned her about, giving her a little push from behind. There was no further argument. Within moments she had disappeared from sight.

Mallory leaned against the faithful tree and sighed. God must curse me for the things I am thinking, he thought passionately. And when enough time had passed since her departure, he too made his way out of the garden.

From the shrubs on the opposite side of the great oak there came a rustling. A man pulled himself to his feet and clambered out of the protective bushes and onto the garden path. Tedric faced the old oak and bowed.

"You must be the most well-informed piece of tree in all this kingdom," he said. "I vow you know more secrets than Merlin. I would stay and hear yet another lover's story, but my head grows soft." He laughed and slapped the ancient oak in apparent friendship. "I had not thought sharing a night with you would be so informative."

Whistling, he left the garden.

All thought it a good omen that the day of the wedding dawned bright and clear. The bride and groom fasted and confessed, repeated their vows with solemnity, and rose to accept the blessings of the many witnesses.

The common folk found the wedding a fine excuse for celebrating. The village was alive with games, dancing, singing and laughter. Sir Medwin provided a huge amount of food for their feasting, and before the afternoon had worn on, the bride and groom paraded through the streets. Rose petals were scattered at their feet and the noble couple threw coins to the villeins. All thought them a perfect pair, the handsome groom and the bright, fair beauty of his bride, the lady of Phalen.

Alaric and Medwin showed no restraint in their celebrating. The old friendship held stronger bonds, and they toasted the bride and groom and the union of their lands as brothers would. Sir Theodoric was not to be left out of the kinship. He joined them with his horn full also and indicated his youngest son, Tedric, who had seemingly cornered Chandra and was in the act of charming her. All three looked in that direction and noted Chandra's bright smile. The aging lords put their heads together and raised their horns to drink to the possibility.

Tedric was not ignorant of women and he knew the way to court a maid. He entertained Chandra first with many tributes to her loveliness and then with humorous remembrances from his youth and travels. Though she seemed somewhat saddened earlier in the day, her spirit was lighter now. He took it as a positive sign.

"I vow your wedding will follow soon. Tell me, maid Chandra, how soon must I return to witness it?"

"Not too soon, I hope, for there is no groom," she returned.

"I don't believe you. I had heard at least a score waited in line to speak to Medwin."

She giggled lightly. "I promise you, I cannot name one. But my father grows tired of his house full of women. Laine goes to her calling soon, and he will be rid of me as soon as he can."

Tedric's smile vanished and he looked at her seriously. "Is there no man, Chandra? No one who has crept silently into your heart to abide there, waiting only for you to claim him?"

She looked into her lap and said quietly, "Nay. There is no one."

He lifted her chin with a finger. "Your eyes say otherwise. In your eyes I see a love lost."

"You are mistaken, sir knight. I cannot lose a love I've never known."

"You have loved no man?"

She took a light spirit she hoped he would not sense was forced. "Do you bid me sing songs better held in my heart? Nay, I will not tell you what a maiden dreams," she said, smiling coquettishly. "Nor will I tell you how many hearts I hope to break."

Tedric did not laugh. "You gave your colors to Sir Conan at the contest of arms."

For a moment her eyes widened, but quickly she smiled. She reminded herself not to react to the name. "I knew of no other," she replied innocently. "Would you have me give no tokens at such a contest?"

"You do not care for him overmuch?" he asked, still serious.

"Of course I care for him. He has married my sister and that makes him a brother of mine."

Tedric stood straighter and cleared his throat. "I should like to speak to your father and make my proposal."

Chandra's heart fell. "We are only friends, Tedric."

"We do not know each other well enough to be more. With your permission, lady, I will speak to Medwin."

Total confusion overtook her. "I tell you true, I am not

prepared for your offer. I must have time to think on the matter."

"I hope not for very long. I grow anxious to take a bride of my own. And I think your father could be persuaded in my direction."

She greatly feared he was right. After all, he had seemed a fair choice for Edwina, whose dowry was much richer. "Surely there must be maids of richer means than I, Sir Tedric. And in your many travels you must have left hearts aching."

"I assure you there have been none to outshine you. Your beauty alone bodes of riches unexplored."

Chandra felt the rush of color to her cheeks. His compliments had not embarrassed her earlier because he did not direct them with such intimacy. "I must be ready to attend my sister, Tedric. May we talk of this later? When the hall is again quiet and I can think of myself?"

"Chandra, where is the need for deep thought? Either you care for me or you do not. My family has as much wealth as yours."

She looked at him in some surprise, for she had not considered wealth or lack of it, and his tone seemed more irritated than before. "You have a fine family," she replied.

"Is it because I bring no great inheritance from my father that you delay?"

"Nay, Tedric. It is my sister's wedding day and there is no urgency in my decision. I have another year at least before I must make haste in —"

"There is no reason for your hesitancy save one: there must be another who occupies your thoughts," he said gravely.

"There is no one, Tedric. And I will give you my answer later. Now I must see to my other duties."

She started away, but he caught her arm to draw her back. "Do not play me as you would a puppet, Lady Chandra. I will not dance on a string for your amusement."

She jerked her arm away, and for an instant he was taken aback by the sharp flash of her blue eyes. Young though she was, she was neither afraid nor intimidated by his anger. She faced him bravely. "If you truly wish my consideration, Sir Tedric, do not act the knave."

He made to snap back at her but bit his tongue as they were joined by a tall, overbearing presence. Sir Thurwell towered over them both. He gave his tawny and unruly hair a shake as if to throw it out of his face and smiled mischievously at them. "Lady Chandra," he nodded. "Tedric," he nodded again, purposely not using the knight's title before his name. "A grand wedding, is it not?"

Chandra did not know him well, but she felt a special closeness to him now, a kinship begun because she knew they both loved Conan and strengthened because he had obviously come to her aid. "Grand indeed," she smiled. "Has the bridal couple returned from the village?"

"Yea, lady, and I venture to guess they've had enough of celebrating. Lady Edwina has returned to her chamber."

"Then I must attend her. Will you excuse me?"

"I would deem it an honor if you would allow me to escort you there."

"Of course, Sir Thurwell. With pleasure."

She rested her hand atop his and they strolled through the garden toward the hall, smiling at those they passed and talking in a lighthearted fashion of general things. It was not until they were in a quiet place in the hall that he stopped her and spoke to her seriously.

"It would appear, my lady, that you had more than you could handle with Sir Tedric. Has he insulted you?"

"I do not know what made him angry," she replied in some confusion.

"He is oft a surly tempered lad," Thurwell remarked. "Have a care when you are alone with him."

A feeling of security washed over her. Thurwell's size boasted of strength, and his age, for he was probably twenty years her senior, spoke of a fatherly and protective nature. She gently touched his arm. "It is kind of you to warn me, but Tedric is harmless, I think."

Thurwell frowned slightly. "Just so that you are aware," he advised. "And if there is a problem, I am at your call."

She smiled her thanks, more appreciative of his offer than she could say, and, patting his arm warmly, she turned to go to her sister.

Thurwell would have returned to the gardens and to his drinking horn, but he was sidetracked in an otherwise empty gallery by Tedric.

"Do you court the lady Chandra?" he asked Thurwell somewhat officially.

"Nay, lad," Thurwell replied in an amused tone. "I only seek to protect her from foxes and wolves."

"Do you challenge my manners with the lady?"

Thurwell leaned back against the wall and scratched his rusty beard lazily. He looked on the smaller man's rigid form with humor. "I think it unchivalrous to accost the lady publicly, but if that is the way you court a damsel, who am I to call you unmannerly?"

"And who are you to question me?"

"I am a knight and my code binds me to protect ladies from braying jackals and fools. That is who I am." His tone was final and his patience was at an end, but he did nothing to soothe the hot-tempered knight. He started to brush past him, but Tedric grabbed a glove from his belt and cast it to the floor in challenge.

Thurwell looked at the gauntlet and laughed out loud. " 'Tis the day of Sir Conan's wedding and I will not play your games. It would be taken as a bad omen to spill the blood of a child on a noble wedding day." That said, he easily moved Tedric out of his way and quit the hall.

Tedric stood in silent rage, his gauntlet lying on the floor. If the challenge had been issued in the presence of others, Thurwell would not have dared treat him so.

This threesome, Thurwell, Mallory and Conan, was the worst irritation to Tedric. They laughed at him, never taking his challenges seriously. Now that Conan no longer served Sir Theodoric, Tedric was not a part of that group. He had hoped that when Mallory and Thurwell left Anselm in the fall they would not return, but he should have guessed that they would continue to be most often at Conan's call, protecting and serving him as if he were a great young lord.

"Someday they will hearken to me," he said aloud, though there was no one there to hear him.

As he stooped to pick up the glove, the knowledge that Thurwell could have easily beaten him was an inflaming thought. He tucked the glove into his belt and vowed to accept the fact that Conan was the stronger in arms. It would be useless to try to prove himself in battle. He must use his wits. "I am smarter than Conan," he thought with growing pleasure. "I can find a way to ruin him without lifting a finger."

He gave his gauntlets a pat and went again to the

gardens. For the rest of that day and the day following, he watched the wedding guests closely. He found first the puzzle and soon after, the missing piece.

Lady Udele walked through the courtyard after breaking the fast. She looked at the flowers that lined the walk. Phalen was not a rich hall, but the gardens were exquisite. She vowed to return to Anselm and make their gardens richer.

"Good morningtide, lady," Tedric greeted with a bow. "I thought the day could not shine brighter until I saw your lovely face."

Udele stopped short and gave the young man a suspicious look. She could think of no reason for him to treat her with such pleasantness. "Good morningtide, sir," she returned casually.

"It is a stroke of luck that I find you walking here, for I have longed for a few moments of your time."

"To what purpose, Sir Tedric?" she asked coldly.

Tedric looked over her shoulder at the women behind her. "Alone, if I might be so bold."

Though she did not think it a good idea, she could not deny the presumptuous knight a moment of privacy, for she wondered at his business. She turned to her women. "Wait for me in the hall. I will be along shortly."

Tedric watched as the women walked away, and then, before giving his attention to Udele, he looked about the garden to assure himself that they were alone.

"This is a place of great conspiracies, madam. Were you aware of the secrets held by the flowers?"

Udele straightened her spine indignantly, her actions urging him to get to the point, but Tedric seemed unhurried.

"Many lovers meet in this place late at night — lovers who cannot exchange their promises in the light of day."

"What is it you wish to tell me, Tedric?"

"I will tell you *first,* lady. And then I will mayhaps tell the world. Conan and Chandra met here last eventide, long after the others had retired. Conan is not entirely pleased with his hasty choice of bride. It seems he loves Lady Chandra —"

"Slander!" Udele hissed. "You are a fool to believe such —"

"I heard him tell her so. He said he could not have known how he would have regretted this day." Tedric shook his head in mirth. "What luck, this, madam. Conan will not look so mighty when he is caught tampering with his wife's young sister."

Udele took a deep breath and composed herself. "You know so little of my son, Tedric. Do not hold your hopes on the event of that. Conan will not weaken to any such lust. His promise is good to the end!"

"You may be right, lady," Tedric said. " 'Twould be in good measure to see Chandra wed to a man who can keep a strong hold on her."

Udele was amused by Tedric's forthright manner. "And who would that be, sir knight?" she asked with a smile.

"Why, I would be honored to have Lady Chandra."

"Then I wish you the best, Tedric." She turned and began to walk away.

"I had hoped you would offer aid," he admitted brazenly.

"I?" she said, turning. "How do you need aid, sir, when your courtly manners and eager pursuit should set the matter done?"

"I have a strong family, true, but no lands and little

money. I lost one bride to a richer groom and do not relish
the thought of losing again. Gold or silver would quicken
Medwin's mind."

Udele laughed outright. "Find another source, sir. And
do not think to threaten me with my son's misbehavior;
he will not shame our family by dallying with Chandra.
He is not a fool."

"Love has made fools of stronger men," Tedric pointed
out, his attitude casual. "Even our king has forgotten
himself on occasion. But then who would reprimand the
king?"

"But Conan —" Udele attempted.

"Yet a knight who casts his honor aside for the brief
pleasures of love — an adulterous knight — that is another
story. It would take the brave Falcon a very long time to
restore his reputation. He would not be among the favorites, that is certain."

Udele turned her back on Tedric. "Conan would not,"
she insisted, voicing more assurance than she felt.

"Conan was not the only one to declare his love in this
garden," Tedric said knowingly.

Udele turned and looked at him with open curiosity,
completely unprepared for what more he had to offer.

"It appears your daughter, Edythe, has also cast her lot.
She is also in love. Ah, love! Everywhere I look I see love!
But poor Edythe! The knight she has chosen is poor and
has so little."

"And who might that be, sir?" Udele asked.

"Why, Sir Mallory, as a matter of fact," Tedric returned
with an air of superiority.

Udele almost grimaced but caught herself. She had long
thought it a handicap to have a daughter. Edythe could
add little to the family estate and in all probability would

only take her portion to another family. That was a fact of life that Udele had come to accept, but she would not accept Edythe's marriage to a penniless knight who would not even add prestige to their name. Mallory would only become one more person to share what had been accumulated.

"I do not think a marriage between them will come to pass," she said.

"Ah, perhaps not, if you are quick, madam," Tedric said. "But I think riches unimportant in Lord Alaric's mind. Reputation is all, and Mallory has acquired a good one — though I suspect it has been through good luck and not good deeds."

"Alaric is not a fool. His daughter will have a rich husband."

"Alaric is not a fool," Tedric mimicked. "And he loves Mallory as if he were his son."

Udele feared that Tedric was right this once. She looked at the young knight in expectation.

"I could tell Alaric this very morn, and Edythe would not deny it. I think the wedding could be done before summer touches the land."

"Perhaps they will tell Alaric themselves," Udele mused.

"Nay, that will not be. Mallory has made Edythe swear to silence to allow him enough time to build a case for himself. He fears Alaric would have him banished. Edythe knows her father better, guessing he would simply insist that they marry. The lass is most eager to be found out. You still have time to find a richer husband for your daughter."

"If you do not betray the lovers to Lord Alaric," she said, understanding Tedric's motives quite well and trusting him very little.

"My needs are simple, lady. Help me into marriage with Chandra and I will hold silent. Not one word about all I have seen and heard will pass my lips."

"Why do you want her if you believe she is in love with Conan?"

Tedric smiled knowingly. "She is property also, though not as rich as what Edwina holds, and, looking at the two, Chandra is more the prize in herself. It will not be hard to possess her."

Udele thought quickly. It would never do to allow Conan the slightest opportunity to lose his head and disgrace himself and their family by an adulterous, even incestuous, alliance with Chandra. And there was no denying the maid's beauty and other strengths. Should Conan lose the battle and succumb to her charms, Tedric would be close at hand to expose them. Conan's strengths and oath would be ridiculed. It could greatly affect his position, which would greatly alter his ambitions.

And the matter of Edythe would not be difficult to rectify if the lass stayed quiet about her love for Mallory. Alaric would not worry heavily over her reluctance to marry. It was an accepted fact of life that many maids found disfavor with their fathers' choice of groom.

The matter of dealing with Tedric caused considerable distress, but Udele was not foolish enough to show it overly much. "You will allow me some time? It is not a thing I can manage in one day."

"A little time, lady, but I am impatient for support."

"I will send word to you in not very long. I think perhaps I can help you, if marriage with Chandra is what you truly desire."

"It is, madam," he said with a smile and a slight bow.

She clicked her tongue. "So you, too, are smitten."

He made a fist with one hand and lightly struck his chest, his eyes twinkling. Udele's response was a grimace of distaste. She did not think it showed strength to be such a victim of love's tender call when estates were more logical. She turned and left him standing alone on the garden path.

"Smitten indeed," Tedric said softly as Udele disappeared from sight. He laughed outright. "And it will not be too painful to hold as my own the one thing Sir Conan loves and cannot touch!"

Sir Conan's absence from Stoddard Keep could not be a long one, not even for his wedding. Many of the things that Edwina loved were loaded onto carts, and the servants whose only chore it was to see to this lady made ready. A litter was provided for Edwina, and her horse, the mare that Conan had gifted her with some months before, was tethered at the rear. Edwina could never ride all the way to Stoddard.

Edwina was understandably tearful at her departure. Laine was to go soon to the convent at Thetford and could not be visited by her family for a long while. It was the last time the sisters would all be together at their father's home.

Tedric had watched the departure of Conan and Edwina and now stood just outside the door of the hall to watch as Alaric's family prepared to go. Pierce, the hulking manservant who had served Lady Udele since before she left her father's house, inspected the saddles and lifted Edythe into hers. He stood ready at his lady's horse, waiting for her to come.

Udele came from the hall with Medwin, chatting amiably about the festivities, promising to keep close contact between Stoddard and Anselm and making Edwina's well-being her personal obligation. As she passed Tedric he bowed.

"Farewell, my lady," Tedric smiled. The eyes he met were not warm and friendly. Bright green brimmed with suspicion, but Udele smiled.

"Farewell to you, Sir Tedric," she said sweetly.

"I am in hopes that our paths cross again soon, my lady. I so enjoyed your company I despair to think of how long it will be before —"

"Perhaps you will have occasion to venture near Anselm," she said. "You must stop to visit with us if you do."

Tedric bowed again, his lips curving in a knowing smile. "I hope that is the case, lady, but of course, if you have need of me, you have but to send word."

Udele's smile vanished. "I have protection aplenty, sir knight."

"Just in that event," he said.

Udele did not answer. She moved past him quickly before anything that would raise eyebrows was said. She went to her mount and was lifted into place by Pierce. Within moments the entire group was moving through Phalen's protective gate.

"She will call for me," he thought with satisfaction. He had been lucky in guessing Udele's character accurately. She had seen the dowry to be gained by urging her son to speak quickly for Edwina. Tedric had himself put that idea into her head, though he hadn't intended to. And she must have already suspected and feared that Conan leaned toward Chandra. Tedric was not overly concerned that Conan would disgrace himself with the maid. The cocky knight would hold firm to his oath regardless of the futility of it.

Tedric knew that Udele's love of money and all the grand hopes she laid on her son's future would bring her willingly to Tedric's aid. She would much rather pay to support Tedric's sure solution than risk losing any of their family wealth on an ill-planned marriage or a knight's disgrace.

Tedric smiled at the thought of the ease involved in obtaining money. No battles, no scars and no work. Now that he had one resource he would set about to find another . . . and then another . . . and another . . .

The crops were harvested and the lord of Phalen proclaimed a harvest celebration for the people of the village, but, in comparison to the wedding seen at the castle the spring before, it was a small affair.

In the summer, Medwin had finally released Laine to the convent, and with her went a potful of silver as her dowry. It was a bittersweet parting, for that daughter was no longer his by any claim. For the harvest festival, Chandra stood alone at her father's side. His dependence on her had increased drastically and he seemed to decline steadily. He often spoke of vassals that could take the bulk of his responsibilities. For Chandra, she could see her goal in sight. "You have need of no one, Father. Not while I am here to help you."

And indeed, he needed no castellan to manage Phalen. Chandra would carry the bulk of the responsibilities. She was seldom seen dressed in her finer gunnas and kirtles, for daily she donned a rough wool gown and set about her chores. She was busy from dawn 'til dusk. She did not have time to think, then, of her state of limbo; a maid of marriageable age, she had no preferred groom and her heart was already locked up tight.

She knelt in the garden and clipped the sage, mallow and nightshade that would be used for medicines. She placed them in a small cloth and tied it tightly for storage. When she had made several such packets, she carried them in her apron to the hall. She came across Medwin, apparently just finishing a conversation with one of his men-at-arms.

"Yea, lord, I will make ready and advise the men. We will plan to leave in four days, as it pleases ye."

Medwin nodded and excused the man. He dropped his arm about Chandra's shoulders and walked with her into the manor.

"Where do the men go, Father?"

"I must send a troop to Cordell to collect the tax and rent. I've left it undone for too long."

"And you do not go?"

"Nay," he sighed. "I am too old, daughter, to be uprooted so often. There needs be someone there to manage in my stead. Why did God grant me no sons?"

"Conan will manage here when he is needed, Father. Never fear."

"King Henry and his sons are enemies. Perhaps sons are not such a blessing."

Chandra did not reply, for her father was more often in a mood to talk, that aura of command now gone from his voice.

"When Henry dies there will likely be a battle for the crown. I wonder how many good men will fight."

"Father," she sighed, " 'tis of no worry now. Henry may yet make peace with his sons." She put her arm around his waist. She did not really walk with him these days — she supported him as he walked. "This is the first summer I have not visited Cordell."

"You love it as your mother did," he returned.

"I think perhaps I love it because Mother did. I loved to go there with her. We would spend the days together. She'd say, 'This is to be yours someday, Chandra. You must learn to manage it.' I didn't mind that Laine and Edwina were allowed to play while I worked with Mother. I loved learning and I loved hearing her tell everyone she met that I would be the next lady."

"We did not think it would be so soon," Medwin said pensively. "You shall go there now. As a part of my deputation."

"But you have need of me here, Father. I should not leave you now."

"I can do without you for a time. And I think if you could visit Cordell for a time I might see you smile again."

"I would like to go," she said, brightening at the thought.

"And there," he said affectionately. "I see that smile already. You have worked too hard to please your father, and you deserve a treat. Go. Make ready. I will send a few more men to keep you safe along the road."

She stood on tiptoes and placed a kiss on his cheek. "Thank you, Father," she said. She left him with a skip in her step, and for the first time in some months he heard her humming as she went.

Usually preparation for a trip was a long and drawn-out affair, but Chandra's enthusiasm for this journey saw nearly everything ready in two days. She was hard at work after that seeing that Phalen was in order so that Medwin would have no problems in her absence. She could not rest until she had planned every meal, spoken to those servants staying behind and checked her plans against those of the men-at-arms staying in Phalen's walls. It was late in the

afternoon, when she was seeking out one of the huntsmen, that she noticed a large troop had arrived and their
horses were being tended by stable boys.

"What visitor is here?" she asked the nearest guard.

"The blazon of the Blue Falcon, lady. 'Tis a troop of
Sir Conan."

She turned abruptly and hurried to the hall. Why had
he come? Was Edwina ill? Earlier that summer, King
Henry had fought Philip in France and Conan had not
gone to war, though many had answered the call. A chill
feeling possessed her. Was he here to bid farewell to his
father by marriage to go off to some faraway war?

As she flew into the hall she collided with Sir Thurwell. "Ho!" he shouted, catching her. "I have witnesses,
lady. You've flown straightaway to my arms!"

"You are returned," she said, smiling. "There is no
more war for the king?"

"For the moment, lady." He smiled. "Henry's love of
fighting keeps us well fed," he joked, looking across the
hall to Mallory, who lifted a cup to his mouth.

"Do you ride with Sir Conan?" she asked anxiously.

"Only lately so. We met him upon the road while we
were journeying to Stoddard and he was coming away."

"And why has he come? What is his news? Is my sister
well?"

Thurwell looked to Mallory and grinned. "Yea, lady.
She is well."

She was about to ask more when Conan and Medwin
came into the room, a burst of laughter announcing them.

"There you are, daughter," Medwin said. "Where have
you been? I sent your maids out for you. Conan bears
good news. My daughter is with child."

"Edwina," she breathed looking at Conan. She could see pride in his eyes. He stood tall. "With child!" she cried, a smile of excitement showing on her face. "A son to bear your arms."

He stared at her in silence for a moment. She could not know how she affected him. Her face was shining and her cheeks were flushed with color. In her simple dress that showed she had labored the day long, and in a rough kerchief, her bright blond locks tied back and trailing down her back past her hips, she was more appealing than other women in their finest gowns. And the look of robust health and energy added considerably to her fairness.

He remembered clearly that time long ago when he had come unannounced to spend Christmas with Edwina, and Chandra had fled weeping to her chamber. He dreaded facing her with this good news for fear she would be crushed under the weight of envy. But this bright little star that faced him showed no jealousy. Her happiness for him was sincere. She knew the importance of an heir.

"Is my sister well?"

He frowned slightly, but decided he did not want to tell her that Edwina was often unwell, and since she was never seriously ill, he nodded.

"I should like to see her," Chandra said.

Conan recovered himself from the first sight of her and now could speak in a more confident and relaxed manner. "When the child is born and old enough to travel, I shall send her and the babe to you for a visit among her kin. And you are always welcome in our home."

"I must send her something. When do you journey back?" she asked.

"Not for some time. I will travel on an errand for your

father." He looked to Thurwell and Mallory. "You're welcome to ride with me as always. It will add a fortnight to our journey to see to business at Cordell."

Chandra's mouth fell open and she looked between Conan and her father.

"He will make a better escort for you, daughter," Medwin said. "I will be assured of your safe passage with Conan's arms to protect you."

Now the surprise was Conan's. He looked sharply at Medwin. "Chandra travels with us?"

"Had I not mentioned it?" he laughed. "Ah, my mind grows weak with age, and in my excitement over your news I did forget to tell you. Aye, Chandra goes to Cordell. The pair of you will make an impressive emissary."

Chandra and Conan exchanged troubled glances. "Father," Chandra said somewhat nervously, "Conan will be anxious to do your business quickly and return to his wife. He would not wish to be bothered with a woman. I would slow the journey."

"You?" Medwin laughed. "I venture it will be the other way. He will likely have trouble keeping pace with you. And since you leave in the morning, are there not things to prepare?"

Conan bowed to his father-in-law. "For myself, my men need a sound meal and a good night before setting out again, my lord. Would you excuse me to my men? I would advise them of this additional errand."

Chandra's brow wrinkled into a frown and she looked down as she took slow steps to the stair while Conan went through the doors of the hall in search of his men. Both seemed heavily in thought and not giving a mind to the duties they were bound to do. Medwin did not notice. He was intent on finding a cold draft to ease his thirst. Mallory walked closer to Thurwell and spoke in hushed tones.

"Did I not tell you there is something amiss in this family?"

" 'Tis not of our concern," Thurwell grumbled, raising his cup to his lips.

"That is the reason for his melancholy," Mallory insisted.

"Unless he asks us to share the burden, say naught." Thurwell lifted his chalice slightly toward the stair. "Do not jest, lad," the older knight advised. "Conan would not see the humor in his predicament."

"Do you forget so soon?" Mallory murmured. "I would be the last to make light of his troubles. I understand his misery."

CHAPTER
6

THE party of men-at-arms, Chandra and two of her maids, and a small number of servants and attendants formed a train that left Phalen Castle early one September morning. The entourage was led by Sir Conan, with Mallory and Thurwell close at his heels. Chandra could easily have kept pace with the men, but she deliberately kept her mount well behind Conan. And he did not fall back to ride beside her.

The distance to Cordell was not great, but the journey was long, for there was no road through the dense forest that surrounded the land side of the manor. They traveled first northeast and then directly south. There were those noble homes along the way that would have welcomed such a party for a night's lodging, but that did not meet Conan's mood.

He was somewhat surprised at having no argument from the women. When they passed the last village of any size on their first day out, he waited for Chandra to question him on his plans for the night, but he heard nothing. When he halted the party at a small clearing in the wood as the sun was lowering, he rode back to her position in the group and threw his arm wide, indicating the place. "This will satisfy our needs for the night. Some of my men will aid you in making a tent for your women."

She looked around as if considering this, her finger touching her lip in thought. He was certain she would complain and ask where the comfort of a roof could be found. Instead she said, "If memory serves me, there is a stream just to the other side of those trees. A strong line and sharp spear could bring us fish for dinner."

The surprise rendered him speechless for a moment. "I'll see to it," he finally grumbled.

That first night he tossed upon the hard ground, feeling when he rose as if he had taken the night on a moving cart. He stumbled into the wood to answer nature's call and heard some soft talking near the stream. Looking through the brush, he saw Chandra's maids holding up a linen sheet in front of the creek. From his vantage point, a bit off the path, he could see Chandra kneeling at the water's edge to wash.

The sight held him spellbound. Her golden hair formed a canopy about her face, and full breasts tempted the strength of her sheer kirtle. Every time he saw her she had grown more beautiful. He turned from the sight with a familiar ache in his loins, and silently cursed this state of affairs. He could not seem to subdue the longing. And if it was not enough that he wanted Chandra, his situation with Edwina left him famished. He could count the number of times he had lain with her, all of them because of his ardent insistence. And always his wife submitted unresponsively to his lovemaking.

He had thought it very noble not to satisfy his longings with some eager and available wench from his own castle, and there were many. Now he wished that he had. Chandra's close presence and his starving passions did not lend him an amiable nature.

"Did you rest well, lady?" he asked as they prepared to leave camp.

"Aye, Sir Conan. My mantle is lined with ermine and it kept me warm and comfortable." He grunted his approval and ended the conversation.

The second night was similarly spent, and Conan's mood was strained. He was miles away in thought and seemed never to hear what was said to him the first time. And his temper was quick. When something was amiss he did not handle the matter with his usual tolerance, but snapped commands at his men to right the situation. His grumbling would have been understood had he traveled with Lady Edwina, for her demands on him were usually constant. But Chandra, who traveled so easily, should not have provoked his temper so. While the men stumbled over each other to offer aid to the ladies, Conan stayed far away. He offered neither his services nor conversation to the lady in his charge. Mallory and Thurwell exchanged many questioning glances.

It was not until they neared Cordell that Chandra moved to the head of this long train. She took her place beside Conan in leading the party into the village. They passed an old and worn sign bearing the blazon of her father.

"We are very near now," she advised him.

"The forest is dense," he argued. "It could hide a fair-sized army."

"I doubt that," she replied.

"And what clearing lies before the village?" he asked.

It was not much farther when he saw for himself. Where the trees ended, a meadow began. The road to the town was clear, but for only a short distance. There were fields, fruit trees and huts. The village was small, oriented around one road that wound its way to a great house built of stone. It was not a castle. The tower was short and stout, reaching just a bit taller than the house. Though the lower floors did not have windows, and a heavy oaken door barred entry, there was no wall, no gate, no parapets from which bowmen could shoot their arrows at an approaching army.

"Wherein lies this town's protection?" Conan asked somewhat irritably.

"The forest and the sea," Chandra replied easily.

" 'Twas the forest that made my attack on Stoddard so simple," he said. "The trees should be assarted and the town held in by a wall."

"Nature is our wall," she told him. "The forest is too thick to hold an army, and the coast, too rocky. The road is the only reasonable entry."

"You give little credence to the possibility that an army would enter the forest from beyond the road, making a camp and clearing a path to your bedchamber. Forsooth, you could be rousted from your sleep by thieves and taken prisoner by any able-bodied lad."

He proceeded forward, not meeting her eyes. There was a firm set to his jaw, and within he felt anger and stress mounting. He knew the reason for his discomfort, but he had not given much thought to its manifestation. He felt her eyes on him and he turned to look at her. There was a sadness there in her eyes, a sadness brought by the terseness of his words. "We will talk of this, Conan," she said quietly.

He simply snorted and directed his attention again to the front. The fields were full of young lads and women harvesting the last of a good year's crops. Those they passed smiled and waved their greetings to Chandra. No one shied from the sight of many fettered knights astride their destriers, nor did the children hide behind their mothers' skirts. The entire troop entered the town without seeing one frowning or slightly uncertain face. It was a different sight from any other village Conan had so entered.

The people as a whole seemed contented and well fed. There was a definite lack of poverty here, which made Conan suspicious. It should have been refreshing, but no armed soldiers lined the path to the keep, and no guards could be seen watching from the tower or the roof.

"They are not worried that you are captured and being led here against your will," he said.

"Of course not," she returned. "When that is the case with me I seldom smile and wave."

"They do not know my arms, yet they welcome me eagerly and without the slightest distrust. Are they stupid or entranced?"

"Neither, sir knight," she told him. "I ride with your troop and for that they will assume that you are a loyal vassal to my father. And you see," she said, "they are right."

The oaken doors to the keep opened, and there was someone at Chandra's side to help her from her horse. Lads ran in to take the horses from the men. Within the lower level there were many servants scurrying about carrying heavy kettles of water to the upper levels, stoking huge cooking fires, toting large bundles of linens and other things.

"A message was sent ahead and they hurry now to make us welcome. Allow your men entrance and they will be bathed, fed and made comfortable."

That said, she made her way to the upper level where

there was a large and airy dining room appointed to accommodate many visitors. There were trestle tables and chests, stools and even a few chairs. Benches were being brought from other rooms to seat Conan's forces.

Conan looked about in appreciation. The room was polished clean, with fresh rushes scattered about the floor. The smell of herbs sprinkled on the floor to ward off odors and the rich aroma of a steaming brewis brought a sense of comfort, but his warrior's mind would not rest. He saw no soldiers and it seemed ill protected.

"You shall have the lord's chamber, Sir Conan," Chandra told him.

"Nay, 'tis yours. I shall take a pallet with my men."

"There is no need. I have a chamber, far richer than yours. It was my mother's and it was designed to do a lady proud. This is in fact the first time I have ventured here as lady of this hall, and the first time to sleep in her chamber." She fumbled with the keys attached to her gold girdle and handed him one. "It is yours, and I promise you will be comfortable."

She started for the stair to climb to yet a third level of this great house. After looking about to see that his men were entering and indeed being taken care of by the servants, he followed her.

The room she entered ahead of him was large, and a fire blazed on the hearth. A wooden tub stood steaming with hot water, though there was no servant. A large bed carved of oak stood rather majestically on one side of the room, and a huge chest stood at the foot of that resting place. On the opposite wall there was a large set of doors which Chandra immediately opened.

The sight took away Conan's breath for a moment. Outside the doors was a balcony, and beyond, the sea. Slowly

he walked to join her on the balcony and the two stood
silently, taking in the awesome sight. This place and all
its trappings could soothe any troubled mind.

After a few quiet moments, Conan turned toward
Chandra, his mood softened now. "Edwina is often ill,"
he started.

She would not turn to look at him. Staring straight
ahead he heard her murmur. "You cannot tell me more
of my sister than I already know. Your confessions will not
ease your mind." Then in a whisper that sounded strained
she added, "You are my brother now."

"I do not curse her name," he said pleadingly. "She of
all of us is most innocent. I do my part to see to her comfort. But do not tell me what I must feel." His last word
was issued harshly and with considerable bitterness. Still,
she did not look his way.

"Whatever you feel, Sir Conan, do not burden me
with it."

He turned again to the sea to keep himself from lashing
out at her. It was then that he heard her voice and knew
that she was looking at him.

"I have a great favor to ask of you, if you will hear me."
He gave her his full attention, turning and looking into
her troubled eyes. "I ask that you pass no judgment on me
nor ask my reasons." He nodded his assent and she continued.

"It is in my mind that a warden for this estate would
be advantageous." He began a protest and she held up her
hand to stop him. "Cordell has been managed by women
since my grandmother. My grandfather had other lands
and this was a part of her dowry. Thus it was with my
mother. She visited Cordell frequently and the people here
respected her word as law. There was never any resistance

to her, but had there been, my father's army would have supported her here.

"I choose not to marry, but I do not choose to lose Cordell. This is mine no matter what. I see no profit in being bound to a man I do not love, but I am not so foolish as to ignore my lack of arms. If you would consent to oversee my lands, my father would have little room to argue."

"Your father will not leave you unwed," Conan said flatly.

"Perhaps he will, Conan. If I am inclined to leave this estate to Edwina's children, he will see it scattered among those he loves. He loves you as any son. If I could count on your approval, I may win his."

"And you would abide here? A woman alone in this poorly protected place?"

"Only when my father is gone and there is no need for me at Phalen Castle. And this 'poorly protected place' is safer than you can guess."

He leaned both hands on the stone wall about the balcony and looked out into the sea, laughing ruefully. "Such a delightful platter you lay before me, Chandra. An unmarried woman abiding alone and under my protection. How can I refuse such an offer?"

"Nay, Conan," she cried. "Nay, 'tis not an indecent thing I suggest. I doubt you would ever be called to my aid."

"And why would you prefer this solitary existence to a proper marriage?"

"I do not need a man to manage my lands! Better to be alone than be bound as the unhappy servant to a man I loathe."

"How do you know you will despise the man your father

chooses? How do you know he will not be a man you will love and long to serve?"

He half expected her to say it was because she loved him, but her reply left him stunned. "Even if he is Tedric?"

She walked away from him and moved toward the door of the chamber, leaving him standing in confusion on the balcony. "I would have you learn Cordell before you make your decision, Sir Conan. And do not be perplexed; I make you no indecent offers. My favors are for no man, and lastly my sister's husband. My chamber is yonder," she said, throwing her arm wide and indicating a door that would lead to her room. "And the door will be bolted. Never again suggest that I would be so easily compromised."

Abruptly she turned, leaving him to stand and stare at the door in wonder. He looked from there to the door she earlier indicated, the one that led to her chamber. As he watched that door, he heard the bolt slide into place. Does she think me some beast of the wood that tears down doors in his rutting fever? he thought. But no sooner had that thought passed than he realized perhaps the locked door was wise.

A maid bearing a tray with a silver goblet came into the room. A gift from the lady Chandra, he was told. The finest wine Cordell could offer to lighten his spirits and bring him ease. He drank of the heady brew and turned his thoughts back to the ocean. The waves crashing against the rocks far below him simulated the feeling in his heart at the moment.

It was not enough that he was committed to years of unhappiness, but now Chandra, so fair and young and good, was left with unpleasant choices: to be alone always or live with a man such as Tedric.

Behind him the maid busied herself in the room, laying out linens and fresh clothes. The wine relaxed his rattled mind and the tub beckoned. He put the goblet aside and began to remove the heavy clothing of his profession. As he struggled with the chain mail, two small hands aided him in lifting it from his body. When the chausses were removed he looked at the young maid. She was still more child than woman, but her face was bright and she was lovely. It was the custom in most noble households to have the women help the men bathe. Conan was accustomed to this, but his emotions were terribly confused.

"Do you have a name?" he asked the lass.

"Aye, milord. I am called Wynne."

"I thank you for your good service, Wynne. I will bathe and dress myself."

She bobbed in a little curtsy and left him. Sinking deep into the warm water, he thought heavily on sparkling blue eyes, long golden tresses and a womanly form that begged to be held. His fantasies were anything but chaste, and in fact he had never indulged himself in such an imaginary romance before. But his conscious resolve was firm. He would never again suggest to Chandra that he would welcome her affections. He would protect her interests and her virtue as if she were his daughter.

The coast was considerably colder in late September than farther inland. The fire burned bright to warm the hall, and many of Conan's men conversed with those servants present. Anselm, in all its greatness, could boast fine feasts and much gaiety. But Cordell, a small and warm keep, had many more servants available to the manor than Conan would have expected, and the quality of food was rich. He was welcomed here in a manner he wished he could apply to Stoddard.

At the table Chandra sat, patiently waiting for him to begin the meal. He took his place between her and Thurwell, with Mallory beyond him. The knights conversed with the lady of the hall, but between Conan and Chandra silence reigned. Her mood was pleasant and easy. In fact, there seemed no tension in the room but for what he felt within himself. He tried aping her casual manner, for her appearance suggested she never thought of him as anything but a friend.

"Your father's serfs are at ease here," he began.

"They are my serfs," she reminded him.

Although he chafed slightly at the thought of a woman in charge, looking around he could see that nothing was lacking here. But he went on, for it was quite an uncomfortable thing for a man to accept a woman's efficiency. "The people here are confident of their safety, yet I see no guards. When my men ask why, they are told the village has never seen an attack."

"That is correct. Even Vikings of yore were not dim-witted enough to attempt our coast."

"Is your village secret?" he asked.

"Oh, nay. Our people travel often to the fairs and trade in Colchester and as far as Cambridge. And though the journey is not an easy one, many have been to London. This village is well known to the outlying towns and we have visitors from the monasteries often."

"There is a rich store of grain here and livestock abounds, not to mention the wealth your fishermen must enjoy. Does no one threaten this?"

"If you were to attack this keep, from where would you come?"

"From the forest, as I did at Stoddard," he replied confidently.

"Then I challenge you to go there and see what protection I speak of. I believe you will find it is impenetrable."

"I will take my men in the morning and —"

"Sir Conan, if you will indulge me a bit: I would have you take only Sir Mallory and Sir Thurwell as you go. Cordell is not a secret, many know of this place. But Cordell is a place of secrets. I know the wood well and I promise you, you need no army of men. And," she added, leaning closer to him and speaking in hushed tones, "I would keep my wood, my moat and wall, from the knowledge of great armies of men."

Her blue eyes glittered like sapphires and his heart quickened its pace. He looked away from her to hide his discomfort. "And what of your father's chores? Those things we came here to accomplish?"

"I need no henchmen to do my father's work. The people will yield their revenues without quarrel. I would have you test the security of this keep so that you can answer my request."

He did not argue with her further. In time she rose and moved about the room, conversing with some of his men and many of the serfs she had not seen for more than a year. She laughed easily as she talked and more than once took a tray from a serving maid and presented it herself to one of the knights. He found himself most distracted by her casual manner.

When the evening had worn on she retired. He was urged to have another drink, and Thurwell raised his glass, toasting the mistress of the hall. "To the lucky fool to win her hand," Mallory added to the toast. Conan did not drink to the salute, which was made more in jest than true appreciation. But his comrades went on to attest loudly to the fair Chandra's more desirable assets, and Conan slumped lower in his chair. He fairly pouted in his wine, considering the burial of his troubles in drink.

What curse this? he thought in confusion. She dwells in every corner of my mind and there is no room for another in my heart. No room for a wife who will bear a child, no room for even a saucy wench who would ease my urges. Yet she is at ease with the torment, prepared to live a quiet life alone, wanting me not as lover but as brother. And even knowing how I feel, she is insulted at the meagerest hint of any advances. And she has such little faith in my chivalry that she must bolt the door against my pursuit.

He left the men in the hall to seek some comfort from his bed, thinking Chandra had successfully overcome the agony of this unrequited love.

As he passed by the door to her chamber, it was in his mind to knock and draw her into a short conversation. He would show her, as best he could, his own casual and unaffected manner. He would ask her of his journey into the wood and calm her thoughts on the matter. As husband to her sister, he could be depended on for whatever protection she needed for Cordell.

But from the other side of the door he could hear her broken, jagged sobbing. He listened even as it tore at his chest. He longed to cradle her in his arms, yet he knew he could never touch her. He had made her burdens less in his mind and her tears brought clear to him the realness of her pain.

He went into his own chamber heavy of heart after a few of the most disquieting moments he had spent in some time. He stared into the fire. "I was wrong, my love," he said somberly. "There is no comfort in knowing you are as tortured as I."

Dawn roused the lazy village. Mallory, Thurwell and Conan were up at the first glimmer of sunlight and were about the chore of fixing their armor and other battle gear to venture into the wood. They had expected to eat a simple and quick morning meal and be on their way, but they were distracted by Chandra, who had also risen. She came to where they stood in the courtyard with horses ready.

"Come into the hall," she bade them, ignoring any proper morning greeting. "There is some information I would have you take to the forest with you."

She turned as quickly as she had come, and they looked at each other in bemusement. Finally Conan shrugged his shoulders. " 'Tis her wood. Until she leads me astray, she will have her way."

They found her seated in the same place she had taken the night before. As they drew chairs about her, a pork brewis, steaming and tempting, was thrust before them.

"No armor or horses for the forest, my knights," she told them. "Wear your mail if you insist upon it, but leave behind your spears and lances. A heavy broadsword will serve all your needs, and a horse would slow you, for the paths, such as they are, are narrow and crooked."

"Without horses, how are we to carry our provisions or bring back game?" Conan asked.

"Packs to be carried on your backs have been prepared," she said, pointing to the bundles by the door. "There is enough provender for a few days, should you need it. And as for game, there is no need, since my huntsmen keep us well supplied. Bows and arrows have been set aside for you, and I suggest you venture together lest you come across an angry boar."

"Bows and arrows," Conan choked. "By God, Chandra, we are not simple serfs sent to bring food to your table! We are knights and —"

"If you believe my words, I think you will fare the better," she advised.

He would have argued further, but one of his men entered the hall and stood before him, impatient for a word.

"Sir Conan, I thought you should hear of the situation in the village," he said uncertainly.

"Did you receive a night's lodging there? Were there problems?"

"Nay, my liege, no problem. Indeed, 'twas the finest lodging we've chanced upon in some years. And the women there treated us with much kindness. We all did as you bid us and no one pressed any maid from the town, but you should know: there seem to be very few men."

"How does this matter to me?" he questioned.

"I only thought it important, my lord. We heard you advise the lady of the lack of safety in this keep, but in my mind 'tis worse than you suspect. There are mostly old men and young lads. The only stout men abide at the shore and set out early with the tide to fish and collect seaweed. Once the sun has risen, there is scarce a man in the village offering protection. 'Twould be a simple matter to take the whole village with ten stout men."

Yet the village had survived many years without a battle. He looked between Chandra and his two friends with uneasiness. She offered no solution to this puzzle. "Set your men to guard the house and the road leading into the village. Be sure someone watches from the tower, and rest assured: I will not leave Medwin's lands as poorly fixed as I have found them."

He finished his breakfast quickly and rose to leave. Chandra followed them outside and pointed in the best direction for them to enter the wood.

"I mean what I say, my lady. This hall and this land have been run by women a trifle remiss in considering what dangers may lie beyond their kens. While your rooms and your table boast of your good service, your walls would crumble around you from the weakest foe. I am surprised at you, lady. You have seen attacks on your father's strong walls and know the sufferings of those women and children not adequately protected."

"Take yourself about this village at your leisure, Sir Conan, and when the time comes for you to leave Cordell, you have my support in taking any protective measures you deem necessary."

He could find no further reason to lecture her. And the forest waited. That was the first place he would consider in building a better defense for this hall. He centered his thoughts on the assarting of more of the wood and building a wall about the town, trying not to admit that it was because Chandra wished to live here alone. As he entered the wood, the thought of this plan of hers made him even more uneasy than before. Even Tedric's protection seemed safer than her isolation.

"The lady knows more of the wood than you will allow," Thurwell said as they entered on a narrow path. "She is right in her advice to travel light, for this is a thick wood. Do not mistake this for a hunt or other adventure in a forest thinned by many travelers."

Conan yielded with much more grace to Thurwell's remark, for he knew these two men well. They knew the
ways of the forest better than he. Though they had never
confided the details of their earlier days, Conan thought
it likely that before they earned the right to wield swords
in defense of the king, they spent long periods of time in
royal forests dodging the king's henchmen for crimes of
poaching. The penalty for shooting a deer in such a wood
was more often than not death by hanging. Nobles were
allowed to hunt, specifically huntsmen commissioned to
hunt for the lord to provide for his table. Commoners
were not. Neither of these two were born to noble families,
but had fought long and hard to achieve their positions.
He already knew that they made their way to honorable
knighthood as mercenaries, a profession not looked upon
with much adoration.

"We'll find nothing on this heavily traveled path," Mallory grumbled, cutting from the worn trail and using his
sword to clear away the brush as he went. The others followed. They encountered no clearings or animals but for
an occasional rabbit or fox darting past them into the deep
brush.

They came across a shallow stream and for a time followed that for convenience. They walked silently on until
the sun was high in the sky.

"How sits this wood with you, Conan?" Mallory asked.

" 'Tis a thick wood, but I see no reason an army could
not enter and make a camp. And I wonder how the huntsmen furnish food for the hall. Do they dine only on
chicken and pork?"

"This is not a primitive wood," Thurwell said confidently. "It is inhabited, Conan, but I say with beasts of a
two-legged type."

"Men? But there has been no sign," Conan argued. "No camp, no broken fires, no sound."

"Game would drink at the stream and we would have encountered a group of deer by now, but that smell of man lingers all about us. I've seen a fork in the path more than twice, but covered with brush." Mallory walked nearer Conan and dropped an arm about his shoulders. "Had you not wondered at the many small children in the village when there seems to be a certain lack of men?" He let go with a loud riotous laugh that echoed through the trees, and Thurwell joined in. "Aye, Lady Chandra needs no wall to keep her safe."

Conan looked in confusion to his amused friends. "They are a crafty lot, are they not?" Mallory nodded in agreement while Conan stood perplexed. Finally Thurwell attempted to explain his hunch. "Sir Conan, you command a sturdy troop of men, none of them overly ugly and all paid generously for their services. But the womenfolk did not greet your men-at-arms with great eagerness."

"And they would have been soundly beaten had they dared," came a voice from behind.

They turned as one to view a man coming through the trees. Conan's hand went directly to the hilt of his sword, ready to fight, but the man smiled and held up his hands as if to ward off this aggressor.

"Nay, Sir Conan," the man said good-naturedly. "I am bidden by my lady Chandra to guide you should you become lost."

"And who are you?" Conan questioned, looking the man over. He wore naught but a leather tunic, with only a hunting knife at his waist. A rude bow rode his shoulder and a bundle of arrows was handy at his back.

"I am called Sir William," the man said, bowing.

"Sir William?" Conan echoed.

Mallory stepped near to Conan and said softly in his ear, "The master of the lady's guard, is my guess."

"Master of the guard," he mimicked. The man certainly did not have the look of a knight, and there seemed to be no order of men. But just as he was about to voice his confusion, the trees bled men. An army donned in simple clothes, bearing no more than the hunting knife and bow, surrounded them on all sides. Conan spun about in wonder, surveying the massive number of ready warriors. And then Chandra's words rang through his mind: *I would keep my wood, my moat and wall, from the knowledge of great armies of men.* Suddenly aware, Conan threw back his head and laughed loudly.

In the following days, Conan learned of the dynamic and subtle protection of Cordell. The men were certainly not noble lords or knights, but men of the town who had been raised partially in the wood. While many were always about the forest, many lived with their families in the village unless called. When a large party of knights or other travelers ventured down the road toward Cordell, they were seen by those who kept a constant vigil near the only reasonable entrance. At the first call, others came from the village and watched the town from the forest. They were an unknown force. And Conan learned that the fishermen watched the coast as carefully as the huntsmen watched the land side of the manor.

It was a system long in practice that worked ideally for this small burgh. Visitors who queried those in the town about their lack of guard went away unsatisfied, for it was a ploy that worked only as long as no outsiders knew their methods.

Conan learned, in the course of seven days, the ways of

the forest that surrounded the keep, and the village and shore. There were caves along the rocks that were known only by the fishermen, entrances to the forest, out of sight of the keep or the road, known only to those who guarded the wood. And all this was shown to him by order of the lady of the manor.

When Chandra's duties at Cordell were done, she did not dally. Preparations for her return to Phalen were made at once. The carts stood ready outside the keep and the knights mounted their horses. Sir Conan took Sir William's hand and grasped it fondly.

"I give you my word, Sir William, that your secret is safe with me. If ever you have need of my troop, you have but to send word to me."

"And in like, my lord," William answered with heartfelt fondness. "If you have need of my aid, you have but to ask."

When the troop was departing, with Conan and his comrades again leading the way and Chandra and her women again at the rear, one of the lesser men-at-arms rode to the front to speak to his lord.

"Sir Conan," he ventured carefully. "You've left no men behind, and there was no talk of sending men-at-arms to Cordell. I thought it was your plan to leave it better protected than you found it."

"And so I have," he said, a smile playing about his lips.

"And how, sir? I see no protection for them."

"Nature protects them. The forest and the sea."

CHAPTER
7

THE lady of Anselm ventured as often as her serving women into the village. She frequented many of the shops, though she did not go to make purchases. The weavers, carpenters, bakers and smithy would all come to the hall for her needs, but in the town there might be a peddler or traveling friar. Besides bringing spices and unusual fabrics, something apart from the linen and wool that made up nearly all of every person's clothing, they would bring news from other towns. The traveling friar was better, for he would bring mainly news and would be found lingering in the village streets to talk to the peasants.

And of course Udele wanted to visit the lacemaker. The lord was not ignorant of his townspeople, nor was he ignorant of Udele's visits to the lacemaker's shop. Alaric, quite simply, thought little of it. The village priest, Father Ambert, a young and determined man, asked Alaric to put a halt to Giselle's incantations and predictions. Alaric turned to Udele.

"Do you visit her shop often?" he had asked.

"As often as any other," was her reply.

"Do you think her a dangerous unbeliever?"

"Dangerous?" she laughed. "As dangerous as a butterfly, my lord. She plays and does no harm. Let her be."

"Have you asked her for predictions?" he queried.

"Aye, a few times," she said without much concern.

"And?"

"Sometimes she is right. Other times —" Udele shrugged, pretending disinterest in the subject. To put an end to Alaric's questions she told him things that would make it seem that Giselle was often inaccurate. "She told me I would bear you two children. Another time she warned me that Edythe's birth would be difficult, which it was. But the villeins put more stock in her predictions than I, and if it gives them hope I say she does no harm."

"Udele," he asked seriously, "have you asked her to perform spells for you?"

She laughed lightly and admitted without much fear that she had asked Giselle to give her potions to make her first child healthy and strong. "I see no harm in that, my lord. I was so lonely that my greatest fear was that my child would die. But," she went on in her sweet and seductive way, "I was not lonely for very long."

It was not difficult for Udele to help Alaric out of his suspicious or angry moods. She knew the way to his heart and was the greatest sorceress in her own right, using her cajoling and alluring nature as her potions.

But he was lord and the responsibility was his. Though he would have the matter done, he made one further attempt to find fault with the lacemaker.

"Father Ambert says that you take predictions quite seriously, and that you are most often in her shop. Her potions are a sacrilege."

"Father Ambert! Are not our confessions private? That good priest is the confessor of many more young maids than farmers, and does he not love his wine and hold a sizable portion of the tithe for his own purse? He is a jealous and selfish man and Giselle is a Jewess. He would burn her for a sorceress, but she abides under your protection. He hates her for that, my lord, not for the games she plays with her sight."

The matter as it stood held Alaric silent. He did not meddle with the church. It was a power he never wished to defeat; and the sins of those in service to the faith were not his concern. If it was true that Ambert was seen coursing the streets in the late hours, Alaric did not wish to know. That the priest was handsome and held himself nobly attracted the women and perturbed the men, but not much else was said in criticism. And Alaric would be the last to say anything against him.

The subject was closed in Alaric's mind, but what he had failed to see was the possibility that it was not toward Giselle that Father Ambert directed his vengeance, but toward Lady Udele herself. It was his spiritual duty to denounce sorcery, and he knew, as did many others, of the mortal spells Lady Udele had cast using information she had forced from Giselle.

Father Ambert was a young man and the sensual aura his good looks gave him was his curse. He hated Udele for seeing this in him. And he hated her for the fact that he found her tempting, her beauty spellbinding. And the worst of it was that she seemed to know it. She taunted him with his humanness, asking if he wouldn't like to be more than her confessor. Father Ambert was filled at once with desire and hatred, which he found equally unsettling.

But just as Father Ambert could not speak to Alaric about his wife, neither could any other. To discredit the faithful and beautiful Udele to the lord took not only courage, but a monstrous lack of good sense. Because Alaric wished them to honor and worship her, all the people of the village, including the priest, made it seem as though they did. In truth, they feared more than admired her.

As Father Ambert knelt to his prayers this cool September morning, he felt a chill pass through him. His mind went momentarily blank and his eyes opened and shone with a strange light. At that same moment, in the village, Giselle opened her door to the lady of Anselm and bade her enter. The priest went back to his prayers, wondering at the strange sensation. Giselle locked the door to her shop and pulled the curtain over the window. The crystal stone sat majestically on its scarlet cloth.

"I awoke with a feeling this morn," Udele said. "I want to know about my son. Where is he now?"

The battle of whether or not to inform Udele of Conan's acts or future had already been lost. Now the seer was making what attempts she could to buffer her information, giving enough to satisfy without giving away any real clues as to what was to come. But with this she took increasing care, for Udele was not only shrewd: it was almost as if she had absorbed some of this gift.

"He is only miles away — on his way to Anselm."

"He is! Somehow I knew. I could feel him riding toward me!"

Giselle thought for a moment and then bravely she blurted out the rest.

"He is anxious to see his father. He will stay only one night."

The priest rose from his prayers, the ill feeling still with him. He covered his head with his hood and went into the village, being drawn toward trouble, though he did not know where he was bound.

"Conan went to London on behalf of my lord husband and Sir Medwin. Many nobles went. Henry has made an alliance with Philip of France and they talk of Crusade."

"They talk," Giselle said confidently. "Henry will not go on Crusade."

"Thank God," Udele breathed. "Conan must not Crusade. I will not lose him to the infidels!"

Giselle bit her tongue against what she saw. "Even I do not know what strange alliances will be formed between King Henry and his sons and Philip. A pledge to Crusade today will fall apart tomorrow under the strain of smaller battles."

"Where has he been? Has he seen Medwin?"

"Yea, to deliver the news that his wife is with child."

"Of course," Udele conceded. "And Medwin would be pleased."

"As you must be, madam," Giselle replied, hoping they were finished for today.

"I expect him to keep her belly full. What else can Edwina do for him but bear his children?" It was not a question but a disdainful statement. She had chosen Edwina because she could hold no strong charm over Conan, yet held her in contempt for the same reason.

"What of the wench, Chandra?" Udele asked brazenly.

"*Lady* Chandra," Giselle said, straightening. "She serves her father in all things now, for Medwin is growing old and weak. She does more to manage his home and lands than he does."

Udele's mouth twitched in distaste. To learn that Chandra was good and strong did not whet her appetite for the maid. "Well, what does she feel for Conan now? Does she still lust after him?"

"I cannot tell, madam. I cannot see into her mind, you know that."

"Then for Conan — what does he feel for her? You have the shirt I gave you, do you not?"

Giselle had to break her mood to fetch the clothing. When she was seated again, caressing the shirt, she saw into the mind of Sir Conan. Her eyes stung with tears she would not shed. She felt his struggle as acutely as he felt it. He loved beyond all reason and beyond all good sense. He felt for his wife an indifference that was often turned to scorn for her lack of effort in her wifely obligations. With the scorn came the guilt that tore him end from end. Honoring her as his bride brought him pain and sorrow.

And for Chandra his passion grew stronger. First it was her beauty and vitality that drew him near loving her, then it blended into a more confused combination of desire, respect, admiration and appreciation of her many admirable qualities. And again the guilt — for his feelings. The earth and stars knew they would find each other. He had been cast by a meddlesome mortal into a mold he could not fit.

From outside this psychic world Udele prodded Giselle to tell her what she was seeing.

"This garment has been a long time from the knight's body, madam. It is weak and my vision is not clear."

"I will bring you something new. For now, try harder."

Giselle felt the intensity of their struggle during the long stay at Cordell. She felt the pain of their parting when Chandra was delivered home to her father. Conan's words were so loud she wondered if Udele heard them. "I must hasten to your sister. She will fret the more while I am away." And Chandra, soft and melodious: "Care for her

166 , THE BLUE FALCON

well, Sir Conan. I love her dearly and want her happiness above my own." There was a touching of hands, one tortured touch that was too much and too little and left both souls hungering and aching. And he rode away from her.

"Conan is greatly appreciative of Chandra's many capabilities, but as I can see, his oath is the same: to be a good husband to Edwina."

"Aha!" Udele shrieked in delight. "Now you must see the wisdom in what I have done! It does not matter that he does not love Edwina. This business with Chandra will come to naught. My son's word is his life."

Giselle looked at Udele sharply. "I did not say Lady Chandra was the one for Conan."

"No, you did not say, but I am no fool. It was not difficult to reason. But I think," she said thoughtfully, "it would be best if Medwin saw her wed."

Giselle was still in touch with Conan's feelings, and she could see what would come to pass. Within this dark cloud of unhappiness there was still a glimmer of hope. Sir Conan could not know that hope existed. She struggled for an answer that would dissuade Udele. She struggled for a lie. "Though I cannot see her mind, her beauty is no mystery to me. She will marry soon enough, madam."

"Not soon enough to give me peace of mind," Udele snarled, rising from the table. She dropped some silver onto the cloth, payment that was plenty, but that became less with every visit. "I must make ready for my son."

The sun was setting over Stoddard's walls when the herald announced the approaching army of men. The blazon of the Blue Falcon brought the bridge crashing down and opened the gates wide to the returning knight.

The sight of Sir Conan as he rode with his falcon on his shoulder still awed the people here, and the serfs and children came running to stare with wide eyes at this warrior leading many men of battle into the small keep.

"Boy," Conan called to one of the bystanders, "have the fires stoked and meat brought forth to feed my men. The night is cold and they would eat in comfort. By my order, lad."

Edwina was sitting before the hearth waiting for his arrival and jumped to her feet when he entered. "Welcome home, my lord," she said.

Conan smiled at her, but it did not mirror his feelings as he looked at her. He fought to keep his pain from showing on his face. He wanted to look at Edwina and be overcome with love; but as he looked at her he felt so little.

He pulled her near and placed a light kiss on her cheek. "I saw Medwin and he sends his best to you. News of the child brought him joy." He looked down at her barely swelling tummy. "Are you well?"

Edwina smiled. "I am well, my lord," she said softly. "Water for your bath is drawn."

"My men would eat, lady. Have trenchers of meat brought and bread. The road was cold, and I for one am more hungry than dirty."

"I fear more time is needed in the cooking, Conan."

"Let the others wait that these men may eat." He turned from her to draw an ale.

"Conan, your messenger arrived only this afternoon, barely ahead of you. The meat is being cooked now, but our provender is low."

Slowly he turned and looked at her in some confusion. "What is low?" he asked.

"There were many mouths to feed in your absence. You left more men than you took." She shrugged and her eyes began to tear. "There was little I could do."

Mallory and Thurwell entered the hall and stopped short, sensing a problem. Both went for ale, trying to bring little attention to themselves.

Conan stepped closer to Edwina, keeping his words hushed and trying to keep from showing any anger. "Edwina, tell me what has happened to affect our supply of food in my absence."

"Come to our chamber, Conan, and let me aid you in your bath," she said.

He could clearly see her upset, the emotion entering him as it seeped from her. Something was amiss in this hall. "Tell me what you can. Tell me what has happened here."

"I was ill, Conan, but I am better now. While I was abed the food was prepared and served without my presence, and when I rose again I found the supply low, and the huntsmen complained that the game was too far into the forest for good meat."

Conan could feel his muscles tense. "How have you fared?"

She shrugged. "Much on porridge of egg and pork and bread, Conan. I fear I have failed you."

"You have not failed me, lady," he said, turning slowly to look around the hall. His men were entering and sitting heavily, tired and hungry. The servants moved about the hall with speed and nervousness. Not one dared look in his direction.

"They do not fear me as they do you, my lord," she said.

He looked at her closely. She did not appear to be in the best of health. She seemed thinner at a time when she should be adding weight to her frail frame. "Edwina, tell me truly, are you feeling fit?"

Her eyes held a dull cast, but she smiled again. "Conan, I so wanted you to be pleased upon your return. Don't worry for me, I am fit. These people, I fear, serve you poorly."

"What do you hear in the keep? Do they mourn for Rolfe?"

"I am not certain, Conan. I hear nothing. They do not slight me in any way, but they move slowly to my requests."

"That will change," he said in a low voice.

"I fear it is my fault. My manner is too quiet. Their lady needs be of a stronger —"

He lifted her chin with a finger and smiled consolingly at her, though the condition in which he found his wife and his hall was causing his anger to build. "This is my hall, Edwina, and you are my lady. Your order is law in my absence, and whether you appeal to them softly or harshly, it is their lot to hearken to you quickly and without question."

Edwina smiled and touched his bearded cheek. "I have no doubt you can see them better trained, Conan. Sometimes I think you would have it easier with a stronger woman at your side."

"I have chosen the woman to stand at my side, chérie," he said gently. "I have not asked you to change, and what is amiss here is not because of your manner. These serfs must learn their good fortune. It is not often the lady they must serve is so forgiving and gentle. They will learn."

"I had not wanted to bring complaints to your ears, my lord."

Conan laughed softly, but in his eyes there was a cold gleam. Edwina knew that he was angry.

"It is unfortunate for these serfs that I understand things here must have been much worse than you will tell me. I hope it is the last time I leave and return to find this hall so poorly kept."

Conan turned to the men in the hall. "Tonight will see a meager fare. Fill your stomachs on what is put before you and tomorrow we will hunt. Then you will see a feast worthy of your work." A slow moan filled the room, for there was not one eager for yet another hard day. "Whoever wishes to feed through the winter on bread and honey is welcome to stay in this warm hall on the morrow."

"Conan," Edwina beckoned softly. "What will you do?"

"I will instruct these serfs carefully on the manner in which I wish this hall to be kept, and tomorrow they will be allowed a test of their efforts. They will not fail me again. They will see the lash the next time."

"I fear they will hate you," Edwina said.

"They may indeed," he said, taking her hand. "Come, you need not worry with it now. It is important that you rest."

Edwina pulled back. "Whatever your intent, my lord, I will not lay abed while you dole out punishments. I will stand at your side."

Conan felt a certain pride in Edwina's support and looked at her with pleasure. "Very good, lady, but there will be no lashings tonight. On the morrow, before I leave this hall, they will know better how to serve their master."

Conan could see Edwina relax. The tension he had noted etched into her fine features was disappearing, and he could see how tired this left her. She had worried over the many problems he would find on his return, unable to mend the ways of these serfs and unable to give the impression all had been well in his absence. She wanted to please him. And Conan felt the weight of his responsibility to her grow heavier.

"Lady, I think it best if we retire to our chamber now. You have grown tired. I was too long away."

Edwina smiled and reached for his hand. "A day would be too long, Conan. And I am weary."

The tub stood ready in the lord's chamber and Conan began to remove his clothing. Edwina moved around their chamber in a slow and docile manner, putting things away and laying out a fresh linen shirt for her husband. He felt a flicker of emotion as he removed the linen gamberson that Chandra had mended for him while they stayed at Cordell.

He turned his thoughts toward Edwina. There was much about her to love: she was loyal, kind, and there was no doubt that she loved him. She did not respond to his ardor with the enthusiasm that he had hoped she would show, but it was not her way to respond to any situation with great passion. She was gentle and slow, a soft and delicate flower that would sway with the breeze. She was made to be respected and protected, to be held on a pedestal and carefully tended.

But there was that other one, the younger sister that he could never put out of his mind. It was she who stirred not only his blood, but his mind and his very soul. Chandra could show a gentle and feminine side, but there was little about her that required a man's protection. Yea, she could smile and move in that same soft and delicate manner, but under that feminine mien there was a strength that could not be ignored. Conan doubted he would have returned to such confusion in Stoddard Keep had Chandra been managing during his absence. She would have found a way to make these people work hard to please her.

He sank into the tub and reminded himself for the hundredth time that it was an unfair comparison. These people would come to adore their lady's compassionate nature and work to please her because they would soon come to love her. That she was not energetic and tough did not mean she was not strong. There was strength in her kindness and loyalty. He would be her strong arm, and they would, together, make a prosperous life.

He leaned back into the tub and closed his eyes. He wished she were as bright and eager as —

"Conan?"

He opened his eyes to find Edwina kneeling near the tub. When had she come? Could she see in the depths of his eyes that he had been thinking about her sister? Did she see now that he was tortured within because he had violated his own heart and could not feel passion for the woman he had pledged his life to love?

"I've brought you a trencher of bread and meat," she said with a smile.

He nodded once and sat up to scrub weeks of grime from his body. "Good. There was precious little upon the road."

Edwina took his sponge from his hands and wrinkled her nose as she lathered it. "You may be hungry, my lord, but you are in sore need of bathing."

Conan leaned forward that she might scrub his back. "What you smell is the odor of hard work, my lady. With luck it will keep you fed and well gowned. Show respect as you scrub."

"Yea, lord," she said in feigned chagrin.

Conan would have preferred a quiet evening, but the

lord of the manor was allowed little leisure and less privacy. He ate quickly and donned clean clothes to begin making his rounds. He spoke to nearly every servant, stable hand and huntsman within the keep. He rousted some from what they thought would be a long, restful night. He explained, with careful precision, what he expected when he left the keep on some pressing business. While he spoke he smiled, but his eyes held theirs and most shrank back from him a little. There wasn't a person here who had not heard of his reward for Rolfe.

"You and your family reside in this village and have for a very long time?" he would ask the serf he was speaking to.

"Yea, lord," came the expected reply.

"And you reside here, earn your bread here, for as long as the lord chooses."

"Yea."

"And you work hard on my behalf?"

"Yea, lord," they would answer, tension building in the reply.

"But I am returned to find that service to this hall and my lady has been poor. The serfs are lazy and do not worry with their chores. I consider this to be a treason to my rule."

"Not I, my lord!" every worker questioned would reply. "Nay, I have not erred! I worked 'til weary while you were away. Perhaps another, but not I!"

Conan would smile snidely in every case, as if he knew otherwise. "That is good. Good. I am glad to know there is at least one in this hall that I can trust. But there are so many. I dare not ride away again lest every man sleeps in the sun while I am gone and this hall goes to ruin. From now on, I leave at least one knight with my privy order to manage this hall and see my lady well cared for. But you

need not fear this one whom I will choose, for he will punish no one. All punishments will be dealt by my own
hand."

"Yea, lord."

"I am glad to know that it will never be necessary to have
your back bared for the lash. If you have always worked
hard for the lord of this hall, you will do so again, without
question."

"Yea, lord."

" 'Tis good. I weary of warnings. I am known to give but
one."

The business had not been unpleasant, but bothersome.
And Conan did not assume that his warnings would be
heeded. He thought perhaps he would return from the
hunt with beatings to dole out. Because of his youth and
routinely calm behavior, the serfs were unprepared for the
fury he could display when angered. He did not storm and
shout at those in his service; it was not his way. He walked
softly, saying little, making his demands in a quiet but determined way. These people would learn, before too long,
that his rule here was not to be ignored just because he
behaved in a controlled fashion. Sir Conan would not
hesitate to use his strength when necessary.

When he returned to his chamber, Edwina had been
prepared for bed and he warmed at the sight. He had not
had the slightest taste of any woman upon the road, though
his men had done their share of wenching. He dismissed
Edwina's servants and drew her close to taste the lips he
owned, but when she was near enough for touching she
turned her lips away, and his kiss fell on her cheek. She
withdrew from him and climbed into the bed.

He disrobed clumsily, tossing his clothing aside. He no
longer cared one whit about the disorder in the hall, nor

did he feel the anger that earlier had possessed him. He hungered for her, and all other thoughts fled his mind. The fact that he found little invitation in her lips did not hinder his advances, for it was often this way as he approached her. He kissed her neck, her eyes and her temples, and when he imagined she might be of like mind, he asked her to remove the soft linen nightdress she wore.

"I beg to decline, seigneur," she whispered faintly. "I do not feel well."

Conan raised himself onto one elbow and looked down at her. "What troubles you?" he asked as gently as he could.

"I beg your forgiveness, Conan," she said softly. "I would not torture you. Truly, I feel ill."

Concern for her health caused his brow to wrinkle. "What is it, love?" he asked. "What has made you ill?"

"It is naught to trouble yourself with, Conan. This sickness that comes with the babe often passes when the child begins to move. The castle women tell me that it is a passing thing. I do not fear. But I cannot give you ease. I fear the sickness. I trust it will pass."

"Can I help you? I can bring you herbed wine or —"

"Oh, please," she moaned. "I dare not think of eating or drinking."

Conan withdrew slightly. He gave her hands an understanding pat, though his frustration by now was complete. He relaxed into the feather tick and lay quietly beside her, knowing she did not sleep any better than he. He could not lash out at her — it was his child that made her ill — but it took every ounce of his composure to keep from stomping like a spoiled child. Making love to Edwina would have been the one solace in an otherwise troubled day.

Visions of himself as the landholder and warrior flashed

through his mind. His shield was respected and often praised in these parts. His handsomeness was declared by many women who openly swore their desire. His chivalry and courtly manners brought him attention from earls and dukes. But here, in his own home, he met with discord. His keep was not well managed in his absence, when he was hungry he could not find food, and when he sought to ease his troubled mind even his seduction could not be answered here. He held himself back from cursing this marriage and his hopeless lot, for the child growing in his wife's womb was the start of a promise that answered a vital need within him. For that reason he could not be angry with Edwina. He held dear the fact that she suffered bravely with his seed.

He rose from the bed carefully so as not to disturb her sleep.

"Conan?" she questioned softly.

"Rest, love," he murmured.

"Where do you go?"

He turned to her guiltily, leaning over to place a kiss on her brow. "I find it difficult to lie beside you, love, and not take you in my arms. I will walk about the hall for a time."

"Conan, I know I have failed you," she whispered. "I will not question you. Go where you will."

"Edwina, I do not leave your side to seek out another woman."

"I could not be angry with you —"

"But have I shown myself to be a man of little faith? Have I given you cause to think I do not hold my vows dear?"

"Never, Conan. But neither were you faced with so many disappointments in earlier days. I tell you now that I understand."

"Then understand this, lady. I care only that you are resting and nurturing the life I gave you to carry. My other problems I will manage without ever bringing a slight to your name." And as he spoke the words, he felt them in his heart. He knew he could never hurt her. She, who would willingly give him to another who could serve his needs better, had learned the way of truly unquestioning love. Would that I could return it, he thought with some discomfort. But his mind was firm. He would do all he could to show her the same unselfish devotion she showed him. "I would do nothing to dishonor you, Edwina. Rest easy."

"You are a good man, Conan," she said sleepily. "I could not have known how fortunate I would be."

Wearily Conan made his way to the lower level of the hall, feeling more than seeing his way, for he had no torch or candle. There were a few who had made pallets in the hall, but many had found other lodgings for the night. There was one man still awake and sitting before the hearth, his dark mantle shrouding his face. As Conan approached, Mallory turned and looked. Neither seemed pleased with the other's company.

"The fire has died down," Mallory said.

"Dawn will come soon enough. Will you be ready to ride with the rest?"

"Have I ever made you late, my lord?" he returned somewhat angrily.

"Never," Conan replied, staring back into the glowing embers. "The game may already be deep in the forest. It will be a long day — longer still to ride with a man plagued by some reluctant maid."

Mallory's head snapped up in surprise, and the look he

gave Conan was not one of fondness. "What makes you think I am troubled by a woman?"

Conan laughed and drew himself up. He rummaged about a bit to find two mugs and filled them both from the pitcher. It was a sight that would have left a simple serf bemused, for to see two great knights sitting upon the rushes before the fire quaffing ale was a rare sight. Conan was usually surrounded by much aplomb, taking the highest place in the hall, the lord's chair. Serfs and peasants were the ones to sit on the floor.

Conan took a long pull on his drink. "You have no family to worry you, and Thurwell is no more surly than ever. He has found some wench from the village to warm the night, but what of you? The women upon the road never saw your smile, and you turned no favors their way — to their good fortune I am sure, for no doubt you would have disappointed them greatly."

"You should pay such close attention to your horses," Mallory grumbled.

"Who is the fair dame?"

"Do not burden yourself, my lord. I have not touched the maid."

Conan laughed and then whistled low. "More the bite! Will she have none of you?"

Mallory trusted in Conan's friendship and understanding, but those could easily give way to wrath once Conan learned 'twas Edythe that dwelt in every corner of his mind. He sighed. "Her family is wealthy."

"Ah," Conan acknowledged. "Does her family not see the merits of having a knight of Henry in their household?"

"I've had no dealings with her family on that score," Mallory returned sullenly. "Nor do I intend to. I am not a suitable match for the maid."

"And what of the maid? Has she nothing to say on the matter?"

"Nay, she will not speak of me, because I forbade her and she will honor me. I begged her hold her tongue so that no suspicion of ill doings would lay heavy on her father's mind, though I tell you true, I have not spoiled her. Yet I would stay in the family's good graces. I know they cannot have me."

"You have not thought of acquiring the wealth needed to buy her hand?"

"There is no time. Her father's wealth could bring her a fine lord, and a year of full moons could not bring me the livres to buy her."

"Perhaps her father would allow you the time."

"Without a family name to lean upon? Nay, he would not be so foolish."

"She must indeed be a goddess, for I have never known the dame that could leave you with such a low opinion of yourself. What is her preference?"

Mallory sighed. "She swears she will take the veil rather than the choice of her father. 'Tis a burden of guilt greater than I had hoped to bear, since I cannot free the maid from such an oath."

"A better fate for her, I think, than should her wish come true."

"By the rood, Conan, 'tis a poor time for jesting —"

"Jest? Nay. In truth, the maid's determination outpaces your own. If you love her, find a way to have her. What more risk than laying your life in your king's hands? For a damsel worthy, I would risk all."

Mallory looked at Conan closely. He could easily guess what problems Conan had. "What would you risk, Conan?"

Conan was quiet for a moment. Working hard and fighting would not bring him his love. That was no longer an option. "I am pledged to my lady wife and I would risk all for her — on my honor."

Mallory made no response. Both men stared into the fire for a long while. Conan finally broke the silence. "We ride at dawn's first light."

"I will be mounted with the rest," Mallory returned, rising to leave.

Conan stayed before the fire, considering the events that had led him to this position. His decision to marry was hastened by his mother's advice and warning. He regretted his haste now. Regardless of the stress of fighting for a maid, he would welcome the chance to try.

As the embers faded, he lay upon the rushes, his eyes closed as he tried to envision how things might have been. By the time the sun cast its first rays over Stoddard walls, he was up and in the stables, preparing for the long day ahead.

Strict orders were left with the bailiff to see to matters in the hall, and the word was passed that Conan would not return until he was well satisfied with the game.

Conan was astride before many of his men had eaten and finished dressing. His head was covered with the hood of his woolen gamberson, and a surcoat and heavy woolen mantle of dull gray were still little protection against the biting cold. His helm was resting on his saddle horn, and he watched impatiently as his riders scrambled to mount their horses before he was far ahead of them.

Two men near the rear of the troop grumbled as they hurried to catch up with the departing troop. "Curse the lady for not keeping him abed until the sun rises," said one.

"He was up the night," said the other. "There must be nettles in his bed."

"And for those nettles we will pay a dear price," returned the first. "He will ride us until we drop."

The game the hunters sought was deep in the forest. They returned with boar and deer, rabbit and fox. Conan kept his troop in the wood for three days, giving himself time to set his mind to his oath again and giving the castle folk time to prove their worth.

As he entered the keep, he thought perhaps he had returned too soon, for he found the hall cold and dark. He could almost feel the lash in his hand, believing the villeins had paid no attention to his warning. He did not wait for any report from the bailiff but strode in, barking orders. Fires must be stoked, pots hung, meat cleaned and applied to spits for cooking. Within moments there was a new light in the hall and a mad scurrying to comply with the lord's wishes. Kegs of ale were swiftly provided, and the men entering met with servants eager to help them disarm themselves and to offer a drink.

Conan had not noticed that Edwina was not there to greet him. A castle woman approached him and gently tugged at his sleeve. "Monseigneur, your lady is ill."

He frowned. Even though the condition of things in this hall had not pleased him when he had returned from his earlier business, the hall had not been so quiet and dark. Fear gnawed at him and he stared at the woman.

"My lord, she calls for you."

"What is her ailment?" he asked.

"She has miscarried, my lord."

His eyes widened in surprise. "The child? Dead?"

"Lost, monseigneur. 'Twas a son, far too early born."

Conan felt an ache creep into his throat. He had never wept, even as a child. A man child was taught early to mask hurt and pain behind a strength that was impossible to penetrate. He looked about the room for some sign of comfort, but there was none. Even this hall held no pleasure for him. But the men were quiet, watching him. The word had traveled quickly.

He turned abruptly so that no one would see the glistening of his eyes. He felt a sudden rush of tears threatening to spill. He moved quickly in the direction of his wife's bedchamber. Just inside the door stood Mallory, watching Conan's flight in confusion. Conan did not pause to explain his sorrow to his friend.

In the chamber above, Conan pulled back the bed curtains to see the pale and drawn face of his wife. Around her were servants and the priest. He found words impossible and cleared the room with a wave of his arm, kneeling then beside the bed.

Her eyes were reddened and dull; her hair, her best feature by far, was damp and stringy. Her lips, the same color as her sallow skin, were dry and cracked. He looked at her with pity and pain.

"Forgive me, my lord," she croaked weakly.

"Forgive?" he gasped. "Forgive me, my love. I should not have left you."

"Conan," she moaned, tears coming to her eyes. "Conan, I could not bring your son to life —"

"Edwina, love, it is not your fault."

"Do not hate me, Conan."

"Hate you? Nay! You are my wife! I love you!"

"My sister, Conan. Please. Send my sister to my side."

His agony increased. She did not know what she asked. Guilt churned within him. Knowing he did not love her totally, even as she lay here suffering with the loss of his child, even as he uttered the words he hoped would give life to her eyes again, he did not know if he could bear the temptation of having Chandra in his own house. As much as he wished it was not so, he thought of Chandra every day, loving her.

"My sister, Conan," Edwina repeated. "Chandra . . ."

He placed a kiss on her fevered brow. "Aye, love," he whispered. "I will send for her at once. She will know how to care for you."

CHAPTER
8

THE bedchamber in which Edwina lay was kept dark and tightly closed to prevent death from making an entrance. Serving women entered and left throughout the day, and the priest from the village kept close guard over her soul. Conan ventured there several times a day, sitting patiently at her bedside. She had no fever and the bleeding was controlled, but still Edwina lay in this weakened state, showing no improvement.

Sitting at his wife's bedside brought Conan the greatest feelings of inadequacy. Fighting a strong and widely acclaimed knight had never made him feel helpless. Managing the burdensome chores of a large hall were not confusing or upsetting. But faced with this delicate woman in need brought out the worst in him. He could not care for her or protect her from the weakness of her body that caused her to deliver the child much too early.

Edwina would awaken from time to time and find him there. She would attempt to smile or squeeze his hand. His heart was torn with guilt. Even as he stood vigil at her bedside he thought of another — and then cursed himself for feeling such emotion. All knights were not so bound to their code, but Conan knew he could find no escape in being a lesser-bound knight. Honor was the blood that flowed through him.

Mallory and Thurwell, his most trusted friends, were the leaders of the troop that rode to Phalen to bring Chandra. He knew she would leave at once and travel swiftly. He was in the hall when the doors were opened for her. He was afraid. He feared the wild and painful wanting as their eyes met. Even with Edwina so ill he could feel no differently.

A woolen mantle of deep green covered her to the ground, the hood hiding her golden locks. Her eyes were alive with the excitement of her hasty journey as she burst into the hall. Her cheeks were flushed and she did not look at all weary despite her long ride.

She bowed briefly and wordlessly. Two maids were close at her heels, struggling to keep up with their mistress and looking tired and worn. She threw back the hood and her golden hair unraveled about her shoulders.

He met Chandra's eyes. It was the same. His love for her pierced his heart and hung there dripping from the wound of wanting her.

"Where is she, Conan?" Chandra asked.

"Her chamber is at the head of the stairs," he answered. He did not offer to take her there.

She smiled at him and moved closer to touch his hand. "Don't worry over her now, Conan. I am here and she will mend."

"Chandra, I —" He looked away briefly and struggled with his words. "I left her alone, though I knew she was not feeling well. I have protected her poorly."

"Conan, 'tis no fault of yours. You could not have known she would deliver the child so early. It is no one's fault that Edwina has earned this sad circumstance. She is so like our mother in so many ways. My lady mother did lose several children before a healthy child was born."

"I fear she is dying," Conan thought aloud.

"Nay, Conan. She is not strong, fair to say, but Edwina will pull through this. I am here to see to that."

"She mourns for the child . . ."

There was a flicker of emotion in Chandra's eyes. She looked up at Conan and he thought perhaps he saw a tear gather there. "As you must," she said softly. Chandra took a breath and braved a smile, looking pert and energetic as quickly as a snap of the fingers. "But you are both young. She will yet deliver you sons."

Without further discussion, Chandra went directly to the stair, looking over her shoulder at the two maids. Impatiently she snapped, "Come, come!" and turned to go, knowing they would follow with a bit less enthusiasm.

It was not long before Mallory and Thurwell joined him in the hall. "The journey was safe?" he asked.

"Aye, and speedy. Lady Chandra travels easily," Mallory returned.

On the first day after Chandra's arrival, there was naught but quiet in the hall, Conan's ear often turned toward his chamber while he stayed mostly away from that room.

On the second day the pace in the hall picked up and there was more light and more movement. Chandra was quick to see that Conan was spending more than the usual amount of time with his horses. She put a stop to the morbidity all about her and snapped many a melancholy servant into action. It was without great labor on her part that the hall was running smoothly and efficiently and Edwina was showing improvement. It never occurred to

Chandra that witnessing her ease in managing a great hall, even one she did not know, tormented Conan the more.

There were no problems in setting a good meal before the men-at-arms, and there was no idleness among the castle folk. Some worked hard to spare their backs the lash and others worked for the reward of her quick smile and praise. She had no time to sit and chat. The people would see her in virtually every room in the hall, from the kitchen to the lord's chamber, never staying in one place for very long. When she was near Conan she paused only long enough to tell him that she was pleased with Edwina's recovery. He usually grunted his thanks and the two parted as quickly as they had come together. In these days, many would exchange bemused stares as they judged Conan and Chandra's reaction to each other.

The chair beside Conan was glaringly empty at mealtimes. Had Chandra chosen to don her best and slip into that chair beside him, no one would have criticized, but she would not presume so much. She was never seen garbed in a fine gunna and gold trinkets, but a rough working tunic, with her hair pulled back and hidden under a wimple. She worked from early morning 'til late at night, taking her meals with her sister and sleeping on a straw pallet beside Edwina's bed.

Chandra found a certain peace once Edwina regained some of her health. They would talk of the way things were when they were children and wonder aloud what life was like for Laine now.

Late on the seventh day after her arrival, Chandra knelt at the hearth and poked at the fire. Edwina was sitting up in her bed and her fingers plucked daintily at a stitchery project.

"I have written to Father that you are better and will soon be managing your own home. He wanted to come with me," she said, looking at her older sister and rolling her eyes. "Traveling with Father has become a chore. He grows old, Edwina. I fear he will not have many years left. And the chatting he wants to do now — Jesu! We must sit and discuss the king and the situation in France every eventide!"

Chandra went to sit on the bed and a little laugh escaped from her. "It would have been your just reward had I brought Father! You would not dare to complain of the ennui of being bedridden. He would —"

Chandra stopped abruptly as she noticed a tear tracing its way slowly down Edwina's cheek. She could remember her sister being beset by illness after illness all through her childhood, but she had not remembered her tears.

She held Edwina's arms and tried to look at her eyes, but Edwina kept them downcast, looking at the little piece of linen she held. Chandra could see that a tapestry face was being worked onto the fabric.

Edwina sniffed back her tears and tried to smile, but the effort was lame. She shrugged as if embarrassed. "It was to be a doll. A child's toy."

"Oh, Edwina," Chandra sighed, not knowing how to comfort.

"Father is growing old and I had hoped he would see the child that would one day earn Phalen by right of birth. It was a son — somehow I knew it was a son."

"There is time, Edwina. You will yet give Conan a son."

"I *must* give him a son," Edwina said softly. "He is such a fine, strong man, so good and so kind. His rewards are so few, having me for a wife. If I can give him a healthy son —"

"You will, Edwina," Chandra said, as if making a promise. "He does not suffer because of marriage with you! You are a fine wife, Edwina!" Chandra felt an ache creep into her throat and she could feel tears threaten. She embraced Edwina and said, "You love him so very much."

Edwina did not respond. Chandra wondered if Edwina could see that look in Conan's eyes, that faraway, pained expression that she had witnessed so many times. For the first time Chandra felt his torture as acutely as he did! Edwina was so devoted to him. She loved and worshiped him with every fiber of her being.

"You need rest," Chandra said softly. "Here, lie down. I will be back in a moment."

"Where do you go?"

"You have not had a moment alone, Edwina. You have been set upon by serving women, priests, castle folk and me. When I feel the need for time alone I run and hide, but you cannot. I will leave you to your thoughts, and if you want me, I am near."

"You are wise, Chandra. Beyond your years. And I love you so."

"And I love you, Edwina," Chandra said in a near whisper.

Chandra left the room and stood outside the chamber doors for a moment to collect herself. The guilt of feeling drawn to Conan had been strong before, but faced with Edwina's devotion, the discomfort was greater, the shame almost consuming her. And there was nothing to be done but to hope that one day Conan could return Edwina's love.

The hall was quiet when Chandra went to the lower level. Conan sat there before the fire, staring into the glowing flames. He turned to look at her as though he felt her presence. She hoped he would not see the stain of tears marking her cheeks.

"All is still," he said huskily.

"You must go to your wife, Conan. She needs you."

He stood abruptly. "Has she worsened?" he asked anxiously.

"Nay, she is improving more every day and soon, I think, will be well enough for me to leave."

"She calls for me now?" he asked.

Chandra shook her head and looked down so that Conan would not see the tears gathering in her eyes. "She weeps for the child. I cannot comfort her. That is your place."

As Conan moved past her toward the stair, Chandra took his place before the fire. Passion did not move Conan to his wife's side, she knew that. Even so, the bonds that held them together, the ties of marriage, responsibility, duty and honor, would keep them tightly bound for years to come. The tears spilled freely as jealousy tore at her. She would rather have that much of him than what she had now.

Am I so wicked, she thought in despair, that I deserve no reward for my labors and prayers?

She buried her face in her hands and gave vent to her tears, hating herself for loving wrongly, hating herself for coveting what was her sister's, and knowing that the one thing that could give her ease in her troubled state was to be held in the arms of the knight she could not forget or deny.

No one was prepared for the arrival of a long train of knights and servants from Anselm. When Conan was given word of the approaching retinue, he went in some confusion to greet his guests. To his surprise he found it was Udele and Edythe who had come.

"Madam," he said in greeting. "What brings you here?"

"My daughter, your wife, is ill. What better reason?"

"I brought her sister here to care for her. You are good to come, but there is no need."

"No need?" she laughed. "Conan, Chandra is a young lass who should be home with her father, making plans for her own wedding. Though I'm sure she is a capable maid, it is unfair to chain her to Edwina's sickbed when she should be home visiting many attractive suitors."

Conan stiffened slightly at the thought. He had not heard of suitors. "She was glad to be called," he said.

"Of course, Conan. She is a good lass and would no doubt care for Edwina all her life, but we must think of Chandra. I know you wish her well and would not have her slave her years away caring for her sister. Now I am here and she can return to her father."

That said, in a manner that greatly resembled Chandra's, Udele brushed past Conan and was into action. Udele was no stranger to work and took charge of the keep. She had a room made for herself and one for Edythe and her women, putting some of the castle folk out of their beds.

She went next to Edwina, finding Chandra near, and, with her most sympathetic smile, relieved Chandra of her chore. But Udele had no intention of personally guarding Edwina's recovery as Chandra had. Instead she installed her own nurse to see to Edwina's many needs.

In just a few hours Chandra felt many changes. She felt like a participant in one of her own dreams. Nothing seemed particularly real. The evening meal found Udele, gowned exquisitely, sitting at the right hand of her son

and presiding over the crowded hall. Chandra rather sheepishly took a chair quite far from Conan, near Edythe. And
Udele's manner seemed unusually gay for the premise of
her journey: to care for her daughter by marriage after
the loss of her child.

Chandra was not ignored by the great lady. Rather,
Udele made quite a show of thanking her over and over
again for her labors and praising her efficiency. "You have
been detained long enough and I can see to Edwina now."

When Chandra went to Edwina's chamber after the evening meal, she found she had been thoroughly removed
and her belongings were put in a small, inferior chamber
with Edythe's things. The maids Chandra had brought
were cast from their closets to make room for Udele's
servants. They were at odds as to what to do and in their
confusion had placed their things with Chandra's. Now
they stood, four of them, in a room that could never accommodate them. Chandra sent her women on an insignifi-
cant errand, and when they were gone she turned to
Edythe in a quandary.

"Edythe, what am I to make of this?"

Edythe shrugged in embarrassed apology. "My mother
is accustomed to having things her way."

"I do not think she hates me, yet I am being cast from
my sister's side, now that she is nearly recovered and there
is little left to be done. I know that Conan sent word to his
parents when the child was lost, yet I have been here for
ten days and she has not come. If it is aid she wishes to give,
why was she so long in coming?"

Edythe shook her head. "She saw no need when the message arrived with the sad news of the child. The second
message prompted our journey here."

"The second message?" Chandra asked.

"Conan sent word that you had arrived and were taking good care of Edwina. He reported that she was doing well and there was no longer any reason to fear for her."

"Then it is so?" Chandra half questioned. "She thinks it unfair that I am heavily tasked with my sister's illness?"

"Part of the reason perhaps," Edythe offered.

Chandra stared at the younger girl in confusion.

"I see the way my brother looks at you," Edythe said gently. "Perhaps my mother has seen this also."

Chandra felt the flush creep to her cheeks. "But she cannot fear that he would dishonor me!" she argued. "He is a good man and he is devoted to Edwina."

"I do not think that is her fear," Edythe said. "But I think it possible she fears you would be a greater influence on him. She has allowed no other that position, not even Father. She guards Conan's decisions closely, when he will allow her."

"How can I influence him? How can I claim to be his friend and counsel? I am young and unmarried and of little experience."

"If what I see in his eyes is true, he would listen to you. And what we have found in this hall does not speak of a lass of little experience. You manage as well as my mother ever has."

Chandra held her gaze. "If I have worked hard and done well, why is it still impossible to please her?"

Edythe laughed softly. "Madam has no friends, Chandra, nor has she ever. I have seen her treat women of a higher station with care, but when they are gone she speaks unkindly of them. Madam holds herself above all women, and those who are her match she treats scornfully. I think perhaps she fears you."

"That cannot be so. There is nothing I can do to cause Udele to fear."

"You can give my brother your love. You can make him promises and urge him to give up all that he has acquired and take you for his own."

"And would I do such a thing?" Chandra asked in disbelief. "Can anyone imagine that I could shame my family, tear my sister's love from her arms, and beg Conan to dishonor himself and shame his family? Edythe, if I loved him, would I do that to him?"

Edythe only shrugged by way of an answer, for she knew very well the desperation of love. "My mother envies youth and beauty and strength. Beware of her, Chandra. She will never let you near to what is hers."

Chandra thought heavily, straining to recall every detail of her few brief encounters with Udele. She had admired the great lady from afar, Udele's many strengths drawing Chandra's attention and actually giving the young maid something to pattern herself after. Chandra had many times hoped she would be as Udele was: strong, capable, beautiful. She had never thought herself even near having those qualities. Even now, though what Edythe said was true and Udele seemed to scorn her and push her well out of Conan's sight, she could not fathom the reasons. Chandra could do Conan no harm.

"What will you do?" Edythe asked.

"I will take myself home. And I will not come to my sister's aid again. This is not my place."

The sun set and was replaced by a bright moon, a sphere of ivory that escaped the drifting clouds to shine brightly upon the earth, giving moments of light to the darkness. Chandra asked many squires and attendants the whereabouts of Sir Conan and was finally directed to the stable.

A lantern provided his light as he brushed down Orion, speaking softly to the beast as he tended him. Mars was on his nearby perch and was often the recipient of some comment or a light stroke of his feathers.

At the far end of the stable two squires sat polishing Conan's armor and hammering out the dents. She watched in distracted interest, wondering what fight upon the road had earned those marks. The thought of him meeting an enemy and raising his sword in defense gave her a feeling of excitement and discomfort at once.

When she looked back to where he was working, his eyes were on her. She felt her stomach jump as it always did when he looked at her. His eyes held a warm glow, something she had not seen in a very long time. They had encountered each other only a few times since he took Edwina to wife, and in those meetings his eyes had been pained, reflecting the struggle between his honor and his desire. He did not frown at her now, but with careful slowness, he measured her form with his eyes from her toes to her brow. She shuddered with the cold, only now aware that she had no mantle to warm her against the chilly night. In her eagerness to have the matter behind her, she had come quickly to the stable.

Conan called the squires by name and they looked up to see Chandra standing just inside the door. He sent them from their chores and closed the door behind them. He was sure in his action and different somehow. He seemed older and, if possible, more determined.

"You should not close the door, Sir Conan," she said. "There could be too much curiosity in our privacy."

"There is curiosity in our every meeting. Don't you know what echoes through my halls? Idle hands have quick eyes. They say I am in love with my poor wife's sister."

Chandra felt a boulder drop into the pit of her stomach. She was a fool to think even her most private feelings secret. They were suspect and they had done nothing. "Now that my lady Udele is come, I shall leave. I have little to prepare. I can be upon the road as quickly as your men can travel."

"You do not have to go," he said huskily. "If you choose to stay I will arrange it. It is only fair that you be allowed to see your sister's complete recovery, if that is your desire."

"It is best that I go," she said, looking at the ground.

"Because you wish it or because you feel you are being cast from this house?"

"Edwina will be well soon. I am not needed."

He lifted her chin with a finger. "I am not concerned about Edwina. Do you wish to stay?"

"So that they can say I am here for the few precious moments that I can share with my sister's husband? Is there not trouble enough over my being here?"

"Do not punish yourself, Chandra. This is not your fault and you have been strong."

"And my strength diminishes with each passing day. Nay, I beg of you, do not make it difficult for me. Give me escort home."

"Of course. It will be as you desire. You can ride on the morrow."

She turned as if she would leave, but found he had her arm and was drawing her back to him. So swiftly that she could not stop him, he had locked her in his embrace.

"Conan, nay, you must not hold me so. If someone —"

"I will hear if anyone approaches," he assured her.

"But 'tis wrong! You must not touch me so!"

"Chandra," he murmured, brushing her hair away from her face. "I am prepared to live with the ties I have made for myself, but I have wondered for too long. I must know if I am greedy in my heart and crying out like a babe for more wealth than I already have, or if there is something real between us."

"Nay, Conan, you must not."

"One kiss, I pray," he said softly. "By the blood of God, I wouldst do you no harm and never would I soil you. One kiss, for that is all I may ever know of you."

The soft and sure determination in his gaze showed her he suffered no confusion. She shook her head negatively, but he held her fast with his arms and eyes. She was certain she should not assent, but she could not find her reason. His touch and scent, his eyes, so loving and warm, gave her to wonder what harm there was in a kiss. Could the longing ever be more? The future any better or worse for a kiss? Slowly her eyelids dropped, and her mouth, half opened in expectation, met his.

His arm tightened about her waist and her head dropped back to be cradled in his hand, her thick hair woven about his fingers. His sigh was deep as he consumed her with his kiss, his blood racing through his veins as he tasted response, so sweet and so welcome. He felt her quiver slightly and the inexperience of her lips made his fulfillment even greater. What he suspected was confirmed as he held her. Their love, given a chance, could rival the stars in its brightness.

With great reluctance he let her go, and she moved quickly away from him lest he be tempted to more. They both knew this one kiss had not only confirmed the heights their passion might reach, but the danger in being too close.

"You must heed your words, Sir Conan," she said, somewhat shaken. "You must live with the ties you have made. You must never touch me so again."

He looked at her with confidence. "I give you my word. I will not dishonor you. My love must never hurt you."

"With your permission I will leave at morningtide."

"I will advise my riders."

Chandra reached for the stable door, though her hand was weak and it took every fiber of control to keep from running into his arms.

"Chandra," he said to her back. Weakly she turned and looked at him. "I will not touch you again, nor will I seek to weaken your resolve, so you need not fear me." She shook her head and it was truth: she did not fear him. It was something growing within herself that she feared. Conan continued, "I may never again feel your lips close to mine, but be sure in your heart that my love is real and will endure. It will be impossible for me ever to love another woman as I love you."

Tears came to her eyes, though she fought them. "Do not watch my departure, my lord," she said with a tremor in her voice. "And do not fill your nights with dreams of what can never be." With that said, she threw open the stable door and rushed into the night. The door, unlatched, banged in the wind. She did not return to close it and he did not move to secure it.

Soon there was nothing where she had stood — nothing but the wind causing the door to crash against the outer wall. He stared at the memory of her. "I will not watch you go, fair lady, for that would pain my heart. But I will savor my dreams. That is the only peace there is for me."

Early the next morn, while the village was just coming alive and the smoke from the rekindled fires was swirling about Stoddard's walls, the party of riders that would escort Chandra home was assembling about the carts in the court-yard.

Conan stayed in his chamber, vowing to himself that he would not venture to the courtyard to bid them farewell. But his plan was not to be. It was Mallory and Thurwell who drew him out and asked for a moment of his time in the courtyard.

"I've taken much to heart the advice you gave me, Conan. You urged me on to find a way to make some claim that would please my lady's father. I think I have found the way," Mallory said. "It may not please you."

Conan's brow arched in question and he looked to Thurwell. The only answer he saw in his face was that he would go with Mallory, to whatever fate. They would not separate now, after such a long friendship.

"What is your plan?" Conan asked with some reluctance.

"In some ways it would be better not to tell you, Conan. We could ride out with the lady this morn and you would learn our intentions soon enough. But neither of us could see the worth of leaving your hall without a word and have you think us traitors to your cause."

"I have no cause," Conan grumbled, "save the cause of the king."

"Aye, Conan," Thurwell said solemnly. "Henry lies half alive and half dead in France. His health is as tender a thing as a slender branch under an eagle's nest. He re-fuses to name Richard as his rightful heir. What Henry does in this is wrong. That father and sons should fight each other is wrong. But we go to Richard. We will pledge to him."

"Richard will gain his due with Henry's passing," Conan

said. "He is a strong warrior and will win his right. What use in defying the king who saw you knighted?"

"Because Richard will be grateful and will likely reward those who defend his right."

Conan could see clearly now. Mallory would find his fame and wealth by choosing his army carefully. "But it can be called by no name but treason," said Conan.

Mallory shrugged. "My honorable friend," he said with affection. " 'Tis easy to be steadfast when your family name and wealth are your tools. Aye, treason, for a fortnight or a year, whichever is the length of Henry's life. It will be called treason while the king lives, but when Richard is king it will be called wisdom."

"And if there is war?" Conan asked.

"There has been war," Thurwell replied. "There will be war again. And again."

"And if I am called? My father and my wife's father stand firm in their allegiance to Henry. Unless I cease to call myself a son and leave all my possessions behind to travel to France, what prevents us from meeting opposite each other on a field of battle with swords raised?"

Mallory laughed and looked at Conan much as he would regard a younger brother. "My good friend, I would expect you to fight. And do not expect my breast bare to your blade. But you must see, Conan, that your loyalties have been fed to you like a midday meal. Though you have the right to choose them, you take the offered ties and 'tis your right to abide or deny them. You will do what you have to do, and if that means raising a sword to a friend, you must fight to win. And I will do what I have to do.

"But I think it more likely we will be reunited under a new king," Mallory continued, "for Henry may yet acknowledge Richard's right. And if he does not, and Richard comes to the throne by right of arms, I doubt he would punish those who served his father well. Most of England would dance from a gibbet if he dared."

"Is there no other way?" Conan asked. "My father urges me to find a castellan to tend and support Stoddard with arms. I could make that decision in your favor and he would be pleased."

"Lands not even my own? Conan, this of all things cannot come as a gift from you."

"Then what of Edythe's dower lands?" he asked, not noticing Mallory jump in surprise at the sound of her name. "My father has long said he would greatly reward a hardy man who would act as guardian to that estate. It was my mother's and has been neglected because of the resistance of the Welsh neighbors."

Mallory smiled indulgently. He wished he could tell Conan that he hoped someday to be one of Alaric's strong arms, not to acquire wealth but to serve his lady and his father by marriage. But he only said, "There must be pride in the gathering of a fortune or it means naught. And if I do not make haste in building my wealth, I will find the maid gone."

Conan laughed. "I remember a time when women did not matter. I remember when our passing words were not so sweet and noble."

"Other women do not matter," Mallory said with seriousness. "Only one."

And in his heart Conan agreed. For every man at some time in his life, there was only one. And that one could bring joy untold or a heart weeping with longing. He could not begrudge his friend his chance. "Would that I could see the dame who drives you so hard." Then he chuckled in spite of himself. "Would that *I* could drive you so hard."

"You haven't the proper swing to your skirts to give Mallory such will," Thurwell laughed. He grasped Conan's hand firmly. "God speed, friend."

With some uneasiness Conan faced Mallory. "Do not say anything to my riders. They are loyal to me and thus to Henry. There is no need to tell them where you are going. Go from Phalen in secrecy and I will hear of your departure from my returning troop."

"Go with God, Conan," Mallory said.

"Good fortune, friend," Conan said, grasping him by the hand and upper arm. It was his intention to go back into the hall so as to be spared the departure of his friends and Chandra, but she came with her ladies to the courtyard at the very moment he would have fled.

"I have said my farewells in the hall," she said quietly.

"I wish I could properly thank you for the service you've given, Lady Chandra. I fear there is no adequate reward."

"I seek no reward but that you think kind thoughts of me, sir knight."

She looked past Conan and saw Edythe in the courtyard behind her brother. She brushed past Conan and embraced her fondly, murmuring in her ear. Edythe nodded and whispered to Chandra.

Conan could not escape, so he stiffened his back and took Chandra's arm to lead her to her horse. He lifted her to her saddle himself, helping her find the stirrup with her foot and positioning her knee about the pommel. A servant stood near with a woolen blanket and Conan took that, tucking it about her lap.

Their eyes met for a moment as he looked up at her, hers

with a hint of tears and his with naked adoration and longing. He touched her hand. "Thank you, fair lady."

"Good-bye, monseigneur," she replied with a trembling voice.

He handed her the reins and she looked straight ahead, her eyes brimming. He knew her agony and would not prolong it. He stepped away from her horse and raised a hand to the gatekeeper. The creaking and snapping of the portcullis signaled their parting. He waved to his friends and felt his breath catch as the three people he loved most in his life rode away from him. He stood beside his sister until the gate began to close.

"They will be safe upon the road," he said, half to himself. " 'Tis too cold for even the hardiest thieves."

He looked down and met Edythe's round green eyes, which were filled with tears that glistened beneath the sooty lashes. "Aye, brother. They will be safe." Her voice was barely a whisper. She turned from him and, pulling her mantle tightly about her, went back into the hall.

Conan looked again at the Stoddard doors that had seen his friends' departure, then he looked at Edythe's disappearing form. Edythe? he asked himself. Could Edythe be the maid that Mallory struggled to win?

My brain grows thick with romance and knows not beef from grain, he thought. He ran a hand through his thick, dark hair and shook his head. If war does not come, he thought, I will make a better poet than a knight. He turned in the direction of the hall and with long, determined strides made his way to his wife's chamber.

PART

II

CHAPTER
9

I
N the pale glow of dawn, the beasts and critters of the
forest were already awake and about their morning
work. Mice skittered from hay to brush; rabbits darted
from tree to hole. Sir Conan stood in the field outside
Anselm's walls with Mars perched on his gauntleted hand.
Though the hood had not yet been removed, the great
bird sensed the morning and was eager to be set free; his
jesses pulled and the bell tied to them tinkled.

"No patience this morn, eh? Ready, then . . ."

The hood was removed and the feathers close to Mars's
breast tensed and stood out. His beak opened and he
roused. Conan's hand jolted him into the air. The great
bird soared, tucked his head when he spotted his prey,
and flew to a brown spot that stood out among the golden
layers of hay.

Conan rode to where his falcon had lighted, lifted the
bird, and fed him a piece of meat, the meat of a domestic
dove. "Fine catch," Conan said.

"My lord?"

Conan turned abruptly at the sound of a woman's voice.

"Edwina, what are you doing here?"

"I beg your forgiveness, Conan, but the boy in the mews
told me where you might be found. I hoped it would leave
us a moment alone to talk."

"And it could not wait?"

She was quiet for a moment, her sad eyes looking down and not at him. Conan steadied himself. It was not her fault, he reminded himself. He was to blame. He had done her a great injustice in seeking her so quickly, thinking so little of her needs. He had been moved by her beauty, her estate and a vengeance that would not allow him to stand by and give all that to Tedric.

He replaced the hood over Mars's head and faced his wife with more gentleness. Perhaps he had protected her from a worse fate. Their marriage had not been rich or fruitful, but for her goodness he loved her.

"Come, love, what troubles you so early this morn?"

" 'Tis no trouble, my lord, but you have been surrounded by family and men-at-arms. There is never time for a wife to speak."

"Edwina, you are my lady. When you have need of your husband, send the others from us and speak your mind. I am at your call."

"Conan, I am your lady, but I am not the lady here. You may have the courage to send Lady Udele and Lord Alaric from the room, but I dare not presume so much."

Conan laughed lightly. "I can see your problem. Clearly, you would have a difficult time ordering my mother to do anything."

Edwina grimaced slightly at hearing her husband speak with such light affection of his mother's overbearing nature. In over two years of marriage, she had not learned the way to please Udele.

A second miscarriage had been Edwina's fate. Shortly after Conan returned to their marriage bed she had come with child. A few months later the child had been lost, this one too early to tell the sex. Edwina had not suffered so this second time, except for the agony she knew at letting Conan down again.

Lady Udele came quickly to manage Stoddard and care for Edwina. She convinced Conan that another attempt might endanger Edwina's life, and for a time Edwina should reside at Anselm where her health could be carefully guarded.

Thus Edwina had been living with Conan's parents, seeing Conan only when he could leave Stoddard and other duties for visits. They had not shared a bed and did not even sit beside each other at the dining table when Conan was in residence.

"Conan, after the coronation, will you return to Stoddard?"

"Aye, you know I must."

"I have been frightened of Stoddard," she said quietly. "It was a dark and lonely place when I was there. And the memories — the children I could not give you . . ." Her voice trailed off for a moment. She took a deep breath and looked at him. "But my place is not here, Conan. If I am not to live with you at Stoddard Keep, might I go to Phalen?"

Conan stiffened slightly, wondering if this was indeed the end of their marriage. He could let her go to Phalen and she would be his wife, but there would be no marriage, no children. "What is your preference?"

"I should like to go with you to Stoddard, but Conan, I would understand if that does not please you."

"Why would I be displeased? You are my wife. Your place is with me, in the home I call my own, not with your father."

"I am of little use to you. I cannot promise that the next time I bring your seed to fertile ground I will deliver you a live child."

"Does this mean that you would like to try? You are not afraid?"

"I am not afraid," she said softly. "It will be as God wills it."

"Then you shall have Stoddard," he returned.

"There is another thing I would ask, if you will hear me. When we return from London, I should like to travel to Bury Saint Edmunds and pray for a healthy child."

The shrine, almost directly north of Cordell, was a place of miracles. Women who could not conceive and women already with child prayed and made offerings there. The spirit of Saint Edmund was said to be so strong as to strike down thieves who would pillage the shrine, killing them on the spot.

"I will take you there myself, after London."

"And then to Stoddard," she said, smiling now. She was lovely when she smiled. He remembered that sweet and shy smile she gave to him when he first spoke to her of marriage and the alliance of two powerful families. The estate the marriage brought would be mighty and strong and would need sons to carry it on.

"Stoddard shall have its lady again," he said, touching her cheek with his hand.

Edwina pressed his hand harder to her face. "Conan, I know I am not your match. I am not the lusty wench who can return your passion in a manner that would please you most. But Conan, you have been good to me. I want only to serve you well, to give you a son."

"Edwina, do not torture yourself — I have not complained. I know you wish to serve me well. And there will be sons."

"The dowry means so little if you are not given children to support you."

"There will be children, love, in time. Worry will not bring them. You must not blame yourself for things that are not your fault. Let us look ahead to more fruitful days and forget our past sufferings."

Edwina looked at her husband with adoration shining in her eyes. She brought his hand to her lips and pressed a kiss into the palm. "I love you, Conan."

He put his arm around her and walked with her toward his horse. "We have not been allowed much time to think about love," he said quietly. "You have been kept here, though I did not think it was against your wishes. And I have been set to the task of bettering my name, representing our fathers in every council and conference. They will have to allow us a brief space of time for family matters."

He remembered the feeling that came to his breast when he first learned that Edwina had conceived. Though their marriage had many weaknesses, he was filled with joy over the prospect of a son. It was a great strength in their relationship, a common bond and goal. He had a vision of the boys that would bow before him, seek him out as teacher, master and father. It was the only grasp at immortality that a man had, the truest reason he could find for hard work: to pass his possessions and his high standards on to his sons.

But the first two children his wife carried were lost, and lost too was Conan's reason for toiling. He had become a stranger to his wife's bed and had come to think there would never be a child of this union. This was the first time, in more than a year, that he heard his wife give the slightest indication that she wished to feel his weight in their bed again.

"You have walked a great distance to speak to me," he said softly.

"Had I waited for a mount, you might have already returned. I ran most of the way."

He arched a brow as he tried to consider this, for Edwina's pace was quite slow in the most hurried instances. He chuckled to himself and mounted Orion, offering her a hand to pull her up in front of him. With an easy motion she was raised to the saddle and he pulled his mantle tightly around her shoulders.

Edwina leaned back against him and sighed her contentment and sense of security. Conan held her closer, acting as her protector and strong arm. There would never be great passion in this union. But as they rode toward Anselm together, Conan finding warmth and devotion in his wife's manner and giving back to her as much caring and love, there was a certain peace.

Conan clicked his tongue and urged Orion slowly in the direction of the rising stone wall that surrounded the hall and hamlet that would one day be his. The steed stepped daintily through the field of rye, moved around the rows of vegetables nearer the wall, and finally found the dirt road that led through the gatehouse into the courtyard with almost no direction from his master. *She worries that she is not enough of a wife,* Conan thought. *Were I more of a husband she would know a total love, and it would make her strong.*

He hoped, for the hundredth time, that they could give each other more, thus finding contentment in their marriage.

The next morning Conan took Mars again to the field for their morning exercise, and when he returned to the hall he found his family seated to break the fast. He placed the hooded falcon on the back of his chair, and a servant brought him a horn of milk. Pork and coddled eggs were placed before him to tease his nostrils and start his stomach juices working. He felt fit and fine.

"I sought you in your chamber this morn, but you were not there," Udele said. Edwina's face flushed and she concentrated on her meal. Edythe looked up and listened with interest. Alaric's eyes focused on his wife.

"I was with my wife," Conan said easily, mopping up the yellow of the yolk with bread. "You will find me in her chamber henceforth."

"Do you think that wise?" Udele asked pointedly.

Conan looked at his mother and smiled in spite of himself. "Yea, madam, I think it wise."

"Edwina is not strong, Conan. You should not press her."

Alaric cleared his throat and frowned at his wife. She did not notice. Conan shrugged and declined further comment.

"And if she proves with child?" Udele asked.

"That is our wish, madam, that Edwina will prove with child. And though it was not my intention to inform you of my plans this very morn, you might be interested to know that after Richard is crowned in London, we will travel to Bury Saint Edmunds to make an offering and pray for a healthy son."

Udele grunted in disapproval. "You must make the offering generous," she sneered. "And I shall have her bed ready when you return."

"We go to Stoddard," Conan said.

"Stoddard! And who will care for Edwina there? Will you shirk your duties to take care of her when she is stricken again? You have obligations. How much will prosper by sitting at your wife's bedside?"

Edythe went back to her breakfast with a sigh. Alaric put his goblet down with a loud bang and glared at his wife, hoping Conan would stop her as well he should.

" 'Tis Edwina's wish to go with me to Stoddard, and rest assured, madam, she will be well cared for. 'Tis time we lived as man and wife — duty will always be close at hand to reclaim me."

Something of a snort escaped Udele and her mouth was twisted to show her displeasure. She looked at Edwina until the latter met her eyes and blushed in discomfort, and then she glared at Conan. "I had not thought you fool enough to bed her when all you will gain is a burden to keep you from giving good service and bettering your reputation here and —"

"Madam!" Alaric shouted. "Still your tongue or I shall still it for you!"

Udele fell suddenly quiet and picked at her meal. That was a command that could not be ignored. Though Alaric loved her and openly adored her, he would allow her to move only within the perimeters of his design.

She would not beg pardon for her bad behavior, but she was silent for many moments. It was not until conversation had resumed in a light manner that Udele spoke again, careful that her voice was pleasant.

"Word came from Medwin late yesterday and I only just remembered the news." Many faces turned her way. "Following the coronation there will be a wedding. Chandra will marry Tedric and we are all invited to attend."

Edwina smiled, but the other faces that were turned toward Udele were stunned and expressionless. Udele laughed as if in confused embarrassment. "Does the thought of a wedding distress you all?" she asked, looking mostly between her husband and son.

"Chandra deserves a richer man than Tedric," Alaric finally said, signaling a page with his empty mug. "I have long loved Theodoric and his sons, but that that one is a disappointment even his father cannot deny."

"But Tedric has done well for himself in spite of his lack of inheritance, and he stayed by King Henry's side through his death and served him well. I am to understand that he has accumulated considerable wealth," Udele argued. "Chandra's estate is not worth much and she should be grateful."

"Tedric stayed by Henry as a friend to that fiend, Count John," Conan said testily. "He hoped John would inherit the crown he did not deserve, and in the end he was not by Henry at all, but fleeing to Philip's side with that worthless whelp, John. Though the king unwisely would have risked all to save the crown for his youngest, that ungrateful wretch abandoned him. Tedric was no loyal knight, madam, but the same undeserving leech he has always been. You can be sure this is not a marriage born of love and tenderness."

Udele's jaw had a firm set. "I knew there was no great love in your heart for Tedric, but I had not thought you hated him so."

"Hate him?" Conan asked. "It is more that I can only abide him when I can see him. When he is out of my sight I keep an eye turned to my back. He cannot be trusted, and the oath he took to protect the code of chivalry is a sham. I would have hoped for better for Chandra."

"Will you celebrate his wedding?" Udele asked.

Conan looked at his wife, whose eyes were now downcast. In his blatant defamation of Tedric's character, he had forgotten that Edwina once considered marriage with him and did not think him such a terrible wretch. Perhaps she had even felt some happiness for Chandra, not thinking that perhaps Chandra was being taken advantage of by a knave. "Edwina will want to be with her family — with her sister — on that occasion. I will not shame my family with improper behavior, but I think I shall find little joy in it."

His hunger seeming to have vanished, he took a last drink of his milk and rose from the table, leaving the hall to seek out a quiet place to try to regain his good spirits.

Medwin did not feel that he was selling Chandra into some torturous bondage. He saw Tedric as a decent choice and a heaven-sent redeemer in this time of need. The tithe he had to pay to finance the crusade against Saladin had bled the wealth from Phalen, and Medwin was hard pressed to meet his obligations. And now that Richard would be king and leaving soon for the Crusade to the Holy Land, Medwin would either pay his scutage for the privilege of staying behind, or he would have to yield men for war. The men could not be spared, for they were already few, and the scutage was hard to meet. Tedric, though he would not confide his means, backed his marriage proposal with much money.

Chandra looked about her chamber. It was adequate, to be sure, but there were no new fixings or furniture. She possessed the same oaken coffer that had been her mother's.

It functioned as a chair, space for clothing and linen, and a table to write at when a stool was set before it. There had been no new gowns and certainly there was no money for jewelry. Two tapestry wall hangings kept her chamber from being starkly naked.

Chandra did not long for riches, but she had wants. A chair with arms carved from oak for her sleeping chamber would be a luxury item, or a bed that was raised from the floor, like the one in her mother's chamber at Cordell. And the few clothes that were being hurriedly made for her to take to her marriage brought her little pleasure.

She remembered the conversation she had had with her father, though it had taken place months before.

"But I do not love him," Chandra told Medwin.

"That is the least of your problems," he had replied. "Many a maid marries a stranger. If you will allow, you could learn to love him. He loves you."

"He does not love me," she spat hatefully. "He loves the land I hold and I do not need a man to manage —"

"Were it a man you loved, even if he be of lesser wealth than Tedric, I would yield to you. But this notion of living alone, putting yourself above other women whose needs require that they marry, I will not condone. I am an old man and have not much time. I will not leave you without proper protection."

"But Conan has given his word that he would act as warden to my lands and I would gladly see his heirs inherit —"

Medwin's face had reddened considerably as she said this and she could see that he was angrier than ever. "Have you no shame?" he stormed. "Your sister's husband! When will you abandon your designs on that man?"

"Nay, Father. Nay! 'Tis not bent of desire, I swear on

my mother's grave! Only that I would rather live alone than as Tedric's wife. I loathe him!"

"Loathe him? And why? He has been nothing but generous with you and courts you as if you were a queen, when in truth you are the daughter of a poor knight! An aging lord with little to give! What he has lent me amounts to more than your precious Cordell is worth. Would you have me sell that parcel and leave you as a ward to the sisters, penniless and without even a title?"

Weeping, she could only hang her head, for she knew how it hurt him to speak that way to her.

"One daughter lives with her husband's mother and might never give me a grandchild. Another daughter took her dowry to the convent and is useless to me as she serves the Lord, but this I accept without complaint for I have done little enough for the church in my life. And you, my last hope, would have me sell my home to the crown that you might have your Cordell and live without marriage. And for what? To save you from a man who treats you better than you deserve!"

"But, Father, I fear Tedric uses you dishonestly. He has acted the part of a love-smitten swain, but that is not how I have seen him in years past. He is not known as a good knight among his peers and —"

"And because of past deeds must ever bear the curse of wagging tongues? I say to you that he is older now and has learned more honorable ways. I could not expect more from the youngest of Theodoric's brood and I dismiss his youthful pranks in lieu of the more honorable man he has become."

"Pranks? Father —"

"Chandra! I am out of patience with your many complaints! You will wed the man as well you should, and you will act the lady or feel the weight of my own hand. I leave you the right in your betrothal contract to manage your own lands, but if you resist me again I shall give that right to your husband."

"Nay, Father, you must not!"

"Do not tempt me further. And for every insult you lay to Tedric, that generous knight, you push me closer to that end. He promises to give you his heart and his strong arm for a lifetime!"

Such a threat had stilled her tongue and forced her into proper acquiescence. The wedding would be in London following the coronation of Richard when so many friends and acquaintances would be gathered there. She felt a slight jump in her stomach because she knew she would see Conan. Just the thought brought the color to her cheeks and she felt herself burn with shame, for little had changed in her heart. She was able to contain her misery and did not appear to be a brokenhearted maid, but she longed for him still. She prayed every night that morning would bring her at least a feeling of indifference. But it was not to be. He invaded her thoughts and she was often caught daydreaming. He conquered her dreams, and many times she would awake so certain that he was there beside her that she would reach for him. She did more penance for her thoughts than she had ever done for sinful deeds, and the village priest had grown frustrated with her fixation, though she would not confess the identity of this man whose image was inescapable, even in sleep.

Just as something deep within her would not allow her to feel the slightest affection for Tedric, there was something unearthly about the way Conan had taken complete possession of her heart. She knew that it was not a simple infatuation that besets many a young maid. Even the total impossibility of their circumstances, even the shame that she felt at the thought of Edwina being his wife, did not lessen the strong love she felt for him. She longed to abandon the feeling. She tried everything from prayer to hard work to developing fondness for any other man. But it was futile. She came to think of it as a curse.

About a year had passed since she had seen Conan last. He had journeyed to Phalen to see what service he could do for Medwin. Though he stayed only a few days, and they had had little time alone together, she had been left suspecting that he suffered as she did.

Medwin had spoken fondly of Tedric to Conan, but Conan was direct and honest, saying he thought Tedric an unsuitable choice for marriage because of his lack of inheritance. While his family might well back his defense of any keep, Tedric's protection alone would be weaker than that of many other knights. And where would Tedric's family be when an attack came? Waiting behind Tedric to lend aid? Nay, they would be scattered throughout England and France on their own estates. The power of Theodoric and his seven sons might indeed cause some invader to think twice about waging war on Tedric, knowing that that great family would certainly take its revenge, but that alone was little reason for alliance. There were other knights and lords that could serve Medwin's family better.

But Conan had no way of knowing that Tedric would bring so much wealth to the proposal. He left convinced that he had swayed Medwin away from his choice.

One morning Chandra had found Conan in the Phalen gardens, and, while she had avoided his close company earlier, she rushed to him then.

"You came to my colors and stood up to my father for my sake, Conan. Thank you."

Because no other could look so deeply into his eyes, she saw the sadness there. In the presence of her father he seemed distant and uninterested. "I spoke only the truth, Chandra. I have no love for Tedric and would not support his wish to marry into this family. Medwin is my father now. I could never call Tedric brother."

"And if another knight were courting me through my father, what would your advice be?" she asked.

"If he were worthy of you I would urge Medwin to accept." She looked down, not watching him as he spoke. "It would not change the way I feel."

Her words were almost angry then. "If that is so, how could you help any man into marriage with me?"

But he did not react to her anger. His voice was strained and hoarse. "How valiant would I be to choose for you a life alone rather than hope someday you could learn to love the man who takes your hand in marriage? Ah, Chandra, I have regretted so much and I am a young man. If there is a chance that you might yet find love, I wish it for you. But I am wicked, for I would rather have you spend a lifetime in lonely solitude than to have to think of you sharing a bed with Tedric."

"I am sorry, Conan. It was cruel of me not to think of you. Of course I do not suffer alone."

He turned from her then and stared out into the roses and trees. "I do not think Medwin will allow you to remain unwed, however little you need a husband. Edwina is not likely to bear a child, and this he knows from her letters. You are his last hope that he will live on. If you would avoid marriage to Tedric, you must find another man worthy and profess your strong love. Scream it to the heavens and think naught of me, for you must convince your father of a better choice."

"But Conan, there is no one," she murmured.

He turned back to her and she saw the forlorn look in his eyes. "Lady, you are of beauty rare, and Cordell is worth much. There are other late-born sons with little inheritance, but of honor and strength. I cannot have you and I cannot help you."

Chandra thanked him humbly and left him alone, for she could not bear the sadness in his eyes. She knew that her sister was well and that she had been living with Conan's parents since recovering from her miscarriage. She did not have to wonder what complaints Conan could have brought to her ears.

Now the fault was hers because she did not heed Conan's advice. She let the young men pass through Medwin's hall without a flicker of favor for any of them, and when Medwin's patience was at an end, Tedric rode into Phalen with saddlebags filled with money. She pleaded then for a chance to find a young man for whom she could feel some love, but too late. Medwin had watched her turn away suitor after suitor. And her father needed the silver that Tedric offered to meet the needs of his keep plus a liberal loan to meet his debts. The marriage contract was made and the time for arguments was past.

In her chamber at Phalen Castle, Chandra stood gritting her teeth and trying to still her agitation as the hem of her pale blue wedding gown was being cut to the proper length. Her arms were crossed in front of her and her lips were pursed. She often let out a slight grunt of discontent and shifted her weight to the other foot, thus swaying the skirt.

"Lady, please," Wynne pleaded. "If you cannot be still I shall have your knee showing in the front and the gown dragging behind."

"You can slit the vulgar thing to ribbons and it would suit me fine," Chandra said hatefully.

"Oh, lady," Wynne said. "You do Sir Tedric a grave injustice. He is a fine knight — so chivalrous and kind."

"Would that you could take him in my place," Chandra snapped, looking down at the maid.

Wynne only sighed her answer, and Chandra knew the maid would swoon at the very thought. Wynne, daughter to Sir William, master of the guard at Cordell, had been promised this position as maid to Lady Chandra. Now at thirteen she was the perfect maid, for her training had been rigorous. Her mother, Agnes, lived in Cordell Keep and had been managing that house for many years. Wynne had been taught how to attend a lady since early in her youth. She was gay, bright and quite pretty.

"You must not flirt with Sir Tedric so," Chandra scolded. "You do not know him well enough to be certain your gestures will be treated with propriety. He may surprise you."

"Yea, lady," she said softly.

Chandra knew the lass did not believe that Tedric could be anything but gracious. He often sent fine gifts to Phalen to woo Chandra, and on his one visit just months earlier he was at his very best, displaying his courtly manners and behaving in a careful, courteous way. Even when Chandra made a most embarrassing display of refusing his offer of marriage, he reacted only with a disappointed frown and never did he raise his voice or attempt to subdue her. Medwin, however, promised her a sound beating if she did not hearken to his word and abide by his decision.

She kicked a small slippered foot at the floor and groaned at the frustration of her circumstance.

"Lady, please . . ." Wynne begged.

"Are you nearly finished?" Chandra asked tartly.

"A moment more, lady," the maid said patiently.

There was a knock at the door and Wynne rose slowly, her legs stiff from sitting for so long on the hard, cold floor. She opened the door a bit to see who the intruder was, and then opened it to admit Medwin.

He paused just inside the door and let his eyes behold Chandra. The pale blue gown swirled about her feet, clinging to her hips and fitting tightly about the full bosom that had come with womanhood. Her golden hair, contrasting so beautifully with the color of the gown, fell over her shoulders. More adornments would be added later — jewels and gold — but Medwin did not need to see that for more effect. His eyes glowed with appreciation. He couldn't remember, in all his lifetime, seeing a woman of greater beauty.

He walked toward her, limping now from the pain in his joints that became worse with every winter. He reached his hands out to take hers and she tried to smile for him.

"You will be a radiant bride," he told her. "The queen will be jealous, for even in her youth she was no match for you."

"Thank you, Father," she said, but she knew that she could never be a radiant bride. Not unless she could find a way to conceal the blackness of her heart.

"I hope you are nearly finished. We must make London before the rest of the countryside if we are to find a suitable hall."

"I am nearly ready," she told him.

"Don't make us late or I will accuse you of misbehaving. I have never known a woman who could make ready and travel as quickly as you do. I would know you wish me only ill if you dally."

"I will be ready," she promised.

Medwin lost the shimmer in his eyes as he looked into hers. She could act in the manner he demanded, but she could not hide her unhappiness. And in this she hurt for him, for she knew his love for her was real. He wanted her happiness and security above all else.

He shook his head in resignation and left the room, his limping bringing an ache to her heart. As she looked at the door that closed behind him, a tear slowly crept down her cheek.

CHAPTER
10

TRAVELING frequently between Anselm and Stoddard had become a tired habit to Sir Conan, and he was relieved that his wife would once again live under his roof. But in one way he was thankful for these forced visits: they gave him a new opportunity to know his brother and sister.

Galen, a strapping lad of fourteen, had returned to his family for a brief visit from the north of England. His training under the care of a strong knight, Sir Boswell of Tarringwood, had been the best medicine for a boy trying to match his successful brother's reputation. In two years Galen had grown tall and strong, his shoulders broad and his arms developed into strong weapons. His chin sprouted the fine growth of what would be a thick, dark beard and his skin was beautifully bronzed from the long, hard days in the summer sun spent jousting, hawking, tilting and learning the theory of chivalry.

Conan embraced him now as a true brother, seeing for the first time a promise that they could support each other in strength and work together to make the name of de Corbney a respected one in England.

One of Conan's greatest joys came from watching Edythe grow into womanhood. She had grown tall, as Alaric's sons had, slender as a willow and graceful as a cat. Her thick, dark hair made the contrast of her radiant green eyes more overwhelming, and now, at sixteen, her blooming body spoke more of the joys of lovemaking than the folly of children's games.

For Edythe, many young knights had been beckoned to Anselm, but she scorned them all. Udele was becoming increasingly impatient with her daughter, for Edythe could not find a desirous quality in any of her suitors.

"Among the great many that ride through these gates," Conan observed, "you have not seen one to meet your fancy."

"Knaves all," she replied flippantly.

"Some have money," he replied.

"And what need have I for money?" she asked. "When the knight who can best you in a contest of arms rides upon me, I shall take him without hesitation. Money does not move me, nor youth and beauty. I will await a knight with enough years to his credit to protect my holdings well. I will wait for a man I can respect."

"And you have not seen the man who could capture your heart?" he asked.

"I did not say that, brother," she smiled. "Indeed, I have seen him."

"Then call him to Anselm and let the wedding be soon."

"But Conan," she said, her smile coquettish and her eyes twinkling, "I do not know where he is. I see him every night in my dreams, and sometimes when I ride he lingers at the wood just beyond my reach. Or by the stream in the morning when I go there with linens to be washed, he is there, across the water, where I cannot run to him." Her eyes held a quality he had not seen until now. She was a woman in love and the glow on her face promised an eternity of loving. "I wish to call him home, Conan. But

I cannot. And what am I to do with these other suitors Father brings me?"

Conan looked into her eyes, the deep emerald pools begging him for understanding. And he did understand. His own love was lost to him now and he could not recapture it. This talk of building empires, this custom of bringing young men and women together to unite families and render power and wealth, what did it bring? For him, only misery. His chance was gone, but not Edythe's.

"Knaves all!" Conan exclaimed, cupping her chin in his hand and lifting her face to place a kiss on her brow. "Name the man you love, and I will capture him and bring him to his knees before you."

"Conan," she said seriously, "if he is good and strong and gentle of heart, does it matter that he is not rich? Brother, tell me truly, if he is a capable man of untiring spirit and stands by his oath without wavering even so much as an ancient oak on a windless day, does it matter that his name is not known through all Christendom?"

"This man, Edythe — is he common? Is he a farmer?" She shook her head negatively. "And he is a strong knight of good repute?" She nodded quickly. "And you love him?"

"Conan," she breathed, tears coming to her eyes, "I love him. I love him more than life itself. And if I cannot have him, I will have no one."

"I am of the mind that naught will come of a marriage ill planned, and the best fruit falls from a tree grown in love. If he is not a criminal or unbeliever, then he is, in my mind, a good choice." He touched her cheek with his hand, his thumb caressing her smooth skin. "And because you love him, he must be good."

"Will you stand by me, Conan?" she asked.

"Aye. 'Til the end of time."

Edythe stood on her toes to kiss his cheek. "You are a good brother, Conan. When the time is right I will ask you to help me."

Moments like this alone with Edythe, or hawking with Galen and sharing a close kinship, filled a place in his heart that had been empty. He promised his support to them both and found that adding these burdens to his already hefty load did not sap his strength, but made him feel stronger, surer. His loyalties had become many and varied. They fed his hungry soul.

He could not have guessed that his loyalty to his brother and sister would create ill feelings within the keep. Udele watched and worried with Edythe's closeness to her brother. She could see that not only might Alaric encourage Mallory as a husband, but Conan might also. Udele cursed her daughter.

Lady Udele had delivered her second child only to see him die a few days after the birth. Her grief was felt throughout all of Anselm. She came with child as soon after that incident as possible, and Edythe was born. Her lost son had not been replaced, and she had no joy in her daughter's birth. "What good is a girl?" she cried. "What can she bring to our estate?"

"Beauty and grace," Alaric had returned angrily.

But Udele did not hold her daughter or nurse her. Before very long, Udele behaved in a more appropriate manner, accepting the baby, though in a more distant manner than she had with Conan. But Edythe never tasted the milk of her own mother.

Two years later, Galen was born to Lady Udele and she was more pleased with this addition to the family, but by this time Conan was nearly eight years old and had already shown his elders that he was of superior stock. He had been with Sir Theodoric for two years and had the promise of being a powerful fighter and leader. Udele had put all her hopes and dreams into that youngster. He would inherit, become rich and well known. She could relax in wealth and prestige, for Conan would never forget his mother. Edythe, Udele decided, was useless unless she could marry into a rich and prestigious family and give the de Corbneys a strong ally. Galen she saw only as a helpmate to her older son, not as a son to divide the estate. The fact that Galen was already proving to be a fine hopeful as Conan's match did not alter Udele's ambitions for Conan — or herself.

Udele was engaged in a serious discussion with Alaric when Conan entered. His mother sat in her chair before the hearth and Alaric paced up and down before her. Conan had only just left Edythe and her problems still lay fresh in his mind.

"I say the time is now. You needn't allow for her approval, she is your ward. Select the one you deem best, remembering the state of the young man's family, and let the wedding follow the coronation. If you truly care for her future it would be wise to insist she marry soon, before these wealthy young men lose patience."

Conan stepped nearer the discussion. "Of whom do you speak, madam?"

"Edythe. She is past five and ten and must marry."

"Must, madam? She will soon enough wed, and what purpose in a swift decision when patience and careful consideration can better guarantee her happiness and profit?"

"I see no need to be hurried," Alaric said. "And the lass will be hard pressed to keep herself a maiden for long. The men all watch her now. She is beautiful."

"Father," Conan offered, "Edythe has spoken of marriage to me and in her heart she is wise. She seeks not power and wealth but a man of honor and deed. Those first to call bring their family names and their father's money. Names lose their power and money can be lost. My sister seeks a more certain future. When all else is gone, a man's honor becomes his strength. I say the lass will come to a wise choice in time."

"The matter could be done now," Udele argued. "What point in awaiting a silly maid who knows nothing of worldly ways?"

"Have you spoken with Edythe, madam?" Conan asked his mother. "I found her not a silly maid but a young woman of wisdom. And she alone knows her heart. Why betray her future to a man who can show his courtly manners in this keep, when in truth he may not be worthy? Edythe knows best whom she can live with."

"Betray her? Am I not to be given credit for my ability to judge the character of a man asking for my daughter?"

"Aye, madam, for what you can see. But if there is no room in Edythe's heart for the man you deem worthy, what chance has she for happiness?"

"Aye," Alaric agreed. "Edythe is a bright maid. She will not fail me. And if she tarries too long, I will encourage her. If I have to choose for her, I will not hesitate."

"You cling to your children, my lord," Udele said scornfully. "You keep them too long in your nest and coddle their whims. They will become spoiled and unfaithful, that will be your reward."

Alaric laughed outright. "Aye, madam, I can see before me the problems I have bred up," he chortled, slapping Conan on the back.

He looked long and hard at Udele, ever wondering how

she could find any fault in all that she had. Her riches were many, her beauty was enviable, and her children were fine and well bred. "I think I shall not worry about the wretched children I have sired. Rather I shall enjoy them, for I have more than most men."

He turned to Conan, stroking the falcon on his shoulder. "I ride to the wood today to inspect a dam built by my woodsmen. Will you ride with me?"

Conan turned and walked with his father out of the hall.

Udele sat a moment longer and then signaled the man-servant who was ever near to answer her call. Pierce came quickly to her, the same blind devotion that he had always felt showing in his eyes. Udele did not see it. All that mattered to her was that he was loyal to only her. He would carry out any plan or deed she designed and would not argue.

"Will you take a message for me? In your own hand?"

"Yea, madam. Have I ever failed you?"

"You are good, Pierce. Your reward will come."

That was a frequent promise, but it had little effect on the loyalty he showed her. His reward was in being close to her every day, serving her every whim and protecting her against every villain. As he had promised her father when he came to Anselm, he would make her dreams and ambitions his own.

"I cannot deal with Edythe now," Udele was saying. "My lord husband will not hear me again. But there is another matter that cannot wait. I must take money to London for a debt I owe. But Alaric knows nothing of this and I cannot carry the sum. You will carry it for me."

He would not ask to whom she owed the money. It did

not matter. He would gladly do as she bade him, however it compromised his own integrity.

Conan and his father were returning from the wood at a relaxed pace, their chore having been accomplished without problem. There was a thing that lay heavy on Conan's mind, and in this private time he brought the subject to his father's attention.

"Edwina has received a letter from her sister. It is as I suspected. Chandra will wed Tedric much against her will."

"Pity," Alaric said with a shrug.

"He buys Chandra's hand with considerable wealth. Father, have you ever known Tedric to have money to call his own?"

"I have not followed the lad on his journey to France. Mayhaps he met some wealthy lord there and did a service for him."

"Would Theodoric finance him in his pursuit of Chandra?"

"I have known Theodoric for a long time, and while he has given much to his sons, he has been most stubborn in his insistence that they make their own way as far as they can. He has complained that Tedric expects gifts he does not deserve. If he has given Tedric money, I would be surprised."

"There is money he boasts as his own for the betrothal, but more, he has made Medwin a substantial loan. Is it possible that the money he loans Tedric is not his own?"

"Who, then, would give him money to secure himself a bride?"

"Jewish usurers?"

Alaric digested the possibility. "Whose name would he borrow in? Theodoric would have none of that."

Conan did not like the alternative possibility and he did not wish to bring a slight to Medwin's name in the presence of his father. He knew they had a long and valued friendship. "Medwin could have consented to the loan. Medwin has lands."

Alaric frowned. "If that is the case, Medwin has been cheated. He has either lost Cordell to Tedric or promised Phalen twice: once to you through your marriage and again to usurers. I have never known him to borrow from the Jews. He traded with them fairly, but never borrowed."

"I am not concerned with Medwin's reputation; he is old and can be pardoned for his poor judgment. I fear he has compromised his daughter and fallen to the trickery of that knave, Tedric."

"His sight has been dimmed by the brightness of gold. It has been hard on all of us to meet the Saladin tithe and keep our towns from starvation, but I would not think Medwin would sacrifice one of his own to meet the cost." He shook his head sadly. "Medwin has suffered many losses in recent years. Millicent was taken from him and she was his best advisor. Edwina is gone and he fears for her health. Laine's commitment to the sisters is a burden he has borne with strength, but I know he was displeased. I think his motives are right but his actions misguided."

"Will you confront him, Father? Advise him yourself?"

Alaric nodded, and they rode on in silence for a time. Finally Alaric spoke again. "You show great concern in this matter. Is it because you so dislike Tedric?"

"Oh, I dislike him, Father, but it is not for that reason that I bring this to your attention. Tedric has been beating a path to Chandra's door for some time, and she confided that she feared her father would insist they be wed. She does not love him."

"Chandra's battles are not yours," Alaric advised.

"Should I ignore an injustice? If I fear Tedric lays a trap, shall I watch silently as Medwin falls into it?"

"And if Chandra had desired Tedric all along?" Alaric asked.

"Then I would not feel a fox sneaking along the ground in pursuit of unknowing prey. But if that were the case, Tedric would have but to pledge himself to Medwin and his daughter. I do not recall him offering so much wealth when he had bidden for Edwina."

Alaric slowed his horse and Conan did likewise. Father looked at son and tried to see what more there could be to his concern. The younger's blue eyes showed only his characteristic cool and confident detachment.

"And if she loved him, you would not be concerned?"

"I would be concerned in any business of Tedric's, for I think little of him. But I would hold silent."

"Three years ago you asked me if I would be pleased with Edwina as your choice of bride. I asked you if you loved her. You spoke of good faith, honor and oath. You spoke of desire and a pledge. You were a young man and I knew your word was your life. I will ask you only once, not because I doubt you but because I am your father. You have spoken for Edythe and your reason was love. You speak now for Chandra, your reason the same. Do you know now what love is?"

"No, my lord," Conan said easily. "But I have learned what it is not."

CHAPTER
11

B Y the second week in August the London streets
were teeming with visitors for the coronation. Merchants found themselves rousted from their homes
as nobles moved in and claimed them, tossing them
a sack of money for their trouble. Even so reimbursed,
they could not buy space in the city, for every stable and
house was filled to the brim. Still, in this madness and
confusion, every horn was raised in toast to Richard. And
the excitement mounted as his entry into the city drew
near.

Friends who had not met in some years found themselves
together in the streets of London, making the most of the
market and shops, enjoying parties and sports. Others did
not find each other for days, the crowds were so great and
there was no way of knowing where their acquaintance had
found lodging.

The latter was the case for Medwin and his daughter.
They had secured a fine hall from a merchant who could
house many without putting his family to any great discomfort. Medwin sent out servants immediately to locate
Theodoric's and Alaric's families, but neither had been
found. Medwin had begun to think he would not be reunited with his old friends until he saw them at the coronation banquets.

He had kept his daughter within the confines of this London manor, for the pressing mob bothered him greatly, but he could contain her no longer. Chandra begged for a chance to shop and barter. Along with prizes that could only be found at the grandest of country fairs, the merchants brought news from faraway places and fascinating tales to tell that caused Chandra to be nearly hypnotized with interest. She skipped from shop to shop to stand, to examine goods and argue with the peddlers. Merchants who had traveled to the East took advantage of the many visitors to London to bring out their wares. There were spices, brass, pewter and gold, ornately carved wooden furniture, stoneware and silver goblets and pitchers finer than any that could be fashioned in the small English burghs.

She could not pass a fabric for sale without touching and caressing, viewing for the first time the many luxurious silks and satins brought to the city by these widely traveled merchants. She leaned over a long length of silk and purred quietly as she touched the precious piece to her cheek.

"Cut the amount the lady desires," said a familiar voice.

She turned to look into the eyes she remembered — the deep blue beneath his dark brown lashes. His hair was cropped shorter, his beard trimmed, his face bronzed. When his lips parted to smile at her, Chandra felt the same rush of joy and excitement that swept over her at every meeting.

"Conan," she breathed.

"The cloth, Chandra," he said. "As much of it as you would like. 'Tis yours."

"You must not, Conan," she advised. "It is too generous." She looked about a bit nervously to see if any member of their families looked on.

"While I'm able, Chandra," he said softly, "let me make you this gift. 'Tis not nearly what I would like to give you, but cannot."

Flushing slightly, she turned to the merchant and gave him a measurement. The little man frowned slightly at the humble yardage and looked to Conan to see him hold up three fingers, ordering triple the amount. The merchant beamed and handed the entire bundle to Chandra, taking Conan's silver eagerly.

"Thank you," she murmured, tucking the fabric beneath her mantle for safe keeping.

"Unless you are asked, you needn't mention it," Conan told her, sensing that she attempted to hide the piece. "But don't worry, Chandra. No harm can come from my simple gift, I will assure it."

Quickly he inspected some fabric displayed and purchased some for his wife and his sister.

He took Chandra's arm to lead her out of the shop, and in doing so he leaned near and whispered to her, "Do not think my gift a casual thing. Remember that I cannot easily show you the way I feel."

"I will cherish the cloth, Conan," she said, smiling.

"Your father waits," he urged.

"And Edwina? Is she with you?"

"Nay," he said, shaking his head. "She would not venture into these crowded streets. She is afraid of the mobs."

"Poor Edwina," Chandra sighed. "She misses so much of life because of her weaknesses and fears. Pray be gentle with her, Conan. I know she needs you."

"She is well cared for, Chandra. I gave my word to that, and so I keep it. As for needs, what of mine?"

"You are strong," she said softly. "I am strong. We can endure."

Medwin stood against the wall of a hastily constructed merchant's stand trying to escape the bedlam of carts, horses and people. Beside him stood Edythe, obviously left in his care while Conan looked for the shop where Chandra could be found.

Edythe rushed to Chandra to greet her, kissing her cheek, but she obviously had something else on her mind. She did not wait for the exchanged niceties.

"Knights of Richard, Conan. I heard a passing man say knights of Richard approach. Please, please, let us see!"

Conan smiled and took her hand and drew her to Medwin. "Edythe longs to see the army approach, my lord. Will you come?"

"In this madness? Bah! My time is better spent in a warm hall away from these maniacs. Nay, Conan, I will find my way home."

"I'll go with you, Father," Chandra offered.

"Do you wish to see the army, daughter? I would trust Conan as your escort, if that is your desire."

"Oh, come with us," Edythe begged. "Later Conan can take us home and you may visit Edwina."

Chandra looked between Conan and her father, and, when assured Medwin would allow this, she smiled and nodded. "I won't be long, Father. Will you go to Alaric's house?"

"They're coming!" Edythe shrieked. "I hear a trumpet, it must be they! Hurry, Conan, I want to see them come!"

Chandra was barely able to wave to her father, she was so quickly drawn away through the crushing mob. Conan held fast to her hand, he being pulled by Edythe. To become lost in this city would be a nightmare.

They were pressed together closely, among the last to respond to the call. They could not see past the other spectators. Edythe wailed her complaints until finally Conan grasped her at the waist and lifted her above his head, laughing and trying to escape the skirts that threatened to smother him. But Edythe found a perch on his shoulder and was quite content. She called down to them how many knights she could see, what banners she could make out, and finally she wiggled in excitement and screamed, "Mallory and Sir Thurwell!"

"Where do they go?" he shouted.

"I cannot see. I don't know where they will stop. The palace?"

He brought her down to her feet and looked at her. "Westminster, I would think. Would you mind if we went there?"

She did not notice the teasing glint in his eyes. Her mind was filled with the number of days it had been since she had last seen Mallory. "I would not mind," she answered him.

Conan led them toward Westminster. Being unfettered as he was, no one would know his rank, but the richness of his surcoat and the emblem of the blue falcon made him out to be at least a knight, and the crowd parted for his passage. The ladies fared the journey through the masses poorly, their dresses being caught on spurs, their wimples being tugged and finally lying askew atop their shoulders. But neither minded. They giggled and struggled to keep up with their escort.

Edythe stopped the moment she could see the rising structure of Westminster beyond the many heads that blocked her vision. "Lift me, Conan," she ordered. "I will tell you what I see."

Without thought he lifted her and she sat still, looking in all directions, finally tapping him on the head so that he would bring her down. Her eyes were downcast and her excitement seemed drowned by some other emotion.

"Do you see where they stand?" he asked.

"Aye, Conan, many of the knights have dismounted. Sir Thurwell was still upon his horse and Sir Mallory was leading his."

"Clearly in sight?" he asked. He raised her chin with his finger and saw the gathering tears in her eyes. "Can you lead me to them?"

She nodded and her chin trembled slightly. "Conan, they wear the Cross."

Conan knew at once that all his suspicions had been accurate. She had hoped Mallory would return to take her to wife, but he returned prepared to go to war. "Can you make your way to him?" he asked gently.

She nodded as one large tear traced its way down her cheek.

"Go then. I will follow."

Her hand came up to caress his cheek and then she stood on tiptoes to kiss him. Her eyes met his for an instant and her gratefulness glowed there. Then she lifted her skirts and darted through the people. Conan's last glimpse of her was her dark brown hair bouncing down her back as she ran to meet Mallory.

"Conan," Chandra begged, "Conan, where has Edythe gone?" She had to tug at his sleeve a moment longer before he looked down at her. She frowned in confusion and then her eyes widened to see his misting slightly.

"She has gone to her knight," he said softly.

"Her knight? I did not know Edythe was betrothed."

"She is not. But she has chosen. And Sir Mallory is her chosen one."

"Mallory?" Chandra was surprised.

"Come. We must join them. I would give her the moon, but I dare not give her more than a moment alone with Mallory."

Before Chandra could digest this news, Conan was pulling her again through the crowd. Soon they were among the many horses that had delivered the knights into the city, the large beasts forming a maze that was difficult for even a tall man to see through. When Conan found them he stopped, leaned casually against a horse's hip and crossed his arms in front of him.

Mallory held Edythe clear of the ground, burying his face in her neck and filling his hand with her hair. She clung to him as fiercely, her small feet showing from under her gown. Thurwell was the one to see Conan, and he squirmed a bit uncomfortably, clearing his throat and getting no response from Mallory. Then with his elbow Thurwell jolted the happy couple apart. Mallory turned on his friend with a growl, but he was directed by Thurwell's eyes to Conan. The anger left Mallory's eyes and was quickly replaced by concern. Gingerly he walked the short distance to where Conan stood.

"Pardon, Conan," he said with a half bow. "My word, I have not harmed the lass in any way."

"Oh? Methinks you've greatly hurt her."

"Nay, by my oath, I have not —"

"You've taken the Cross," Conan interrupted.

Mallory stiffened with pride. "Aye, Conan. 'Tis my intention to fight for Richard and God, and with what I gain I will make my offer to your father. I hope to marry Lady Edythe."

"When?" Conan questioned lazily. "When you're an old man and finally returned from Jerusalem? I think it a poor proposal."

Mallory seemed resigned. "I cannot blame you, Conan, but I will not rest so easily with your refusal. I will face my lord Alaric in any case."

Conan laughed easily and drew his sister from Mallory's side, rather enjoying the older man's discomfort as he did so. "Betrothal? Before you venture off to war? Nay, I would not sell my sister into such a bargain." He looked down into Edythe's pleading eyes and smiled devilishly. "I say you marry her now or not at all."

With a cry of gladness, Edythe threw her arms about her brother's neck and hugged him so tightly that he could scarcely breathe. Choking and gasping, he disengaged himself from her wild embrace and looked into Mallory's smiling eyes.

"You are a generous friend, Conan," he said, extending his hand.

"Oh, I am that," Conan laughed. "But you have yet to meet my father. My approval means nothing."

"It means everything," Mallory argued. "How long have you known?"

Conan thought about how long he had hoped Edythe had chosen a man such as Mallory, but answered honestly. "For a fragment of this past hour," he said. "And now I know that for years you have been courting her. She was too young when you began."

"Nay," Mallory laughed. "She has been courting me! Tugging at the heart I swore would not be tethered. From France I heard her," he claimed, drawing Edythe back to his side.

"Rest assured that I support your desire to take her to wife, but seeing her as a woman is a matter that has taken its toll on me. And I will not leave you with her long, for I know more than I like of your ways with the wenches."

"All that is past, Conan," Mallory promised, though he could not suppress his smile.

Conan turned to Thurwell. "Our friend has good cause to go to war, but what of you?"

Thurwell smiled. "It is war, Conan. What more reason?"

Conan stood still for a moment, his eyes fixed on Thurwell's. He envied them both, these two friends going off to war. He had come home to his father's lands prepared to be his loyal vassal, and now he was farmer and bookkeeper, spokesman for his father and his wife's father at political conferences, hunter, and breeder of horses. Three estates, Phalen, Anselm and even Stoddard, depended upon him for protective arms and management, for Alaric and Medwin were growing old. And there was Edwina. He would have taken the Cross, but he was pledged and could not in good conscience abandon a wife who he feared could not manage without him.

He had been trained to fight and was among the finest knights in all Christendom, but he could not forsake his duties. Though he longed to test his sword and his skill in war, he was obligated to his position as landlord and vassal to others.

He shook off his musings and turned abruptly to Mallory. "Friend or foe, you will treat her well and do her honor, or I will make you wish you had."

"I know better than to test your threat, Conan. Have no fear."

"Then let us go straightaway to Alaric," Conan said. "He will be glad to see you, though he knows nothing of the favors you will ask."

The two knights proved to be more than adequate protection for Edythe and they went ahead, the spectators parting and bowing to the large symbols of the Cross on their chests. They cleared the path for Conan and he extended his arm to Chandra. She looked up at him with her warm blue eyes, a sentimental half smile on her lips. "You are wonderful to help them, Conan," she said.

He smiled and touched her cheek. "Why should I not wish to help them, chérie? I must take my pleasure from the happiness of others, since there is no way I can help myself."

Her smile faded to a frown and she could not look at him, feeling again the guilt of knowing they loved wrongly. "Conan, there is no help."

He could not abide her sorrow. He pulled her along with something of a carefree attitude. " 'Tis true, maid, there is no help. Well, we've been tricked by fate, and all of heaven has turned its back on us. For that I feel dread and sadness. But your smile no one can take from me." He winked at her as he pulled her past the crowds of merchants, beggars and warriors in the magical London streets. Finally she smiled up at him, unable to frown into his happy face. "And your eyes. In them I see the blue of the sky, and it speaks of eternity — a forever about you, damsel, that gives me hope and fills my emptier nights with blissful dreams. So it's true that I cannot have you, nor you, me. But there is something I can have of you. I will know in the worst of times that I have your heart — and upon occasion, your smile. If I must content myself with that much of you, I will. 'Tis better than having nothing of you at all."

Chandra stopped suddenly and looked up at him. She did not share his contentment. She often thought she would be better off having never known him at all, having never felt his gentle touch. And the torture no longer came from the fact that he belonged to her sister. Now it was a more vicious demon that held her from hope. "Conan, I am to marry Tedric. Soon," she reminded him.

The warmth was gone from his eyes. His pupils shrank to pinpoints, and he stopped walking so he could look at her. "That, my love, takes even the joy of your smile from my heart."

The reunion in Alaric's house was heartwarming. Medwin had arrived and happily greeted his daughter Edwina and old friends. The embraces and hearty laughter from that reunion had barely subsided when Edythe arrived with Mallory and Thurwell, and again cups were filled and raised. The first toast was barely drunk when Chandra and Conan returned. The sisters had not seen each other since that time two years before when Chandra had traveled to Stoddard with Conan's men to tend to Edwina's health. Lady Udele was the only member of the household not present.

Alaric plagued the two knights of the Cross with questions of Richard's plans and news from France. He did not seem to notice Mallory's gradually increasing tension. Conan exchanged amused glances with Chandra.

Edythe became impatient with talk of politics and war. "There is another matter, Father," she finally said. Alaric looked at her in wonder, and the lass blushed slightly. She had not wanted to speak for Mallory, but she suspected this task might be more distressing to him than fighting. Fighting was natural to him, she told herself. Begging the hand of a maid was not. "Sir Mallory would have a word with you — privately."

"A private word?" Alaric questioned.

"Nay, it need not be private," Mallory returned nervously. "There are naught but friends here." He stood and faced Lord Alaric and bowed clumsily but respectfully. "My lord, 'tis the matter of the marriage of your daughter," he said, stopping to clear his throat twice in just those few words. "My family is not well known and there are no lands, but I go to fight with Richard and would gladly yield whatever prizes of war I will claim to the betrothal contract if you will give me Edythe's hand."

"You?" Alaric asked softly.

Mallory cleared his throat again, feeling as though he were alone, though his friends were behind him. "Her dowry of course will be hers for her children and I pose no argument to that. Likewise any marriage gift — Edythe's for her own dowry. And I would gladly pledge myself as vassal to your lands, if you ask it of me."

"Vassal," Alaric mimicked, somewhat amused.

"Vassal," Mallory repeated. "If you choose."

"And of these riches you intend to bring home?" Alaric asked with a faint smile.

"To bargain for the bride of my choice, my lord. To be part of the estate that supports Edythe or as a gift to you for her hand, as you will it. I will pledge it now, before it is won."

"A betrothal? Now?" Alaric asked.

Mallory cleared his throat again. It had begun to feel raw and sore. "I am not needed until Christmastide, my lord. We depart from Vézelay, in France, after Easter. I would marry Edythe now and give you my word that upon my return you shall dispose of the prizes of war as you see fit."

Alaric scratched his beard and looked quizzically at the knight. "And if there are no prizes of war?"

Mallory straightened himself. "My lord, there will be."

Alaric chuckled. "Aye, there will be."

"You will see upon my return that my promise is no passing fancy. I will return with wealth enough to make the bargain more than fair."

"I believe that," Alaric said, pushing his bulky frame out of the chair and rising slowly. He came to Mallory's height when standing erect, and he looked into Mallory's eyes. "She is a slight lass, and young," Alaric said, indicating Edythe with his eyes. "I have seen you meet men in the contest of arms with less halting than now, and I for one have never feared Edythe."

Mallory smiled with more confidence now, for he could plainly see the twinkle in Alaric's eye. "Then you have not felt the sharpness of her tongue, my lord. She seems a gentle maid, but the fate she promised me if I failed to please you made me quiver in my boots."

Alaric's voice dropped to barely a whisper and there was a smile on his lips. "She is not so fearsome," the old lord confided. "It took you a very long time to heed her warnings." Mallory responded with only a look of confusion. "I am old, but I am not an old fool," Alaric said softly. "I long ago decided I would be proud to call you son."

Mallory's heart was touched by Alaric's approval, and when the old lord extended his hand, Mallory took it gratefully. When Edythe saw the two men clutching hands in friendship, she guessed her father's approval and jumped to her feet with a squeal, wrapping her arms around her father's neck, then Conan's, Thurwell's and finally Mallory's. Another toast was raised and more laughter and congratulations followed.

The door to the lodgings opened and Lady Udele entered with her manservant, Pierce, close behind. Udele greeted all her guests warmly.

"Bring a goblet to my lady," Alaric called to a servant. "She will want to toast the occasion."

Udele looked immediately to Conan. "Occasion?" she asked with a faint smile.

"Sir Mallory and Edythe have spoken their preference for each other and the wedding will be soon," Alaric announced.

"Sir Mallory," Udele choked. "But — they — Mallory has been in France! What of all the others who have spoken for Edythe?"

"In her mind, madam, there have been no others."

"But he is to go to war with Richard!" She turned to Mallory, shocked. "You will wed the girl now and leave her with her father, probably heavy with child, to go to war? What assurance have we that you will not be killed, leaving a widow and child for me to see to?"

"You have my promise, madam," Mallory said as respectfully as he could. Edythe moved closer to his side, frightened that her mother would change her father's mind. Mallory slipped a protective arm about her waist while all others in the room held silent.

"What proposition is this?" she asked her husband. "Sir Mallory is a good man, to be sure, but what of Edythe's future? He is a poor knight, with no family with arms to support him and —"

"I am not concerned with her husband's wealth," Alaric said with a shrug. "Galen's bride will bring lands to our family when he marries. Edythe's dowry is not grand and she will give children to her husband's family. I think he provides for her enough."

"What?" Udele asked testily. She looked about the room. She alone opposed this, that much was clear. And what of Conan's loyalties? She had planned so carefully, so painstakingly. *He* would take the bulk of this estate and Udele would live in comfort. But he was giving his support and pledging himself to so many others: Edwina, Chandra, Medwin, Galen, Edythe, Mallory . . . "What does he provide her with?"

"Protection when he has returned. A strong arm. Love. Hope. Things that are more important than riches, lady," Alaric said easily.

Conan could contain himself no longer. "Madam, I see this as an advantage for our family. More than one vassal will be needed in time to keep safe the lands we gain. By the grace of God, more vassals than you have sons. Should Edythe be given to a rich knight with lands of his own, we could not count on his support. But with Anselm, Phalen, Stoddard and the surrounding lands, 'tis a blessing to have another son not bound to his father. We can bring him into our family's service and count him as another strong arm."

"But wed to a man soon to go warring in some faraway land? Alaric is old and it is time for him to see his children well fit, not a time to add more burdens to his shoulders. Who will see to our daughter's welfare if she is left widowed with a child?"

"Whom do you suspect shall, madam?" Conan asked tartly. "If I am to be lord of my father's lands, I can speak for my sister's welfare. She shall always have her place with me, if need be. And if there is a child, his welfare will be mine as well. No further promise seems needed."

"Have you not pledges enough?" Udele asked angrily. "You've pledged to your mother, your wife, your wife's sister has become your concern. And now another ward, mayhaps two —"

"Methinks you bury the knight too soon, lady," Conan

said sharply. "It chafes me sore that I cannot travel with my comrades into battle but must cleave to England for the sake of my family. They make me a tree with many blossoms and I see no harm in adding yet another to the branches for my protection. I think I can easily bear the weight." He steadied himself and took a breath. "Were my father already gone, God save us, and the decision mine, I would give Edythe to Mallory. I know his ways and his skills, and no finer knight is asking."

Udele saw the battle lost. Tears came to her eyes and she sought a way to hide her disappointment. She turned to Edythe and reached for her hand. "Edythe, dear child, can you be content, a woman alone while your husband is at war? If you have but a moment as his bride and he leaves you heavy with child, can *you* bear the weight?"

Edythe, somewhat touched by her mother's tears, smiled. "I know Sir Mallory must go, madam, and I will not bemoan his absence but pray for his safe return. I could not be content any other way."

Udele brushed a tear from her cheek. "That is all I need know," she said softly. She turned and took the goblet of wine that had been brought for her and raised it, though in her heart she was not pleased. She had hoped for so much more. "You may have your knight with my blessing."

As if yet another battle they feared had been won, Mallory and Edythe were again rejoicing. When Mallory bowed over Udele's hand to thank her and promise to prove himself a good husband, it was difficult for Udele to smile and wish them her best.

So, she thought in anger as she looked at her son, you have surrounded yourself with your wards. And what will be left for you when you have sworn to support so many? Indeed, what will be left for me?

Alaric's arm dropped around Udele's shoulders and she looked up at him with tears still brimming in her eyes.

"Do not worry for Edythe, lady," Alaric said gently. "She will be happy and that is all I ever wished for her."

Udele nodded, knowing better than to argue now. But her thoughts were a turmoil as she struggled to count what might be left for her when Conan divided all that he would inherit and scattered it about his many pledges. What you need, she thought angrily, are fewer burdens.

The coronation was still a few days away. The London streets were as dangerous at night as they were busy during the day. All sensible shopkeepers closed their doors and windows tightly when the sun lowered in the sky.

Udele walked toward Westminster with Pierce close behind her to offer protection. It was dusk and most of those people hurrying through the streets were on their way home. Udele's step was quick and her hood was pulled over her head. Inside the mantle she could feel the weight of a heavy sack of silver.

A solitary figure leaned against the castle wall and he straightened as he saw her approach. He would not have been certain it was her but for the presence of the huge manservant.

"What is the meaning of this?" Udele hissed.

"I wanted the balance to come from your own hand, lady." Tedric shrugged. "I will no longer do business with your henchman and lackey."

"You do not deserve the balance! Your silence has not aided my cause, since Edythe is now betrothed to Mallory!"

"Ah, but I have eliminated Chandra from Conan's pursuit. Had she been allowed to remain unwed or wed to any other, Conan would still be in her company often. He will not visit my house. You need not fear he will create a scandal."

"And since you have done half the job, why not graciously accept half the sum we agreed to?"

"I did all I promised, lady. 'Twas you who could not carry out the plan. Your influence did not touch Alaric's will. And the word is that Alaric has long suspected romance budding between Edythe and Mallory. And he has long approved."

Udele's eyes grew wide and she stared at him in wonder. "I had not heard this. For how long has my lord husband known of Edythe and Mallory and their love?"

Tedric snickered. "As Sir Mallory tells it, since it began — long before I overheard them in the garden."

Udele's piqued temper quickly turned to sharp anger. "How dare you cheat me with your offer to —"

"Lady! I did not cheat you! I was not aware that Alaric awaited his daughter's whim! I guessed he would approve, had he known, but he kept his secret well. Now the debt is yours. When we agreed on the sum I promised the same to Medwin — half with the betrothal, half with the wedding."

"And now that Edythe marries a poor knight there is no money bid for her hand and I cannot repay my debt!"

Now the surprise was Tedric's. "The money is not yours?"

"I have managed to save a pittance, but not nearly the amount you demanded," she said bitterly.

"Then how have you come by it?"

"I have traded with the Jews on occasion," she sighed. "There are those who will lend money to a lady in distress."

Tedric laughed uproariously, holding his sides as he

thought of her predicament. He did not attempt to contain himself until Pierce stepped closer to Udele's side.

"Pardon, lady," he said, tears of laughter gathering in his eyes. "I thought your position delicate enough. I knew the news that you had paid me to hold silent would anger your husband, but I cannot imagine his wrath when the Jew comes to his door for payment!"

"They do not *know* me," she said. "Do you think I am fool enough to go to them myself and ask for silver?"

Tedric saw the dawning. "Ah! Once again Pierce does your bartering and borrowing. Then where is your problem?"

"It has taken me a very long time to arrive at this position," she said tersely. "They do not hand money out to serfs and servants. For the sum I needed, there had to be years of borrowing and trading for the Jew to give Pierce the money with no fear of having it lost. Now I shall have to begin again, with another usurer. And there is always the chance that Aaron will find Pierce at Anselm. I do not need Alaric's suspicion."

Tedric clicked his tongue in mock sympathy. "Poor lady. I had no idea Alaric was so selfish with his money."

"He does not approve of all the bargains I strike," Udele returned.

"I doubt not," Tedric returned with a laugh. "I cannot give you back the money, madam, as I have use for it. And perhaps I will need more."

"There is no more!"

"You will think of a way!"

"I will not give you another —"

"And when I tell Alaric that you have borrowed from the Jews to pay me? I tell you, madam, many have asked where I came by the money I needed to buy Chandra's hand in marriage. They are a curious lot and hard to convince." He scratched his blond beard lazily. "Some think it hard to imagine that I have labored hard for the sum."

"You are a knave!"

He shook the bag and the sound of silver brought a smile to his lips. "A rich knave at that," he added. "I will not bother you for a while, lady, for I think it would be difficult to demand more money now. But you will think of a way to get more. You do not like being without money."

"Do not push me too far, Tedric," she warned. "If I do find a way to money, mayhaps I will use it to have you killed."

"Oh, I think not, lady, when Pierce would oblige you without payment. But I will be wary not to test your good nature. I should like to bargain with you again."

He bowed briefly and smiled at her. "Thank you, my lady," he said, holding the silver before her. He shrugged off her hateful glare and turned to go, quite pleased with his business for the night.

CHAPTER
12

O N the third of September in the year 1189, a
procession of clergy dressed in copes of purple
silk led the way to Westminster Abbey, carrying
holy water, cross, tapers and thurible. They were
followed by the abbots and the bishops, then the noblemen
bearing the cap of maintenance, the spurs, the rod topped
by a dove, the sword of state and the scepter.

Next came a party of six barons, Lord Alaric among
them, carrying the chequer board with regalia and robes;
then the earl of Essex with the crown; and finally Richard
himself, duke of Normandy, flanked by the bishops of Bath
and Durham, walking all the way upon a white linen cloth
and protected by a canopy of silk supported on the lances
of the four barons of Cinque Ports.

Richard was a sight to quicken the hearts of many as he
moved with grace along the coronation route, for he
seemed to tower at least a head above all other men, and
his reddish gold hair and piercing blue eyes added to his
regal bearing.

Never had London seen such a coronation. For all that
Henry II had hated pomp and display, Richard loved it.
His was by far the grandest and most regal of coronations.

Within the Abbey, where only the most prestigious of
guests were present, the *Firmetur Manus Tua* was sung and

the king brought his offering to the altar. Then the litany, the oath, and the pious utterings of prayers of consecration were said: *Omnipotens Sempiterne Deus; Benedic Domine; Deus Ineffabilis.* A long and holy ritual ensued: the oath, the hallowing and anointing, the insignia, coronation and enthronement. If there had been any doubts as to who was king, they were surely diminished by the ceremony of his coronation, which was so long and dramatic it nearly guaranteed his heavenly sovereign right. The king was then taken back to his chambers in procession.

Though it seemed the coronation itself could not be outdone, the preparations for the banquet to follow were even more pompous. Nearly two thousand pitchers, nine hundred cups and over five thousand dishes were purchased for the occasion.

The magnificence of the hall, decorated for pure pageantry, was presided over by Richard, who was surrounded only by the men in his service: the bishops and lesser clergy, the knights and nobles. No women were allowed in the hall and they did not take part in the celebrating. It was very like Richard to exclude the gentler sex. Women, excepting his mother, had never played a significant role in this warrior king's life.

The noblewomen of London, then, were for the most part without escort for that eve of the great coronation feast. They had the protection of what men-at-arms their fathers or husbands had left behind, but the knights and nobles of high repute were all at Westminster Hall attending Richard.

Though Medwin had found more than adequate lodgings, he took Chandra to Alaric's house on this night so that she might enjoy the company of the other women while the men were engaged. No one questioned the fact that Tedric did not offer his company for the evening. Although he was not a part of the delegation of sons Theodoric took with him to Westminster, he was not expected to spend his time with women and servants.

A fire was needed to warm the hall when the sun was sinking. The four women formed a half circle about the hearth and worked their stitchery. The large house was nearly void of men but for four guards, Pierce and the landlord, a little man so intimidated by the elite personage using his home that he asked constantly and irritatingly if he could be of service.

"And after Bury Saint Edmunds where do you go?" Chandra asked her sister.

Edythe looked up from her stitchery and listened as the sisters talked.

"We return then to Stoddard," Edwina replied.

"Bury Saint Edmunds is not far from Cordell," Chandra said.

Edwina flushed slightly, not wishing to hurt Chandra. "Conan has duties awaiting him at Stoddard. Perhaps we can journey to Cordell another time for a visit."

"Perhaps."

Udele laughed sharply. "Chandra, how foolish you are. Do you imagine Conan will be bringing Edwina to visit you at Cordell? Or perhaps you think Tedric will take you to Stoddard for a visit!" She laughed again. "I cannot imagine Conan and Tedric sharing a cup and calling themselves brothers!"

Chandra stiffened indignantly and Edwina focused her eyes on her needlework.

"Tedric has promised me visits to Phalen," Chandra said to Edwina. "We could arrange our visits at the same time."

Edwina reached for Chandra's hand and fairly whispered her reply. "It's true that our husbands may never be friends, but neither, I think, will deny us our time together."

"Is there proof that you are with child?" Chandra asked softly.

"Nay," Edwina replied. "Not so soon."

"You will be more fortunate this time," Chandra said hopefully. "I will pray as well, and we must send word to Laine at Thetford so she can offer the prayers of the sisters. I am sure the next child will be born healthy and strong."

"I hope you are right, Chandra," Udele said without looking up from her sewing. "Conan will be hard to abide should this attempt fail as well."

Chandra stared coldly at Udele. She no longer wondered at the woman's tactlessness. It had become clear in the past several days and evenings they had been together that Udele was careful with her tongue in the presence of the men and hurled her nasty comments at the women.

"Sir Conan is not alone in his disappointment when a child is lost, madam," Chandra said tartly. "Edwina is pained with the thought as well. I think we should all think only that the best will occur. Let us not dwell on past sorrows."

"Indeed not!" Udele returned. "Most certainly, we must think the best." She looked back to her sewing, and it was a few moments before she spoke again. "Edwina, I think you would be wise to persuade Conan to bring you to residence at Anselm when you prove with child. I cannot rest worrying that you are not being properly cared for."

"Do not worry, madam," Edwina said. "All will be well."

"Dear heart, he is so reluctant to leave your side when

you are under his care. How will Conan better himself if he is ever tied to your skirts?"

Chandra's face grew red and her lips white. "Conan is a rich man without lifting a finger," she returned saucily. "A few months at Stoddard to watch his wife's health closely should not beggar him."

"I think not," Udele returned easily. "At least not a few months. But a lifetime of tending his sickly wife will not add lands to his estate and virtuous attributes to his knightly reputation." She sighed heavily. "Your father was a lucky man. He managed to do quite well for himself in spite of the many hours he spent attending Millicent in her illnesses."

Chandra smiled slyly. She was beginning to understand better Udele's baiting game. "Father was never fooled by the gift of physical strength. In all things there are strengths and weaknesses. Better a woman of meager strength who is kind and wise and loving than a mighty body and a shrewish heart."

Udele's head snapped up and her mouth opened, ready to hurl her angry retort, when Edwina rose suddenly.

"Chandra, I am weary. Come with me while I make ready for bed."

"Of course," Chandra said, rising. She faced Udele and offered a brief curtsy. "By your leave, madam," she said.

Udele's eyes were cold. "Guard your words, Chandra. Take care that you do not make me angry."

"Oh, madam," she gasped in mocked chagrin. "Beg pardon if I have ever been less than kind. I could not pardon myself if anything I said offended you!"

Udele glared at her relentlessly. She could see she had underestimated the maid's assets. Chandra was as quick and stubborn as Udele had ever hoped to be. Were she my son's wife, Udele thought, she would see me dressed in rags and begging my bread.

Chandra and Edwina went alone to the chamber aloft, and by the time they reached the room Chandra was seething.

"How do you abide that woman?" she hissed under her breath.

Edwina laughed softly. "Though it would be a fancy sight if you were ever near to protect me from her, I doubt I could bear the strain. Jesu, should the two of you ever live under the same roof I dare not guess which would survive."

"Have no doubts who it would be, Edwina. I would never allow her wickedness to prick my tender skin. Why do you not speak to Conan about the evil way you are treated?"

"Conan is fond of his mother." She shrugged. "It would hurt him to think she does not always serve his best interests."

"And so you have lived with her shrewish nature for all this time without ever telling Conan what insults she lays to you?"

Edwina shrugged. "I have only lately told him that I am not happy at Anselm and wish to live with him in his home."

"Oh, Edwina, you should not let her treat you so badly!"

"But what is to be gained by fighting her? It will not change the way Conan sees his mother, for she puts on her best face for him. And it would surely cause him to doubt me. Nay, I would not complain and make life hard for Conan. It is hard enough for him now. Better I bear what Udele flings at me as quietly as I can and let it affect me but little."

Chandra calmed considerably with her sister's reasoning, seeing the truth of it. It *would* be a disaster if Udele was Chandra's mother by marriage. She knew she could never abide the woman's haughty barbs quietly and remain unaffected, even if her heart told her that would be best. Chandra was much too volatile for that. Had Udele realized that? Chandra wondered. Long ago, when Chandra had gazed at Conan with love in her eyes, had Udele seen that Chandra would not be intimidated as easily as Edwina could be? She shook the thought from her head — it was too late to consider that now. No matter Udele's motives, the situation was beyond cure.

"He is lucky to have you, Edwina. You are a good wife."

"Lucky," she laughed. "He has so many disappointments to bear as my husband. But he is too noble ever to make me suffer for the trouble I am to him. Had I known how I would love him, I would have never married him. I would have begged him to find a stronger woman, one who could promise him sons and would live to see them raised. *You* would have made him a better wife than I."

Chandra felt the sting of tears in her eyes. Once again she was guilt-stricken when faced with Edwina's quiet devotion and unselfishness.

"Edwina, never say that. It just isn't so!"

Before another word could pass between the sisters, there was a sound from the window that made them both turn their heads to listen. First there was a scream and commotion below them in the streets. Then came louder shouts. They looked at each other and then quickly moved to the window.

Men were running, yelling as they went, with other men chasing them and brandishing clubs and swords. When caught, they did not fight back but fell instantly. One man seeking some haven from his foe darted into a doorway, his back flush against the wall as he attempted to hide in the shadows. His pursuer, wearing the blazon of a lord or knight, saw the man hiding and, with great malice, clubbed him over the head until he slumped, bleeding and motionless. Still the aggressor continued to beat the fallen man with his club.

Edwina blanched, covered her mouth, ran to the corner of her chamber and leaned against the wall to retch. Chandra could not turn away.

There was no sense to the brutality she saw. Another unarmed man fell to a sword held by a man on horseback. Two men lay bloody below her. Many more were fleeing. They were commoners, from all Chandra could discern; weaponless commoners being chased by well-garbed men coming from the direction of Westminster.

"We've bolted the door," Edythe cried, rushing into the room. She ran to where Chandra stood at the window, watching the wild scene below.

As they watched a man running, they saw a horsed warrior, a fettered knight, cut him down with a ready lance. Chandra gulped convulsively. She had never witnessed anything to match this in all her life. It in no way resembled the death of a convicted criminal. It was a macabre slaughter for which she could name no cause.

"They are Jews," Edythe shuddered as she noticed the clothing the pursued men wore.

The Jews were granted few favors in the English burghs and villages. On the insistence of the church, they set themselves apart from Christians by their style of dress so that no Christian would unknowingly become involved with them. They were harassed and called infidels and unbelievers; their punishments for lawlessness were most often harsher because they were not Christians. But they lived under the protection of the king and therefore were handled with care.

"They must have attacked," Edythe whispered.

"Nay," Chandra said, shaking her head. "They have no weapons."

Edythe pointed to the street and Chandra looked to see the same thing: men fleeing and being senselessly slain. Looking again, she gasped. "Tedric!"

She watched him as he grabbed the man he chased, spun him about and drew his sword. She screamed, but her sounds were drowned by the noise below. Beside the window on a bedside commode there stood a basin of water for washing. Frantically she grabbed it and flung it out the window. The water drenched Tedric, and as he looked up for the source of this soaking, the man in his hold slumped to the ground, leaving Tedric holding the bloodied sword.

Chandra stared down at him in awe. She watched as he turned and disappeared into the night.

In the great hall where Richard feasted, a page crept nervously toward the king, but was halted by the archbishop at his side. The page whispered in the ecclesiastic's ear. Immediately the holy man crossed himself, turned to the king and spoke softly and quickly. Richard slammed his goblet down on the table with such force that the hall fell silent. All looked toward the king, whose face reddened with rage. The archbishop continued to speak. Richard stood, his long legs taking him quickly to the edge of the table where he spoke to the earls of Pembroke, Essex and Gloucester.

Word was being passed from the king's table down to the other tables, through hundreds of knights and nobles, the men being jolted upright as they heard, wondering whether to flee or remain with Richard.

Alaric rose from his table to find out what chaos had interrupted the coronation feast. "London is afire," he heard. "Fighting in the streets," he heard someone else say. Finally he heard the accurate explanation. A group of London Jews bearing gifts for the king were fallen upon by Christians at the palace gates. Rioting even now was ripping through the city, causing great bedlam.

"Go quickly before you are missed," Alaric told Conan. "By the back halls, and find our residence to be certain the women are safe. The king's fury will strike down those involved. Turn your mantle lest anyone place you in the riot, and lay sword to no man, Jew or Christian."

Mallory and Thurwell met Conan at the door, and before leaving the palace gates they turned their tunics and mantles inside out so that no symbol of the Cross or emblem of demesne was visible.

To go quickly and without violence was their intent, but before they had traveled far, they found the need to draw out their weapons. Frightened Jews raised clubs in self-defense, while nobles were ready with their own blades, eager to kill or maim any person of Jewish descent. Madness swept the streets, and flames from the Jewish quarter lit the skies.

It was not far to where the women were housed, but on this night the streets were so littered with crazed rioters that the journey took the better part of an hour. And when the house was finally before them, no amount of pounding could persuade the men protecting that house to open the door.

" 'Tis Sir Conan of Anselm," he shouted until he was hoarse.

"Break down the door," Mallory urged, anxious to be sure the women were safe.

The bodies of those slain nearby proved that the door was bolted with just cause. Conan heard the bolts moving and the ram being lifted from the door. Gingerly it was opened just enough for a man to peer through and see who the intruder was. Conan was in no mood to wait patiently for his identity to be checked. He pressed his way inward the moment the latches were slackened, nearly taking the door from its leather hinges.

"Conan," Chandra gasped, flying from the stair into his arms.

"You are unharmed?" he asked quickly.

"Aye, we are safe, only frightened. What madness plagues this city?"

"Edythe?" Mallory asked.

Chandra pointed to the stair, for by now all the women, maids and servants and noblewomen, had huddled together in one bedchamber above. Mallory rushed past her to see for himself that all were safe there.

"A misunderstanding," Conan heard himself say. "Of the greatest magnitude."

"Conan," she breathed, "Tedric was a part of this. I saw him murder —"

"Have you come to our aid, my son?" came a voice from the stair.

They turned together to see Udele, unbelievably cool

for all that had happened in the past hour. Conan let his arms fall from Chandra's. "Aye, madam," he said. "Are the women safe?"

"Your wife waits yonder. She would benefit from your reassurance," Udele told him.

Conan quickly passed her on the stair, making his way to Edwina, who by now was terrified and lay weeping and trembling on her bed.

Chandra followed him, returning to the chamber she had had to fight her way out of when she heard voices and pounding at the door below. She found her arm seized by Udele and looked into that woman's eerie emerald eyes. The two women were nearly the same size, since Udele was a slight woman and Chandra, possibly having grown to her full adult height, was also small. But the eyes of these two would have been better placed on giants. Neither would give way and neither would so much as blink. And in that meeting of snapping blue and chilling green, there was a mutual hatred so intense it could have shaken the ground on which they stood.

"What would Medwin think of your whorish pursuit of your sister's husband, I wonder. Or Tedric," Udele hissed, her breath hot and brash in Chandra's face.

The arm that held her was relentless in its grasp, but Chandra would not wince or attempt to pull away. "Do not hope to intimidate and threaten me as you do poor Edwina, madam," she returned with venom. "I know enough of your wicked methods to best you at your own game."

"You are a slut," Udele spat.

"I?" Chandra said, and then smiled knowingly into Udele's eyes. "And what would Conan think of your cruel games, lady? His loyalty has been a steadfast thing, but I should think you would fear for the day he learns you have made a mockery of his trust."

"You cannot discredit me to my son. He would believe nothing —"

Udele stopped as she noticed Chandra's smile: as superior and cunning as her own could be. "Whom would he believe, madam?" Chandra asked. "Indeed, between us, whose love does he hunger for?"

"You will be punished for your sinful lust," Udele said through clenched teeth, taking her hand from Chandra's arm.

With poise and dignity, Chandra took a few steps past Udele, turning and looking down at her to speak for the last time, to hurl the last stone. "When the punishments are being given out, madam, the one of us who knows a sinful lust best will fall the hardest. I think mine will be the lesser crime."

She did not look back at Conan's raging mother again but went on to the chamber above. I am wicked, she thought as she climbed the stair. I depend on his love — love that I have no right to claim, even as it tears at his heart.

She looked into the bedchamber that was now crowded with people, the women chattering in fear and confusion and the men leaning out the windows to look out on the turbulent city. Edwina lay in her bed, her face pale and drawn, as Conan leaned over her and tried to assure her that she was safe now.

If I were stronger of will, Chandra thought hopelessly, I would find a way to make him hate me, to free his heart for the woman whose right it is to claim it. Tears collected in her eyes much against her will. But what little bit of his

love I have known is my only treasure — and I need — his
— love. . . .

The morning's light showed the Jewish quarter to be a
smoldering ruin. Panic still was rampant and the women
did not dare to venture out from their homes.

King Richard had offered his protection to the Jews,
for he depended on their wealth for his Crusade. His journey to the Holy Land to rescue the Holy Sepulcher was an
obsession — he saw himself as the greatest knight to live,
the one man who would take his army and finally rid the
Holy Land of the infidels.

Rumors of the king's fury trickled down through the
streets and reached all the nobles. The news that nobly
born Christians had been the ones to overreact and attack
the gathering Jews further angered the king, and he was
intent on punishing those who had participated. He
threatened banishments and possibly hangings. And while
the king's rage sent every noble scurrying about to gather
names, it was well known to all that he was angry not because those unfortunates were unjustly slain, but because
they could have filled his purse with wealth. Richard
declared that any money owed to the Jewish usurers who
were slain must be repaid to him.

Conan and his father walked toward Westminster,
Mallory and Thurwell close behind.

"You are certain this is the course you wish to take?"
Alaric asked.

"If I lay any importance to my oath to uphold justice, I
must face Richard with the truth. Chandra saw Tedric
kill a man, a man well known here and in the north as a
moneylender."

"We could take the accusation to Sir Theodoric —"

Conan stopped short. He eyed his father and there was anger in his stare. "I have long loved Theodoric, but he is shortsighted where Tedric is concerned. He treats Tedric's treacheries like boyish pranks. Nay, if I left the punishment to Theodoric, he would take a switch to Tedric!"

"It would be better if you took Richard more proof," Alaric counseled, walking on toward Westminster.

"Where is the proof beyond a witness? Tedric has given Medwin a large sum of money for Chandra's hand and refuses to confide his source. I must believe the money came from the lender he killed. If Richard has assumed receipt of those debts there would be a record."

"Your witnesses will not help you. Even though Chandra and Edythe saw Tedric, Richard will put little stock in women's reports."

"And for that I am grateful. I hate to think of either woman enduring this confrontation, and especially Chandra. I accuse the man she is to marry."

"I reason that is the purpose of this," Alaric said.

Conan did not reply. He walked silently on, looking straight ahead.

"Do you hope to see justice done and Tedric properly disciplined, or to save Chandra from a marriage she does not desire?"

"Both," he said simply.

"Your motives may be questioned. Are you prepared for that?"

"She is my wife's sister. If Tedric were a man of honor and chivalry, it would matter little to me that Chandra does not love him. But if I am to serve my wife and Medwin as I promised to do, I cannot stand idle while she is given in marriage to a thief and murderer. One day,

Father, Tedric's sword will be turned on me. It will pain me to have to kill Theodoric's son."

"That will change," Alaric said. "When this is done there will be little love between our families."

"While that is truth, it will never change the way I feel about Theodoric. He taught me justice and honor."

Many swarmed the halls of Westminster on the business of the riots. All were there to capitalize on the insult Richard felt when his coronation ended with this ruinous event.

When Conan and his father were finally admitted to the king's chambers, they could see that Richard had not tired of his rage. His eyes were bright and piercing, and energy seemed to seethe from every pore of his powerful physique. He was again surrounded by clergy.

Years earlier, before he had been knighted, Conan had met Richard on two separate occasions in France. Conan's appearance had not changed drastically since then, except that his beard was thicker and darker, but his surprise was genuine when Richard recognized him. He bowed before his king.

"Sir Conan," Richard acknowledged. "What is your complaint?"

"None, Sire. You called to have justice brought to those who murdered Jews. I know of a man who was seen in the riots killing a lender."

While Richard's eyes remained angry, he handled the business with formality and serenity. Conan told his story while a scribe copied the details slowly and carefully. When the telling was done, Richard spoke.

"A part of justice is to give the accused a chance to speak. You are excused and will be called when Sir Tedric is found and records from the lender who was murdered are brought to me. I hope, Sir Conan, that you are not wrong."

"On my oath, Sire, I would not dare so much if I doubted. Tedric has been in possession of large sums he will not answer for, and the lender was murdered below his bride's window. She is my wife's sister and fears marriage with this man."

"And you have taken the position of matchmaker? I can think of better work for a knight of the realm."

"To protect women is a part of the code, Sire."

Richard nodded, though his lips were curved in a snide smile. With an impatient gesture of the hand, Conan was excused and the next man to see the king entered.

It was two days before Conan was called back to Westminster, but the time was well spent. Mallory and Thurwell had learned that the lender's name was Aaron and he was well known in London and York. He was widely traveled and had made many loans to nobles, charging for the privilege of borrowing. His home in York was not terribly far from Theodoric's lands. His records would cause some furor, the names would cause Richard to raise his brows. Most nobles forced to borrow tried to keep their debts a secret and were not bent to a cause so sanctified as the Crusade.

Tedric and Theodoric were already present when Conan and Alaric arrived at Westminster. Theodoric did not speak or look at Conan. His face was stony with displeasure. Tedric growled his greeting.

"Will you stop at nothing to spoil my reputation on English soil?"

"There is no blood on my hands, Tedric," Conan answered confidently.

"You could have come to me for an answer to this charge, but the king! You are wrong, Conan!"

They were admitted to the king's chambers, and the bishop at Richard's right hand read the charge.

"Sir Tedric is accused of taking part in the riot and the slaying of Jews. The man slain was called Aaron, a lender known in London and York. The witnesses were Lady Chandra, betrothed of the accused, and Lady Edythe, daughter of Lord Alaric de Corbney."

Tedric stood calmly as the accusation was read.

"How do you answer these charges, Sir Tedric?" Richard asked.

"I did in fact slay a man that night, Sire," Tedric said calmly. "I was not a part of the coronation, and when the riots began I took myself quickly to the home of Lord Alaric, knowing my betrothed to be there. I found a man trying to gain entry and I could not name him Jew or knight. When I pushed him aside he drew a knife and I killed him. I had not seen him before and did not know his name."

Richard raised a brow and studied the young man before him. He had heard similar charges and answers in the days following the riots. He was not oblivious to the possibility that old feuds would be tested on this ground. It was a choice situation for one man to discredit another.

"Why did you flee if you were innocent?" Conan asked. "You did not enter to see to the welfare of your betrothed, but ran."

"A fair question," Tedric answered easily. He casually touched a place on his head, drawing apart the gold locks to expose an undergrowth of his yellow hair stained pink from a bloody gash. "I was carried away from Alaric's door by the mob and soon after found a quiet doorway to rest my weary bones." Richard allowed an amused smile for the accused. "Forsooth, I did not rise to see to my betrothed's safety until dawn. But you were there, Conan. Did you find the lady well?"

Conan squirmed slightly but faced the king again. "Sire, Sir Tedric weaves a pretty tale and no doubt a believable one, but I state again that he has given his bride's father a large sum, money whose source he will not name. And the lender who was killed lives not far from Tedric's home. I believe the murder was given much thought and the riots offered the hope that it would go unnoticed."

Richard looked to Tedric, who at this moment seemed ill at ease. "Sire," he said softly. "I have not borrowed from a lender and I have not wished to tell my family or my bride's from whence the money came. Truth, Sire, I fear to tell you, but better I am punished for poor judgment than murder. I looked long and hard for labors that would bring me the silver to buy Chandra's hand, for her estate is my only hope of prospering — I am the last born of seven sons. Count John paid me a large sum for my support when he was in France. Though I realized my error in judgment and have pledged myself to your cause, the shame is more than a knight can bear to lay to his family."

"Then something was gained in your hasty loyalties, Tedric. You've at least realized where your allegiance belongs. I will forget that you were opposed to my sovereign right and can plainly see why you would be hesitant to name the source of your money."

"I will accept any penance you lay to me, Sire. But I did not borrow from the Jew or kill him with malice. 'Twas in self-defense."

"Some of Aaron's records could not be found, but those

kept in London were saved from the fire. No member of Theodoric's family has borrowed from Aaron. There is a chance a record is still kept in York."

"Nay, Sire," Tedric said. "I have never borrowed, I swear. Sir Conan accuses me now in hopes that I will be cast from English soil and the wedding will not take place. He is in love with Lady Chandra, Sire."

Richard's eyes were not sympathetic. He looked sharply at Conan for an explanation. Conan did not lie easily, even when it was necessary.

"The lady betrothed to Sir Tedric is my wife's sister. She fears the marriage, for she knows Tedric to be dishonest and she was the one to see him murder. He paid the maid's father a sum Medwin could not turn away, for with the Saladin tithe and scutage, Medwin is in need. I acted in her defense, as I would any woman in danger."

"But you come with charges you cannot prove. It smells of vengeance," the king said hotly. "My chamber is opened to you for the sake of justice, not as a forum to renew hostilities."

"Sire, Tedric has attacked unfairly in the past, and there have been witnesses to his treachery. I could not let this incident go by without testing Tedric's guilt. Sire, he is not a trustworthy knight; others would attest to —"

"Had you received your answers from Sir Tedric, would you have troubled me today?"

"Had I known what pretty tale he would weave, Sire, perhaps I would not have brought the charge to you. Tedric is skilled with lies."

"Yet I see no proof that you speak the truth," Richard returned.

"My allegiance has always been firm, Sire."

"And do you travel with me to the Holy Land?"

Conan's face took on a darker hue. "Nay, Sire. But I willingly meet the scutage. I am the lone able protector of my family and my wife's family."

"And you?" he asked Tedric.

"Nay, Sire. My father chose four of his sons, the ones best known for their knightly skills. I was not chosen, but my scutage has been paid."

"Sire," Theodoric put in. "My youngest son asked to be supported with arms for the Crusade and I refused him. He is better with his mind than his sword. The other men will do you better service."

Richard looked to Alaric. "And do you send sons to this cause?"

"Nay, Sire. I have not been given seven, but two. There is Conan, and Galen, a lad of only four and ten."

"I will call this matter done," Richard said. "Bother me again when you put as much importance to God's work as you put to a damsel's plight."

"Sire," Conan protested.

"It is done! I am interested in men's games, fighting and causes more important than your preferred choice of husband for your wife's sister!"

So dismissed, Conan bowed and left the room, Alaric behind him, with Tedric and his father following at a distance. Conan's pace was brisk with anger and humiliation. In the gallery near the exit he would use, Mallory and Thurwell waited. The look on Conan's face told them all.

"So he has escaped you again?" Mallory asked.

"And worse," Conan explained, looking over his shoulder to see a victorious Tedric and stony-faced Theodoric approach. "He managed to make me look the fool to Richard. The fox earned sympathy for his allegiance to John and failure to answer Richard's call to arms. His father told of how Tedric begged to go and Theodoric would not release him to join the Crusade."

"He would not go to war if Richard demanded it of him," Thurwell retorted. "Does Theodoric lie for his son now?"

"I cannot believe he would. I must believe that Tedric asked, knowing Theodoric would refuse him."

Theodoric and Tedric passed Conan and his friends without speaking, moving out of Westminster quickly, making clear that the ties of friendship had been severed.

"By the rood," Conan said, "I know that Tedric is guilty! I would stake my life on it!"

"I think not," Alaric said. "I would not stake anything of much value on Tedric's defeat. You have already staked your reputation — and lost."

CHAPTER
13

H AD Medwin been able to afford a wedding on a grand scale for Chandra, the occasion would have been an awkward one. It was just as well, then, that Medwin was lacking in ample means. His poor financial condition served as a good excuse for a modest celebration when his youngest daughter was wed.

In the hall that Medwin leased in London, there were sufficient decoration and plenty of food and entertainment. Those friends already in London for the coronation attended the ceremony and partook of the feast. Medwin, of course, was not responsible for making the arrangements. That chore fell to Chandra. Most of these preparations were made before she left Phalen, and once in London it was simply a matter of assigning last-minute tasks to others. Chandra did only what was necessary so that her father would not be embarrassed.

Garlands were strung, a minstrel was hired and birds were roasted. But there was no saving the day. No amount of primping, decorating or feasting could rescue the affair. It was common knowledge that the bride had been forced by her father into the marriage. She had accused Tedric of murder, and the man to come to her colors had been Sir Conan, her sister's husband. And Tedric had openly accused Conan of trying to stop the marriage because he loved the bride. That there was any rejoicing at all was a surprise.

She knelt beside Tedric in the rushes in the manor house that Medwin provided. The pale blue of her gown would have brought out the sparkling blue of her eyes, had she been able to raise them. A jeweled girdle that was a gift from Theodoric on her wedding day adorned her gown, but she could not smile her pleasure, for though the gift was generous, this was the blackest of days for her. Tears gathered in her eyes against her will as she spoke her vows. She knew that her appearance was not at fault, that her gown and jewels were envied by many, but the words that left her lips brought despair. She could not suppress the memory of Conan and Edwina as they knelt before a priest. The words she spoke now for Tedric she wished only to pledge to Conan. She wished, with an ache in her heart, that she could present this richly arranged wedding outfit to him; and that she could feel joy in her heart as she pledged her troth.

During the feasting and singing she was quiet and solemn, while Tedric raised his horn for every toast to the couple. His gaiety, Chandra believed, was due more to his triumph over Conan than to his great pleasure in having her as his bride.

In spite of the harsh allegations against Conan and Chandra, and the general attitude of disrespect displayed toward Conan in the wedding hall, Conan and Edwina were present. He would not shrink away in embarrassment and thus give the impression that the accusations he had levied were untrue. And Edwina was the bride's sister; without her presence Chandra would have even fewer supporters at her own wedding.

It was a strange day for many. In the past, Conan had

been the highly sung hero, with Alaric standing proudly to accept compliments on his son. Now he seemed scorned and beaten by Tedric, and Theodoric was the one standing proudly, for he boasted seven fine sons, four of whom would journey on Crusade. Alaric and Theodoric did not speak, and Medwin's position was uncomfortable. His two sons by marriage could barely abide being in the same hall with each other.

A lame falcon, long having been the symbol of good luck at a wedding, seemed to hold a double meaning as the crippled animal was displayed for all in the hall to see. At one point Chandra could bear the snide remarks and animosity no more, and with tear-filled eyes she turned to her new husband.

"My lord, I beseech your goodwill. Please speak no more ill of Sir Conan. He is my sister's husband and family in my father's house."

Tedric grinned. "But chérie, he has brought serious charges against me, and before the king! Would you have me treat him as a brother?"

"But Tedric, it was I," she murmured mournfully. "I could not think I was mistaken in what I saw, and Conan only wished to help me. I beg of you, let your punishment fall to my shoulders. I cannot bear to see Conan treated so poorly."

"Ah, the proud cock rooster does not strut so well now! He has basked in the glow of glory for a long time, chérie, when he deserved little of it. I have waited a long time to see the falcon shown for the lame coward that he is!"

"Tedric, please —"

He placed a finger under her chin and lifted her eyes to meet his. "If you did not hunger for him so, you would not beg me to cease," he accused.

Her pleas were ignored. Tedric raised his horn high to toast those brave enough to follow Richard into battle. There were not only four of his brothers present who would go, but other knights, Mallory and Thurwell among them. To toast the Crusaders was noble, but Tedric's only motive was that he might see Conan wince in shame.

Chandra watched Conan's reaction as well. He did not act mortified as Tedric hoped; rather, he raised his horn high and joined in the salute to those going to the Holy Land. Alaric's response was not so gracious. Though the hour was still early, he said his good-byes to Medwin and the bride, taking Udele and Edythe with him. Mallory and Thurwell, hard pressed to offer any more salutations to Tedric and his bride, followed close behind. Within moments Conan's supporters were gone from the room and Chandra wondered what stubbornness provoked him to remain. She would not have blamed him for leaving in an angry state hours before. And then the reason struck her: Edwina was to attend her to the bridal chamber.

It was a moment she dreaded more than any other part of the day, but Chandra could not bear to think of Conan standing alone to absorb any more subtle insults from her husband and his family. She leaned closer to Tedric.

"My lord, I beg you excuse me now. I am weary and would find our bed."

"So soon, chérie?" he fairly sneered, a knowing gleam in his eyes. "If you cannot bear the wait, so be it! I will join you there soon!"

Chandra shuddered at the thought but raised herself with as much dignity as she could muster and bade her father a good night. Edwina came quickly to her side and walked with her to the chamber above them.

There was no one in the room and Chandra went directly to a stool before the hearth and lowered herself tiredly, looking into the flames. She folded her hands in her lap, and tears coursed her cheeks to fall onto them. Edwina allowed her a few moments of quiet to calm herself. There was nothing Edwina could do to ease the hurt.

Edwina spread a delicate white nightdress on the bed. She smoothed the fabric, remembering her own wedding night. She had been nervous and distressed, but her husband had approached her with gentleness and compassion. It was her first taste of love. Her sad luck with carrying his seed to term had lessened the blissful moments for them, but when he did lie beside her at night, the warmth and glow of those moments stayed with her for a very long time. It made the weeks and months that they could not share a bed more bearable. Now, casting a furtive glance at her weeping sister, Edwina was pained to think of what Chandra might find on her wedding night.

"Come, dear heart, let us not anger him by delay. You cannot escape the wedding night."

Chandra turned to look at her sister. "You must hate me," she said sadly.

Edwina rushed to her, kneeling before her and taking Chandra's hands into her own, bringing them to her lips. "Hate you? Oh, my love, my sweet Chandra, why would I hate you?"

"For the things they say about Conan. That he helped me because —"

"Oh, my dear! Would I let what spills from jealous tongues eat at my heart? Chandra, I begged him to help you! After all you have done for me, all you have endured because of me, would I listen to such cruel lies?"

"But Edwina —" Chandra attempted.

"Nay! I hold you above all others! And it pains my heart to think of all you have been through because of me!"

"I have never suffered because of you," Chandra said in confusion.

Edwina reached out and touched Chandra's golden hair, looking with love into her eyes. "I am not blind to what you have sacrificed for me, dear heart. I know that long ago when I was prepared to take Tedric, you longed for as little as a kind word from Conan. It was his mother's doing that he noticed me at all. And it was a long while before I realized it had broken your heart. And never have you begrudged me my happiness! Never have you complained of what might have been!"

Feeling less than pure and not deserving of Edwina's sympathy, Chandra looked again at her hands and felt the tears fall onto them.

"I have had naught but kindness from my lord husband," Edwina went on. "Kindness and love he showers on me, though I do not deserve so much. I have been a disappointment to him. I cannot give him sons, and I know it is because of me that he does not go with Richard. Oh, Chandra, I did not always think Tedric so undeserving, but now I see him for the knave he is. Do you think I could have survived as his wife?"

Chandra raised her eyes and looked at her sister.

"You have always been the stronger one, and you have always taken my burdens. Now you will spend your life serving a man that was almost given to me, while I have the prize. If you can forgive, I pray you will forgive me for the many times you have slaved for a lesser reward while I have profited."

Chandra sighed, wishing she could convince herself that

there would one day be a prize for her, but she felt more permanently removed from happiness than ever before. She rose to begin to ready herself for her husband. Talking about her troubles seemed to worsen them in her mind, and delaying the inevitable could not improve her circumstances.

"I will not see you again for a long time," Chandra said. "I know that Tedric's promise to let me visit Father may be forgotten."

"Chandra, don't worry so. We will be together again. And I will pray that Tedric learns the value of what he has and changes for the better."

It was that thought that gave Chandra a glimmer of hope. She wondered how he could change if she would not allow it. Perhaps if she showed she was tractable and could be a supportive wife, they could come to an understanding.

I must show him I am willing, she thought desperately. Perhaps he does hold some love for me and is only injured by my reluctance. I fear I cannot love him, but I am strong enough to act the part of a loyal wife. In time, I pray, there will be peace between us.

It was with that resolve that she could settle herself and try to steel her mind against ill thoughts.

She could not muster a seductive or intimate smile for Tedric when he came to her; to show that she was resigned and willing was the very most she could do.

He leaned over the bed and drew her toward him, kissing her lips gently. Chandra yielded to the kiss and tried her best to return the affection. When his lips left hers he was smiling, a smile of pleasure that momentarily convinced her she had done well.

"The beautiful Chandra," he said softly. "The maid the

men all want for their own. You are accustomed to being desired, my love. It is a thing you will have to learn to live without."

"Tedric, you must forgive me if I have hurt you and let this be a time of starting over. We are pledged, you and I, and there should be kindness between us."

He laughed loudly at that. "And so you are ready to play the wife?"

"I will do my best," she murmured, confused by the look in his eyes.

"But chérie," he protested, "I was not awaiting your approval. Whether or not you are prepared to try, you are mine."

She lowered her gaze for a moment, not wishing to argue with him further, when he reached out and grabbed the sheer cloth of her shift and rent the fabric to expose her from her breasts to her thighs. She gasped as she unconsciously clutched at the cloth.

"Do not cry out, chérie," he warned. "It would be the crowning glory to Conan's shame should he hear your screams and run to your bridal chamber to save you from your husband."

Rage replaced the shock in her eyes as she glared at him. "Why do you seek his humiliation, and always at my expense?"

"Why? Because, chérie, he wants you. I have waited a very long time to take something he values from his reach and watch him stand helpless to prevent me."

Chandra rose to her knees and clutched the cloth to her heaving bosom. "You will not cease, Tedric! As I lie here regretting that I hurt you by wrongly accusing you, you treat me with greater cruelty!"

"Wrongly? Nay, love, the charges were not false. I did

indeed kill the Jew. I chased him fairly an hour, and it was a strange twist of fate that I caught him beneath your window. But then mayhaps not so strange: you should have learned to fear me, at least."

Without thinking, she cowered from him. How could she have doubted what she saw with her own eyes? "And your injury?"

He clicked his tongue and made a half frown. "It was a wretched crowd that night . . ."

"You are vile!"

"Hush, chérie! While Conan is chivalrous enough to accuse me twice, Richard will not hear him twice. It would be more shame for that poor crippled falcon to bear."

"And you *did* borrow from the Jew?"

Tedric chuckled, but there was a hardness to his eyes that would frighten a stronger maid. "In a manner, chérie, but it will never be proved."

He turned from her and began to remove his clothing, tossing it about the room carelessly. Chandra's mind whirled with anger and fear, trying to think of an escape from him: a way she could resist him without bringing any more innocent protectors' virtues to question and without gaining yet another reprimand for being an unwilling bride.

When he turned back to her, there was a feral gleam in his eyes.

"Remove the shift, my love, or I shall tear it from you."

She clutched it more fiercely to her bosom and bore through him with her eyes. He leaned closer and she felt the chill of his words.

"It will not be easy to show you your master tonight without badly bruising your tender flesh, but I will find a way. We travel to Cordell soon where there is nothing to prevent me from beating you. The marriage is to be consummated here and now, and I do not make idle threats."

Chandra felt the indecision for but a moment, and then with something of a haughty air, she pulled the shift from her body with one more tear and flung the thing away.

"If you resist me —"

"It was in my mind to meet you midway in this marriage, Tedric," she spat. "I will not resist you, but it is not my own punishment I fear, but what you lay to others to make my suffering worse."

He pushed her down onto the bed and covered her with his weight, drawing her arms up over her head and holding them there. Her earlier fears did not approach the terror she felt now. He did not condescend to give her even so much as one gentle caress. She willed herself to think of a faraway place and forced her body to become limp and lifeless so that she would show neither resistance nor encouragement.

"Do not mistake this for fondness, my love," Tedric said hoarsely. "Yet it is the only duty in our marriage that I will not despise."

"Do not mistake this for acceptance, love," Chandra mimicked through gritted teeth. "I shall despise this duty of our marriage enough for both of us."

For a moment Tedric looked into her eyes, his cold gray clearly showing hatred. "You are a bitch, Chandra, but you will learn."

With an angry hand, Tedric parted her legs, and she felt the burning ache spread through her pelvis as he plunged himself into her resistant flesh. She could not suppress the gasp of pain and the faint whimper that escaped her. Tears she could no longer hold back spilled from her eyes as the blood of her virginity stained her thighs.

"You will learn," he laughed again, his pleasure increasing greatly with her agony in yielding.

"You are mine, Chandra," he finally said, rolling away from her. "You are mine, and you will never be allowed to forget that."

Chandra felt the tears of her violation hot on her cheeks. "You claim me by right of law and strength, Tedric, but we will both always know that I am not yours! Never!"

By the time Edythe and Sir Mallory were ready to exchange their vows, there were few family friends left in London. A grander affair could have been planned to take place in Anselm, but Edythe could not wait a day. She preferred the small, intimate gathering. And there was more joy in this ceremony than had been seen in any of the other family weddings over the years. Indeed, the glow in the eyes of the bride and groom made it the grandest wedding by far.

Even though there was gladness in this union, Conan's mood was not light or gay. He was sullen and quiet, and Alaric grew more concerned with every passing day. It was not until Conan was alone in the stable tending to Orion that Alaric found the opportunity to speak to him.

"Sir Mallory and your sister will not travel with us to Anselm. Mallory has taken a modest house in the city and will deliver Edythe to me when he is ready to meet Richard in France."

"What of Thurwell?" Conan asked with little enthusiasm. "Does he stay in London with the bride and groom?"

"I hope not," Alaric laughed. "I believe he intends to offer his services to you for a time."

"Good," Conan replied. "I can use another man, even for a short time."

Alaric stood back and watched his son move around the stable, gathering a feed bag, pitching hay into the stall, brushing Orion's shiny coat. For a long time neither spoke.

"You do not find much joy in your work," Alaric finally said.

"There is little challenge in it," Conan replied.

"I have not asked you to stay behind," Alaric said.

"But you allowed King Richard to think that as my father you chose to keep me in England to serve you," Conan said, looking at his father now.

"I could have urged you to go and did not," Alaric replied.

"And if I go, what then? What of Stoddard? There is little time to find a vassal for that land. Medwin grows less capable with every day — what of Phalen? And Edwina — she tells me there is life within her womb: a son? How would she fare in my absence?"

"She would live. And Medwin has another son by marriage to give him aid."

"I should trust Tedric to manage lands that will be mine?"

"Would you trust me?" Alaric asked.

"My lord, I would trust you in all things, but you need no more burdens. You carry more than is fair now."

"Who makes me out to be so weak of body and mind?" Alaric blustered. "By the rood, I am capable still, and should I learn that I am your excuse, I will show you by my own hand whom you call old and weak!"

"You alone? Nay, Father, but a host of others that make

me feel the ties of England, and they are strong ties. I doubt Edwina could bear the separation. She is not strong —"

"How you deal with your wife is none of my concern, but I could see to her welfare. I am to tend a house filled with complaining women in any event; one more will not tilt the cart."

Conan straightened and looked at his father. "I have given madam, my mother, my word that I would not go to war. She fears for my life and the estate that should fall to me."

Alaric stood erect and quiet for a moment. "That is her reason?" he finally asked.

"And that there will be estates left floundering by nobles who do not return. She is right: it could add plentifully to our lands."

"Is that wisdom — or greed?" Alaric asked softly.

"Her motives are not selfish. Too many lean upon me for me to leave them to fulfill a private desire. There will be wars enough that I cannot avoid."

Alaric did not know how to advise his son. Conan would be no less a man for not going on the Crusade. He would still be a powerful lord in his own time, and he would not forget the ways of fighting. But a broken spirit would hinder his future, and that was what Alaric feared.

"You are an honorable man, Conan," Alaric said. "There is only one thing I have not been able to teach you. I shall never be able to teach you."

Conan looked at Alaric with a quizzical expression.

"There comes a time in every man's life when he can no longer meet all of his obligations, when his loyalties are too far-reaching for him to maintain them properly. It is as precarious as scaling a high wall, his own desires causing him to lean one way and the needs of others forcing him to lean the other way. To and fro he stumbles, balancing the weights."

"Until he falls?" Conan asked with little enthusiasm.

"You scale that wall now. The *wants* of those you've pledged to support could be confused in your mind with *needs*."

"I can abandon those who depend on me and seek my own adventures, but will I find happiness in breaking my word?" Conan asked sullenly.

Alaric chuckled. Although Conan was not yet twenty-five years old and had already burdened himself with many demanding dependents, that was not the cause of his misery. Rather, it was his reluctance to stand up for his own desires, to choose the best direction for his own life.

"When all these that you serve are gone, who will you serve then?" Alaric asked.

"There will be others," he replied testily, aggravated with his father's riddles. It was a habit of Alaric's to weave these little webs and let Conan struggle for the answers. He could never just give his advice and be finished.

"Ah, there will be others," Alaric confirmed. "For as long as you are so willing to please, there will be many to offer you the chance to do them service. But there is only one man, I think, who can reward you justly for your honor."

"The king? When he thinks me a coward and a fool?"

"Not the king," Alaric said.

"Who then?" Conan demanded impatiently.

"When you find him, son, and begin to serve his needs

faithfully, you will find the burdens others would have you carry just a bit easier to bear."

On the day before Tedric and Chandra were to depart from the city, Tedric took Chandra to Alaric's home to visit Edwina. It was a gesture of goodwill that amazed both Chandra and Medwin.

Once there, he spoke to Alaric. "My lord," he said humbly, "it sits ill with me that I have angered you. If my ways were roguish, I pray you forgive me."

Alaric was taken aback by the apology and looked at Tedric skeptically. "A once-fond friendship has been rent apart," he said. "The door between your father and me is closed."

"I cannot accept blame for that," Tedric said. "You would have closed that door had I falsely accused Conan. But our wives are sisters. There must be a peace that is at least livable."

Alaric nodded once. "I will not close my house to you when you seek only to reunite family. But Tedric, I will not try to mend this break with Theodoric. And I cannot speak to Conan for you."

Tedric smiled and bowed, excusing the old gentleman. Conan would not stay in the hall and left immediately after wishing Chandra well, without a word to Tedric.

Udele would have escaped also, for she, most of all, wished to avoid Tedric. But when he begged a moment of her time she could not refuse him, fearing he would state his business while others were near enough to hear.

"Your debt is free, lady," he said in a hushed whisper.

"So you show your true colors," she hissed. "I should have known you did not come here on a mission of kindness!"

"Richard has claimed the records of the lender's debts," he advised her. "Yours will be included, I suspect. Though the king might not easily find the man who borrowed for you, I could help him. A bauble or two will keep me quiet a while longer," Tedric whispered.

"I have nothing!" she insisted.

"How well is your future fixed when Alaric and Conan learn of our dealings?"

Udele's eyes were alive with the hate she felt for him.

"Do not ask too much of me, Tedric," she warned. "Do not make the anger of my husband and son seem a better bargain."

Udele watched Tedric leave with hardened eyes. She was one of the few to know just how trapped Chandra really was.

CHAPTER
14

S IR Tedric was fortunate in that the silver he owned
had lent itself to a practical use. There were men
to be found who did not relish war but would swear
to serve a young knight in England. He paid his
scutage to Richard, and with twenty new men-at-arms
Tedric rode into Cordell. Chandra rode behind him. She
did not smile or wave. But Wynne, feeling the exuberance
of coming home, beamed in pleasure to those villagers
who watched them enter.

Tedric was most anxious to view this holding and set
out immediately with some of his men to look through
the town. When he was gone, Chandra turned to Wynne.
"If you tell Sir Tedric one word of our forest guard, I will
beat you myself!"

"But lady, he is —"

"I am lady here and he is my husband. I rule this burgh.
You will abide by my laws. Do not question me."

"Yea, lady, but I think —"

"For the time being, Wynne, don't think. I must see
your father at once. Bring him to me before Tedric
returns."

Shaking her head in confusion, Wynne left the hall to
go to the small house that her father, Sir William, kept.

Chandra looked about the room. It was orderly, and

more benches and trestle tables had been supplied by
Agnes, William's wife and loyal caretaker of Cordell.

"You have always pleased the nobles in this hall, Agnes.
I have no doubts about your talents. I have sent for Master
William. When he comes, send him to my chamber."

Then, with a great deal of worry on her mind, Chandra
went to the storeroom to draw out some money and placed
it in a bag. She noted with pride that the sum kept at
Cordell was not touched by any of the castle folk or residents of the village. And while she hoped this action she
took was unnecessary, she greatly feared that Tedric's hand
would find its way into this vault and allow himself more
than he deserved of Cordell's revenues. She intended to
avert that from happening.

Not much later, in her chamber, Master William entered and stood before her. "We have not much time," she
said, indicating a chair opposite her, a table that served
as her writing desk between them.

"My husband, Sir Tedric, has brought men-at-arms with
him," she said.

"I saw them, lady."

"I believe he will use them as guards," Chandra went
on. "I think we will let him do that without argument."

"And the forest guard? And the men on the coast?"

Chandra sighed. "For the moment, I think it best to
show my husband little of Cordell's secrets. Use care in
sending your people in and out of the wood. And this,"
she said, pushing the purse filled with coin toward him,
"should be put in a reserve for a day when some emer-
gency arises."

William raised one brow. "You do not trust the new
lord. Your marriage . . . ?"

"Much against my will," she said, looking down at a

parchment and writing, though she did this only to escape William's eyes. What she wrote did not make any sense to her later. "I dearly hope that he will prove a good lord and gentle husband, but in the event that the opposite is true, we must be prepared."

William's frown bore down on her.

"Perhaps my words do not give Tedric his due, William. This will be his burgh too, as he shares it with me. He has in good faith lent me the right to manage my dower as I will, but I have known Tedric to be cruel and wicked, and I fear he can be again. Do you know why I warn you?" she asked coyly.

"I think so, lady," he replied.

"Clearly, an arrow perfectly placed from the wood or the town might well end my troubles as I see them, but it would serve no good in this burgh. You would swiftly see the town in flames. And Cordell would no longer belong to my family."

"Aye, lady," he said, rising. "And there is no one to avenge us under misrule?"

"Medwin is old. Those men-at-arms under his command can protect Phalen Castle well, but I cannot depend on his support now."

"And Sir Conan?" John asked.

Her eyes became glassy and looked past him to some distant place. Then she caught herself and looked again at her parchment, taking up the quill and making some marks on the page. "I would not lay that burden to Sir Conan now. You do not know the extent of the fief wars that could follow."

"Aye, lady," William replied, but he did not know. The battle would reach a great deal farther than Cordell. It could easily grow to include all of Alaric's holdings against all of Theodoric's. Conan could lose everything. And she would not ask him to take that risk.

William stood and tucked the purse into his belt. It was not well hidden, but neither did it seem to draw much notice. He was bowing to leave, when the door of her chamber swung wide and Tedric entered.

Chandra rose. "My lord," she said, still uneasy with this title she must lay to him now. "Master William is our head huntsman. You can count on him to bring anything you request from the forest. His talents supply much of what our tables bear."

"Food does not concern me," he said, throwing his gauntlets onto her desk. "I can see your father's eagerness to see you wed. This town is like sleeping prey. My men will see it better kept from now on."

"Thank you, Master William. You may go." She turned to her husband. "I will rest easier knowing you have seen to the protection of this burgh," she said. She heard the door close softly as William left them.

"It is small, as I was promised. But it will do," he said.

"It could be larger," she offered. "We could easily extend the farming land —"

"I can't see the need to waste my time trying to make this piddling acreage into something grand. There are other lands to be had."

"Tedric, your dreams are bigger than your ability —"

"The beautiful Chandra," he said sarcastically, reaching out a hand to caress her cheek. "The fair damsel. You've grown accustomed to hearing about your beauty and strength, haven't you? You've learned to enjoy the worshipful look of every young lad that passes. In time you will feel less like a goddess." He turned to walk toward the door that joined their chambers. "Send Wynne to me," he said. "I have need of her."

"Tedric, she is a young lass and does not know the ways of —"

"Never mind, Chandra. The lass knows more than you credit her for. She would not thank you for your interference."

"You must not take advantage of her naivete. She does not know —"

"Very well, I will find her myself," he said, leaving the room.

With a touch of panic, Chandra ran hurriedly to the hall below, where she found Wynne with her mother. She brought the girl to her chamber and made her stay close. For several days Tedric gained a fair amount of amusement from the way Chandra kept the girl under her protective wing. She even had the girl place her pallet beside Chandra's bed to sleep there at night, until Tedric strode in and asked Wynne to leave them in privacy. Tedric was not gentle, and he used her body to please himself just as he used her land to get him the money he needed for more profitable ventures.

She warned Wynne to be careful to keep herself from being alone with Tedric. "I am afraid he will take advantage of you," she said. "He looks at you in a way that frightens me."

But Wynne's look clearly said she pitied Chandra for so badly misjudging a good man. "You do Sir Tedric wrong, I fear. Lady, he has been nothing but kind to me."

She could do nothing to make the girl see. In truth, while the castle folk were a bit wary of their new lord, as they would be with any new lord, Tedric had done nothing to cause them to fear or hate him. In the time he took to acclimate himself to Cordell, he did not act any less than a chivalrous and honorable knight.

But hardly a week passed before Wynne came to attend her one morning with eyes downcast, dark circles under them. She had been crying.

Chandra sat on the edge of her bed while Wynne knelt to hold the slippers to her feet. She put a finger under the maid's chin to raise her face. "Wynne?" she questioned softly. She gasped at the large bruise on the maid's cheek.

Wynne let her head fall into Chandra's lap, and all her pent-up anger and humiliation bled itself out in tears. Chandra lightly stroked her hair and back, knowing what had probably befallen the lass. It was a long time before Wynne's crying ceased.

"Did he hurt you badly?" Chandra asked.

It was a moment before Wynne could speak, and when she did, she could not look at Chandra. "He did not beat me much," she said.

"Look at me, Wynne."

"Lady," the girl choked, "I cannot!"

"Lift your eyes. It is not your fault."

"Lady, how you must hate me. How foolish I have been!"

"I do not hate you," Chandra said consolingly. "You could not see Tedric's cruel nature. He kept it well hidden."

"You tried to warn me," she sobbed.

"I should have done more. I should have sent you from this house when I suspected. Truth, I thought he would seduce you to his bed. Even I did not see that he might take you by force."

"I am so ashamed."

"You needn't feel shame. You had nothing to say in what happened. Now you must stay close by me and out of his way as much as you can."

"What does it matter now?" Wynne asked weakly. "I am already spoiled for any marriage. He cannot hurt me any more than he already has."

"You need not be his slave," Chandra said sternly. "You are a servant to me, and your duties do not involve Tedric." But she feared there was little she could do to prevent Tedric from taking what he pleased.

"Your parents, Wynne. Do they know?"

Wynne shook her head and yet another tear fell from her eye.

"I will have to attend to that," Chandra said resolutely.

In the hall later she encountered Tedric. He leaned against the wall and smiled lazily. He took perverse pleasure in assuming that his act had been discovered. Chandra's glare proved he was right.

"Where do you go so early this morning, my lady?" he asked insolently.

"I go to ask Master William not to avenge his daughter's rape. I pray he sees the wisdom of my pleas."

Tedric threw back his head and laughed heartily. "Revenge? From a simple serf!"

"You are a bigger fool than I imagined, my lord," she said through clenched teeth. "Had you not given thought to an arrow as you rode past the wood? A knife while you knelt at mass? Tedric, your guards cannot protect you from everything. They offer little protection from the simple villagers you pass every day in your own halls."

"Should any harm come to me, do you think my father and my brothers would allow it to pass? When will a common serf free himself from my lordship with the point of his knife?"

Chandra met his cold gray eyes with determination in her own. "When there is nothing more you can take from them, Tedric. That is when."

The season of Christmas drew in on the land with blowing cold and swirling snow. The town of Stoddard did not have the look of a gay village, for the people there labored hardest just to keep their small huts warm. And the hall was likewise very cold, the servants working constantly to keep the fires blazing. Many townspeople sought haven in the hall if their homes were inadequate against the storm.

Lady Edwina served a steaming brewis by her own hand to some who huddled there. The fur lining of her mantle kept her warm, and she had drawn from her own coffer certain cloaks to warm those in the hall.

It was not often that the hall was crowded with people. There were no grand dinners or parties at Stoddard, and visitors were few, mostly travelers who could find no other lodging for the night. The town had no inn.

The door to the keep opened, and the wind from without blustered into the hall. Conan stood brushing the snow from his mantle, a froth of white glistening on his beard. He threw off the cloak and a servant snatched it up to lay it before the hearth to dry. Edwina approached him immediately.

"The first thing we must do in the spring to assure these people the use of their homes through the winter is to rebuild much of this burgh. None of these folk could survive the night in this storm. The child, there," she said, pointing to a lad lying before the hearth on a straw pallet, "he is nearly frozen. Why did they wait for so long to come to the hall?"

Conan smiled with affection as his wife spoke. Her concern for the people of the town warmed his heart.

"The hall is more theirs than mine," he said. "I have told them in time of trouble they are welcome here."

"I would have you send some men into the village before nightfall to be certain there are no others who should be here."

"Very well, madam," he returned, his eyes shining.

"Conan, you must be cold," she said, pulling on his arm. "I've kept you here talking when you should be warming yourself. Come."

The moment he stood before the fire, she went to kneel beside the youngster and put a hand to his brow. She spoke quietly to his mother and then rose to some other chore. Conan watched her as she moved about the hall, taking a cup to one and talking to another. The storm would not last long, there was no cause to fear. But he gained much pleasure in seeing his wife show such concern for the people. Conan was just beginning to see what had been missing here while Edwina kept residence at Anselm.

When the day became darker and evening was upon them, Edwina sank to a chair before the fire and held a mug of hot wine to her lips. In her slightly rounding tummy there was a fluttering and churning. A smile came to her lips. The child was strong, she told herself. It moved early, and it must be a son. She had not felt well in the early days of pregnancy, but that had passed and been replaced by the first faint movements. His thrusts and kicks became stronger with each passing day. This time, she assured herself, she would carry the child easily.

"You are tired from your labors, madam," her husband said.

"Aye, Conan. It has been a long day."

He knelt beside her and brushed a wisp of her blond hair back from her brow. She took his hand in hers and guided it to the obtrusion that was his child, and he felt the movements there.

"All through the day the child was still," she told him. "And the moment I can rest he begins his antics. This will be a lively son, mark my word."

"You have made me proud, Edwina. I would not have thought you capable of doing all that you have."

She laughed lightly and brought his hand to her lips, placing a soft kiss in the palm. She looked at him with a sparkle in her eyes that he had not seen before. "I would not have thought it myself, my lord. I am only lately finding joy in rest well earned. The burdens of this hall have become a blessing." She smiled at him and said softly, "I have never known such happiness, my lord."

"You have indeed earned your rest. Come now and let us find our bed. You must take care of my son: that is your first duty."

The night was too frightfully cold to dally with nighttime grooming rituals. Edwina let her hair fall down from her tightly coiled braids and untangled it with her fingers. She quickly donned a heavy muslin sleeping gown with long sleeves and climbed into bed. She snuggled close to Conan for warmth, and he received her gratefully.

He was more patient with her than she could ever remember. Though he had always been kind and tolerant, in the last two months he seemed to show her more affection than ever before. He stayed close by her side and complimented her every effort sincerely. The extra pounds the pregnancy brought somehow found her face, usually long and thin, and it became rounder and more healthy looking. And she found such relief in being here in her own home rather than managing in Udele's home. She laughed more often and found great joy in pleasing Conan. She felt, finally, that she was of some real value to him.

As she lay in bed beside her husband, his arm encircling her and her head resting on his shoulder, she felt the security of love. When my son is born, she thought just before drifting off to sleep, my husband will teach him honor and strength. And I shall teach him love.

The storm left a cover of crisp snow in its wake and the dreary skies of winter prevailed. The people of Stoddard were able to labor out of doors once again, and all were busy preparing for the celebration of Christmas. Breads were baked and ale was brewed. It was a time of great community, and if the people had been indifferent in their feelings toward their lord and lady before, now they were steadfast in their respect and appreciation because of the generosity shown during the early winter storm.

The roundness of Lady Edwina's belly brought the women ever to her side to give her aid, and all noticed that her smile was quick and her eyes aglow with the wonder of a mother-to-be. And Sir Conan showed in his manner a contentment that his people had not previously seen. A man who had long been beset with nervous energy and a quick pace, he had seemed to learn the art of relaxing. He no longer sought to work late into the night, but retired early to a bedchamber where warmth welcomed him and brought him rest.

Sir Conan received by messenger a letter telling him

that his mother and sister were coming to give what aid they could to Edwina during the Christmas celebrating. Sir Mallory had left just after King Richard early in December, and Edythe, being at loose ends and missing her husband, wished to be with them during this gay season.

"Conan, you must write them and tell them I do not need any help. I am managing very well," Edwina said tremulously. The thought of Udele's coming caused her insides to churn in apprehension.

Conan laughed lightly and touched her cheek. "She does not come so much to help, chérie, but to assess our situation. She does not have a high opinion of Stoddard."

"I don't believe she would come if you were not here," Edwina said.

"Indeed not," he laughed. "She loves nothing so much as thinking she manages my life. And for as long as I live, I imagine that she will be ever near with her advice."

"And this does not bother you?" she asked.

"Her interference has more than once upset the normal routine," he said with a shrug. "If it gives her pleasure, I can bear the burden."

But I cannot, Edwina thought in near despair. "I do not manage quite as well when Lady Udele is near," she sighed. "I do not think she likes me."

"Nonsense," he replied. "She would not come to see that you are well if she did not like you."

"But that is not why she comes," Edwina blurted.

Conan looked at her in confusion for a moment while Edwina stammered and twisted her hands, not knowing what to say. It had been a very long time since he had seen his wife act thus. He raised a suspicious brow as he queried, "Why, then?"

"She has not always been kind to me, Conan," she said haltingly.

He folded his arms across his chest and waited for something more.

"She has said cruel things to me because of my frequent illnesses, yet it was she who insisted I be put to bed most often — especially when you were near. She chided me for not giving you a child, yet became angry when we again shared a bed. And then she questioned me every morning about our most private moments. Conan, when you were near enough to hear, she was kind to me, but when you were away she was cruel. She hates me. I cannot please her well or ill, no matter how . . ."

He was quiet for a moment as Edwina's complaints dwindled low and she finally ceased.

"Are you certain it is not larger in your mind?" he asked.

"Oh, nay, Conan. Edythe has often witnessed her hostile manner with me."

"And why have you never told me of this problem before?"

"Oh, Conan, I know you love her. And truly, she has always treated you with so much fondness and devotion that I feared" — she hung her head and her next words came very softly — "I feared you would not believe me."

He lifted her chin with a finger. "You have never lied to me. Why would I not believe what you tell me now?"

"Because you have never seen your mother as anything less than a great lady," she said sadly. "And she is a great lady — in her hall, with her family. It just seems that I cannot win her favor."

He smiled. "She plays her role very well," he said easily.

"But I have seen her push her authority too far and I am aware of my mother's less desirable traits."

"Will you ask her not to come?" she asked meekly.

He kissed her cheek tenderly. "Nay, I cannot. She would be badly offended and my father would question my manners. But you are lady here, Edwina. And madam will treat you well or she will be escorted home."

"Will you stay in the hall?" she asked.

"As often as I possibly can," he promised.

The first few days that Udele and Edythe were present were easily passed. Then quite suddenly there was a strange occurrence. Edwina had felt slightly ill while going about her chores and took a moment to sit and rest. The ill feeling persisted and she felt hot and flushed. She thought to move from the fire and stand before the door to let the cold draft cool her face, but before she reached the door she fainted.

Conan carried his wife to their chamber and stood at her beside while a cool damp rag was being fetched. There was no fever and Edwina was quickly revived.

Conan questioned her anxiously. "Are you ill?"

"I think not," she sighed. "I feel fine now."

"You will stay the rest of the day in bed," he ordered. "I will be assured of your good health before you are allowed up."

He stayed with her while her women undressed her to help her into her sleeping gown. There were red stains on her shift and kirtle. A feeling of fear and horror swept over them both.

"It will not be so," she whispered with determination that was impossible to ignore. "The child will *not* be lost! If I have to lie in this bed until Eastertide, the child *will* be born!"

At Edwina's insistence, the Christmas feast went on in her absence. She kept cautiously to her bed, though she was feeling quite well. The child moved within her, and those reassuring flutters kept her spirits high. There was a small amount of bleeding, but she felt no pain. She was determined she would not miscarry again.

"It is good that I am here," Lady Udele said. "Sometimes a mother knows when her children have need of her."

"I will trust you to treat Edwina with the utmost care," Conan advised his mother sternly. "Say nothing that will upset her in any way, and do not even suggest the child might come too early."

Through the twelve days, Edwina kept mostly to her bed. Conan on occasion carried her to the dining hall to take a meal so that she might be in the company of the other castle folk. In spite of the unhappy circumstances, Edwina was marvelously bright.

"I am well," she insisted. "My mother was plagued with difficulty in bearing children and was often put to bed. It is worth the bother."

"Your mother delivered no sons," Udele remarked.

Conan frowned at his mother and looked at her closely. "And if there are no sons for me, madam, my daughters will bring lands to great families," Conan said tartly. "And Galen will do his part to carry on the family name."

Udele stiffened in indignation at her son's harsh tone. She could feel that the bond between husband and wife had strengthened: she had not foreseen the possibility of that.

"I am not afraid, madam," Edwina said with confidence. "I will give Conan a son. One child we lost was a son, and I know myself capable of bearing another. And this child is safe within me. He moves daily and there is no pain. You will see: come Easter, you will be a grandmother."

Udele's spine straightened and her mouth was set in a grim line. She stared at Edwina for a long moment. "I hope you are right, darling. I do hope all goes well."

Edwina, so pleased with a kind word from her husband's mother, smiled back with genuine affection. "You must not worry. It will be so." She laughed softly and touched her husband's arm. "And I am learning to manage this household from my bed, as my mother did in such times."

"A strong woman, Millicent was," Conan said matter-of-factly. "Though she may have been weak of body, she was a strong lady for Phalen. And Edwina grows stronger with her years."

Udele smiled at the young couple, but inside, disgust gnawed at her. She remembered Millicent well. Medwin had worshiped her. It was not a part of her plan that Edwina would be like her mother. And she could not accept Conan as a doting and solicitous husband. She had expected him to be ambitious, busily seeking greater riches, not bound to this beggarly hall. He could be swayed, though it was hard to influence him when he was set apart from her, as now. She could easily convince him, as she had in the past, that she knew what was best for his future.

"Mallory has been gone more than a month," Conan said to his sister. "How fare you now?"

"It is lonely," Edythe said softly. "But I am grateful for the time we've had." She smiled with the maturity of a woman secure in her love. "And I look forward to the time ahead, when he is home."

"You are welcome here whenever you wish," Conan told her. "And you, madam," he said, turning to his mother. "You must be thinking often of Father, alone in Anselm Keep. I imagine you are anxious to make your way home."

Udele looked up, startled. "How can I leave when Edwina is still confined to her bed?" she asked incredulously.

"You cannot do more for her than the servants are already doing," he remarked. "If I am called away from Stoddard I can send for Edythe. She needs the chores to keep her mind free from worry, but I strongly doubt that I will have to leave in winter."

"Conan, you must consider bringing Edwina to Anselm so that I can closely guard her health," Udele argued.

"I'm afraid that is out of the question, madam. She does not wish to live apart from me, and my place is here."

"In this wretched place? I raised you for much better than this, and Anselm is your home! Put a castellan in charge here and come home to serve your father. He needs you."

Conan laughed at his mother. "Madam, I used the better part of a year riding between Stoddard and Anselm, and never did I find Father in grave need of my help. He manages as well as he ever did. If you are so worried about him, you must hurry home to see that he is well."

Udele's face flushed with anger. "Soon you will have to come home, Conan. Though you may not see it, your father ages. I would be the one to know."

"It will not be very long before Galen can be of service to you at Anselm," Conan replied without much concern.

"Galen?" she asked.

"I did not say I would give him my inheritance, but I have Phalen, and Medwin, I fear, will have more need of me than Father. Remember, madam, that you have two sons, and Medwin, none."

Udele's green eyes were lit by a strange fire. "I fear telling your father of your plan. It may kill him."

Conan smiled leisurely. "You insist on worry. Father knows, and agrees it is wise."

Her eyes blazed. "And it was not mentioned to me by either of you? When Anselm is to be my home for the rest of my days, no one saw fit to ask for my thoughts on the matter?"

"Indeed, madam, your position was considered very carefully. Were you old and less capable I would take personal responsibility for Anselm. But you will be a great help to Galen. You could manage without the aid of a man, and I have known you to do so."

"But Conan," she pleaded, "if you are willing to leave a castellan in your charge here at Stoddard, consider the many possibilities! You could be free to pursue the gain of more land, adding to your estate. And Anselm is the richest, and therefore should be the only one managed by you — you've no need for a castellan if I am there and your visits are frequent. Put Galen to better use: send *him* to Phalen and use your skills to —"

Conan shrugged to show his lack of interest before his mother could finish. "I find myself with a full bevy of duties already. Should the day ever come that I can manage what I have with such ease as to find leisure time, perhaps there will be a desire for other lands." He laughed. "I doubt I have much chance of seeing that day."

"You leave me ill fixed, Conan," Udele said bitterly.

"Nay, madam, you will always be well cared for. I gave my word to that. But your preference that I am ever close to your counsel and in constant pursuit of more wealth is not a part of the bargain. My mind is made."

The meal passed with Udele saying little and most of the conversation passing between Conan, Edwina and Edythe. Edwina did not dally in the hall but allowed her husband to guide her slowly up the stairs and help her into bed. Edythe followed, and Udele was left alone.

And this is how it will be, she thought angrily. He will treat me like a worthless old woman before my time! The great and honorable knight has no interest in lands, power and wealth, after all I have done to guide him toward a position of greatness! After all I have sacrificed to help him rise to a position to build an empire, he will closet himself with his sickly wife and live out his days in Medwin's meager hall, never seeking more, never improving on his lot. . . .

She rose to go to her chamber and met Conan on the stair as he was leaving Edwina. "Mother," he said quietly, "you will feel better about Father's fitness when you are with him again. It will not take you long to prepare to travel back to Anselm."

Udele looked at her son closely. Her eyes were bright and turbulent. She did not answer him but turned and continued down the hall to her own chamber. She had not foreseen this when she had put so much effort into Conan's grooming. She had not considered that he would not go along with her plans and goals for him.

CHAPTER
15

THE weather had turned crisp and clear with the new year, and, while cold, there were no storms brewing in the sky. Lady Udele's journey to Anselm could not be delayed any longer.

As she looked about her room at the ready parcels, she felt a sinking feeling in the pit of her stomach, although her anger had cooled somewhat.

Udele went to the small window and brushed the heavy cover aside to look into the courtyard below. Conan was helping Edythe to the back of a dapple-gray mare and then mounted his own steed so they could go for a ride together on this cold winter day. It was only the second time during the visit that Conan and his sister had allowed a small space of time to be together and talk, but to Udele it was the greatest affront. How carefully he tended these young women! Edwina was tucked safely in her bed, and Edythe was counseled and eased through her lonely state. Did he think at all of business, of politics, lands to be acquired?

Her hand came to her breast as if to ease the twisting feeling in her heart. If she could only have more of his time, she could make him see what greatness there was to be had!

She tore herself from the window and, with long, determined strides, made her way to Edwina's chamber. Sitting up in her bed, donned in a deep-green velvet robe, she did not look weak or sickly. There was a healthy flush on her cheeks, and her shining golden hair streamed down onto her shoulders in glowing torrents. She smiled as she saw Conan's mother enter, and her eyes danced with new life.

Despite the gloominess of her feelings, Udele still had her wits about her. She saw that her one chance of reaching Conan would come from making Edwina her ally. She returned Edwina's smile and kissed her brow.

"You are looking fit, dear heart," Udele cooed.

"I feel fit, madam, but I have no wish to worry Conan. I will keep my place a few days longer."

Udele looked about the room. There was but one serving woman with Edwina. Udele turned to her with a smile.

"It is still so cold," she said pleasantly. "I would dearly love a cup of hot milk on such a day."

The serving woman nodded and left them alone. Udele sat on the edge of Edwina's bed and took her hand. "Edwina, my love, I have tried to help you in the past and you must do your part for me now. Urge Conan to return to Anselm, to his father and me."

"Madam, he knows his father's needs, and rest assured, if Lord Alaric had need of him, I would not detain him here. I would certainly insist that he serve his father first."

"Edwina, listen to me," Udele said in a tone that was much more humble than she was accustomed to using. "Unless Conan returns to Anselm to live, he will not see that Galen is not strong enough to manage that holding. We must show him that Anselm, the largest and richest of all that he owns, is his first concern. You must help me."

"Madam," Edwina said with a sternness Udele had not

previously heard, "the matter is for Conan and his father to decide."

"But this notion of taking Phalen Castle in lieu of his own Anselm is foolish! What whim is this?"

"The need is greater at Phalen," Edwina said calmly. "Lord Alaric agrees."

"Alaric, that old fool!" Udele spat, forgetting her plan to form an alliance with Edwina. "He would have Conan take the Cross and go off to some heathen land to die by an infidel's sword! He gives no thought to estates to be gained in England. You can thank me for the fact that Conan stays. 'Twas I who urged him not to abandon his wife for a foolish war!"

Udele rose and walked away from the bed a few paces, turning only to find Edwina smiling calmly. "A foolish war, madam? For Christ?" She shook her head sadly. "'Twas not for me that you urged him to stay, for I would have sent him off with my prayers had he chosen to go. It was for yourself."

"You ungrateful wretch," Udele hissed. "You cannot thank yourself for this rich marriage you've made. 'Twas I! You would be bound to that idiot Tedric even now if I had not encouraged my son to take you for his bride!"

"I know that," Edwina said. "And even now I wonder why."

"For Phalen! I could not stand by and let Conan take a pauper bride while Tedric moved into the lands adjoining ours! What future for my son then? Should he sit idle while Tedric becomes richer?"

"Had you left Conan alone, he might have married a richer woman —" Edwina started.

"Richer? Hah! What riches see you in Cordell?" Udele

looked in shock at Edwina, for she had not thought this argument through carefully. The words spilled from her mouth haplessly in her frustration at not being able to make Edwina see their plight.

"Cordell?" Edwina questioned. A smile came to her lips as she looked at the rattled woman. "Oh, madam, did you fear he would marry Chandra and bring a modest keep to the family?" Edwina laughed suddenly. "She had eyes for him, to be sure, and you took that to mean he would marry her?"

"Oh, you stupid wench! He loves her still!"

"My lady," Edwina said, shaking her head with amusement. "Conan is fond of Chandra — he has always thought highly of her. But you need not fear! We *all* love her dearly."

"You are a foolish child!" Udele said hotly. "It is not so innocent as you suspect! Tedric heard them himself, in the garden on the eve of your wedding. Conan unburdened his heart to her. He told her he deeply regretted his choice and wished to undo it, but alas, he would never break his word! Edwina, I have saved us all from shame. In time, Conan surely would have yielded to his passion!"

Edwina frowned slightly and looked closely at her mother-in-law.

"Edwina," Udele said. "Do you not notice the way he looks at her when she is near? Your halls are alive with the gossip: Conan loves your sister!"

The frown in Edwina's brow deepened. "Madam, how have you saved me from shame?" she asked suspiciously.

"I was the one to help Tedric into marriage with your sister! He could not have managed that alone. And now you need not fear! Tedric will never let her out of his sight."

"The money he gave my father for her hand," Edwina said thoughtfully. "I would not have thought you had such great sums."

"It was not difficult to come by. It was what I had to do, for Conan and for you!"

"For me? But madam, I have never worried that Conan would stray from my side." Edwina thought for a moment and then with a half smile she hoped Udele would warm to, she spoke again. "But you were good to think of me, my lady. However did you raise the great wealth it took to sway my father?"

"I have traded with the Jews on occasion," she said easily, not remembering the trouble she caused the last time she let that information slip. "But you must not tell Conan. He would not understand that I was thinking only of him."

"Of him? Of course, madam, you were worried for him. And how will you ever repay the sum? Is there a way I can help you?"

Udele did not sense Edwina's ploy. "The debt is canceled. The usurer was killed in the riots."

Udele folded her hands across her chest and watched leisurely as Edwina threw back the covers and sat on the edge of the bed. "It was not perhaps the same Jew that Tedric was accused of killing?"

Udele's eyes grew wide as she realized her mistake. She feared the worst — that Edwina would not keep her secret. "Don't be foolish, Edwina! Conan has loved Chandra. I feared you would be abandoned and left to watch as your husband claimed your own sister. Chandra did not want to marry Tedric. And why? Because she is in love with Conan — still!"

"Madam," Edwina said, rising and finding her slippers,

"you have been badly fooled. Tedric invented his story to bleed you of money; and you believed him! Now you have not only the money you gave him to burden your conscience, but the blood of the lender is on your hands as well. No doubt Tedric killed the man to free you of your debt."

"Fooled? Nay," Udele protested. "Nay, he was not lying! I have seen Conan's eyes when he looks at your sister. Edwina, can you really be so blind?"

Edwina shook her head, refusing Udele's pleading. "You have been tricked, madam, and worse, you've sold my sister into marriage with a murderer. I only hope there is still time to help her."

Edwina began to walk to her chamber door and turned suddenly at the sound of Udele's laughter, a chilling and eerie sound that was not born of mirth. When she looked at her mother by marriage, she found the woman facing her with arms outstretched and palms up. The fear was gone from Udele's face and there was now pleading.

"But, dear Edwina, I had nothing to do with the Jew's murder," Udele said confidently. "There is no record bearing my name for the loan. You see, I am innocent in this affair! You could claim that I feared Conan was in love with your sister, but why? Where would the good in it be? 'Twould only serve to further upset your husband, and there is nothing more he can do. And as for the murder, would you have Conan attempt his accusation of Tedric again, when there is no proof of any wrongdoing? Such a fuss, and for what?"

Edwina looked with pity on her husband's mother. "After all the wrong you have done, you worry only about causing a fuss — Oh, madam!" Edwina's hand touched the latch to her chamber door.

"Edwina, dear heart —" Udele attempted, grasping at one more chance to save herself.

"Never mind, madam. It will be difficult, but perhaps it is not too late to undo what you have done."

Edwina left the room and walked to the stair. Udele followed, her mind racing. Edwina would go to Conan! And what would he do with this story? Would he ride directly to Theodoric? Alaric? Richard?

As Edwina took the first step, she swooned slightly and clutched at the wall, leaning backward on the stair to counterbalance. A dizzy spell? A sudden weakness from the excitement of their confrontation? Udele looked behind her. They were alone. There was no one at the bottom of the stair. Her hands came out and pushed at Edwina's back. Edwina gasped in surprise and lost her footing, falling and striking her head and then rolling, the swishing of her gown and the thumping of her limbs on the stair the only sound.

Udele screamed, an involuntary shriek of horror, more at what she had done without even thinking than at the sight of her son's young wife falling down the hard stone stairs. Her hands trembled uncontrollably and tears sprang to her eyes, tears of fear and desperation. She screamed again for help and ran to the bottom, finding Edwina in a heap there, her head bruised and her legs twisted in an unnatural position.

The servants, summoned by Udele's screams, arrived to find Udele hovering over the motionless form of their lady. Udele lifted Edwina's head into her lap and, while weeping and shrieking, stroked her hair away from her smashed brow. "She fainted on the stair!" she cried over and over, but within herself all the tears and trembling came from the knowledge that she had pushed the woman

— instinctively, grasping at her own survival, without a thought.

She put her cheek next to Edwina's nose. No breath came from her. She was dead. Udele felt a shudder run through her as she realized that she had murdered. Her wails became louder, and she let her head fall to Edwina's still chest, clutching her as if she had been a dearly loved child.

Lady Udele had to be pulled from Edwina's still body. The lifeless form, a small bit of blood running from her brow and ear, was carried to the same chamber that she had just left. The servants laid her on the bed with measured care, straightening her clothing and arranging her limbs in a comfortable-looking position. Udele shortly freed herself from those holding her and ran sobbing to the same room, falling to the floor before the bed and resting her head on Edwina's cold hand.

Fear and revulsion made composure impossible for Udele. She looked up several times at Edwina's face, where a look of horror was etched, her wide-open eyes staring straight to the heavens and her mouth still open in a silent scream. Gently, with trembling fingers, Udele brought the lids of her eyes down and pressed the gaping mouth closed. Edwina's look turned almost peaceful. *I never meant for her to be dead,* her mind tried to convince a jury that might descend on her and smite her as suddenly and thoughtlessly as Edwina had been smitten.

Servants crowded around the weeping Udele, but she did not notice their presence. Neither was she conscious of their slow and quiet withdrawal from the room as a taller and much more commanding figure entered. As she felt Conan's presence behind her, she turned red, swollen eyes up to him. He stared straight at the form that was his wife.

His back was straight, his arms stiff at his sides. The blue of his eyes seemed sheathed in ice, anger and horror fixed his mouth into a straight line, and his temples pulsed with the rapid beat of his heart.

"Conan," she began, rising to him.

"Leave me," he said in a hoarse whisper, his eyes never moving from his wife's face.

"Conan, let me comfort you —"

"Leave me!"

Udele rose shakily to her feet, a slight and trembling form beside him. She looked into the cold harshness of his eyes and thought she saw a tear beginning to form. "Conan, she fainted on the —"

With a sharp snap, his head jolted in her direction and stilled her attempted explanations. He stared at her with nothing less than hatred, and the guilt in her turned to fear that he would know what had happened. Cautiously she turned and made her way out of the chamber, pausing to lean against the closed door to collect herself.

The guilt and terror began to ease as a sense of order returned to her befuddled mind. No one had seen what happened. She had not pushed Edwina with enough force to leave marks on her back. Indeed, she was swooning on the stair. She might have fallen in any case. And Conan would need her now — he would need the support and comfort she could give. Only she knew how to give that support! He would suffer grave disappointment, for he certainly wanted the child. For a time he would feel lost and need —

A wail, loud and ringing with agony, came from the chamber within, stopping her thoughts and causing her to jump in surprise. Udele's eyes became round and she almost panicked from the sheer passion and anguish of the cry.

Finally she moved down the hall toward her own room, a dazed look on her face. Does he grieve? she asked herself. Did he truly cherish her so much? Did he learn to love her and finally forget the other woman? Giselle had said a lovely blond woman with strength and passion — Edwina had certainly never been that! Never! But, had she begun to fulfill that destined role? Was she the one after all?

Stoddard Keep was kept quiet and dark through the evening. No one spoke above a whisper, and while food was put on the table in the hall, few felt the desire for it and Conan ignored the tray placed outside the chamber door. Murmurings spread through the hall that Sir Conan had closeted himself with his dead wife. Some feared for his well-being, others questioned his sanity. Not one person within the keep slept easily.

Morning brought Conan from his private hold looking haggard and worn, but his eyes were of that clear and determined blue that his opponents saw in a contest of arms or battles. Udele found her son in the dining hall moments after he had arrived. Clearly her task at hand was to show Conan she would never fail him.

"Prepare Lady Edwina's body," he told a serving woman. "I will take her home to lie near her mother."

"Then I will prepare to ride with you —" Udele started.

"Madam! For the love of Christ! You are not needed at Phalen Castle! Take yourself and your train of servants to my father and bring this sad news to him!"

He turned on his heel and left the hall, the brisk morning air rushing in as he opened the heavy door, catching the soft, light fabric of Udele's gown and causing it to billow. I must hasten, she thought. I must take myself to Anselm quickly. He will come to me when Edwina is buried and have need of my comfort. He will soon see there is no other more able.

Before the sun was very high in the sky, Udele and Edythe, with horsed men and many servants, were on the road to Anselm.

In the cold of January, when the ground was more like rock than soil and the wind threatened to rip a man's skin from his face, a place was rent in the merciless earth for the body of Lady Edwina de Corbney of Phalen, Stoddard and Anselm. A slow tear touched Medwin's cheek, but that was all the pain he allowed to show. On one side of him stood Sir Conan, and on the other side was Lady Chandra, her husband next to her.

Later, in the quiet of the hall, those same four sat around the lord's table, and with a saddened and quiet mien they partook of an evening meal. Tedric, while cautiously quiet, was the only one who could find his appetite.

"You have delivered the tithe now without beggaring this estate," Conan said to Medwin. "Thanks to Tedric."

"You need not fear for Phalen now, son," Medwin said wearily.

"I do not fear. I know that the money was necessary for you to exist. Should other problems with money arise, I would have you approach my father. I have allowed a substantial sum for emergencies."

Tedric looked up from his food and glared at Conan. Conan returned the stare.

"I am to inherit this land, this keep," Conan continued. "It is not necessary to rely on any other for the help you need."

"You do not trust me even now," Tedric said. "You are advising Medwin to take nothing from me!"

Conan looked at Tedric closely. "Nay, Tedric, I do not trust you. And I do not want you to help Medwin with any matter concerning my estate."

Tedric's jaw twitched in muted anger and Chandra seemed to withdraw slightly in apprehension. Even Medwin was uneasy with the fact that these two men were forced to share a table after the event of Edwina's death.

"My lord," Conan went on. "I ask only one thing of you. In times of trouble, seek out my father or Galen. Either would work hard and honestly to preserve this estate for me."

Chandra sat a bit straighter in her chair and a look of surprise came over her face.

"And why would I call on them when you are heir to all this?"

"Because I leave shortly to join Richard. I will go to war."

"Now?" Medwin choked. "Now, when so much rests on your management?"

"Aye, now. My father grows old, but he commands a strong army still. And Stoddard has benefited from my labors and is a fit place for Galen to learn his duties. As for Phalen, your army is not weak and you can hold this hall. Should that prove difficult, my father and brother will support you."

"But 'tis your presence in England that gives me peace of mind!"

"My presence?" Conan asked with a raised brow. "Nobles who once praised my skills call me coward now. And my strong arm here is abused. While I am anxious to serve, I have found myself used as an errand boy for two aging lords, and a lame bird to be mocked before my fellow knights. I could not leave England while Edwina was heavy with child; but she is gone, God rest her soul. And I have a matter to settle with myself — lest I come to doubt my own worth."

Medwin raised his tired eyes to Conan and nodded. "There is nothing here for you now, is there, son?"

Conan looked at Chandra, then Tedric. He returned his gaze to Medwin. "I do not take the concerns of my inheritance lightly, my lord, but wealth has never been of supreme importance to me. There is much I cherish here, I cannot deny that. But what is worth holding will keep faithful until my return."

Chandra raised crystalline blue eyes to meet his. A faint and almost imperceptible smile touched her lips. Conan felt the comfort of her support. Any love that was true would not vanish with his leaving. Love would wait faithfully — as would battles to be fought.

Medwin sighed and rose. "My youth is not so long past that I cannot remember the stirrings of a young man. I hope you find what you seek."

"I would take your blessings into battle, my lord, rather than your reluctance to see me go."

The old man moved to Conan's side of the table and dropped an arm about his shoulders. "I cannot give you men, but there are some things you might take with you. Come and look at the leather goods kept with the horses. Those who will pledge to ride with you will have need of sturdy stuff."

The two walked together to the rear of the keep. Chandra looked down at her hands and felt the tears collect in her eyes, but she did not dare let Tedric see. She longed to wish Conan well, to promise her prayers.

Tedric gave a short laugh and looked at her. "Your hero is leaving you."

Chandra stiffened. "Does this not finally convince you that he has no great longing for me?"

Tedric laughed outright. "Do not let your pain at his parting show, ma chère. He goes now because there is nothing he can do to have you. But Conan is never long without a plan. Perhaps he thinks that riches and fame won in war will allow him a better chance at wresting you away from me when he returns — if he returns."

"Your jealousy and greed eat at you, Tedric. He does not need to return to battle you: you will meet your own end through all this evil —"

He grasped her arm tightly, and she was stilled and forced to look into his steely gray eyes. "There is no one here to protect you, chérie," he said slowly. "Have a care with your words."

Galen rode swiftly to meet his brother at an inn in Canterbury, following the message from his brother allowing for his rather premature release from the service of Sir Boswell. He walked with a proud gait, his head held high. He was certainly a de Corbney. Conan saw him enter the common room and look about. As Conan approached him, Galen gave a sign of greeting and then fell to one knee before his brother. Conan's hand on his shoulder and a gentle but firm command bade him rise.

"You are young, Galen. Not yet five and ten. But you are strong. Sir Boswell speaks well of your talents."

Galen smiled in embarrassed pride.

"You are too young to be knighted," Conan said.

"If I work hard I will gain that honor by eighteen." And then more quietly he added, "As you did."

Conan laughed lightly. "But we have not the time. Are you prepared to pledge your fealty to Richard our king, myself and our father?"

His mouth slightly agape, Galen could do nothing but nod the affirmative.

"You will shortly take my place at Stoddard Keep until such a time as a proper castellan can be installed there. As for Lord Alaric, you must serve Anselm at his whim. In good time, Sir Medwin may have need of you: I have asked him to seek out you or our father in times of crisis, for that land is mine. You see, Galen, you must continue to learn as you rule. It will not be an easy task, but one I believe you capable of."

"Conan, who will follow me?"

"Any man who loves or fears me. The first you will find easily. The latter will find you."

"Is the need so great that I am called home to give you aid?"

"You will be my aid, Galen, to be sure, but I will not be near enough to counsel you. When you are installed on our home ground as our father's strong arm, I will leave for France. From there I will go with King Richard to the Holy Land." He smiled proudly. "When I am returned, you will have to share your empire with me."

Galen's eyes grew wide. He would protect these lands for Conan. Or die trying.

Before the Archbishop of Canterbury, Galen was knighted, one of the youngest ever. Then Conan made his pledge and oath to the Cross. Before leaving for Anselm, Conan discarded his faithful colors and donned the gray of the Crusaders, with the white cross covering his chest.

The total number of men-at-arms serving Anselm and Stoddard together totaled about three hundred. Of these,

Conan would take twenty of the strongest and most willing, along with horses and the instruments of their profession.

The banner that was raised as the small party reached the gates of Anselm Keep was not that of the Blue Falcon, but of the Cross. The gates were opened immediately, for the soldiers of the Cross would always be admitted. Lord Alaric and Lady Udele stood in the courtyard ready to greet the Crusaders.

As Conan and Galen dismounted at a fair distance from their parents, a slow smile formed on Alaric's face. He stood tall and easy as the men approached, one wearing the red and blue of Anselm and the other wearing the Cross.

Udele's eyes widened and she slowly shook her head in silent denial. He was to stay in England, ready to take on the lands of nobles and landholders who did not survive the war! Now, without a sickly wife to hold him back, he would finally be able to pursue the acquisition of lands! Her lips formed a silent no. The color drained from her face as a new thought came to her: if he did not survive the Crusade, there would be nothing! Nothing! Before her husband noticed or her sons reached her, she fell to the ground in a faint.

Eight men already selected from the guard at Stoddard Keep arrived as prearranged with horses and gear to travel with Conan to Vézelay. Twelve of Anselm's finest prepared for the journey as well, offering Conan his troop of twenty sound knights. All was in readiness within two weeks' time.

In the short time that it took Conan to prepare to leave, Udele began to look her years. She would not bid her son a decent farewell and refused to give her blessings to a war that would not promise profit and risked death.

"Do not be concerned," Alaric told his son. "She fears for you as any mother would and will be praying for your safety before the sun sets on this day."

"Edwina, God rest her, would have yielded to my leaving with more grace than madam shows," Conan said.

"And it was Edwina's passing that made your decision final?" Alaric asked.

"The pain of her death was greater than I could ever have foreseen," Conan said softly. "And she died knowing that my name was despoiled before my kind — before my king. For her devotion I must reclaim my good name. I cannot hold what is mine when no credence is given to my honor or strength. When I am returned I will finish what business I have left undone."

Tired blue eyes crinkled at the corners in an affectionate smile. "You have found the man you must serve with the greatest loyalty," Alaric said. "You have found yourself." Alaric grasped Conan's upper arms. "Go with God! Return victorious!"

PART

III

CHAPTER
16

THE rains washed away the memory of winter, but for those who had suffered more privation than ever before, the easing of the weather with spring did not heighten their hopes. The energetic smiles that had once greeted those who entered the small hamlet of Cordell were gone, and now the village looked as many others, its citizens moving through their chores and duties without much pleasure or satisfaction. Sir Tedric had proved to be a leader bereft of compassion and decency. During the cold winter, he had collected a heavy tax to pay the scutage that freed him from service in the Crusade, and had hoarded the winter supply of food, yielding nothing to make the villeins more comfortable. His discipline was swift and harsh and his guards were as cruel as he was.

Chandra felt her strength begin to slip away many times, but she mustered her reserves and attempted to show courage if only for the sake of her people. Everywhere she looked she saw evidence of Tedric's selfishness. Her people were left wanting and frightened. While she could not undo the trouble her husband had caused, she did what she could to encourage them all to endure and wait for a better day.

As she leaned over the small pond in the Cordell gardens, she looked at her face. She had not lived so very many years, and the bruise from her husband's hand in one of his recent rages was healed, but her face had changed. Etched in the fine, delicate features, she could see the passing of her sister, the slow deterioration of her father as he learned of her miseries, and the slow destruction of the home she loved and cherished. And more closely, in the deep blue eyes, she could see the sad memory of sending a lover off to war. She turned away from what she saw. Her beauty was not marred, but what emotional wounds lay beneath the flawless skin would take a long time to heal.

"Lady," Wynne said softly.

Chandra looked up to find the maid standing near, twisting her hands and looking down. Chandra stood and lifted her chin with a finger, looking into the innocent brown eyes. "Raise your eyes, Wynne, and straighten your back. Of all, you are least responsible for what has befallen you."

"It will take time, lady," she said softly.

"You have your dignity as long as you cling to it. Remember that."

"Aye, lady," she murmured, her eyes lowering, a habit for her now.

"Wynne," Chandra insisted, "do not face me with your shame. I too feel shame, for I was unable to protect you. Had I sent you far from here the moment I suspected Tedric's lust, I could have spared you."

"I do not blame you, lady. You could not have done more."

"He is gone now?" Chandra asked.

"Aye. He has only just left."

"Did he take many of his men?"

"A goodly number. More than I would have guessed. A dozen, perhaps."

"We have that much to be thankful for. With so many of his brothers gone to war, Theodoric has need of him more often. And there is always hope that his father will see his wicked ways —"

"He does not go to Theodoric," Wynne said. "I heard him tell one of his riders that the message was not from his father."

Chandra looked perplexed. "Do you know where he has gone?"

"Nay, he did not say while I was near enough to hear. Lady —" Wynne started softly, unsure.

"Hold up your head, Wynne. You must be strong. Someday you will have your revenge."

"I do not seek revenge," she said timidly, tears smarting in her eyes.

"Do not fear him, Wynne," Chandra ordered. "If he sees your fear he will take pleasure in frightening you."

"I do not fear him, lady. I fear God."

Chandra laughed lightly and stroked the girl's arm. "Even God would not condemn you for hating him, lass."

Brown eyes bright with tears looked into caring blue. "Even if I carry his child?"

Chandra's shock was evident. But she should have expected this much. That Tedric had robbed the lass of her virginity weighed heavily enough on her mind: she had not even considered a child. The fact that she had not come with child herself as a result of their intimate encounters, however infrequent, had removed that worry from her mind.

She reached out and touched the hand that hung limp at Wynne's side. She smiled kindly. "If there is a child, in spite of the sire, he will be only as good as his mother's love. Do not despair," she said, smiling even though this news brought pain to her heart. "Do not despair now, while there is a child growing within you. Now you must be strong and proud — if you wish your child to be."

Wynne looked into Chandra's eyes. "My father, lady. I fear his anger once this is known."

Chandra sighed. "I stayed his vengeance once; I will try to do so once more."

In the afternoon of that very day, Chandra donned her mantle and covered her golden locks with the snood. She left the warmth of the hall and made her way into the village streets. More men than usual were visible during this time of year. Cordell's protective scheme was at a disadvantage during the winter months when the foliage in the forest was meager, but during the cold months the men stayed mostly in their homes. Now, while the rain drenched the wood and new leaves began to show, there were many in the village to help with the planting. Soon, as the protection of the new foliage concealed those in the wood, only those unable to act as guard would till the land. The able-bodied men would go into the forest.

Women were seen kneeling in the dirt to tend the tiny seedlings carefully. Whereas through the winter months the animals shared the shelters with their owners, now the children drove the animals farther out to their pastures. Monks from the neighboring monasteries began bringing their carts into the town again, offering to trade or sell their religious relics, carvings, animals and homegrown vegetables for things they needed. Their appearance brought the villagers into the streets to hear what news would be brought from neighboring cities and towns.

Wynne's father, William, was not really a knight — not in the true sense of the word. He was spoken of as Master William around Tedric and the other guard, but the people who knew he led the forest guard respectfully prefaced his given name with "Sir." He had earned at least that much, Chandra thought ruefully.

William's dwelling could be found at the farthest edge of the town, and there he would be tilling the land and watching over what little livestock grazed nearby. Chandra found him thus and quietly approached him as he worked. When he turned to see her, he bowed.

"I would have come at your call, my lady," he told her quickly.

"I know that, William." She smiled. "I chose to come myself rather than send for you." She looked around her. His humble home was not rich, but was kept in a good state of repair. He had made neat rows in his garden in preparation for planting, and a goat stood tied to his fence. Leather flaps were the only guard against the cold entering his windows, and the roof was recently reinforced with fresh sod. He cared meticulously for what he owned and obviously took pride in this humble acreage. "Will you offer me a cup and a seat?"

"Here, lady?"

" 'Tis your home, William. I would be honored."

He shrugged, somewhat surprised. It was not unusual for the lord and lady of the manor to venture into the village to view the commoners' way of life, but to pay a social call was quite rare. Proudly he led her into the small hut and brushed the crumbs from his morning meal onto the floor, offering her the only chair at a modest trestle table and taking the stool for himself. There was a pitcher on the table filled with ale, rather bitter and stale, but the best he could offer. "I have no fine cups, m'lady," he apologized.

"Take up your own and I will use another."

He poured what remained of the last user's ale onto the
rushes and set the cup before her, filling hers and his own
to the brim. On a board on the table sat bread and cheese,
and in a wooden bowl was honey. He gestured with his
hand that she should indulge.

Chandra picked up the bread already cut from the loaf
and dipped a corner into the honey, tasting it slowly. It
was stale and dry, and the honey contained a few of the
usual pests, drawn there by the sweetness. She daintily
removed those she cared not to eat and chewed, washing it
down with a sip of ale.

William joined her in taking a bite of cheese and bread,
grinding it much more easily, for he was accustomed to its
hardness. His, in fact, was one of the finer homes and his
table more generous than most. He watched her slowly,
wondering what matter brought her here. She might have
him think this a pleasant social call, but he knew better.

They sat thusly for several moments, chewing and drinking, Chandra politely admiring some things about his
home and he thanking her for her compliments.

"You have acquired some comforts for your family,
William. You must be proud of what you have."

"My family has lived comfortably. We have been content."

"Has my family aided you in any way to accomplish all
that you have?" she asked coyly.

"Aye, lady, you know that. Without the confidence your
mother placed in me I would be naught but a simple
farmer here. I owe your family a great deal."

She reached out and touched his hand, and he felt the
dark stain of a blush rise to his cheeks. He had never
touched a noble lady but to aid her in mounting her horse
or help her in some other way. Certainly never with affec-

tion, as she touched him now. "There is no debt, William. Your loyal service and great strength have helped me and mine, and in times of trouble you have been my most dependable vassal." She took a breath and looked at him for a moment. His eyes were bright with anticipation. He knew she was leading to a serious confrontation. "I bring you news that will be most difficult to bear. I ask you to summon your strength."

He nodded once, his eyes narrowing.

"Your daughter, Wynne, is with child."

The lines on his face deepened as he clenched his eyes and mouth tightly. Finally he looked at her again.

"You come to me in friendship like this," he said slowly, "in hopes that my rage can be quenched by your —"

"I come to you in friendship! And the rage I hope to subdue is not for my sake, but for yours. And the people of Cordell."

"Do you deny that this village would be better off with Sir Tedric gone?" he shouted, his fist hitting the small table with such force that the cup holding Chandra's ale tipped and spilled onto her mantle. She ignored the spill and quickly covered his clenched fist with her own small, white hand and looked beseechingly into his eyes.

"An arrow from the forest can end Tedric and remove him from this burgh, and who would know from whence it came?" she asked urgently, reading the man's mind more accurately than she could know. "But it will not take the stain of Wynne's defilement from her, nor will the child she carries vanish. It would remove one villain, William, and leave us one much worse — the sin of killing."

"This was once a good and peaceful place," he said.

"It will be a good place again. With God's help."

William turned and looked at his lady. She was not very much older than his own Wynne, and she looked meek and frail, an illusive covering to the strength he knew her to have. Indeed, she had borne much of the insult of Tedric's cruelty on her own tender frame, without complaint or tears.

"Do you fear I will act out my rage and slay your lord husband before the sun lowers in this day's sky?"

"Nay, William. Sir Tedric is gone and will not return for many days."

"So, you hope to see my temper cooled while he is gone."

She nodded. "But I have held no secret from you, William. Wynne came to me only this morn."

He nodded, but he could find no words to pledge to Tedric's safety.

Chandra knew better than to expect more than a curt nod from a man so greatly wronged. She pulled her mantle about her and rose. William stepped away from the door to allow her departure, marveling inwardly at the poise she could maintain even in this troubled time of her life.

As she left the little hut he watched her. At the edge of his small lot she turned and looked back at him. They communicated with their eyes for a moment and William knew he could never defy her. She owned him as totally as he could be bound. He was tethered to her. And to Cordell.

"You are well schooled in duty, William," she said. "I am also. But I can no more forgive this wrong than I can forget my duty." And she turned to go, not looking back at her most loyal vassal.

William stood at the gate and watched her walk away. She stopped suddenly and William saw her look up. He followed her gaze to see a falcon rise in the sky. It could be some farmer's bird or even one of the keep's own falcons, but to Chandra it must have reminded her of something more. She watched it for a long moment until it flew farther and the sight of it was blocked by the rising walls of Cordell Keep. She crossed herself and moved on.

"Aye, lady," William said to her vanishing form. "I, too, pray for his safety. If there is any hope for this burgh, it is in the Blue Falcon."

When Lent is past, Chandra thought just before drifting off to sleep, I will send word to Edythe and invite her for a visit. But as the thought came, she quickly dismissed it. She could not allow Edythe here. Tedric would likely take great pleasure in having a captive guest whom Conan treasured. Just as she· had failed to protect Wynne, she could not protect Edythe. And with Lady Udele watching over Anselm closely, would the message even reach Edythe? The walls between them were built tall and stoutly.

Perhaps I can make a pilgrimage to the convent and bring my love to Laine. But that thought, too, was struck away. Tedric had not allowed her to travel even to a nearby town without his escort, so afraid was he that she would flee from him. If he did not have business near the convent, he would not be pleased to take her. And there was not much to draw him to Thetford.

She sighed in peaceful rest. For this brief space of time that Tedric was away she could sleep without worry. She needn't fear that some member of the village had been unjustly punished, and she knew Wynne was safe in her bed. She closed her eyes on a long day and turned her mind to her prayers.

"Father, forgive my many sins and be my father's

strength. Forgive his error and give him peace in his old age: he sought not to hurt me or these good people. Give Edwina's soul rest and let her not be restless in her grave. O Lord, forgive my weakness, and even so, protect the Falcon. Make his eyes sharp and his hand quick! Let him move within Your care and keep him safe. . . ." Her mind fell from prayers and into dreams as the mists of early spring enveloped the keep and the fires grew dimmer.

A rock on the seaside slipped and bounced to the water below, down a long drop of cliff.

A tower guard jumped. "What was that?"

"I heard nothing," the other replied.

For a few moments they were quiet and tense, waiting for another suspicious sound, but nothing came. The crickets in the wood sang their nighttime song, and the keep soldiers did not find their slumber disturbed.

A chill breeze invaded the bedchamber of the lady of the manor. Chandra unconsciously pulled her cover closer about her. She was not cold. A feeling encompassed her and her eyes slowly opened. She looked into the burning blue eyes of a memory that could not be dissolved in her mind — his thick, dark hair curling about his face and his beard stiff and thick, parting only to show the bright smile that she remembered from happier days. Her hand moved to touch him, her fingers feeling the white Crusader's Cross on his tunic.

"You are cruel to invade my dreams so often, my love," she whispered faintly.

The image would fade and blend into a familiar fantasy of what life might have held for her had her lover not —

But her hand was held in one much larger, warm and

secure against his sturdy chest. He squeezed her fingers gently and then brought them to his lips. The crisp beard and moist lips could not be mere imagination.

Her eyes opened and her lips parted in astonishment, for if he was not real, it was by far the most vivid dream she had ever known. She dared not speak lest she break this unearthly spell. She needed, more than ever in her life, to be near him.

His arms came around her and his mouth lowered to hers. She drank in the deepness of his kiss, straining against him, moving against the insistent mouth with an urgency of her own. She tasted his mouth and caressed the bold, mailed chest, finally bringing her hands to lock into the thick hair at the base of his neck. She was filled with his entire essence: the smell of the wool, leather and horses, the taste of him, the warmth of his breath in her mouth.

Tears coursed down her cheeks and fell into her hair. A sob escaped her and her breath came in ragged spasms. Her breasts, pressed hard against his mail, smarted from the desperation with which he held her.

When he released her mouth she reached for his face with shaking fingers, marveling that he had not faded into the midnight mists. "You are real," she sighed in a weak whisper.

"Real," he murmured.

"Hold me," she begged, hungry for the protection of his arms. But that security lasted only a moment before she broke away and looked at him with wide eyes. "There is danger in coming here," she whispered.

"Your door is bolted."

"More than that," she breathed. "If you are found here —"

"I will fight, in that case. I could not leave you without a proper farewell."

"Tedric is not here," she confided.

"I know that. More the pity. I should like having him find me here. I would take more pleasure than is right in killing him."

She shook her head sadly. "If he learns you have been here, he will likely kill me."

"He would not dare. I would come from hell to see him pay. He knows this well. He claims you only because he wants to keep you from me. How he knows that I desire you is a mystery to me."

"Who knows you are here?" she asked, fearing the whole village guarded a secret that could change the course of her life.

"Only Sir William. And he would die before confessing."

Again the tears came, and she closed her eyes against his image. He touched her cheeks and hair, gently brushing the moistness away. "I cannot stay you, Conan," she breathed.

"I know," was his soft reply.

"I have no will left. It has been torn away. I cannot deny you."

"Don't. Don't deny me. There have been years of restraint, never yielding. Has it earned us reprieve or grace? You are bound to a man who does not love you but uses you. I have buried a wife and am bound to war. What more could be dealt us now? Chandra," he moaned, clutching her to him, "what has happened to us? We have loved since the first and were never given our day! We suffered and refused to commit the greater sin, holding all that we felt from each other! Has there been any reward for such strength and conviction?" He looked closely into her eyes and let his lips rest lightly on hers. "Yield," he whispered hoarsely.

Her tears were gone and the trembling that possessed her now was of a different emotion. She relaxed into the pillows, and a smile, tender and loving, graced her lips. He released her gently and moved away from her to struggle out of the heavy mail and chausses, soft leather boots and spurs. When he stood again at the side of her bed in all his naked majesty, she glowed at the beauty of his body. His tall and sturdy frame was not only a result of the burdensome clothing of his profession: he was as awesome bereft of his clothing.

As he leaned over her again, all thoughts of restraint fled her mind and she opened her arms to him. A fever of passion such as she had never known filled her. His hands on her brought to life a dream that had been nurtured in the private chambers of her mind, and so quickly that there was no conscious thought leading to the act, she was all of him and he was all of her. Blended together in body and spirit, there was a power to their lovemaking that rivaled the crashing of the sea against the rocks below.

As if the greatest hunger were finally nourished, the driest thirst quenched, they lay together, touching that tender ground so often dreamt of but never walked

"Are we truly miles removed from each other and only dreaming the same dream?" she whispered.

"For once it is not so," he returned. He raised himself on an elbow and looked down into her eyes. In the dimness of the room he could see the gloss of tears. "Love, do not weep. The blame is mine —"

"Blame? I do not weep for something lost, Conan, but for what I've found. Could I have pain from the only touch of love I have known? Could I feel anger for the only joy I have felt? Oh, love, I weep for the beauty of a moment — and the pain of parting."

"Then you must hold the moment," he told her. "You must keep the memory safe in your heart, and it will come again. On my word, Chandra, I will find a way."

She shook her head sadly. "I fear to hope for so much."

He lowered himself and touched her lips softly, weaving his fingers through her hair. "Our time is brief," he said against her lips. "But our joy will be great, and the bond is forever. Hold dear what little we have, love, and hope. I swear, I will find a way."

"So much stands between —"

He silenced her with his lips, his hand making one long caress of her body, her flesh coming to life under his touch.

"You tremble, love," he whispered in her ear.

"Conan," she groaned. "Do not leave me soon . . . Do not leave me too soon . . ."

"Eternity would be too soon," he returned.

The weight of his body pressed her down, and his lips traced a fiery path along her flesh. The thirst returned, the hunger raged, and she answered him with a passion wild, a side of herself she had not known existed. His laughter echoed from deep in his throat as he tasted her response. A glow from his touch covered her, tortured her, consumed, devoured — and was spent. As if their two souls had been entwined, she feared to release him.

"The sky will lighten soon," he said.

"How did you manage your entrance?" she asked.

"Easily, through the lord's chamber."

"You should not attempt the halls, Conan. Since Tedric's coming, there are guards posted."

"I did not come through the halls. I came from Tedric's balcony, across the cliffs."

Her eyes grew round as she considered the drop had he lost his footing for even an instant. The balconies were twins, but separated by a distance equal to a man's height. Every consideration was given to protection during the building of the manor house. If any attempt was to be made on the town from the sea, there was no place to bring up a boat near the manor or town. The only suitable entrance was much farther up the coast, and that stretch of coastline was watched by the fishermen.

Conan shared Chandra's concern. The climb he had made was precarious indeed. "I will stay for a few days. Can you come to me from now on?"

"How will I find you?"

"Make your way to the wood. I will find you."

"I am chaperoned on my every excursion, whether to the wood or shore, but I will find a way. But how have you come? Word was that you were preparing forces in France."

"Aye. Even now if I am missed it will be difficult to explain. But we are safe. Richard does not concentrate heavily on my whereabouts, and I left my men in good company. Time is short, love."

"I never dreamt there would be this much."

"This could be all we'll have, love, until I have found the way to claim you."

"Conan," she started, perplexed, "if you truly love me as you say, why have you chosen war?"

"What will Tedric do while I am in England? While I am able to protect my possessions? He would hold you fast and take pleasure in my envious stare. But if I am gone from here, holding you from me will lose its flavor. When I return we will set this troubled destiny aright."

"You must return, Conan," she breathed.

"Do you think even the angel of death could keep me from you now?"

"Please," she begged. "Go quickly."

He rose to find his clothing, carelessly scattered, and donned the chausses, mail and tunic as quickly as he could. He returned to her side to place a soft kiss on her lips. "The wood," he breathed.

"The wood," she murmured.

She watched him go through the door that would lead to the lord's chamber and then to the balcony. She went quickly to her own balcony, the breeze from the sea chilling her naked body. When he appeared on the opposite balcony she raised a hand to him. She watched as he climbed carefully over the balustrade and clung like a spider to the ridges in the stone wall of Cordell Keep. From there he would have to scale a thin and delicate ridge of rock high above a still inlet of water. She could not see him because of the darkness and would not hear him if he fell because of the noise of the sea below. She would not consider that he might not succeed. She sighed deeply and returned to her bed.

There was a new flush on Chandra's cheeks. She was careful not to smile more quickly than usual at the villagers. In the forest, no fire could be made to warm the night. A meager hut, an inadequate tent covered with branches, was the easily hidden home for their clandestine meetings. With Wynne as her accomplice, Chandra drew no notice to her absence at night. The maid closed the lady's door early in the evening and took a place in the large and comfortable bed. At morning's first dawning,

before all the castle folk had risen, Wynne would walk
the distance to her father's house with a basket on her arm.
Within, there would be a clean kirtle, of a color noticeably
different from the one Chandra had worn the day before.
Before the inhabitants of the keep would join together
to break the fast, Chandra would have returned.

The bed they shared was the ground, the closeness
natural. When the sounds from the forest animals warned
that dawn would be breaking, Chandra would slowly
rouse. Most often she would find Conan's eyes already on
her, the cover of animal skins that kept them warm
pulled away.

"You never sleep," she accused.

"Nay. There is no time for sleep. I study you. I must
remember the way your eyes look when you awake, the way
your skin glows in the darkness, and especially the way
you reach for me. I must never forget that even in your
sleep you reach for me."

"It is morning, Conan. Will you walk with me to the
stream?"

"I watched you once as you washed beside a stream."

She questioned him with her eyes.

"When we journeyed to Cordell from Phalen. The
one night that we made camp I rose early and followed
the sounds of your women. They helped to conceal you
with a linen wrap, but from where I stood their cover did
no good. I could not find the will to turn away."

"Conan," she scolded. "You spied on me!"

He leaned back and put a hand to his brow. "Aye, and
the sight caused me to ache for days. What torture the
sight of you brought me."

She pulled herself to her feet, trying to suppress a
laugh, and picked up the cover of skins to keep herself

warm as she walked to the stream. " 'Twas a misery of your own making," she said playfully. "You should not have been spying."

She moved away from their shelter and through some shrubs to reach for her basket. When she knelt to retrieve it she felt Conan's presence close behind her.

"William is a good servant," Conan said. "I do not hear him come or go."

She stood, but her eyes were downcast. "I am certain it is a hateful task for him," she said softly. "William would not easily be drawn into such a sin."

Conan lifted her chin with a finger. "He showed me the way to reach your chamber. He offered his aid, love, and will not remember seeing a strange knight in the wood."

"I cannot bear to see it end," she said. "I knew it long ago: that a fine manor and wealth meant nothing. I have known more joy sleeping on the ground than I have ever felt in the warmth of my chamber. Conan, without this, there would be nothing for me; there would be no way I could hope."

"Be thankful this once that King Richard and King Philip quarrel so often. At least we do not leave from France at Easter. But soon. And I must return to Vézelay to be ready."

"Had Edwina lived, you would not go," she said.

"Perhaps not," he admitted. "But to fight well for Richard can in no manner hurt me. He is not fond of men with no taste for fighting."

Chandra looked at the modest hut in the wood. Mars was tied to the perch within and Orion was tethered to a bush outside. It was the meagerest dwelling she'd ever visited, but it would have contented her for the rest of her days. She touched his cheek. "And you have a strong penchant for fighting."

"Nay," he said. "For winning."

On a crisp morning after the most rudimentary tasks had been accomplished within the great stone house, Chandra went to the garden to inspect the clearing and pruning she had ordered done. Her heart raced in anticipation of the evening. Every nighttime flight into the wood she feared would be her last. Though they had both refused to shorten the beauty of the moment with promises or farewells, she knew there would be no denying the necessity of parting phrases. Three days would bring Easter. The morrow was Good Friday. Tedric would likely return and Conan would have to go.

In his coming, she thought, he has given me reason to endure and to hope. He has delivered me the love I have been wanting and he has risked his life to secure what moments could be ours — perhaps the only ones in all of eternity. He must know I am grateful. He must know he has been the only joy I have known. And though it will hurt me to tell him, he must know that I will not bind him to what has passed between us. He has made no promise to free me from Tedric's bonds, and if I am to be forever tied to that unworthy knight, what we have shared will be enough.

I will not cry, nor will I cling to him. He goes to do what he must, what he has been bred and trained to do. I must tell him that I trust his life to God, that I am not afraid. Even, heaven help me, even if he is snatched from me now, I have had that which I longed for, and my life is richer and fuller because of it. I will make him believe in my strength as he believes in his own, and in a moment of heated battle he will not be plagued by fear that I cannot survive his absence.

Before another day is spent, I will tell him all that I feel. I will give him words of hope and love to carry onto a field of battle. I will bid him farewell and promise that come what may, he will have my heart and my prayers. Before another day —

"Lady," Wynne's gentle voice beckoned.

She looked up, startled, wondering if she had been talking aloud.

"Sir Tedric, lady. His banner approaches."

She jumped to her feet and raced to the hall. Through the galleries and chambers she flew to the door of the keep. She could see the soldiers, some twelve perhaps, who had ridden with Tedric. She twisted her hands into her gunna and looked toward the wood for some sign of Conan, but of course there was none. In a panic, she felt the urge to flee to him quickly before Tedric was upon her. She could travel with him to the ends of the earth; a bed on the ground with him would be more desirable than a fine bed with Tedric. Enduring war would be easier than living with Sir Tedric. She could stay in France, perhaps, and await his return . . .

But even before the knight's party was near enough to see her standing in the door, she realized it was impossible for her to leave. She could not turn her back on the people here. She was their only protection from Tedric. Without her to stay him, he would leave nothing but a wasted land where a thriving village had once stood.

She fought for composure. She was not a fool. She did not smile as Tedric dismounted and came near her. He would not be impressed by such a show, and by the looks of him it was plain he was not pleased to see her.

"Did you see your father?"

His grimace was sour, his manner angry. "Never mind my business, dear lady. Just be glad that I am home."

"Whatever, it must have been an unpleasant chore," she ventured, more than a little suspicious as to what Tedric might be up to now. But he would not stand for her questioning of him. He brushed past her and his men followed.

She looked down the road, past the houses and fields toward the wood, straining to catch a glimpse of a horse and rider, or even a man standing alone among the trees. And then her eyes found the message she sought. The falcon soared high into the air, and a whistle, shrill and loud, split through the trees. The great wings of the bird folded, and it dove into the wood, disappearing from sight. Just as Mars signaled her that Conan had come, so he signaled his departure.

A tear fell from her eye. "Be safe," she breathed, the ache in her chest leaving her barely enough strength to return to the hall.

CHAPTER
17

THE scent of Easter flowers filled the air. The mass was sung and the villeins brought eggs to their lord as was the custom. From Easter until Hocktide, a week following, the villagers were freed from their labors. They ceased their farming and fishing chores. Other duties, however, were worked out in the privacy of village homes late at night. Master William brought tidings of his plans to the lady of the manor.

"We've begun to move men into the forest, lady. Younger men that could wait another year plan to go, unless you bid me otherwise."

"As long as the fields can be worked, take the number of men you deem necessary. Make their numbers unknown, as far as that is possible."

"What will your reward be for deceiving him?" William asked.

Chandra took a deep breath and looked directly into his eyes. "I imagine he will beat me soundly."

"There needs to be protection for you in this hall —"

"But there is not. Just protect our town from the wood."

"If he lays a hand to you —"

"If I am not here to give you orders," she snapped, cutting him off, "you have my leave to do whatever you must to preserve Cordell." She calmed her voice and went on with more composure. "Until that day, let us take care not to start a family war."

William lowered his eyes and spoke softly. "You have reason to fear Tedric."

"I have reason to be wary, William. I do not fear him yet."

"Do you know where he was on his last journey?" William asked.

"Nay, he would not say. Up to no good, I am certain."

"I cannot say that Sir Tedric played a part in it, but there was rioting in Bury Saint Edmunds on Palm Sunday. Many Jews were slain. There was great destruction."

Chandra's eyes grew large as she considered the possibility. Tedric would do anything, including being a party to murder and rioting, to ally himself with nobles he thought powerful. Should Theodoric learn of his association with such men, the family support would quickly vanish. On the other hand, for Chandra to bring such an accusation against him without proof would only make matters worse between them.

"It chafes Tedric no small bit that the people of this village take their orders from me. Keep your suspicions quiet for now. Go, do your work, and bring your news to me here — when Tedric is not in the hall."

The village was now divided between two armies: a man's army to protect and serve him, and his wife's army to do the same for her.

She stood in thought, watching the sea. Beyond its vastness Richard's army would be bound. She knew not when. Perhaps they were already setting out. Perhaps there was yet another delay and they were still safe in France. She crossed herself and mumbled a quick prayer.

I must remember every word, she thought, every touch. I must not forget the smallest detail. You will be so far away, my love, and even if fate betrays us again, already I know that you live on —

The door to her chamber opened and she whirled in anger at the intruder. It seemed she could not call the slightest moment her own, with all the problems laid upon her by so many people unable to think for themselves.

As Tedric stepped into the room she relaxed her scowl. He, of course, would not knock. It was not because she had invited him to come and go as he pleased, but because he used this aggravating habit to show his ownership.

"What can I help you with, my lord?" she asked.

"You can tell me when these churls will be working. Everywhere I look I see the lazy dolts leaning on fences and sleeping in the sun."

Chandra turned back to the sea. She was grateful for this much: if she must be prisoner, at least she was being held in bondage in Cordell, where she had the sea, and the forest . . .

"Do you have an answer for me, madam?"

"The answer is the same, Tedric. The villagers must be allowed their holidays, especially the church days and saints' days. They are broken enough."

"They live like kings —"

She whirled back to him. "They live much more poorly than they were accustomed. True, this has been a rich burgh and the people have had more than many a poorer town, but you have already taken more from them than they are in the habit of giving."

"I cannot be blamed for the taxes that —"

"Taxes? Or the high fee you pay to be allowed the

luxury of resting on your manor while other nobles go to war to —"

A hand came out hard against her cheek, wrenching her neck and sending her reeling into the doorframe.

"And tell me, my fine lass: what is England to do while all of its finest trot off to give their lives in a fruitless battle? And is a man not a man unless he loves war? Jackasses, all of them, for they will surely die. Indeed, few will survive the journey!"

She caught her breath and stared at him, her mind raging that it would not be so. They had a good cause and they were strong.

He laughed cruelly at her indignant stance. "Fear not, damsel," he taunted. "I would rush to you with the word of Sir Conan's death. We shouldn't have to wait very long."

She closed her eyes as if that would block out his words.

"I shall have to leave you again, madam," he said. Her eyes opened. Almost too happily, she gave him her attention, but there was a gnawing fear in her heart that she could not answer. "You look pleased, Chandra. Do you enjoy my absences so much?"

"Where do you go now, Tedric?"

"I go to Normandy for a meeting with Count John."

Her heart skipped a beat. Tales were circling England about what John might be tempted to do while his royal brother fought the Crusade. It seemed that John's reputation was fixed. He was known as a power-hungry liar and opportunist. It would befit his reputation to begin making plans to overthrow the kingdom before Richard was even gone from France.

"Do you think it wise to —"

"Align myself with John?" he asked, stealing her words from her. "With the heir? Wise and profitable, madam. I ask you again: do you think every soldier bitten by the war bug is protected by some heavenly force of arms? Many will die. Richard could well be among them. Being close to the man who will be king one day cannot hurt my cause." He laughed at her horrified expression. "Do you think Cordell alone will be enough to satisfy me? Trust my plan, my love. There will be many a castle without a keeper when the stricken army returns. I plan to be prepared for lordship. I shall use my wit to gain a greater prize."

"I think, Tedric, that you would do anything for wealth and power," she said softly.

He raised one brow, considering her statement. He turned and walked to a bench where a pitcher sat. He poured ale into the only goblet and drank. He would give no answer. He would divulge nothing. She was already aware of much more than he would have her know. He had murdered. He punished harshly in the village, collected more than his due in rents and taxes, snubbed his nose at the church and refused everyone their due.

"Someday, Tedric, someone will stop you."

"Who?" he questioned blandly.

Chandra turned back to the balcony, rubbing her upper arms with her hands as if suddenly chilled. Who, indeed? The people would not dare. Chandra cautioned them to overlook his many shortcomings, and his crimes thus far were unpunished because of lack of proof. To fight him now would bring worse destruction than Tedric could deliver alone. As for the fact that he would strike her without thought and use her badly, she was his wife — his chattel. There was no law to protect her, no one to defend her. Who would stop him?

"Where is Wynne?" he asked curtly. "I would have the lass with me before I leave again."

Chandra turned back to him. "Wynne is with child, Tedric. She is not well. Spare her."

"Perhaps she will fight me less if she is ill," he remarked, walking toward the door.

"She has four brothers in this shire, Tedric. Her father is my head huntsman and has served the lady of Cordell for many years. The family is held in high esteem by all who live here. I have stayed one blade from piercing your breast when you robbed her of her virtue and made her unsuitable for marriage. I stayed that blade another time when I had to tell her family she carries your child." With a hand flung wide, she indicated all outside her chamber. "They do not love you here, Tedric. They serve you only because I caution them against the many deaths that would result if they should fight. Do not delude yourself that you would have an easy victory here."

"You warn me of a handful of farmers?"

"Four hundred in all, all strong from their labors, the men skilled in the use of the bow and hunting knife, knowing the forest as well as they know their fields, and with a will to tear this keep to shreds rather than preserve it for someone who will deprive and torture them on any excuse. Tedric," she snarled, "you are lord here only as long as I am lady. With a word, I could have you slain."

"And your reward for that would be to see this village and every living soul ground to meal. And you! You would not survive it!"

She smiled and met his eyes. "Neither of us would sur-

vive should we come to blows, Tedric. If you are killed,
I will suffer the same fate. And if I am slain, hide yourself
quickly. These people would prefer no village to a village
such as you would have for them."

He grunted and turned away from her, but she would
not leave the matter as it stood. "We sit, you and I, high
upon a wall, the wind blowing and tilting us from side
to side. Your murder will bring mine. Mine, yours. Which
of us will slip and fall first?"

His anger began to dissipate. His scowl relaxed and his
eyes ceased to glitter. "Someday, my fine wife, you will
regret having curbed this power in me now."

He bowed briefly and smiled indulgently. "Have you
won, fair Chandra? One battle for the lady? I will give
Wynne rest for the moment, but I've developed a taste
for her, so don't plan to keep her under your wing for too
very long." He paced about the room restlessly. "I have
no desire to cast about looking for a wench. You may
have one sent to me."

She lowered her eyes. "You have a wife," she muttered.

She did not see his surprised expression, but his startled
laugh came quickly to her ears. "Have I, now?" he asked.
"You offer yourself, Chandra?"

She ground her teeth miserably, wondering how she
could endure his touch, knowing she must. It had been
a very long time since she had shared his bed. "If you
want none of me, Tedric, then go. I will not find a wench
for you to bed."

He leaned against the wall and crossed his arms over
his chest. "Let us see what you have to offer. Take off
your clothes."

Her blue eyes flashed as she looked at him, but there
was no escape. He did not frequent her bed, knowing that

if he used another woman to ease his need it chafed her the more. Yet she needed to submit — to protect herself. And others.

She closed her eyes as she removed her gunna, letting it fall to the floor. Next her kirtle fell and finally the light shift she wore under her garments. She did not hear him approach and she flinched as she felt his hand on her breast. Her eyes flew open to see him watching her closely, studying her every expression.

"Let down your hair," he commanded.

With trembling fingers, she plucked at the ribbons that held her small coil in place, and the lustrous golden locks fell over her shoulders and down her back. A chill breeze caused her to shiver. He gathered a handful of the silky gold in his hand. "Yea, Chandra, you are beautiful. It's no wonder you create battles between men."

She found his eyes. "If only you would profess your love, Tedric —"

"I do not love you, nor have I ever. I take pleasure in owning you because other men want you."

"And what do you want, Tedric?" she asked quietly.

"You cannot give me what I want. But with your help I will have it all. All." He made a sweeping bow and allowed her to lead the way to the bed. Her knees threatened to give way; the journey there was long.

Her breasts, already swollen and tender, ached under his careless touch. She dared not anger him now but lay acquiescent to his will. Yet she refused to show him any eagerness, for he would grow suspicious. That was something she could not fool him with. Instinctively her hands came up against his chest to resist him, and it was enough to arouse his hunger for her. He quickly discarded his clothing and roughly forced her down onto the bed.

He found his greatest pleasure in holding her down and forcing her to meet his will. He enjoyed her struggles, and the gasp of pain she released as he entered her brought a smile to his lips. His lust was quickly spent, and without the briefest kiss or caress, he left her.

She turned her face into her pillow and wept. There was never a decent moment between them. Always, it was some struggle for power or nothing at all. Even being bound to him in marriage did not lessen the insult of his violation. But the pain was something she could endure better now. It was the memory of another man's tender and volatile touch that caused her weeping. And to fix that memory more firmly in her mind came the suspicion that she had conceived and part of him grew even now in her womb.

Great numbers of soldiers had gathered to prepare for the Crusade. The tension of postponed departure times and presence of both French and English knights frequently caused dissension among the troops. To further complicate the situation there were German mercenaries, soldiers speaking yet another language.

Within Richard's own army there were problems, one of which Conan was forced to deal with directly. Because of the rivalry between Conan and Tedric, Conan's troops and those of Theodoric's sons often came to blows.

It was in the summer heat in the camp that the feud came to a peak. Conan was walking from the makeshift stables to his own tent at night. He passed the pavilion of Blair, Theodoric's second son, the mightiest and most successful in knightly skills of all the sons.

As he passed, he heard a sound and saw a man huddling in the darkness beside the tent. Conan stopped, strained to see in the darkness, and kept silent. It was obvious that the culprit was up to no good. A moment later there was the sound of the cutting of cloth. Conan reasoned that the tent in which Blair's gear was stored was being entered, though for what purpose he couldn't guess.

Conan crept up behind the man and, grabbing him by the back of his gamberson, spun him around and pinned him to the ground, striking the knife from his hand. The man gave a shout of surprise before he fell, and a grunt of pain as Conan's knee hit his chest. Then, as Conan looked at the subdued villain, he saw the face of one of his own men.

"What are you doing here?" he demanded angrily.

The man did not answer, but looked up fearfully at Conan. Conan repeated his question, but the answer was more clear now.

"Sir Conan," he pleaded. "He is your *enemy!*"

"*You* are my enemy! You would see this battle drawn to dangerous lengths, two troops fighting among themselves, never able to join together to fight one foe!" He stood and dragged the man to his feet. "Despite my orders you will not cease in goading these knights into a larger battle!"

"Sir Conan, let me go and no one will know," he begged.

Conan looked at the man, one of the best in his troop, and then looked at the tear in Blair's tent. "I will know," Conan said.

Half dragging and half pulling the man to the front of Blair's tent, Conan shouted, "Sir Blair!"

Torches were lit outside the front of Blair's pavilion, and within moments the knight he called stood in the dirt before him, chausses and linen shirt being the only clothing he wore. He looked in some confusion at Conan and the man he held.

"This man would have damaged or stolen from you, Sir Blair. He is one of my own, though he was not ordered to commit this crime." He gave the man a push toward Blair. "He is yours to punish and will not ride with my troop again."

The man fell to his knees before Blair and hung his head. Blair looked down at him, angry but still confused. "How can I be certain this man does not work by your order?"

"I am certain he thought to win my favor by causing your anger, but I have ordered all my men to cease in their bickering with your knights, and the knights of your brothers."

"It is a well-known fact that there is trouble between our families," Blair said scornfully. "The battle has reached France and will likely reach the Holy Land."

" 'Tis not so by my choice," Conan said.

"Yet before long there will be injury and perhaps loss of life. Our animals have been tampered with and there have been fights among our troops."

"I have had like troubles," Conan returned.

"How will you stand behind your claim that none of this is ordered by your hand?"

Conan bowed briefly. "I will accept any challenge you lay to me," he said.

Blair laughed suddenly. He was over thirty years in age and a hulking man of experience. "You've had no trouble in besting Tedric, but we have never ridden against each other, Conan. Do you think I could be as easily beaten?"

"Nay," Conan said evenly. "It would be more difficult."

"Aye," Blair laughed. "I don't deny it would give me great pleasure to take you down."

Conan cocked one brow. He had spoken with these sons of Theodoric when he first came to Vézelay, for he could feel the animosity when he entered the camp. Now he looked at Blair's wide grin and knew that the knight had grown impatient with this feud as well.

"A pleasure because of the accusation I brought against your brother?" Conan asked.

"Nay."

Conan bowed again. "I am at your call."

"The challenge is better placed at another time. I fear it would satisfy too many in our troops to see us come to blows. The charge against Tedric grates on me, as it does on my brothers."

Conan inhaled deeply. "I believed I was right in making the charge. I cannot remove it."

"Neither can you prove it."

"I cannot," he affirmed.

"Then it is best laid away," Blair said. "For the time being we must fight together. What we settle later on English soil will be final." Blair kicked the dirt and formed a cloud of dust. The man before him choked. "Lay the lash to him yourself, at the first light of dawn. I will assemble my men to stand witness, if you will bring your troop. Then banish him from your men-at-arms. That should stop future pranks."

"And you believe Tedric innocent? You will stand by him?"

"He is my brother."

"But you will not oppose me here and now?" Conan asked.

"I knew you as a boy, Conan," Blair said. "It does not

366 , THE BLUE FALCON

sit well with me that you and Tedric must battle as you do, but I have never known you to be unfair or dishonest, even in your youth. You must believe Tedric guilty, though I fear you are mistaken. Yea, I will lay away this feud while we fight a common cause. I think I can convince my brothers to do the same."

Conan nodded. "The man will meet the lash at sunrise."

Conan turned to leave. "Conan," Blair called. Conan turned to look at him again. "I cannot promise what battles we will fight when we return to our homes. Time and old feuds may yet see us raise swords against each other."

Conan looked at the man long and hard, remembering when he had lived in Theodoric's house, remembering the closeness he had shared with all the members of that family. His quarrel with Tedric had torn away at the friendship, but the memory of what it once was had not yet been destroyed.

"Then I will expect you to fight hard and well," Conan said, turning and tugging at the arm of his man.

Edythe knew that the lacemaker in the village was said to have the power of sight and that her mother often visited the shop to hear Giselle's predictions. Like most of the other villagers, Edythe thought it harmless enough. Giselle had even been kind enough to predict some happy events in Edythe's future: a new gown, a present her father would give her.

Early one summer morning, when Udele was preparing to visit the lacemaker, it occurred to Edythe that she had not gone there in quite some time. Edythe scurried to her chamber and fetched her mantle. She had been warned by the village priest that consorting with one who made predictions was a sin, and for that reason she did not dare visit Giselle. Even though her worry over Mallory was constant, she would not give in to the urge to ply Giselle with questions lest her reward be greater danger for Mallory. Edythe was certain that Udele was going to ask after Conan's safety.

Edythe crept quietly along, a great distance behind her mother. Had Udele's mood been even passable she might have asked permission to accompany her, but she feared doing even that small a thing. Udele's moods were variable and unpredictable. One moment she seemed nearly kind and soft-spoken, and in the next breath she was wild with rage. Edythe tried to avoid being in her path for fear of a sudden outburst.

There was a place behind the lacemaker's cottage where Edythe crouched beside a stack of firewood. Through the narrow slit of a window, she could hear her mother's voice.

"I would know of my son's fate in battle, and tell me quickly lest I yield to the urge to strike you mute and senseless."

"Your anger is misdirected, madam," Giselle said easily, her voice smooth and warm in spite of the hostility she faced.

"You could have warned me that this would happen!"

"I could not warn you," Giselle corrected. "I could not see what you would do."

"You told me the wench would not live long! You never told me that Conan would flee to war upon her death!"

"I gave you the truth. Sir Conan would have stayed by Edwina's side through her life. You cut her life short."

There was no sound from Udele. Silence reigned for many moments.

"I could not have spent so many years granting your wishes and reading your future and that of your son without being seared by your deed. I have warned you, madam. You have pushed your mortal power too far in killing your son's wife."

"What difference?" Udele asked with little feeling. "The end would have been the same."

"She would have lived longer than you allowed."

"Never mind, she was spiteful and jealous. She threatened to ruin me in the eyes of my son."

"She was kind and honest. She threatened you with the truth," was the reply. The sharp sound of a stinging slap rang through the small cottage. Edythe jumped at the sound. She had more than once been on the receiving end of Udele's rage. Edythe's heart raced and her hands were cold. She quaked with the horrifying truth. Udele must have pushed Edwina to her death.

"If you breathe a word of this — laying a crime to me that cannot be proven — you shall meet your own end quickly."

"It is with great sadness that I promise you none shall hear of this from me," Giselle said firmly. "I promise this not out of loyalty, but rather because my purpose is not yet met. I must guard my own life a bit longer."

"Then speak of this no more. How will Conan fare this war?"

"He will return to England."

"Will he bring riches? Will Anselm be his home?"

"Not until you are gone," Giselle replied.

"How so?" Udele cried.

"You have lost him, madam. You have worn his loyalty thin. Your persistent interference has done what I promised you it would. He will do his duty to you, but he will not think of you when he turns his hand to conquer."

"That will not be so!" she raged. "How dare you! He would never cast me aside, nor would he put me behind others!"

"Lady," Giselle said softly and with patience, "he already has."

The silence that followed was split suddenly by the slamming of the cottage door. Edythe sat stunned for many moments, finally rising and gingerly making her way home.

Edythe kept herself to her rooms the rest of that day, vowing not to cross her mother's path until the evening meal when Alaric would be present. She prayed that Udele would not find a way to escape the accusation. She knew she would not be safe in her own home if Udele could excuse it as slander.

Edythe sat near the small window in her room as the sun lowered in the sky. She heard her door open and turned to see her mother enter with Pierce. Her heart thumped a bit faster, though Udele wore a pleasant smile and bore a tray with two goblets.

"There you are, dear heart," Udele said sweetly. "I have not seen you about today."

"I have been here all day," Edythe said defensively.

"All day? And you have not been out at all? But, my dear, surely some happening of interest occupied you this day."

"Nay, madam," Edythe replied, turning and looking out her window, straining her eyes for some sight of Alaric. "There was nothing special about the day."

"Truly?" Udele questioned, setting her tray down on

370 , THE BLUE FALCON

a stool beside Edythe. "You did not even find an adventure outside the lacemaker's window?"

Edythe turned abruptly and looked at her mother in horror. Udele pulled a strip of cloth from the pocket of her gunna and held it before Edythe. The torn piece matched Edythe's gown.

"This was found on the firewood outside Giselle's cottage. I fear you've snagged your gown," Udele said.

The surprise on Edythe's face lasted only a moment, and then, turning away from her mother abruptly, she refused to comment. While her back was turned, Udele reached into her pocket again, this time withdrawing a handful of a powder.

"Won't you tell me why you were there, Edythe?" Udele asked.

Edythe did not turn, but sighed heavily, trying not to let tears spill. "I thought you would ask after Conan, and I wanted to listen."

"Then you heard?"

"Nay," Edythe said too suddenly. "I could not hear."

"But you did," Udele accused. "Had you heard nothing you would not be so frightened of me."

Edythe suddenly turned back, her eyes brimming with tears. "I wish I had not heard," she said, her voice catching. "Madam, I cannot believe what I heard!"

"Ah, then my secret is told. And what will you do, Edythe, dear?"

"I must tell Father," Edythe said resolutely, though her voice was shaking.

Udele nodded her head solemnly. "I suppose you must." She raised her eyes and smiled at Edythe. "My fate is sealed then. He will have me cast out at the very least."

Edythe looked at her mother in confusion. "You are not frightened?"

"Nay, 'tis what I deserve. I have suffered with the sin long enough. 'Tis best that I accept my punishment."

Edythe sat on her stool next to the window and looked at Udele in wonder. She could not believe her mother's relaxed, accepting manner. Udele smiled with a sweet sadness.

"Madam," Edythe said earnestly, "perhaps there is still a way you can be forgiven —"

"Nay, I think not." Udele raised a goblet and handed it to Edythe. "This may be the last time we share a cup, daughter. Join me?"

Edythe took the goblet with shaking hands and watched in complete awe as Udele sipped from hers.

"Drink?" Udele asked her.

Edythe raised the thing shakily to her lips, taking a slow drink. The wine was bitter in her mouth, but she hoped for some soothing effect.

"You should have stayed in your rooms today, Edythe," Udele said, her voice no longer pleasant and kind. "You should not have spied on your mother."

Edythe felt her head begin to spin giddily, but she was not so sorely beset that she did not know she had been tricked. "The wine —" she said haltingly.

"Aye, the wine." Udele laughed suddenly. "You have always been so foolish, Edythe. Did you really think I would let you take your news to Alaric?"

"Father —" Edythe whispered weakly.

"Alaric has gone to Stoddard Keep, dear heart. He will not hear your tale." The goblet fell from Edythe's hand, clanging on the hard floor. Again Udele laughed and then lifted her own goblet to her lips and drained it, a small dribble of wine falling from her mouth, staining her bosom with a bloodlike darkness. "You have heard that I killed, Edythe. Did you doubt that I would do so again?"

"Madam . . ." Edythe breathed, her head growing heavy and her body weak. "Mother . . ."

Edythe's eyes slowly closed, and her limp form fell from the stool to the hard, cold floor.

Udele turned to Pierce, who had waited silently just inside the door. "Take her from here tonight, but be not long about it. I would not want your absence noticed."

Pierce looked at his mistress with pained eyes. "Aye, madam."

"Do not face me with your righteousness, Pierce. Even if Lord Alaric were to hear and pardon me, Conan would hear of it and ever wonder. You would see me beggared and groveling for the merest crust of bread in my own hall. If you defy me now, I am ruined."

With that she left the room.

The heat of late July chafed at Chandra as the weight of the child within her grew more burdensome. Tears threatened to spill from exhaustion and sadness. She had not slept at all the night before: she had attended Wynne in childbirth.

She knocked softly at her husband's door and entered when she heard his response. He was donned only in chausses and did not turn from his washbasin to greet her. Her hand rested on her own swollen belly as she spoke to his back. "Your son, my lord — was born dead."

He ceased his washing for only a moment, finally turning to her as he dried his face with a linen towel.

"And when will our glad day come?" he asked.

Chandra caressed her stomach. Wynne's labor had been torturous, her child born limp and still. It was horrifying for a woman nurturing her own babe in her womb.

"My heir, madam," Tedric pressed, "is well and strong?"

Chandra's chin trembled. She nodded and looked away.

"When?"

"I am not sure," she replied with practiced nonchalance. "Sometime early in the new year."

"You are not sure? Are you sure of the father?"

Cold and snapping blue eyes darted to his face, and Tedric laughed at her anger. "And who would it be if not you?"

"Were Conan not so far away, I would wonder."

"But he is far away. How long will you accuse me?"

"Until he is dead," Tedric replied easily. "And that will likely be soon, lady. He will find war less pleasurable than chasing pretty damsels."

Her child moved restlessly within her, and Tedric's cruel words could not be hushed.

"I will be leaving this morn," Tedric advised her.

She nodded, keeping silent. She feared the tears would come. She turned and left him to dress, fleeing back to her chamber and leaning against her closed door. It was first a shudder and then a single tear. Conan must live, she thought helplessly. The child. The child will be healthy and strong. Within moments she was racked with sobs, her head falling against the oaken door to her chamber.

Much later in the morning, she was called away from the weaving room when a small troop of men from Anselm had been allowed to pass and waited below to see the lord or lady of the hall. As she went to see them, her heart thumped wildly. By the time she reached the courtyard, her face was white with fear and she bade them tell her quickly what their purpose was.

"We seek out Lady Edythe, lady. Might she perhaps be here?"

Confusion replaced the fear in her eyes and the color came back to her face. "Edythe?" she replied in confusion. "Here? Edythe is not here."

"Your pardon, lady, your word is good, to be sure. But I dare not carry that alone to my lord Alaric. He asks that we search with our own eyes every corner of England."

"Why do you seek Edythe? Why is she not with her father?"

The young man shrugged. "We cannot say, madam. Only the Lord knows why she has fled her father, but she cannot be found. No one saw her leave the hall, and no village between Anselm and hell saw her passing. We find nothing. No matter where we look nor whom we ask. Nothing."

"And what does Sir Mallory say to this? Does he perhaps have his wife?"

"Nay, madam. Sir Mallory does not know his wife is missing. Lord Alaric sent messages of other matters to Vézelay so that his men could search for Lady Edythe, and she was not there. Her husband cannot leave the king's service now, and Lord Alaric greatly fears that news of this would cause Sir Mallory to commit an act of treason in leaving the Crusade, or at least show less care with his own life."

"Then Conan does not know?" she heard herself ask.

"Nay, madam. May we look through the village and hall?"

"Of course," she said softly.

Chandra watched as the men filled her hall and questioned each passing servant with care. Every room, anteroom and hallway was looked through carefully. These men were quite serious in their search. The keep suddenly became stifling, and she fled to the courtyard, hoping the fresh air would clear her mind.

Edythe would not flee. There was no reason. Why would Edythe leave the protective walls of Anselm alone? Someone must have taken her away to do her harm. But who would wish to injure Edythe?

Chandra shuddered suddenly, but it was not from cold. Conan left England for war because even his close guard could not protect those he loved. He could not save Edwina with his nearness and he could not aid Chandra. Now, the moment he was gone, Edythe was missing. In her mind, Tedric was suspect.

"Oh, my love," she whispered miserably, "how many more tragedies will you find on your return?"

CHAPTER
18

THE first time Chandra saw her childhood home since her wedding was at the burial of her dear father. Sir Medwin of Phalen had been ill, his health steadily declining as he realized the losses in his life. He had buried his beloved Millicent and given his Laine to the convent. Next, he had buried Edwina, who had passed on leaving no issue. His last hope was his youngest, Chandra. Medwin had thought her marriage contract through carefully, placing her well-being in the hands of a family that was known and trusted in England. But it was not long before he could see that in this too he had failed.

Sir Tedric stopped pretending loyalty very soon after his wedding. Chandra was abused and mistreated in her own dower home of Cordell. Despite Tedric's promise, she was forbidden visits to her father at Phalen. Though aging and often in ill health, Medwin had visited his daughter twice: once when she was swollen with babe and again when her son was born.

Chandra could not hide from her father the fact that she lived with a man whose demands were great, love for her little, and whose cruel rages came often. Tedric's demands on Medwin became greater as well. "I have given you your only grandchild," Tedric reminded the old man,

"Will you let Conan take Phalen and pass it along to the issue of some future bride, or will you hearken to the fact that his right to Phalen is gone — gone with the passing of your daughter?"

Medwin held to his oath to let no one but Conan take Phalen, but in the final days of his life, Tedric pressured him mercilessly. When Tedric returned to Cordell from yet another visit to Phalen Castle, he brought the news that Medwin had died in his sleep. It was a cool spring night in the year 1192.

There were not many visitors for the burial. Even though Medwin was a respected man in England, nobles were struggling out of a long, hard winter and many were still away with Richard. Sir Theodoric did not journey to Phalen to attend Medwin for the last time. Lord Alaric and Galen did go. It was difficult to tell whether their interests were to put a good friend to his final rest or be assured that Conan's property was secure.

The weight of grief that pressed on Chandra with her father's passing was difficult to bear. He died in great sorrow. On their last visit together, when he had journeyed to see Hugh, his only grandchild, he begged forgiveness from his youngest daughter. He had failed them all, he wept. Chandra could do nothing to give him peace of mind. He had made a mistake in forcing her to marry Tedric, and whether or not Edwina and Laine had been failed also was not certain, but they were both gone forever.

It was for her father's sadness when he died that Chandra wept. And there was the fear that now, with Medwin gone, there was no one to stay Tedric's hand.

Chandra watched cautiously to find a moment to ask Lord Alaric for word of Conan, a moment when Tedric was not near. She worried that Alaric would brush her spitefully aside and refuse her any information. It was early on the morning that Alaric prepared to leave that Chandra saw her chance and went to him in the courtyard, clutching Hugh close to her.

"My lord," she beckoned. "What is your word of Sir Conan?"

Alaric smiled kindly. "You have heard nothing?" he asked.

"Nay, my lord. Tedric brings word of the Crusade from time to time, but nothing of Sir Conan. I know he would tell me if —" she stopped, looking down and wishing she had not said so much.

Alaric reached out and touched her cheek. "Aye, lass, he would tell you if Conan were dead." Chandra looked up at him and saw the kindness in his eyes. "There is nothing I can do to help you," he said softly.

Chandra straightened her back and blinked to clear her eyes. "I manage well enough, my lord."

"I can imagine," Alaric snorted. "Is this the first time you have been allowed to leave Cordell since your wedding?"

"Yea, but I am safe there. He guards me well, but he does not hurt me overmuch."

Alaric shook his head sadly. "It pains this old heart, Chandra, knowing how you suffer; knowing how we were unable to prevent this."

"Sir Conan, my lord. Is he well?"

"This war is an ugly thing, Chandra. He will be greatly changed, I vow. But he will return; he is well." Alaric looked closely at the babe Chandra carried. He was a sturdy child, his skin more bronze than the ivory of his mother's. The shining pate was just barely covered with a dark fuzz. "Tedric has a fine son," Alaric remarked.

"The child is a great joy to me," Chandra said.

"He is dark."

"My father was darker of hair and skin than I," she replied.

Alaric did not respond to her. "You will have to be prepared for the change in him, lass. He will not return the same man. But he will return."

"That is the only important thing, my lord," she said quietly.

Alaric looked toward the keep. "Go inside, lass, before you are found here and chastised."

"My lord? Should you send a missive to Sir Conan, tell him —" She paused and looked down again, shaking her head negatively.

"Tell him —" Alaric urged.

"Nay, there is nothing."

Chandra felt his hand under her chin as he raised her tear-filled eyes to meet his. "Give me something to tell him, lady," Alaric said.

" 'Tis cruel. There is nothing he can do. He must not hope —" Chandra could not look at Alaric, she could not face him. She wanted to send word that she loved him still, that there was a son — his son — but Conan would be burdened with the weight of duty to them both. If he loved her still, he would come to her of his free choice — not out of duty. She could not plead for his aid.

"Chandra? What may I tell him?"

"Please, monseigneur, tell him that I am well. Tell him I pray for his safety."

"Is that all?"

"Aye," she said, sniffing back her tears. "That is all."

Chandra could not send her love to Jerusalem. She cuddled Hugh closely to her and rushed away from Alaric so that her tears could be private. Within the keep, she leaned against the closed door and the wetness coursed down her cheeks. It had been two years — two very long years since Conan had climbed to her chamber and promised he would return to her. He left a part of himself with her then, and he did not know there was a son. No one knew, although Wynne must have suspected.

Conan would return to find England itself had changed. The land was wasted by the sacrifices made to finance the fighting. Count John, first banned from England, had returned and been given by his sovereign brother the right to rule a large accumulation of land in the central part of England. Those living under his rule were a saddened lot, for John's insatiable hunger for power, combined with his cruel and harsh disciplinary hand, left many a sorrowed soul in his path. And while Richard had given him land and power, he continued to surround himself with supporters and warriors, conquering and holding more land to call his own.

Those eager for money and power were willing to pledge their fealty to John in return for his promise of support. One such individual, unsurprisingly, was Tedric. Tedric had powerful friends now. He was no longer the lowly son of little inheritance.

When Conan returned, he would also see the guards who surrounded Chandra, and the improbability that he could ever wrest her away from Tedric's tight hold. She could not send her love and beg him to free her. The desire must come from his own heart. And his heart may have changed: on some faraway desert manor there might have been an emperor's daughter whose eyes were more a promise than a memory.

Chandra dried her eyes and made her way to her chamber to begin the preparations for traveling back to Cordell. Clothing had already been placed in trunks, and when she entered, Wynne gratefully took Hugh from her arms. "My lord husband?" Chandra questioned. "Did he tell you when we leave?"

"Nay, lady, only that we are to make ready."

Chandra picked up a small jewel coffer containing a few things that had been her mother's and held it reverently. She prayed Tedric would not take these and sell them as he had done with some of her other things. There was not much of value within, but the gems were precious in a sentimental way. She opened the coffer to look at them and found it filled with parchment, many pages rolled together. She lifted the pages in confusion, carefully unrolling them to see what this missive was. It was sent to "Father" and was signed with a scrawling "C." It took her only a moment to realize that it was a letter Conan had written to Alaric. And Alaric had found a way to give her word of Conan even before she asked. He must have stolen into her chamber when no one was about to hide the letter among her personal things.

Quickly she closed the lid and fetched her cloak, covering her shoulders and hiding the coffer beneath the folds.

"Wynne, keep Hugh for me. I will be back soon."

Chandra went swiftly down the stairs and through the keep, nearly colliding with Tedric as she was leaving the hall.

"Pardon, my lord," she muttered, attempting to pass him.

"Where do you go?" he demanded.

"To visit my parents' graves once more, Tedric, if you will allow it," she said with cautious respect, but her eyes dared him to stop her.

"Make this the last time, lady," he warned. "We will leave here early on the morrow."

"Has Lord Alaric gone?" she questioned.

"Aye, but he leaves Sir Galen here to protect the keep." Tedric laughed suddenly. "No one would *dare* trouble the *knight!*" Tedric walked away from her, laughing, and Chandra hurried to the garden, to the place where her parents were buried.

She cast a furtive glance over her shoulder to see if anyone was watching her. The small cemetery was almost completely concealed from the hall by bushes and trees, and she knew no other place to go. Tedric was not interested in watching her as she sat and stared at the earth, as she let her mind commune with the spirits of her family in this place. She knelt on the damp ground and opened the coffer to take out the parchment. She did not have time to savor every word, but the comfort of seeing writing in Conan's own hand brought a warm and tender feeling to her breast.

He wrote of the violent storms of Jaffa: the hail and winds, the mud so thick the horses could not move and the men could not walk. On the voyage over, there had been much sickness and strife. Men were forced to kill and eat their horses to stay alive. Many landed with sores and ailments requiring weeks of recuperation before they could travel with Richard. The king, no less human than they, was often ill and bedridden. No one could guarantee his survival of the war. There was no greater in battle, no finer mind for the strategy of war, but his constitution was

weak where ailments were concerned, and he was often
beset.

The infidel enemy was a new sort, appearing easy to
best, with their immodest linen wraps and their petite
horses. But they were sleek and fast, their steeds accustomed to the sliding terrain and light weight. And their
lack of armor did not permit them to hold fast and await
return attack. They flung their arrows from the backs of
moving horses and quickly retreated out of range. The
Negro and Bedouin foot soldiers hurled arrows and darts
while the horsed heathens attacked in waves. The first
reaction to this alien form of fighting was paralyzed horror
on the part of the heavily fettered knights. In the end of
the battle of Arsuf there was a victory for the Christians,
but in truth it was a miracle they even survived. And even
so, many a warrior lay stricken and immobilized from
the severe heat and lack of water.

The taking of hostages in battle was common. And
execution was a necessary evil to be dealt with. Chandra
shuddered. Conan wrote his father that he thought he had
hardened himself to the facts of war, to the blood and
agonized cries of the beaten. But the day he witnessed the
slaughter of over two thousand prisoners taken at Acre,
he found that he hadn't.

There were snakebites, the victims writhing in delirium
and pain before dying. The depletion of food stores, a
severe lack of meat and fruit, caused the slow starvation
of some. Illness. There was a new unknown disease in
every heathen village. One local complaint struck both
kings, laying Richard and Philip on their backs. As if a
noble bug had bitten, Conan, too, was stricken. Fever and
delirium reigned, and though he remembered nothing
when he regained consciousness, Conan found that Mal-

lory had closeted himself with his ailing comrade and would allow no other near.

"I could not see his purpose and would rather have had him leave a more expendable servant to the task of tending me," Conan wrote. "But my sister's husband said that the name I called out in my sickness would not have pleased my other comrades in arms."

Chandra's heart lurched as she read this. Could Conan have called out for her while he was ill? Did Mallory worry that Tedric's brothers would hear? She knew that they all lived and fought together in that heathen land — did they also fight among themselves? Because of her?

"I worry that what I hold dear is being abused in my absence," he wrote. "It pains my heart that I can do nothing. But when I am returned there are matters to settle, and rest assured, my lord, many wrongs will be set aright.

"Should you find the right moment, say that I am well, though poorly spirited from this wretched war. And should you have the time, tell those you know I love that I will return to them."

A tear slowly crept down Chandra's cheek. "Would that I could thank your father for allowing me this simple touch," she murmured to the wrinkled pages. "Would that I could hold this to my breast as I pray for your safety, my love."

The earth was still soft where Medwin had been buried, and Chandra scraped away a portion of the ground near the foot of his grave and placed the coffer carefully within, covering it with dirt. "My father would be honored to think he guards your words," she said softly.

Slowly she rose to stand, and as she turned she met cold gray eyes. She gasped and jumped in surprise as Tedric grabbed her wrist. "What little treasures of Sir Conan do you bury with your father, love?"

Sir Medwin was barely cold in his grave when Tedric called his father to his aid to ride on Phalen Castle. A letter, written by Medwin shortly before his death, brought Theodoric to his son's aid. Sir Conan, Medwin wrote, had done little for Phalen Castle in the short time he was married to Edwina. There was no issue, and the many debts that had accumulated had been righted by Sir Tedric. Since Tedric fathered the only offspring with lineage to Medwin, Phalen Castle was to belong to him, and in turn, to Hugh, Chandra's son. A modest sum of money to ease the insult and to repay Conan for the care given to Edwina was carried in a pouch.

Galen did not yield the keep easily, but faced with Tedric's men and those of Sir Theodoric, he could not hold out for long. Those men who had served Medwin were in a state of confusion over who was right — but quickly saw the right in might. Phalen was abandoned by the young Galen, and a few men fell before the hall was taken.

Tedric might have slain the young knight but for Theodoric's presence. Galen returned a week later with his father and a hardy troop of men, but Alaric forged no attack. The two aging lords, once the best of friends, were enemies now.

"The battle is not over," Alaric bellowed to the barbican where Theodoric and Tedric stood. "Upon Conan's return you will see me firmly behind him!"

"And if Conan does not return, old man?" Tedric shouted back.

"I think he would come from hell to set you from his hall!"

Loyalties at home were torn and shredded while the great armies of Richard the Lion Hearted warred in the devastating heat of the Holy Land. Friends were turned against friends, husbands against wives, and in the absence of the Blue Falcon, little was preserved for his return. Those who would have died for his cause were left without even that recourse.

When Tedric returned to Cordell after his conquest, he gloated before Chandra.

"What did you do to my father to make him write that letter for you?" she demanded of him.

"It was simple, ma chère," he returned. "I told him I would have you killed should he refuse me."

"There is nothing to stop you now," she taunted.

"There is but one thing, love. While Conan wants you, he will be cautious. I hold your life in my hand."

"What he feels for me will make little difference, Tedric," she said quietly. "I think this insult may be the apple that tips the cart. He will surely kill you whether he cares for me or not."

As the winds of November in the year 1192 began to cool the land, the soldiers of Richard began to filter into England after more than two years away.

CHAPTER
19

SINCE Tedric had taken possession of Phalen, he had stocked the walls well with soldiers, promising them grandness in good time for their service. The families were in a suspended state of feud, Alaric and Theodoric doing nothing as they awaited the return of their sons.

After spending several months assuring himself that Phalen was stoutly held, Tedric returned to Cordell to stay. He still felt sure that the prize Conan sought was here, in this small village. Chandra could see no reason why Tedric had not moved them all to Phalen, the larger and stronger keep, except that even he saw the advantages of Cordell: Conan could not enter the town without being seen. It was reasonable to assume that Conan's attack would be on the castle he considered stolen from him — Phalen — where he would not find the lady.

Chandra's days blended one into the next with naught but the seasonal changes to alert her that any time had passed at all. She was not allowed to venture from Cordell, and there had not been any visitors.

Early in the morning she would don a heavy woolen gunna and have Hugh brought to her. Her duties were so many and varied that she could not even mother her own son as she wanted to. She smiled as Wynne brought Hugh in.

Chandra bounced Hugh upon her knee and he giggled gaily. His eyes had never changed from the glittering blue he was born with, but his white-blond hair turned to the dark crown of his sire. And the pale, white skin of babyhood was growing bronze and golden, like Conan's. While Tedric was small compared to his contemporaries, Hugh was a large, solid child. She knew the day would soon come when Tedric would question his parentage. For now they were safe, since Tedric took little interest in his son. Hugh could be out of his sight for weeks at a time without Tedric noticing.

"Lady, my brother took chickens to Colchester," Wynne said. "Many a knight has returned."

Chandra did not look at her. She chucked the baby under his chin.

"Lady? Is there word?" the young woman asked.

"Nay. Nor will there be, as I reason." She hugged Hugh close and relished the fresh, clean scent of his skin. He wriggled from her grasp, more interested in walking about the room, examining every article with his hands and mouth, his fat legs taking him more quickly than seemed possible from one trouble to the next.

"Thetford," Chandra said softly. "Remember, if you forget all else, that Laine is in the convent at Thetford. If we are in danger here, you can make your way to her. There are those who would help you, and the coins I gave your father — they are safe?"

"Aye, lady. And no one knows. But I could flee there now and —"

"Nay!" she snapped, drawing a jump from Hugh, who

was just a few paces away. The little chin quivered and tears collected in his eyes. She held out her arms to him and he snuggled close to her breast. "I cannot know what comes with the winter," she said more calmly. "It is a thing we must do when Tedric is engaged in his battle, when he is far from here. Until that time, be brave. I will let no harm come to you or my son." She stroked the dark head and kissed Hugh's soft ear. "If you skitter about like a frightened rabbit, do you think it will go unnoticed? To this day, though no word has come and no contact ever been made, Tedric suspects me above all others. He would be in Phalen Castle now but for his fear that Conan would come here and free me of this bondage."

Wynne nodded. The guard about the hall and along the road was heavy since the first of the soldiers had returned and word of their coming had reached Cordell.

"If Richard is —"

"Richard gave his brother leave to manage his lands without reprisal. While we may hope the king will curb John now, his first business will likely be arranging masses, celebrations and tournaments to raise the funds for his next battle. We are better not to depend on Richard to solve our problems."

"Aye, lady," she said weakly.

Chandra sighed. She knew she had hardened somewhat as a result of the great burdens she had carried the past years. Her strength was more finely honed and her faith less than blind. Her love had not faltered, but she knew the risk was high that Conan would return with some Byzantine mistress with babes clinging to her skirts.

It had been over two years.

Chandra heard soft talking and moving around in the

opposite chamber and quickly handed Hugh to Wynne. "Take him," she bade the girl. "Later, tonight, bring him to me for a while. Please."

Wynne left the room and Chandra continued with her dressing, fastening an anklet around her slender ankle and fitting into place the gold girdle that she wore daily. A few coins would be given to the priest and she placed them in her pouch along with her rosary. She covered her head with a veil, and just as she would have reached for her cloak, Tedric entered the room.

"To prayers?" he questioned with a sneer.

"As every morn, my lord," she answered.

"For what do you pray, damsel? Do you pray that your knight will return and kill your husband?"

She stiffened with indignation. "I can assure you that I have never prayed for your death," she retorted saucily.

"Have you word of him?" Tedric asked.

Chandra sighed. For a long while Tedric had been quiet about this obsession, but since some knights had returned and there had been no attack or challenge from Conan, Tedric was becoming unbearable with the wait. "And how would a message make its way to me, husband? Would your guards let a messenger pass?"

Tedric chuckled at her predicament. "Sir Conan, the great warrior of the Cross! Has he not yet promised to rescue you from your husband?"

Chandra stooped and fidgeted with her anklet so that he would not see her eyes. "I feel certain that any message from Conan will come to you, Tedric. Not to me."

"Ah, my love, your denial does not fool me," he sneered.

"Tedric," she said, raising her eyes to meet his. She felt almost serene. Chandra neared nineteen years, and while the blush of youth might still be evident if she had cause to be gay, there was no trace of youth or naivete in her gaze as she looked at her husband now. " 'Tis no secret that I once desired Sir Conan, but it has been over five years, Tedric, since that possibility was lost to me. There is no reason for me to expect his protection now."

"The Falcon may be a genius in war, but in his follies with women he has been a fool. I wager he wants you still. He will walk into my trap."

"Had he wanted me at the cost of his life, my lord, would he have ventured to the Crusade?"

"Conan is a pompous ass," Tedric spat. "How like him to return as the glorious warrior to stake his claims."

Chandra smiled lazily. "Has he disappointed you and returned alive?"

She would have expected his anger, but instead he laughed cruelly. "You have aged, my fair Chandra," he said, reaching out to touch her cheek. "You are no longer the blushing maid of our wedding day. Your hate has worn on you. He will not be pleased."

She tore away from him, because she knew what he said was true. All that she had endured as his wife showed on her.

"He will have little to entice him when he stares into those passionless eyes, my pet," Tedric fairly crooned.

"Should he have a chance to look upon my face, Tedric, I heartily doubt it will be in passion. Pity, rather, for what has befallen me since you took me —"

He grasped her arm tightly and held her firmly, looking closely into her eyes. Tedric's gray eyes could bolt from dark to pale as his anger built, and now, nearly white with inner rage, he stared her down.

"I will know the truth of his intentions soon, sweet," he said in a low and menacing tone. "If he casts you aside, he must still fight for his lands. If he holds any love in his heart for you, I shall take pleasure in keeping you from him. One way or the other, fair Chandra, I shall have the brave warrior at odds, be assured."

She would not flinch from him but neither would she fight him. She knew her resistance would goad him into more abusive behavior. Eventually he released her as if disgusted and strode to the door. There he paused to salute her with a sly smile.

When the door closed behind him, she caught her breath and sat heavily on her bed. She knew her place in this obscure rivalry. Somehow Tedric would make her the victim.

She had heard nothing from Conan since that visit so long ago. Many times she had beaten down the thought that his stealthy climb to her chamber was made in impetuous lust eager to be spent after wanting and wondering for too long. If she did see him again, she could not beg his protection now — pride would not allow. Pride and love, for if he did not want her, she would free him to another, however painful.

Upon leaving the keep, Chandra passed the villagers returning from church. Those cruel words with her husband had caused her to miss the mass. The church was vacant but for two villagers bent in prayer, and for this much she was grateful. She crossed herself, genuflected, dropped to her knees before the large wooden cross above the altar. She lent her heart to her prayers, the same prayers, laden with fear and confusion, that she had offered for a very long time.

Daily she would pray until spiritually spent, then confess and then listen to mass and take communion. The
rest of the day she would bear as she could. Its problems
would leave her exhausted and she would sleep, usually
dreamlessly.

There was a hand on her shoulder, and she looked up
to see Father Merrick looking down at her. She assumed
he was ready to hear her confession so that he could be
about his other chores. Wordlessly she rose, her rosary
tightly wound around her hands, to follow him. She noticed that he led her not to the small antechamber where
he heard confessions, but toward the rectory, a room for
his private use that she had never seen. Stopping, she
tried to reason this. But the priest smiled, inviting her
with his eyes to follow.

In this small room there were pages of parchment
scattered about a small table. A quill stood ready and a
stool was the only comfort. No rug or tapestries warmed
the room or broke the plainness. As he held the door for
her, she noticed that a brother of the same order was
within. His back to her, this disciple of Christ seemed to
fill the room. His broad-shouldered frame looked immense
beneath the brown drab of his habit. She was accustomed
to the men of the Gospel being small of stature and more
intellectual than muscular. She turned to ask the priest his
business, but found that Father Merrick had turned to go,
closing the door softly behind him.

The figure in the robes slowly turned. His appearance
was swarthy, his face tanned from many months in the hot
sun. His beard had been recently shaven, making his
cheeks and chin stand out white against the rest of his face.
A scar, deep and still red, was carved along one cheek from

his temple to his chin. His dark hair fell over his forehead, and the eyes — the eyes that had penetrated even her deepest sleep — were the same as ever.

Chandra covered her mouth to silence her gasp of surprise and looked about quickly to be sure that she was alone with him. Then quickly she ran the few steps between them and threw her arms around his neck, burying her face in his chest. She let her fingertips examine him, feeling to be certain he was real. She took in the smell of him, the masculine musk that she immediately recalled. Tears blurred her eyes as she pulled away from him to study his face, so there, too, she let her trembling fingers decide his features. She touched his lips, his dark brows, the scar that stood out on his cheek.

It was several moments before she realized that the arms that held her were slack and weak. She pulled away again and looked into his eyes. They were hardened and cold, though he seemed to try to soften them. He smiled somewhat sheepishly, reaching out a hand to caress her cheek. The hand was rough and scratchy on her delicate skin, but she did not wince. Rather, she held it against her cheek and pressed soft kisses into the calloused palm.

"Chandra," he breathed. "You're the finest sight —"

She laughed softly, the tears more controlled now. "I greatly feared you would find me aged and ugly," she murmured.

"You are beautiful," he said. He frowned slightly as he looked at her. "You have suffered through this war." There was a bitter quality to his voice, as if something within gnawed at him. "I had to tell myself daily that you would survive." She tilted her head to hear his coarse whisper, for his voice seemed to lack strength.

"Oh, Conan, I too have longed for this day, but you are

tired and I think unwell. You need rest and time away from fighting. I wish that I could soothe you, but even now I fear for you."

"Seeing you, alive and well, is comfort enough. Chandra, you must understand — you must forgive me for leaving you. It was the only way."

She reached up to touch his cheek, and she smiled into his tired eyes. "Conan, there was never anything you could do to help me. And you see: I am well enough." She paused a moment, and when she spoke again the tears threatened. "Conan, my father is dead."

"I know what Tedric has done," he said bitterly.

Chandra's cheeks flamed and she looked down at her hands.

"I do not hold you responsible. I know there was no way you could stay him. And he alone will pay."

"Conan, he threatened to have me killed if my father did not yield Phalen. My father was not well," she wept. "He should have refused, for Tedric would not have carried out his threats."

"I know why he keeps you alive, why he keeps you here. There was nothing else Medwin could do — nothing else that I could do."

"He has strong allies now," she said. "He is a friend to Count John, and Theodoric still supports him, even against you. He has not changed, Conan. He swears to his father that he is loyal to the king, yet much of his money and men come from John."

"Richard will take care of John, but the king travels by land rather than sea and has not yet arrived."

"Conan, I fear Tedric will prove difficult to roust from Phalen. He has planted a grand army within those walls."

"But he will not fight," Conan said with a rueful laugh.

"As always, Tedric plots my death without meeting me in fair battle."

Chandra looked away, for she could not stand the distance in his eyes. He, in turn, moved away from her.

"You will regain what is rightfully yours, Conan," she said softly. "But you are right to beware of Tedric: he will never meet you honestly." The inner pain and exhaustion that seemed to consume him did not give the picture of the glorious returning warrior that Tedric seemed to envision. He was not the same man, Chandra thought. "You must not think of me as you battle Tedric. Do whatever you must, Conan."

Conan looked at her. "You must forgive me," he said quietly. "You must not hate me for leaving you here, with him. It was the only way."

"Hate you? It is not within my being to hate you."

"Chandra, under my watchful eye, Tedric would not have dared so much, though there would never have been a way to stop him completely."

"Conan, I have never questioned your leaving. You need not explain to me now."

"Had my promises meant anything, I would have done a better job of protecting you."

"I would not hold you to promises made in a moment of passion, Conan. You are not beholden to me."

She looked at the shock registered on his face. "I beg forgiveness, Chandra, for seeing to you so poorly, but I do not decline promises made! Chandra, I have been fouled by a long war: now you want none of me?"

"Oh, nay," she whispered, tears smarting in her eyes. "Oh, love, never that! But you are tired," she breathed. "You must not in a hasty moment meet Tedric — not for me, not for anyone! It has been a long time, mon cher.

England has changed. You have changed! I cannot have you come home to more burdens. I cannot have you —"

"I had to go," he said. "I went for us. It was the only way; though I knew I would return to see how you had suffered as his wife."

He moved toward her, dragging one foot as he moved. She stared at the afflicted member, trying to conceal her horror.

"A heathen blade," he said sourly. "Chandra," he whispered, "Chandra, tell me that you love me before I live another moment."

She came to him slowly, placing her hands on his chest and trying to smile through tears of pain and joy. "Conan, my love, never doubt my love. It was the only thing that gave me hope. But do not let love blind you. Beware of Tedric. He hopes that you love me; he hopes that will help him cut you down. I could not live —"

He grabbed her fiercely, holding her close to him, burying his face in her hair and taking in the fresh womanly scent of her. "The nights were so long," he muttered, his voice cracking. "The days were hellish, and had a vision of you not been foremost on my mind, I would have perished. Twice I fell from my horse, not able to rise on my own mettle. I feared I would not hold you again. And now," he stopped and laughed ruefully. "Now I am grateful that Tedric's presence presses me on."

Chandra did not respond, but rested her head on his chest. It was the only comfort she would have until this feud was resolved.

"England has changed," Conan remarked. "I have changed, that is true."

"When my father died," she told him, "Alaric traveled to Phalen and left behind one of your letters. He hid it in my mother's jewel coffer, the one I was meant to have. I read the letter, Conan. It was the only news I had of you in two years. And — Tedric discovered me. He holds your letter now."

"And how did he punish you?" Conan asked with a bitterness in his voice.

"He did not. He gloats in his possession. He considers the letter proof that you want me."

"And you deny it?" he asked.

Chandra laughed apologetically. "You have more use for a woman alive than a corpse, have you not? Yea, I deny it. And then I confess an impure love and lies. It has been thus for years."

"Have you changed?" he asked softly.

Chandra pushed herself away from him so that she could look into his eyes. "Yea, Conan," she said. "I am no longer that tender lass that pursued you years ago."

"Has everything changed, Chandra?"

"Nay, love. There are some things that go on through all eternity."

There was a tapping at the door, and Conan scowled at the interruption. They both knew the time had come to part again. She quickly reached for him, for one more touch to hold dear.

"Some things will never change, Conan: my love for you, my hope for a better day . . ."

"There will be a better day," he whispered.

"My sins have been many, but I will not add one more to a very long list. I must ask that you spare Tedric's life, if you can."

"And will you hate me if I kill him?"

She looked into his eyes again, the cold blue glistening.

She knew in her heart what Tedric's last sight would be. She shook her head. "God help me, I could not hate you for any reason."

"Tell me you love me," he insisted again.

"I love you, Conan," she breathed. "I love you more than life."

Again there was the tapping, more insistent, rapid. She knew she would not see him until — or would she ever see him again? How would it end? "Do not meet him too soon," she begged. "Rest and regain your strength. And do not fear for me: I will be safe —"

He silenced her in a kiss that did not hold the passion she remembered, but warmed her through and through just the same. She clung to him, tasting his mouth, holding him closely. Then she broke away from him at the sound of more knocking on the door.

"I will love you again, Chandra. And you will not doubt me."

"Go quickly," she urged, tears threatening.

"I would take you now if it could be done safely."

"Go," she choked, trusting him, fearing him.

He folded his hands in front of him, concealing them beneath the heavy folds of the monk's garb. He bent his head so that the hood would cover most of his face. Without, Father Merrick stood nervously twisting his hands and spoke softly, issuing his instructions for leaving. Just before making his final exit, Conan turned and looked at Chandra once more. There in the blue eyes, she saw a new light, the glow of a promise. It had not been there when she first met his eyes. Now, it was real. He was truly returned. Time alone could take away the sting of war, but she at least believed he would recover.

With a lift in her heart, she smiled at him, her eyes mirroring what his had told her. In time, for love and for honor, all wrongs would be set aright.

He bent his head again and was gone.

Chandra took herself to the chapel to kneel again before the altar. Her heart beat so fiercely she could hardly breathe properly. Within her there was a trembling she could not control, of a nature she could not define. It was perhaps excitement, perhaps fear. Seeing him here, on her own turf, under Tedric's very nose, was alarming at the very least. He was certainly weak, and should he meet Tedric too soon, she feared he would not live through the day.

She let her face fall into her hands and wept.

"Fear not, lady," a soft voice comforted. "He is in good hands. He goes with a deputation of God."

"Will God aid him, Father?" Chandra choked out without looking at the priest.

"God's ways are a mystery, but His strength is well known. Sir Conan has come from a battle for the Cross. He is surely in God's grace."

Chandra looked up into the kindly eyes of the priest. *"You* helped him, Father," she said, shaking her head in bewilderment as the impact of this hit her for the first time. "You have issued me penance for sinful thoughts of another man, and surely you know who that man must be. You have listened to my confession time and time again and you must know —"

Father Merrick shrugged and looked into Chandra's moist eyes. "If God has a plan, I will see it to fruition. For that I will pray for direction."

"And you will not confide in my lord?" she asked shakily.

"Not even in exchange for my life."

The tears threatened again. "There was so much I didn't tell him," she wept. "His sister has never been found; his father grows old; Hugh —" She stopped and looked guiltily up at the priest. That much she had not confessed. But Father Merrick only smiled.

"Better he learns these things one at a time."

"You see him as our hope, too, Father?"

Father Merrick looked up to the altar. "I remember when there were rich articles there, replaced now with wooden implements since Sir Tedric's coming." He sighed. "I pray for Sir Tedric's soul, lady. I cannot bring myself to pray for his life, God help me."

"How does Sir Conan leave, Father?"

"So that no guard sees, he travels with the brothers for a distance. His comrades await him well down the road, and when they are reunited, he enters the forest. Don't worry," he said with a smile. "He has more protection than Tedric could ever claim."

CHAPTER
20

THE sun was high in the sky and a brewis was set to simmer on the hearth. Bread was being kneaded in preparation for baking. All fires but for those needed in cooking were low to preserve firewood for the long winter. In the highest level of the manor, Chandra looked over the cloth that was being woven. The women accepted her compliments and heeded her reprimands, whichever was the case. In a far corner sat Wynne with Hugh at her feet, playing with a doll made of rags and twigs and a small ball of wool.

The commotion caused by Tedric and his returning men echoed through the manor, yet even in this high loft Chandra could tell that it sounded strangely different. It sounded far too raucous. Or was it furious?

A page burst into the room. "My lord sends for you, lady. He is in his chamber. He orders you to come at once. And there are injured men in the courtyard."

"Injured?" she questioned.

"Aye, lady. I do not know how this came to pass."

The page, a lad of ten or twelve, had been about Cordell for at least two years. Chandra knew his face and suddenly realized she did not know his name. He was a fair youth and she liked him. Though he served Tedric's men, he had responded to her kindness.

"Lady," the youth said with a worried look in his eyes, "Sir Tedric is angry."

Chandra tried to smile her thanks to the lad for his warning, but her lips trembled and the effort was lost. She turned to the women in the room and found that all eyes, round with fright, were on her. She signaled them with just a tilt of her head to take themselves below and give aid to the wounded. They dropped their spools and went quickly. Her eyes went next to Wynne and the communication was clear. Wynne held Hugh close to her and hushed her young ward. She was prepared to protect the child.

Chandra went quickly to her husband's chamber and entered without knocking. Tedric stood on the far side of the room and drained a cup of wine. He looked at her with obvious rage and filled the cup again, taking another long pull. He then placed the chalice on the chest near his bed and took long and determined strides toward her.

Chandra's eyes were wide with apprehension as he walked toward her. He had often been angry and abusive, but the rage that seemed to consume him now looked to be even more powerful. Studying the silver slits of his eyes left her unprepared for his hand as he struck her hard across the face. She reeled backward and fell against the door, clutching the bruised cheek, tasting blood in her mouth, and stared at him in mute wonder.

"So you've seen him," Tedric shouted. "He comes to you here!"

Terror gripped her. Did Conan lay below injured? But she could not ask. She knew what part she must play — until all was lost. "Who?"

"Your knight! Conan, the bastard!"

"Conan is here?" she heard herself squeak.

"No longer, fairest Chandra," he sneered. "He's made his escape, but not before laying three of my men low. They may not live through the night."

"How so, Tedric? What has happened?"

"Do you play the innocent with me?" he shouted. "Do you pretend to know nothing of this? You knew I would be upon the road, and that is where we were attacked."

"I know nothing of his presence here," she protested. "Ask the servants if I have been in these walls since —"

He jerked her roughly to her feet, his grip tight and painful on her upper arms. "Do not think to make me your fool, Chandra. I know your rote. You have been to mass, and Sir Conan was garbed as a monk."

He flung her away and strode to the other side of the room. He turned then and shouted back at her. "He led a mule, and it was one of my own men who stopped that caravan when he noticed one brother carrying something beneath his robes. It was a sheathed sword. *I* recognized the face of that devil. He would be dead now but that his cry brought his companions to his aid." He looked Chandra over and smiled sardonically. "He did not leave in good humor, my love. He suffered at least one blow before he made his horse."

Chandra held her head up, trying not to show her fear. "I am surprised that you did not follow and slay him," she said.

"We followed," Tedric snapped. "But our horses were weary from this morning's ride, while theirs were rested."

"It could be it was his plan to attack you," she said. "There are those here who resent you, Tedric, for you have been a difficult man to abide. Perhaps he had learned your habits and —"

"How could he learn my habits when there is a guard

around every corner of this town? He did not come to fight me. He came to see you!"

"I have not seen him," she said simply.

"You lie! You alone would dare to betray me!"

"I? I am the one to caution these people to obey you. Truly, without me to hold them back, they would have defied you long ago. I have not betrayed you. I had not the opportunity."

"Nor will you!" he shouted. "Nor will anyone dare to betray me again. Whoever does, will die!" As quickly as his rage had mounted, it began to die. A sinister smile replaced the look of anger, and the insult of Conan's penetration of Cordell seemed to fall away as he devised yet another plan. He was confident again. He walked to the door of his chamber with a direct, unhurried step. He turned at the door and looked at her.

"Do you think I would let you live if not for the fact that he wants you? Aye, chérie, he will risk his stupid neck to have you, and I will be the one to watch him fall. But no more will I allow betrayal in my village. These good and fearful folk will feel the weight of my hand this very day — and be assured, no one will dare to give Sir Conan aid again."

"What will you do, Tedric?" she asked anxiously.

"I would have done with you now, but the Falcon needs a lure," he said, and left the room.

Chandra felt herself shaking inwardly and clutched at composure. She walked downstairs and looked around at the soldiers in the main room, their shields lying about and their gear scattered here and there. They looked at her with nothing less than hatred as she passed through.

Bereft of a cloak, she went out of the hall. There was a commotion within the town, and Chandra looked, first in confusion and then in horror, to the sight of some of Tedric's men dragging the village priest toward a gibbet. With a cry, she ran to that sight and threw herself at the men, pleading with them to unhand the priest.

"You must not obey Tedric in this!" she shouted. "Do you know the sin of killing a priest? I beg of you!"

But her protest was ignored, and one of the men threw her aside with a sharp blow. She stumbled back and fell, and looked from her lowly position to see the men dragging the priest to the platform. There had never been a device for hanging before Tedric came to this town, but since his coming, there had been many lashings and even a few deaths.

Villagers began to swell the street, and someone helped Chandra to her feet. She immediately took flight in the direction of the gibbet and plowed her way through the people. When Father Merrick tripped and fell, the men-at-arms simply dragged him. Tedric stood relaxed below the gibbet with a sneer twisting his lips.

She fell at his feet, tears wetting her cheeks and a look of horrified bewilderment on her face. As she looked up at him, she saw him watching her lazily, his eyes slightly glazed as he gloated in this power he assumed.

"Tedric, are you mad? Would you kill a lowly priest — a messenger of God?"

"He gave aid to my enemy," Tedric said easily.

"How do you know that he did? Did he confess this?"

"Nay, he will not confess," Tedric chortled. "But that will not stop me from doing what I have to do. 'Tis time these people learn that my word is law here. And Sir Conan is not welcome in this village. He means to do me harm."

She shook her head in disbelief. "You wish *him* harm! His intention is not clear! He has only just returned from the Crusade!" She clutched at his legs. "Tedric, let the priest go, I beg of you. Do not hurt him. Anything, I will do anything you ask!"

Tedric raised one brow and looked down at her. He cast a glance over his shoulder and smiled as the rope was fitted about the stoic priest's neck. He looked back at his wife. "Do you know your master, Chandra?"

"Yea," she replied.

"Name him."

"You, Sir Tedric," she humbly responded.

Tedric's shoulders shook with silent laughter as he enjoyed bringing this proud vixen to her knees. "And you would do anything for the priest's freedom? Would you take his place?"

"Gladly," she replied with bravado, though she knew full well that Tedric would not finish her life so easily. He needed her to draw Conan back.

Tedric looked up to the priest. "Did you aid my enemy and conceal him from me, Father?" he shouted.

The priest looked to the heavens and did not utter a word. His hands were bound behind his back and his eyes tilted up, his mouth set in a stern line. Tedric motioned his guards away from the priest's side, and with a wave of his hand, commanded a man to move to the lever that would drop the floor below the priest. Tedric turned his back as the man moved the lever. He watched his wife as she looked past him to the gibbet. Her scream of anguish as the priest fell, the rope jerking his body to a halt, was all that was heard.

Tedric did not look back at the limp form of the priest

hanging from his noose. He looked first at the villagers, who stood paralyzed as their priest was killed. Then he looked at his wife. She turned and looked into his eyes.

"You have ensured your own demise," Chandra said slowly. "I had hoped that before it was too late you would change your ways. But this," she croaked, throwing an arm wide to indicate the lifeless form of the village priest. "This is too much. I think you will not find mercy even in heaven now."

Chandra turned and looked to some villagers standing near and beckoned them to her. Two women and a man walked carefully around Tedric to follow her up the three steps to the raised gibbet to take charge of the body of Father Merrick.

One of Tedric's men approached him and asked for his next instructions. "Let her finish her task," Tedric said. "Then escort her to the hall and see that she does not leave again. My lady will have to do without even her prayers from now on."

Sir Conan, Sir Mallory and Sir Thurwell pulled their horses along a densely wooded path. They were not traveling the well-known road through Colchester and on to Anselm, but were going through the forest until they came to a southern road to Anselm, a route that Conan's enemies would not expect him to take. He had no desire to fight again so soon. That impromptu battle along the road had worn on him, leaving his injured leg sore and throbbing. And in this thicket he could not ride his horse but was forced to walk and lead the animal. They did not stop until the sun was low in the sky. The evening brought bitter cold, and each man quickly fashioned himself a makeshift barrier and huddled within for warmth. The night was disturbed only by the grumblings of men tired of making their beds on the hard ground.

There was a rustling in the shrub, and Conan was the first on his feet with a snarl on his lips. He hoped Tedric had found him. He would take great pleasure in killing him. The pain and weakness in his leg never for a moment worried him.

"Nay, Sir Conan, do not strike," the familiar voice said.

"Sir William! How did you find us?"

The man smiled. "This is my wood, Conan. No one travels here without my knowledge. You did make us walk a great distance, however." He turned and held aside a branch so that some others might pass. "Build these men a fire and feed them. And see to the animals." He looked again at Conan. "You are a sorry lot. I thought I had prepared you for life in the wood."

"I would not send an invitation to Tedric to find us," Conan replied testily.

"You are too far from the keep for him to see. And he has not followed. You are assumed well on your way home."

"We could have stayed on the road," Conan grumbled.

The two men that huddled over a pyramid of dry sticks backed away as the fire took light. Mallory nodded his approval and moved closer, as did others. More wood was tossed on and the fire soon blazed. Conan's temperament was eased considerably by the welcome warmth.

"We do not protect Cordell as in years past," William said. "Tedric's guard does that. For now we only wait."

"That he allows you in the wood at all surprises me," Conan said.

William shrugged. "He is not much of a warrior. Neither is he a huntsman and he takes all the game we bring. Even Sir Tedric gets hungry."

"Tell me then, how well is the town kept? Could a decent army take it?"

"From the road it would be difficult, but with a force to draw out the guard and another force to come from the wood, 'twould be a simple matter."

"It would be the finest pleasure to take Tedric now, before another day passes," Conan returned.

"Why do you tarry?"

"Of our comrades on the Crusade, four were sons of Theodoric. He still supports Tedric, as word has it. If my move is made too hastily, I may have a family war to contend with. I have no desire to meet men in battle whom I stood beside in months past." He looked into the fire and spoke solemnly. "And I've no desire to see Chandra harmed."

"Or the child," William put in.

Conan's eyes darted to William. "There is a child?" he asked hesitantly.

"She did not tell you?" William asked.

"There was little time. She warned me of Tedric's intention, and she pleaded for her husband's life. Now I see her reasons more clearly."

"Nay, Conan, I think not —"

Conan threw a twig into the fire and muttered, " 'Twill be difficult to coddle Tedric's child —"

"Conan," William said, cutting him off, "the child is not small and fair as Sir Tedric is. His eyes are blue, but not like his mother's, and the hair just sprouting forth is dark. His skin is not the pale white of Sir Tedric and Lady Chandra. He is a sturdy child and —"

Conan came to a slow realization and suddenly asked, "When was the child born?"

William laughed outright. "I think I could tell you when he was conceived."

"And yet he lives?"

"Tedric ignores his son. My daughter cares for the child and keeps him well away from Tedric."

"But if the child looks so much like another —"

"Chandra has prepared for the day that Wynne will have to steal him away. Yea, should Tedric become suspicious or hasten into battle, the lad will be taken away."

"How will you get them out?" Conan asked uneasily.

William smiled. "I can steal away anyone from this village, Conan, there is no problem. It is Chandra I cannot rescue. I leave her to you."

CHAPTER
21

THE journey to the Holy Land had taken many months, with delays of many varieties, from political to elemental, slowing them. The return voyage had taken only one month.

Sir Conan had departed England with twenty men and was fortunate to be returning with ten. Mallory and Thurwell were with him still, by the grace of God. As these bedraggled remains of Richard's army rode toward Anselm, they noted the changed look of the land. Those they passed wore a poor look and appeared downtrodden. Some would raise a hand to the returning Crusaders, but there was no cheering or gay welcome.

During the war in the east, Conan had lived his life day by day, not stopping to consider the effects the war was having on the land at home. With so many good men away, the crops were less abundant and the protection against thieves lacking. Cattle seemed sparser, piles of hay smaller and serfs thinner. In Conan's absence, Alaric's land had suffered greatly from yielding money, goods and men to the king's cause.

The guard recognized the returning troop, though Conan did not have his falcon riding his shoulder. Hundreds of horses had been taken and only a piddling few returned. That Mars did not survive the Crusade was no great surprise. The banner, tattered and worn, and the Cross of Christ on the chest of every knight brought the gates open and the bridge crashing down.

Alaric stood in the courtyard in wait. He looked more than three years older. Conan dismounted and walked slowly toward his father, hoping for the old man's sake that he would not notice the limp. But Alaric's eyes went to the injured leg at once and rose again to Conan's face. The impact of it did not register on Alaric's face: the old lord was made of stronger stuff. Even in his declining years he was capable of bearing the weight of this: that his son had been maimed.

Conan bowed before his father. He rose slowly to find Alaric's arms opened to him. He embraced his father gratefully, and the two stood in this closeness for a few moments before breaking apart. The walking staff that had become Alaric's constant companion had fallen to the ground, and when Conan released his father, Alaric faltered slightly, finding that he needed the cane more than he would admit. With a sigh, Conan bent to retrieve it.

Alaric indicated Conan's injured leg with his eyes. "We may move a bit more slowly, but we will walk together again," he said warmly. Then with a sigh and a scratchy voice he added, "There were days that I feared we would not."

"They found success in slowing me, but they could not finish me," Conan replied, proud that he had survived the heathen sword.

"When word came to England that the great James of Avesnes fell at Arsuf, my fear for your life heightened."

"Aye, he fell, but not alone. He took fifteen Saracens with him."

"The leg," Alaric asked. "How long has it been thus?"

"Months," Conan replied. "Since Acre. 'Twould mend, given a chance. But there was no rest until now. Now it will mend."

"Your victory?"

"Victory? Do they call it a victory here? I think it would better be called an escape — escape with some measure of dignity."

"But there is a treaty with Saladin . . ."

"Yea, my lord, a treaty." Conan laughed ruefully. "The two most honorable warriors in all the world formed a treaty. You would have been greatly amused by their strange friendship. While their armies fought, they exchanged expensive gifts. Saladin sent Richard fruit when he was ill, then killed the hostages. Richard wrote letters to Saladin — then attacked one of his cities.

"When we finally reached the Holy City, we had lost many good men, our horses were few, and food was lower than ever. The city was walled and well stocked with warriors. There was no possible way to conquer it; no way to do battle and have one man left to return to England. That was when the treaty was formed and Saladin promised to let pilgrims of the Cross enter the city for the sake of *our* Christ. And now that we are gone, will he honor the treaty? Will the pilgrims of the Cross be treated with respect, or killed?

"I would not fault Richard if there was no choice, and if Saladin does honor his word, we have made great progress in our Crusade. But I do not feel victory."

"And was it all for naught?"

"Time will tell that, Father. When I have settled matters here, we will see if the price of fighting in Richard's war has broken my purse or lined it with worth. Time will tell."

By this time, most of the other men had dismounted and pages were taking their horses to the Anselm stables. Mallory and Thurwell moved toward Alaric and were welcomed as warmly as Conan had been. It was as if three sons had returned to Anselm instead of just one. Alaric's moist and troubled eyes moved over them.

"Come into the hall," he bade them. "Greet your mother and ease her mind. She has been upset since the day you left us. Then we will talk."

Alaric turned and, with slow steps, leaning heavily on the staff for support, led the way into the hall. Inside was Udele, sitting in her chair, a royal and straight-backed throne carved from oak. Her hands, older now, gripped the arms of the chair in fearful anticipation. Lines about her eyes and mouth showed the effects of the last two and a half years. Her eyes opened wide as Conan came into the room.

She stared at him for a moment and, rising shakily, moved to meet him, embracing him fondly and placing kisses on his cheeks. The beard, just growing back, partially concealed the scar that lined one cheek, but Udele found it and touched it gingerly, tears running down her cheeks. "We have waited," she said, her voice breaking.

"I could not send word," Conan replied, setting her from him. His mother's tears bit at him. She had been angry when he left, never wishing him success in battle. He could not warm to her loving welcome now.

"But why have you taken so long to come?" she asked, the tears gone and a hint of anger in her voice.

"I came as quickly as I could. Here, we could use food and drink, and then we will talk." He looked to Alaric. "I have heard the fate of Phalen. I know what Tedric has done in my absence."

"Then you know that I have done nothing," Alaric returned somberly.

"It is the course I would have had you take," Conan said, his jaw tensing and the blue of his eyes lightening almost to the silver of a spear. "It is my battle. I will settle with Tedric. 'Tis a thing I should have done years ago. 'Twould have found us the same end, for naught but hate binds you and Theodoric now."

"Aye, hatred binds us to a fief war and we shall not, in our aging years, sit in our halls and hear of the battles our sons fight. He has done what I would have done. He supports his son. But he does not know that Tedric is not worthy of his loyalty."

"He has other sons," Conan advised, the cold light in his eyes glittering. "They may also choose to support their brother, but they will bring news to Theodoric of our friendship in battle."

"Blood in the vein is more binding."

" 'Tis fair," Conan said. "Tedric will have need of it." He closed his eyes and returned a calmer gaze to his father. "What I feel for Theodoric notwithstanding, Phalen is mine, and I will cut down any man who stands in my path. By the rood, I have paid a fair price for that holding. I did lay to rest three unborn children and a wife!"

"My lord," Mallory interrupted, unable to contain himself a moment longer. "My lady, Edythe —"

"Bring ale to these men," Alaric barked to a nearby servant. "And have trenchers of meat brought. Gravy and bread and whatever can be found. We would have planned a feast could your time of arrival been known." He turned his saddened eyes to Mallory. "Take up a cup, my son," he invited haltingly. "And as you drink, know that you have a place in my hall for as long as you wish."

Tankards were passed all around, and in the commotion of servants running among the men, Alaric found his chair and sat heavily. Mallory watched the aging lord in confusion. Neither drank. "Edythe?" he questioned anxiously.

Alaric looked at Mallory and, with a finger slightly bent from age, beckoned the younger man closer. " 'Tis hard news to bear you. Edythe is gone. She disappeared from Anselm not long after Conan left us. I sent searchers to travel through England and France to find her, but there was never a trace. We tried looking on departing vessels, thinking she might have tried to follow you, but we could find no sign that she ventured even that far. I do not believe she is alive."

"Nay," Mallory argued. "Nay, this is not true."

Alaric shook his head in confusion. "No one saw her pass. We do not know how she left or why. She suffered the expected sadness with your leaving and Conan's, but she was not disheartened. She did not take her own horse, a mount she favored —"

"But I have letters from Edythe!"

Alaric looked up in surprise. "Letters? When?"

"One that Conan brought when he joined us, one later. In both she urged me never to turn my head with worry, that she was well. She assured me she was safe."

The hopeful expression on Alaric's face turned sad again. "The second letter must have been written before she left this keep and the messenger slow —"

"Almost a year? Nay, my lord, that cannot be. Edythe is alive — and I will find her. Where were you when she left this hall?"

"I had ridden to Stoddard with Galen. When I returned, my wife was frantic with the disappearance. Lady Udele had sent riders in search of our daughter and called me home from Stoddard."

Mallory's fist hit the lord's table in frustration. "The letter!" he stormed. "Nay, the messenger was not slow! That could not be. Not so long! She was trying to tell me —"

"You have the letter?"

"Nay. But she urged me to keep faith that there was nothing that could keep her from waiting upon my return. My lord, she could not have written that while she was still here with you. Had she done so, she would have waited to send it with the messenger that brought Conan's letters from you."

"She would not have flown from me with no word," Alaric said. "And if she is alive, my men would have found her!"

"She is not dead!" Mallory shouted, his hand finding the hilt of his sword, a habit a knight develops whenever he feels threatened. "Her letter came to me after the second Christmas I was without her."

"The letter is a mystery. Edythe was not shallow-witted, and she would not have spent what little she had to buy a courier when my letters to Conan went with some regularity. But what purpose in her leaving when all she needed was provided here?"

Mallory's jaw twitched, for those same questions were coming into his mind. "More to the point, my lord: what drove her from Anselm?"

"I share your burden," Alaric said more calmly. "I have, for more than two years, tried to reason her leaving and I cannot find her — alive or dead."

Through this discussion, Udele's face had drained of

color as she listened intently. The letter puzzled her as
much as Alaric. A slow courier was the only answer — she
hoped.

"Edythe must have written the letter after leaving you,"
Mallory said. "You have letters here that were sent by me?"

"Aye, I have saved them to return to you."

"I thought it strange that she did not mention — when,
exactly, did she leave Anselm?"

"It was late in summer. We searched until the weather
would not permit and searched again when it warmed."

"Weather will not slow me," Mallory said resolutely.
"With all respect, Conan, I must ask you to release me
from my promise to help you fight Tedric. I have a task
at hand that cannot wait. In the letter from Edythe, she
talked of the cold, the promise of snow. It could not have
been written before she left here."

"Perhaps the winter before?" Alaric suggested.

"Nay. We did not leave England until after Easter.
Letters would have been sent to Vézelay. This letter was
written just as winter threatened." He laughed suddenly.
"I was sorely in want of words of love from Edythe! She
talked of wet and cold; of clouds ready to spill their
flakes; of wind, icy on her face! She was telling me the
time of year: the time she was alive!"

The picture became clear to Alaric. For the same reasons he had kept the news from Mallory, so would Edythe.
If Mallory could not return and had been preoccupied
with worry of her circumstances, he might have fared badly
in the battle.

"The missive might have cost her her last livre, but it
was sent," Mallory said. "The reason must be that had
you sent word to me that she was missing, I would have

been encouraged by her letter. But had I heard nothing, I would continue to think she was safe. Either way I had no cause to worry."

"And how will you find her, if your theory is true?"

"If there is some reason Edythe fears telling even you where she hides, she will make herself easy to find when she learns that the Crusaders have returned to England. Never fear, my lord, I will find her."

"I will help you," Conan offered.

"Nay, Conan, this time you cannot. You have another task at hand. And should I make this mission short, I will return to help you. For now, you cannot be occupied away from this keep. Your place is here; my place is in search of a damsel."

"You will send word?" Conan asked.

"I will find a way."

Alaric looked over this group. They had all changed a great deal. They were older, their faces showing the strain of fighting in the heat of the sun in that faraway land. Mallory showed some gray in his hair, and Thurwell, while still a hulking, solid man, looked his age of forty. Conan, handsome and tall, seemed tired and worn. In his eyes there was a notable lack of energy but an over-abundance of anger.

"My lord," Mallory addressed Alaric. "I do not lay blame to you, but I must test your story to the limit of my endurance."

Alaric nodded. "I hope that you will succeed where I have failed."

"I can promise that I will try," he returned. Thurwell came forward and put a hand on Mallory's shoulder, indicating that he would be going with his friend. Mallory looked to Conan. "What are your plans?" he asked.

"We have talked of plans on the road," Conan replied, not anxious to say any more in the presence of so many servants. "Above that, I will train a falcon."

"And a horse?" Thurwell asked.

"Aye, though I do not expect a beast such as Orion in such a short time. Neither the bird nor the steed can be replaced, but my priorities in that have not changed. Other loyalties have changed, but for my birds and beasts I have the same devotion."

Alaric nodded his head once and let his eyes rest comfortably on his son's face. A slow smile grew on the aging lord's lips. To his sword, his ability to fight, Conan would be true — for he would not be betrayed.

" 'Tis a time that comes in every man's life. It has come in yours. Do what you will. I will be steadfast."

"Thank you, my lord. I have need of nothing more." That said, he turned and went to the stair, intent on finding his chamber.

There were few returning knights, so that it was an easy chore for Anselm to see them well fitted for the night. All were given rooms. Conan's chamber was richly appointed with tapestries and animal-hide rugs. Pelts were strewn over a fine bed to keep the cold from penetrating his bones and to raise this great knight from the floor. Mallory and Thurwell were not thought after as carefully, but their chamber was not beggarly.

Even in a room kept warm by a blazing fire, with pelts to give him comfort, Mallory could not sleep. His mind twisted in his own private agony as he considered the many possibilities surrounding Edythe's disappearance. And Thurwell, who shared his feelings more closely than any other, tossed on his pallet for a long time before falling into badly needed slumber.

Mallory finally rose and pulled on his chausses and gown. Ever the warrior, he never considered so much as a breath of night air without strapping on his belt over his hips, his broadsword in place. He took no mantle, for he hoped the chill would snap him out of his worrisome musings and into clear thinking. Then, perhaps, he could sleep.

He passed the forms of sleeping servants in the hall and heard no sound as he moved through the galleries. Alaric had a few guards posted about the hall, and Mallory passed them all without being questioned. He walked into the courtyard and found a pile of rocks on which to sit.

He wondered what insanity had prevailed in his absence. He could not even consider that Edythe's last letter was the product of a slow courier. She had written it from some hiding place. He remembered the days before he left England. He had delivered Edythe to her father's house and gone to Stoddard for Thurwell. He had had very little time with her before leaving — time enough only for good-byes. But there was bliss even in this, for they no longer had to steal their moments at midnight in the garden, nor did they have to pretend nonchalance in parting.

She had been strong when he left her, secure in her heart.

"Do not be afraid," he had told her.

"I am not afraid. Never doubt me. Move forward and know my heart."

"It will be hard for you while I am away," he had said.

"Love knows no time but that spent apart. Yea, it will be hard, but I am strong. And I know my reward."

No man could have had a stronger, more determined wife. Her love was steadfast; even in the earliest days of her youth she was capable of knowing her mind and standing by her word.

Dead? It could not be. Alaric must have adopted this hapless reasoning to avoid the truth: there was treachery here. Tedric, who would hurt anyone Conan loved, did not even seem the proper villain in this case. It would have meant too much planning and expertise, and Tedric would not effect Edythe's capture and death to provoke Conan unless he could gloat over his success. Thieves in the night? He could not quiet his mind. But his business was on the road, not musing in the night. There would be no stone unturned before he was finished.

There was no moon, and though it did not rain, the night fog had settled over the keep and the air was damp. Twice, as he walked toward the stables, he tripped over a stone in his path. A torch at the entrance lit the path, but within, there was only darkness, for the stable also housed some sleeping men.

Mallory left the door ajar so that he could see the articles of his profession. He found what he expected. Every bridle and saddle was clean and neatly laid out with other items necessary for his early departure. He closed the door quietly, taking great care not to disturb those sleeping in the stable. The tower stair would allow him a swifter path to his bedchamber, and he moved to the rear of the keep to take that route. A light, faint and hazy through the fog, was the torch that he knew lit the door to the tower stair, and he moved toward that light, mindful of the darkness and possible hidden obstacles in his path.

Suddenly he was caught about the neck and pulled backward into the deeper shadows, where his assailant held him against the wall of the keep. He quickly found the hilt of his sword, but his hand was frozen there as he felt the blade of a sharp knife against his throat. "I know what you seek," a husky voice whispered in his ear. The person speaking was trying to disguise his voice. "The nunnery — Swaffham Bulbeck near Bury Saint Edmunds — will show you the answer." Mallory's hands were on his assailant's forearm, pulling with all his strength to ease the hold on his throat. He felt his temples begin to throb from the strength of the hold, but the attacker did not ease. "Tell not a soul of this warning. Tell no rider your destination. Your life depends on your silence."

Another unexpected move threw Mallory flat to the ground on his face. As he hit the earth, the air was knocked out of his lungs, and he gasped, drawing in not only air, but a mouthful of dust. He coughed to clear his chest and then listened. The quickly departing footfalls told him his attacker had fled.

"Who goes there?" came the voice of the tower-stair guard.

Mallory struggled to his feet and rubbed his aching neck. "Sir Mallory," he attempted, his voice hoarse.

"Trouble?" the guard questioned, giving him aid in standing.

"Nay. I fell. 'Tis the darkest of nights."

"I heard another sound," the guard offered.

Mallory laughed in feigned embarrassment. " 'Twas the sound of a man boasting of too much wine trying to stand up."

The guard laughed. "Sleep will remedy that," he advised.

"Aye. Sleep." Mallory stumbled a bit, and the guard was convinced that Mallory had taken the better part of a keg before his nighttime stroll. The guard chuckled softly as Mallory attempted the stairs. And then the door closed softly behind him.

Mallory stood for a moment just inside his chamber. Someone here knew of Edythe's flight: her purpose and her destination. He was warned to say nothing even as he rode in pursuit of her — as he valued his life. That could only mean that a traitor could be anywhere, even among the men who would ride with him. If she was still alive, someone here had taken her away. If she was dead, her murderer was still within these walls.

It was now impossible for him to sleep. He was up and dressed before dawn and rousing his men and Thurwell at the first light of day. When the horses were ready and the provender loaded, he could not be on the road fast enough. His manner was cool and detached, and he was suspicious of every face.

Those who rode with him knew his burden and were not surprised with his quick and almost angry departure, but the terse good-byes to Conan and Alaric left many shaking their heads in wonder. Even Thurwell questioned this behavior.

" 'Tis no fault of theirs, yet you seem bent on placing blame. And after such good lodging, is it meet to leave them with such poor thanks? And where do we go? You have told us of no plan, no route."

Mallory just looked forward as he rode, his only answer to his longtime friend as short and sharp as his farewells. "Northeast."

CHAPTER
22

THERE was a time when the lacemaker's shop was bright and cheerful. As Giselle looked around her modest dwelling, she could hardly remember those days of happiness. Few of her neighbors visited her, and Lady Udele was the only one to ask for predictions. It no longer helped to support her. Udele was no longer a generous benefactor.

Giselle felt the end of something drawing near. It could be the ending of her own life that she felt, but she could not say. Her sight had become clearer as her body began to fail. She feared death, even in her old age, because she wondered if anyone could subdue Udele when the predictions were finally over. She opted to try one more time.

On her next visit, Udele thrust a shirt at Giselle. "It is still warm from his body and I know you can tell me much."

Giselle knew before she was told that the shirt belonged to Conan. She had developed such a oneness with the knight that she could sense his presence as if he were in the room with them.

"In a moment, madam," she said evenly. "I am growing old and you must be patient."

"I would know where my son has been since he put in to port," Udele snapped. "Don't bother to lie to me."

"He was, in fact, at Cordell, madam. He saw Lady Chandra for only a moment. He warned her that he would meet Tedric."

Udele gave a short grunt and looked away. "And where was the need for that? It is not as if she wouldn't guess."

"He does not blame her for Tedric's crimes. He knows she is blameless in all that has befallen her."

"Blameless? Never! Don't tell me of her innocence. She has lusted after my son for years!"

Giselle felt the anger bite her deeply, but she held her tongue. "Lady, there is nothing you can do about what will be," she said pleadingly. "Some seeds are planted long before a child is conceived. Let matters rest —"

"Bah!" Udele huffed.

"Madam, I have spoken of a plan. For one man, his purpose is done when he has sown the seeds for the winter rye. For another, the purpose is not served before eighty summers have passed. Some must kill that others would be martyred. My sight does not tell me every man's purpose. It tells me what is to be. And Sir Conan will be a great leader of men. One of the most powerful men in England."

"You see so distantly?" Udele brightened, captivated not only by the prophecy, but by the power promised to her son.

"When you carried the child in your womb, did I not tell you he would be a great knight?"

"Tell me what you see," she urged.

"Conan's lands will stretch wide across England, much of his holdings next to what Count John claims. Richard will provide no heir and John will be king — a hard king to abide. There will only be a few strong enough and brave enough to temper a bad king's rule. Sir Conan will be one of them. A hundred angels will guard him from death. His dynasty will be long and closely attached to the royal court. His descendants will emerge in later years to fight in a great war lasting one hundred years. That is where his people will end."

Giselle took a breath. "His future is so well defined, madam, that your attempts to alter it will only prove a disaster. You will fall before he will."

Udele's eyes looked suddenly sad. "I would only ensure my place in his life. He owes me that much. I gave him birth."

Giselle answered in soft tones. "There is a place for you in Sir Conan's life. Your pension will be plentiful, for his justice is well known. Your abode would be rich, for he would not take one pleasure from you. He is a hardened man, but within his heart there is compassion for those he loves. Let Conan be and —"

"He is to be rich — as rich as Count John," Udele said, as though the news had just settled in. "There is still time for Alaric to find him a rich bride. And I am young: I have many years yet to live. I will see him come to power and I will be near enough to aid him."

Giselle lowered her eyes. Her back was aching. Her frustration was intense. She did not know how to help the lady of Anselm.

"I can only urge you as I have in the past, madam. Let it be, and Conan will achieve his destiny."

There was a glassy sheen in the eyes that looked back at her. Udele had come to hate Chandra. In the beginning, the lass was a threat only because of her meager dowry, but later the threat became greater as Udele saw the strength Chandra exhibited.

Udele began to shake her head wildly. First she had maneuvered Edwina toward her son to save him from a beggarly marriage. Then she had borrowed money to pay Tedric to remove Chandra from her son's eye. She had been responsible for one death, and when Edwina had uncovered that truth, Udele had killed with her own hands to silence her. And even her own daughter, she had ordered killed. The lies and murders had multiplied. After all her efforts to deny Chandra a life with Conan, how could she live peacefully under the same roof with her now? Never would Udele be second behind her. Never!

She asked the same question she had asked years earlier. "Who stands by my son's side?"

"A woman fair and strong. A woman whose wisdom reaches beyond her years. Her hair is golden as the sun; her eyes bright as the sky. It is clearly Lady Chandra."

"It has not happened yet!"

"You are wrong, lady. It has happened. She has already borne him a son."

"Nay," she cried. "Nay, it could not be so! Conan has been away —"

Udele stopped suddenly and plunged her hands into her hair. *Tedric* had a son: a child of almost two years. When would the child have been conceived? Before the Crusade? But Conan left for Vézelay to join Richard. Or was he in England, at Cordell, with Chandra?

Chandra might know! Tedric might have told her that it was Udele's tampering that encouraged him to kill the first Jew, usurp Phalen and continue his life of crime. Conan could not claim Chandra *now!*

Udele suddenly began to laugh, a shrill sound that rang loud in the small room. Giselle felt a cold draft, as if evil had suddenly entered the house.

"She is an adulteress!" Udele cried victoriously. "And what do you suppose Tedric will do? How will he reward her?" The laughter rang out again, a wicked and chilling laugh close to hysteria.

"And what of the child?" Giselle asked in near panic.

"What of the child?" Udele retorted.

"Will Tedric let a child of Conan's live?"

"What does it matter?"

"It matters to Sir Conan. He knows he has a son. He cherishes the thought."

"You tell me Conan will live for many years. There is time enough to father more children." Udele rose to her feet and moved toward the door. "You swore my son would marry Chandra, and I saw him wed to Edwina. Your great predictions aren't as strong as my hand!"

"Nay, madam," Giselle said, rising from her stool. "You did not interrupt the plan. He was meant to have Edwina. Edwina brought him Phalen."

A wild look came into Udele's eyes as if she had been betrayed. Giselle had never hinted that this was to take place. "Your sight be damned! I will yet find a way to change your great plans. My son will have his power. But *I* will share it!"

Udele whirled and flung the door open wide. The last sight of her was her swirling cloak as she fled angrily from the cottage.

Giselle suddenly felt a warm sensation encompass her. Her eyes glowed as many questions were clearly answered in her mind. A slow smile came over her face.

"Our end is near, madam," Giselle said softly. "Sir

Conan will have his lands, his love and his power, but you will not share it. Yet you have done your part to secure it for him." She sighed deeply. "The pity is he cannot be expected to feel anything but hate for you."

November passed and December touched England with icy fingers. The doors to the village huts were closed tight against the wind, and there were no villeins about selling their wares or hanging out their laundry. Even the animals that were not sheltered huddled together to stay warm.

Sir Mallory traveled slowly, stopping at every village and country home. His impulse was to fly to Swaffham Bulbeck, but he did not dare to leave this path unchecked.

If Edythe had passed this way, it would have been in summer when the streets were crowded with merchants and travelers. Trying to trace her footsteps in winter proved difficult, for doors had to be opened to the knights before inquiries could be made. Everywhere he asked, he told of the bright emerald-green eyes and the long black hair, features hard to forget. But no one remembered such a woman.

Cold winds and snow slowed the journey even more, and the trip stretched into the third week before they neared Swaffham Bulbeck. Mallory had seen nunneries before, including those of the Benedictine order, whose purpose was to live with hard work and simple means. Still, because he hoped to find Edythe here, he was taken aback with the weak construction of the buildings. The convent was in sore need of repair. Smoke rose above the outbuildings and the doors were stout, but the roof was soaked through and there was no evidence that the convent could boast even a stable.

"What brings us here?" Thurwell asked. "It cannot be your intention to investigate every convent we pass. We leave a dozen behind us."

Mallory ignored the question and went to the door of the first outbuilding, pounding his fist on that oaken portal. There was no response from within. He pounded again and again. Finally a voice answered him. "Who calls?"

"A knight of the Cross. Will you open to me?"

The bolt from the inside slid back, and the door creaked open slowly. An elderly man in a ragged shirt peeked out.

"How can I serve you, sir knight?" he asked gingerly, looking carefully at the white cross on the chest of this visitor.

"I am in need of information. I have traveled far to hear if a maid I seek came to the sisters here."

"There is no maid here," the old man said, trying to close the door.

Mallory's arm hit the door and prevented its closing. "I have come too far, old man, to be sent away now. The Sisters of Saint Mary may have word of her. I have been sent in this direction by one who knows. I will speak with the prioress or I will enter against your will." He indicated the men still astride by a glance over his shoulder. The order would not contain more than a dozen nuns, some aging people cared for out of charity and perhaps a guest or two in need. All totaled, servants and residents would not number over thirty, and they would have no arms to defend themselves. " 'Twould not be difficult to enter and have my questions answered."

"Milord, milord, you know the penalty for defiling the House of God, and these good sisters would —"

"The prioress!" he shouted.

"Aye, milord! I will tell her a knight of the Cross is here. I will fetch her now."

"Be quick," he warned, removing his hand and allowing the door to close. He heard the bolt as it was quickly replaced.

Thurwell came up behind him. "Who sent you to this place?" he asked quietly.

"The eve before our parting I was struck down by a man while walking from the stable late at night. I could not see him nor identify him in any way, but he told me to come to Swaffham Bulbeck. He said that what I seek is here."

"But you said nothing, and you did not come here straightaway."

"He warned me to say nothing or my life would be cut short. That could mean a traitor in our party even now. I never doubted you, but there were too often other ears within our range. And I did not want to leave those villages between Anselm and Swaffham Bulbeck unchecked."

"Whom do you doubt now?"

"There is treachery in Alaric's house. I cannot guess who would betray such a fine family."

The bolt moved again and the door creaked open. In the doorway stood a woman in a black habit, her face wrinkled with age and her hands hidden in the folds of her sleeves. But her eyes were soft and her lips formed a pleasant line. She nodded once to Mallory and then to Thurwell. "It is not kind that you should frighten one who serves our order," she admonished lightly.

"Beg pardon, Sister," he said to the prioress. "I would not allow the door closed on my question. I believe someone here can help me find the woman I seek."

"I must know more about this woman you search for.

If I bid you enter here, will you give your word that you and your men will not disrupt this house? We have no weapons here and cannot defend ourselves. All reside here in peace."

"I give you my word, Sister."

"There is a warm fire and drink within, if you will treat those who serve you kindly."

"I am grateful, Sister." Mallory bowed.

"I don't know that I can help you find the woman you seek, sir knight," the nun said, shaking her head. "Many seek refuge here for a time and then leave. I will help you if I can." She turned and entered the building again and Mallory gestured to his men that they should follow.

The small room was warm and friendly, a place, obviously, for secular visitors to wait for assistance from the nuns. There was another, heavier door leading from the room to where the sisters lived and prayed. He reasoned that few ever ventured beyond that heavy door.

The men entered the warm room and soon the fire warmed and dried them. The nun who had invited them in moved closer to the door that led to the rest of the convent. She beckoned Mallory near that they might talk with some measure of privacy. "When did this woman you seek visit our house?" she asked.

"I do not know that she visited here," Mallory attempted to explain. "She disappeared from her family over two years ago, during the late summer months. There has been no trace of her and no one saw her leave. Her name is Edythe and her home was Anselm. No one knows the reason why she left, nor whether she was taken against her will or if she fled on her own mission. A man I could not name told me to come here in search of her."

The nun shook her head sadly. "I know of no woman,

but I will ask the other sisters — every one of them — if you wish."

"Please, Sister. There must be a reason why I was sent in this direction. Someone must know where she is."

"Why do you seek this one, sir knight?"

Mallory's eyes grew soft and sad. "She is my wife," he said in a low voice. "I took her just before leaving for war. I left her and money enough to support her with her father. I fear her life is in great danger — if she is alive even now."

The nun smiled warmly. "I sense no danger, sir knight. Rest easy for now and I will speak with the other nuns. Have you a name, sir knight?"

The nun's kindly face gave him ease and he smiled. "Yea, Sister. I am called Sir Mallory."

"And I am Sister Agatha."

"I will reward you handsomely if you can help me, Sister. I —" his voice broke slightly and he closed his mouth abruptly to stiffen his chin. "I love her."

"If I am able to help you, Sir Mallory, I will have my reward. No other seems necessary. Join your men and warm yourself. It will take some time to talk to the other nuns."

Mallory sat on the edge of a bench beside Thurwell and quietly explained why they waited. No one seemed to turn an ear toward Mallory's hushed tones. He wondered again if anyone here would betray him.

The better part of an hour had passed and the door to the convent remained closed. When the prioress returned, Mallory snapped to his feet and towered above the little nun, anxious to hear her news. There was a soft smile on her lips. "There is a sister here who has some memory of this woman you seek, but she is old and sickly and cannot come to you. I will take you to her so that you can ask your questions."

"May Sir Thurwell come? He is a trusted friend."

"I see no reason to refuse," she replied.

Thurwell followed Mallory and Sister Agatha silently. The nun led them down a hallway past many doors. When she paused to open one of two large carved oaken doors, Mallory halted in surprise. He had expected to be led to a sickroom to speak to a bedridden old woman. This door led into a chapel.

Sister Agatha stood back and indicated that the men should enter. Mallory and Thurwell stepped into the small chapel. Tapestries hung from the walls and candles lit the altar. The crucifix loomed above a veiled woman kneeling in prayer. Mallory turned to question the nun, but the door softly closed and she was gone.

From the altar, the woman rose and turned at the sound of the closing door. Mallory took two quick yet halting steps in her direction, his mouth slightly open and his eyes hopeful. The dream he had carried with him into war stood before him now. His breath left him in a heavy sigh and he opened his arms to Edythe. He felt tears come to his eyes, and to keep from weeping he held her closely, not breaking the embrace even to look at her face. He needed to fill his arms with her — possess her and not release her.

Gradually his arms relaxed and he looked down at her. There was nothing of the child he married. Womanhood was etched into her fine features. Her eyes were soft and knowing; her mouth curving and inviting. He kissed her long and lovingly, drinking of her devotion.

"I knew you would find me, my love," she breathed against his lips.

He held her away from himself, looking at her closely. He was not ready for discussion, but the mystery of her departure plagued him. Loving would come later. He needed the answers now. "Your father thinks you dead," he said, the confusion showing in his eyes.

She nodded, her eyes showing her sadness. "My brother?"

"He is home, waiting for word that I've found you."

She shook her head as if to say they could not oblige Conan this time. Mallory touched her veil. "Edythe, you did not flee me — our marriage?"

"Nay," she breathed, standing on her toes to touch his lips with hers. "Oh, my love, I would have waited forever —" She looked over Mallory's shoulder to see Thurwell's back. The older knight faced the chapel door, either out of respect for their privacy or out of embarrassment. "Sir Thurwell," she called. The man turned and looked at Edythe with relief. He smiled and nodded his greeting, his cheeks slightly flushed because he felt like an intruder.

"You must both hear my story. Then we must decide what to do."

Edythe settled herself on the floor, for there were no pews or chairs in this chapel. She patted the rushes beside her and Mallory and Thurwell sat as well, their long swords flaring out behind them.

Edythe explained the lacemaker's powers, something these men had known nothing of. She told of the day she had heard her mother's confession that Edwina's death was not an accident. And then the drink that had caused her deep sleep.

"When I awoke, a full day had passed. My clothes were wet from the ground and my mouth was dry. Pierce, my mother's manservant, had been given the chore of ending

my life. He could have seen the matter done before my
eyes opened another time, but he did not. He hid me in
the forest until the sleeping herb was worn away. He
gave me coins and bade me flee from Anselm, telling me
that he could not protect me for another day. She would
have found out I was alive —" Her voice cracked, for the
urge to cry was strong. This wickedness in her own mother
caused her great pain. Two years with the kind sisters had
eased that pain only slightly.

"How did you come here, Edythe?" Mallory asked.

She shook away the urge to weep and went on bravely.
"These sisters once showed Pierce a kindness when he was
traveling. He knew of the place and promised I would
be protected here. I put flour in my hair and wax on my
face. I kept my head low and covered with a dark hood.
Had you looked for an old hag riding an aging mare, more
people might have answered you."

"Could your own father not have protected you from
her?" Mallory asked in anger. "Surely some message to
him could have —"

"I regret my father's sadness in thinking me dead, but
this way offered more assurance that no accident would
prevent me from seeing your return. I do not know how
deep the veins of my mother's wickedness run through
Anselm. Many there fear her. My father is a strong ruler,
true, but he has allowed her a free hand with much of
Anselm. She knows how to have her way." She shook her
head. "You could not understand it as I do, my love. You
have never seen my father's wrath when someone dared to
decry his wife. It is a very old rule," she said, laughing
ruefully. "If he took a course with her out of anger, that
was acceptable. But he would never allow another to accuse her. And he does not want to see that she is cruel."

"Conan must be told."

"And how will you tell him? Will you take me to him now? Will this be finished now?"

Mallory ran a hand through his hair. "Conan has battles to fight. He must know that his own mother is crazed, that she seeks a place at his side, even if it means his ruin."

"What battles?" Edythe asked. Was the war not over *even now?*

"Tedric holds Phalen. He holds Lady Chandra prisoner in her own Cordell, lest she flee him now. There is a child: the child was sired by your brother. Yea, there will be a war, though how great or small cannot be determined. Much of that rests on Theodoric's declaration and King Richard's return. It is our hope that the king will cure the fox of his lust for riches and power, for Tedric is guilty of crimes Richard can call treasonous. He did slay Jews — Jews under the protection of the crown."

"Chandra," Edythe breathed, sorting through this information carefully. "My mother fears and hates Chandra. If there is any way to do her harm, my mother will try."

"I don't think Lady Udele can reach Chandra. Not to help her, not to hurt her."

"But I think the place for us is not Anselm, but near Chandra. We could not go to Cordell, but we could be near." She looked at Mallory and Thurwell with the question in her eyes. "Could we hide ourselves near enough to Cordell at least to watch Tedric's moves?"

The men exchanged glances and each thought for a moment.

"There is one thing I trust Conan to do," Thurwell finally said. "I trust he will be assured of Chandra's safety before he comes to blows with Tedric." Thurwell smiled. "I think the lass is right," he told Mallory, nodding toward

Edythe. "I think we should place ourselves near Tedric for now."

"Aye," Edythe nodded eagerly. "Let us be near Chandra. The lady cannot be replaced."

"I will take the men back to the last village and find them lodgings. They can return to Alaric with a message that tells him there is proof you are still alive and we go on alone to find you. Tie together what you can carry easily and I will return in the morning with a horse for you."

He placed a soft kiss on her cheek. "I will leave you for one more night. It will be the last time."

"I have managed two years, but this night will be the longest."

Mallory gave his message to one of the riders and sent them off early the next morning. Crusader's garb and blazoned shields were discarded. The men dressed themselves in simple clothing, but their size and mannerisms gave the lie to the disguise.

Gold was dropped into the palm of Sister Agatha. Her promise that they would not be betrayed was accepted as an oath, and the three riders left the convent, their mounts leading them south in the direction of Cordell.

CHAPTER
23

C HRISTMAS was a joyous celebration for most of England. With the knights and soldiers returning to their families, the relief turned to gaiety that spread from earl to knight to serf. And with the returning Crusaders came the hope that money and muscle would be spent strengthening the affairs at home.

The exception was at Cordell, where the return of the Crusaders meant an inevitable struggle.

The tension in the hall was as thick as the ice on the ground. Tedric, temporarily immobilized by bad weather, sent messenger after messenger into the cold wind to bring him word of his allies and enemy. Liegemen of Count John were contacted so that Tedric would be assured of his support. Missives were sent to Theodoric for the same reason, and men were sent toward Anselm to monitor Conan's moves. The tension grew as Tedric awaited replies or news. What he learned he did not like.

Theodoric sent word that Tedric's four older brothers were not quick to rally to his side, for they had been, for over two years, close companions to Sir Conan and they thought highly of him. Tedric was not even sure of his father's support, since Tedric's alliance with Count John was met with disfavor by his family.

"If they fail me, I have support enough from the

count!'' he shouted after reading one of his father's letters.

Chandra, hearing this, mumbled a silent prayer that Richard would soon return to England. But that hope was dashed on a cold day in January when another message came to Tedric. King Richard had been captured and was being held prisoner.

Richard had insulted the German Duke Leopold in Palestine. While most of Richard's army had returned by sea, Richard had chosen a land route. Leopold captured him and was holding him in his German manor, seeking a ransom for his release.

Thus, John had little time for private family wars. He had his eyes on more than Tedric's domain: he would have all of England. He traveled to Normandy and Paris, paying homage to those leaders in return for their support. Rumors spread that Richard was already dead, leaving John as rightful heir. England's nobles were confused and frightened, struggling with their loyalties, trying to decide whether to wait upon the return of the king or go with John now, early in his search for supporters.

Alaric declared his support of Richard. Tedric hoped that his father would go with John, but his brothers had fought with Richard and they loved and admired him. They all, save Tedric, supported Richard and would fight John in any attempt he made to usurp the crown. Theodoric's support was slipping further and was present in name only. Tedric was frightened. And with his fear came rage.

February dragged and March brought no challenge from Sir Conan, but word was delivered to Tedric that the knight was not spending his winter idly. Conan too was making inquiries. Through his messengers and his own travels, Conan was asking questions about Tedric's activities over the past two years. And, to add to the insult, he was building an army within Anselm's walls.

"If Conan attacks Phalen and you are here —" Chandra attempted.

"Phalen is stout," Tedric replied. "And do not try to persuade me to leave here and await his whim at Phalen. That is clearly what he wants: to have me stand ready for weeks and even months while he does nothing."

If it was what Conan planned, it had worked. Conan had not even acknowledged Tedric's possession of Phalen.

It was near the end of March when Master William visited the keep. He came to speak to Lady Chandra, but even he was not allowed a private moment with her. He addressed Tedric, but not until the lady was near enough to hear.

"Milord, game is not so deep in the forest and our fishermen are finding more catch near the shore. I would send a hunting party out, since meat is desired."

Chandra smiled to herself. William knew the land and the sky. He would not have bothered for Tedric's permission to enter the forest. He looked for a way to tell Chandra that spring was near. The weather would be warm enough for travel — and war.

Late one night in the month of March, Chandra stood outside her bedchamber and looked up at the first clear sky she had seen in some time. The wind was still cold off the sea, but the sleet and snow would be no more.

She cuddled her son close to her breast, though he was not much interested in being cuddled. There were other things on his busy little mind. But she cooed to him with a sadness in her voice.

"Lady," Wynne said softly to her back.

Chandra turned and, with tear-filled eyes, handed over her son. "Take him quickly," she begged.

"I will guard him carefully, lady," Wynne promised.

She could not bear to watch the door to her bedchamber close behind Wynne and her son. She would not be allowed the luxury of knowing if they made their way to Laine safely. If Tedric should notice the child missing and set out after them, all three might lose their lives.

She looked up at the sky, her tears hot on her cheeks. The pain and fear she knew in sending her son to safety were almost more than she could bear.

Conan, she thought wildly. Will you know your son? Will he ever know a father's love and strength? Am I alone — truly alone — without a protector, without hope? Oh, God above me — am I alone?

While Eleanor, the Queen Mother, worked toward the release of her son Richard, Count John was rumored to be busily plotting his royal brother's death. His treachery was known to be limitless.

In a small village near the Anglesey monastery, there were two returned soldiers keeping meager lodgings through the winter. They called themselves John and Michael. The man called John had a wife, a lovely woman dark of hair, with bewitching green eyes. The three kept quietly to themselves, the man called Michael taking his meals with the couple and sleeping each night in the stable behind the house. They bought their provender sparingly and the men did simple chores from time to time in exchange for a meal or a few coins. The only thing that set them apart from the many misplaced soldiers was the fact that they had stabled three fine horses.

Their secrets were held behind the door of their one room.

"The time is near when we can stay in the wood around Cordell. The nights are warmer and the brush thicker. Edythe, I think it safer that you stay here," Mallory said.

Edythe nodded, though she feared the length of time she might be forced to keep this tiny room. Their money was running low.

"Did you send the message?" Mallory asked Thurwell.

"I paid the man to put it in Conan's hand. And when he returns I shall have to pay him again for his answer."

"What did you write?"

"That one in his house betrays him. I dared not name the lady for fear the message would not reach him. And I wrote the rest: that we await the dove and watch. He should know it has come from us."

"Unless he has grown slow-witted through the winter, he will know where to find us. Edythe, soon he will know that you live."

"He will not guess our mother betrays him," she said sadly.

Few travelers passed through the single street of the small burgh. There was a better road to the monastery and a faster way to Colchester. That was the very reason Mallory and Thurwell had chosen the little farming village. Therefore, Thurwell looked suspiciously at a cart bearing two women and a small child. The wheel on the cart wobbled dangerously and Thurwell pointed out the trouble to Mallory.

"The old hag travels without a man. Mayhaps she has need of help. Soon the thing will topple and spill out the young woman and her child."

"Never mind their troubles now," Mallory returned.

"The woman, Mallory," he murmured. "I have seen her before."

"You lay claim to every wench who passes," Mallory remarked.

"Nay, I have seen her before. Look at her."

As the cart passed, both women kept their heads bent low. Although Mallory was not very curious, when he bent his head to look at the younger woman's face he ceded she was familiar, but since he could not place her he turned to follow Edythe.

"Old woman," Thurwell called, causing her to rein in her tired horse. "Your wheel needs repair."

"I go not far, sir," she said, urging the horse forward again.

"Do not fear I would cheat you," Thurwell said, grabbing the rein. "I will help you."

The child at the younger woman's side began to whimper and tugged at her mantle. Thurwell looked at the child and frowned. Then he looked at the younger woman and saw a pleading look in her eyes. A wisp of the blond hair she attempted to conceal under the hood of her cloak fell along her cheek. The pleasant face touched a place in his memory. With a snap he connected the face to the name. He had many times seen her serving Chandra in the past.

"Wynne?" he asked.

"Please," she begged softly. "Let us pass."

"You do not know me?" he asked in a whisper.

"Nay," she breathed. "Let us pass."

"Wynne," he pressed. "Thurwell. I am Sir Thurwell, Conan's friend."

A tear came to her eye. "Please do not stop us here. No one must remember our passing or we will be found."

"The child?" he questioned.

"My lady's son."

Thurwell straightened and let go of the rein. "Move along," he said. He watched them pass down the street. There were a few simple bundles in the cart, enough to allow Thurwell to guess that wherever they were bound, they intended to stay for a time. He could not guess their destination, but he could reason the purpose. He was certain they sought to escape Tedric.

Mallory approached Thurwell. "The woman," Thurwell said softly. " 'Tis Chandra's handmaiden, Wynne. She flees Cordell with Chandra's son."

"Conan's son," Mallory said.

"She is fearful. She would not talk to me here. Trouble may follow her and we must see her to safety."

They allowed time enough to pass, and then the two knights took their horses and followed the cart. It was not difficult to catch up with.

"We fly to Thetford," Wynne told them anxiously. "My father is taking many men into the forest, and Sir Tedric grows more impatient every day, and my lady was fearful for her son. We seek haven with her sister in the convent."

"Thetford!" Mallory choked. "The child would be safer in the wood. Tedric will go first to Thetford in search of him."

"There is no place else," Wynne said tremulously. "Hugh cannot survive the cold and damp nights in the forest. He needs special care. He is still a baby."

Mallory reached out a hand and pulled back the hood that covered the lad's head and looked at the thick, dark hair and chubby face. He smiled and lifted the little chin to look into the boy's blue eyes. "How has Tedric accepted the boy?"

"He pays little attention to him," Wynne answered.

"He must not have seen him since his birth," Thurwell put in.

"We will take you back with us," Mallory told Wynne. "You will be safer in our room with Edythe than you would be at Thetford."

"I fear being so close to Cordell," Wynne said, worried.

"There is no help for it," Mallory advised. "Old woman, can you make the journey to the convent alone?"

"If the wheel is repaired I have no other fears," she replied.

"Since you have no money for lodgings, Tedric would not look for you anywhere but the convent. I think you will be safe in our room and we will go pay a call on Sir William."

"But I have money," Wynne protested. "Not much, but enough for a time. Enough for some food."

Thurwell reached up to lift Wynne down from the cart. "The money is badly needed," he told her. "And it will be repaid when we are free to join Conan." Wynne shivered slightly as her feet hit the ground. "Fear not, lass, for Tedric will not search long. He has better use for his men. He plans to start a war."

"Oh, nay," Wynne said. "I do not think he will fight. He has men-at-arms, but my lady says he will never meet Conan. He fears him. Tedric will find a way to trick him."

"And how will he do that, lass?"

Wynne's chin quivered slightly. Tedric had overpowered her so easily and treated her with such cruelty that she feared he might succeed. "He keeps my lady within the keep. She has not ventured even into the town since he killed the priest." She shook her head sadly. "I do not know what Sir Tedric will do, but he promises my lady that Conan will die."

"What priest was killed?" Mallory asked.

"Father Merrick — for hiding Sir Conan in the church."

Mallory and Thurwell were silent for a moment. Thurwell began to examine the wheel. "We have tarried too long," he said under his breath. "Let us make haste for Cordell."

Every day just after breaking the fast, Sir Conan would walk the perimeter of the Anselm wall just as his father had done before him. Now it was the Blue Falcon committing to memory every curve of the land and every tree. He would know instantly if there was so much as a bush out of place. Conan had increased the number of bowmen looking out through the parapets and had many men inside the great, long wall ready to take up arms at a moment's notice.

Conan looked out over the land that would be his when his father was gone. He remembered a time when he attached much glory to the thought. But he had since learned that being the ruler of land and men was not a glorious job.

With spring on the horizon, the time for a confrontation was near. He would be cautious. He worried about Theodoric's support of Tedric. Fighting Tedric would be easier than battling those many heathens on the Crusade, but finishing him would only commit two great families to war; not even Phalen Castle was worth that price. But Chandra's well-being was worth a great deal more than that.

As he walked toward the keep, he noticed that his

mother stood, hands held in front of her, watching him. She no longer held her head high and there was no bright smile — nor had there been for a very long time. The face that greeted him was frozen in a sour, pained expression. Udele had grown old.

Conan bowed somewhat stiffly, wondering what problems she would air this time. "Good morning, madam," he greeted.

"I see your army rises," she said, indicating the men moving around them. "They prepare daily, but no one can say for what."

"I have told you, madam, they are ready for a fox that will sneak in the night."

"But will you take Phalen? It is yours. Why do you tarry?"

"I wait, but the time spent is not wasted. A hasty attack could see the lady Chandra hurt or even killed. I will take care with my moves, but when I move, Tedric will have no doubt that I have arrived."

"Chandra," she sighed. "You *still* fret for the wench?"

"And if I give no care to her safety, madam, who will?"

"It is not your concern."

"Nay, madam, others forced her marriage to Tedric and she has suffered greatly. Even now she is abused and without a protector."

Udele raised one brow and looked at her son suspiciously. Conan had never confessed his brief visit to Cordell after returning from war. "How do you know she is abused?"

"I have it on the best authority. I intend to free her."

"Free her," Udele gasped. She reached out a hand and clutched at Conan's arm. "Conan, you must tell me true. Do you intend to claim the wench?"

"Madam, do not speak of the lady Chandra in such a way again," he said angrily. "She is good and kind and never deserved to have such trouble nestle on her own stoop. I have known many women, but there is none to compare to Lady Chandra in strength, wisdom and goodness."

"But Conan, you have other things to fight for! Your land! Your family!"

Conan looked at her closely. "And will my lands desert me if I free Lady Chandra from her bondage? Will my family turn from me? You speak of her as if she is naught but a beggarly camp follower. She is a lady."

Udele lowered her eyes. "She has no family, no wealth. Her name is attached only to Tedric —"

"Is that reason enough not to free her?"

Udele's eyes snapped up to her son's. "Do you mean to have her?"

"I intend to free her from Tedric's bondage and cruelty. What may come later, I will not guess."

"You love her."

"Yea," he said softly.

"And if she is free of her husband, will you take her? Will you bring her here to my home and make her lady of this keep?"

Conan looked into the green eyes of his mother. Make her the lady? He would be proud to have Chandra stand at his side. He loved her true, and he felt her love reaching out to him even from this distance. He prayed there would come a day when all strife would be laid away and he could go to Chandra in love, promising her his devotion and protection. For now he would make her safe.

He was about to answer his mother, but the guard from the tower shouted to get his attention.

"A man approaches!"

As Conan turned to go to the wall, Udele pulled at his sleeve. "Conan, answer me!"

A warrior and lord first, he pulled his arm free from her grasp and went to the wall to view this man before allowing his entry.

Udele stared at her son's back for many moments. Would he dare to bring Chandra to Anselm and place her above his own mother? I am the lady of this hall, she thought angrily. There will be no other lady here while I live!

She turned sharply and her angry steps took her back into the hall. She had waited upon the hope that Conan would ruthlessly attack Phalen Castle, retrieve his lands and have the matter done. But now his intention was clear. He would not sacrifice Chandra. He meant to have her or nothing. And Udele could not allow it. She knew the way to enrage Tedric.

No one entered Anselm easily. Conan was cautious about letting even a lone man bearing a message inside his walls. He expected nothing but trickery from Tedric.

The man was nervous and would not place the message in the guard's hand. When Conan approached, the rider looked him over carefully.

"You are Sir Conan?" he questioned.

"Aye."

"I see no falcon," the man said uneasily. "I was told you would have a falcon upon your shoulder."

"The bird is in the mews. He is new."

"I see no scar," the man attempted.

Conan cocked one brow and smiled at the little man. Whoever had a message for him had certainly described Conan carefully. He leaned closer so that the man might view part of the scar still visible near his temple. The remainder of it was now covered by a beard.

The man shrugged and put the rolled parchment in Conan's hand. Conan broke the seal and opened the missive. The message was short and concise. He started and quickly looked over his shoulder before reading the rest of his message.

"The man who sent this letter," he said to the messenger. "What was his name?"

"I do not know, Sir Conan," the man replied.

"Where can he be found?"

The man shrugged. "I was sent from Colchester, but he does not live there. He will meet me at the same inn for your reply on a day I am not to reveal."

Conan smiled to himself. How cautious they were. He whistled for a page, and a young lad came running eagerly. "Go to the mews and bring me two feathers from my bird. Be certain they come from Mars even if you have to pluck them yourself." The lad's eyes grew round at the thought of his errand, but Conan urged him on.

"There is food and drink for you in the hall and a place to sleep one night if you wish it. Return to your man with just two feathers and tell him that I will know where to find him. And tell him the time is soon."

The man nodded, though he could make no sense of the message. Conan pointed in the direction of the hall and watched as the man walked toward it.

With the parchment rolled up in one hand, he idly struck the palm of the other. A traitor in his house. And they watched for the dove. As in the past, he and his friends would not be parted for long.

CHAPTER
24

ANOTHER lone messenger came meekly to the Anselm gate, a youth of less than twenty years. There were no protectors to ensure that he would return to his master. He called out to the guard, "I bear letters from Sir Tedric, for Sir Conan —" He faltered and choked on the words he was sent to bear.

Many tension-filled minutes passed before he heard the loud creaking of the drawbridge. The doors to the gatehouse opened and the messenger spurred his horse. He rode through the gatehouse, over the bridge, through the great oaken doors and into the huge yard, the bridge raising behind him. On either side of him were lines of completely costumed infantry, all wearing the red and blue of Anselm, all with their hands fixed on the hilts of their swords, completely outfitted in mail and armor.

Conan would take no chance that Tedric's plan was to use his messenger to open the doors to his army.

Trembling, the lad dismounted. He was surrounded by an army, and he wondered if the Blue Falcon, the man whose warrior skills he had heard so much about, would kill him with his own sword, or if one of these many soldiers would be ordered to slay him after the message was read.

He looked anxiously about, his legs barely able to hold him up in the midst of this army. Finally, from the end of the long line of handsomely garbed warriors, a man approached. His red and blue tunic fitted handsomely across his broad shoulders. He limped slightly as he walked, and the messenger wondered if that was the injury he had incurred in the battle of Acre, when he was said to have slain more than twenty heathens whilst his leg dripped blood. A falcon, his jesses painted red against the blue-black of his feathers, rode the knight's shoulder.

The messenger fell to one knee, holding the papers out before him. He felt the roll pulled from his hand. He kept his head bent, looking at the ground, a toe of the great knight's shoe within his sight. He waited. His back stiffened and his shoulders began to ache, but the toe of the shoe was still in his sight. His forehead began to bead with sweat though the day was cool. His legs began to shake and falter under the abusive kneeling. Why had he not been fed to the hungry soldiers all about him? Tedric's missive had not been so long as to cost him this amount of time. Was it possible that the great and powerful Blue Falcon could not read? Nay, it could not be so. He had been advised to deliver the message to his hand, not the hand of a castle scribe.

"Rise," the gruff voice commanded.

Shakily he found his footing. He saw rage in the knight's blue eyes and he thought it would be the last sight he would see.

"You are aware of impending war between Sir Tedric and me?" Conan asked roughly.

"Yea," he returned, his voice quivering.

"And the missive," Conan said, giving the parchment a shake. "Do you know it to be an invitation to war?"

"Yea," he choked.

"But you brought it. I would know why."

The messenger saw no compassion in the blue eyes, but he was without choice. He answered honestly. "My family is in sore need of shelter and food. They have no farm or animals. Sir Tedric promised a reward for my family. My life is forfeit for theirs." He gulped and dropped his eyes from the penetrating stare. Moments passed.

"You show courage. Courage should be rewarded. Make your choice. Stay and pledge yourself to your new lord or return to Tedric."

He looked up in disbelief. He locked eyes with the great knight for a moment. This act of kindness did not soften the rage he saw there. He fell to one knee and bowed his head. "My lord," he said.

"Wise as well as courageous," Conan said flatly. "Your life would have been short with the fox. His days are numbered." Sir Conan turned. "Give this man food and drink," he barked.

The lad found himself hoisted to his feet. He caught a glimpse of Sir Conan as he strode away from his men. The strides were long and quick, the limp less evident.

The doors to the hall burst open as Conan entered the room. Those soldiers not about their duties filled the hall. A sense of order settled over them at the moment of Conan's presence. Eyes and ears were ready for a command from the master. Word spread quickly within the stout walls of the hamlet.

Alaric had heard the news that word had come from Tedric, and he came quickly from the stables. Udele, in kind, had ventured from the uppermost chambers to hear what word came to her son. As she descended the stair, she was frozen in her place by the icy blue eyes of her son, and for the first time, she felt terror. With a sweeping bow, Conan indicated the royal chair for the lady of Anselm. Poised, she walked past him and took her seat.

"Pray, sit, my lord," he said to his father. "Beside your wife."

Alaric perched on the edge of the chair, looking expectantly at his son.

"Tedric is ready to parley," Conan said. "His supporters are few. He holds Phalen still and will meet me there. He holds his wife, Chandra, and her son as hostages. He offers their lives in exchange for the castle and land. He invites me to Phalen to give my word before witnesses that we have come to an agreeable treaty. In exchange for my promise, he will allow Lady Chandra and her son to live."

"The castle means more to him than his wife and son?" Alaric asked incredulously.

"At present. He boasts word from an informer that Chandra is an adulteress and the son she bore is not his."

"Chandra?" Alaric questioned under his breath. Udele stiffened in her chair, her son watching her reaction carefully.

"I am the accused lover and father," Conan said slowly, his eyes on his mother.

Alaric half rose. He had not dared voice that suspicion even to himself.

Conan did not look at his father. Alaric followed Conan's gaze to Udele. "Tedric takes great pleasure in telling me that my own mother had the news delivered to him."

"You?" Alaric choked, bending over Udele. "You would do such a thing? You would betray your own son?"

Conan's hand was on Alaric's arm, pulling him from Udele. Alaric faced Conan. "God's truth," Conan said,

"I am the father of her child. And I have loved her long — long before I took her. Tedric be damned, I will have her and my son unharmed, or all of Tedric's allies will feel the weight of my anger!"

Alaric looked with venom at his wife. Then he withdrew from her side and went to stand behind Conan, giving him silent permission to handle this in his own way.

Conan faced his mother. "Why did you send this word to my enemy?" he ground out.

"Chandra is a witch," Udele said easily. "She makes you look the fool. She would bind you with her rosy breasts and lock you into her spell, but she brings you nothing! She is poor and has no name!"

With a snarl and a grimace, Alaric moved farther from his wife. He felt the urge to strike her senseless.

"Has she betrayed me?" Conan barked. "Nay! Has she thrown herself in my path and tempted me? Nay! I crept to her chamber and begged her merest kiss! But you have betrayed me and I cannot name the reason. Why?"

" 'Twas for your own good," Udele replied, her voice beginning to tremble. Never had she been so frightened of him. His size and strength seemed bent to her destruction. "Chandra would bring you low. She has pranced before you as an anxious harlot while your own wife lay suffering in her bed. She is evil! She is —"

His hand came out hard against her cheek and she fell back into the chair. Before she could clear her vision, he was before her, his arms braced on the sides of her chair so she could not escape his questions.

"You sent this word to Tedric in hopes that he would kill them both?"

Udele sniveled piteously, rubbing her stinging cheek

with one hand and picking at her gown with the other. "You could take Phalen. Tedric is no match for you," she whined.

"You will tell me how you knew the child was sired by me," he growled.

Udele began to weep. " 'Twas for your good. You could not be strong while tied to her charms. She would bind you with her evil seductions. You would bring her here and make her lady of this hall. I am the lady of this hall! I am the lady —"

"Madam!" he shouted.

"Conan, my love," she whimpered. "She is wrong for you. One taste of her lips has sent you crazed, thinking naught of your family and lands, but only of her! Don't you see? She would rule your existence, and there would be nothing left for you. Nothing but a shadow where a great warrior once stood!" She broke into more choking sobs. "Nothing left for you, nothing left for me . . .

"I am young still," she continued. "I would see your hall managed perfectly; you know that I can do that. You need not share your plenty with so many! There is time yet to find a rich wife: a wealthy woman to add lands to ours! Anselm is yours! Phalen! Stoddard! If Cordell is your desire, take it! Who would stay you? For Galen, to be castellan to one of your estates is enough; he does not need more. Edythe is gone and will take no share."

Galen, who was standing near his father, turned his back sharply, unable to look at his mother another moment. Alaric's fists were clenched at his sides.

Conan spoke again, slowly. "Edythe. My God, what have you done?"

" 'Twas her plan to accuse me! She would have turned

my own husband against me! And she would have taken all that we worked for to a knight of no means! They would attach themselves to you like leeches, sucking your power and dividing your lands!"

The door to the hall opened and Udele's servant entered. He looked at the gathering, observing Conan's rage and his mistress's distraught manner. The news had traveled quickly. There was pain in the manservant's eyes as he faced Conan. "Sir Conan, I would speak," he begged humbly.

Udele's eyes shot to the servant's as she heard his voice. "So," she spat, "even you would betray me."

"Lady Edythe is alive," Pierce said to Conan, glancing hesitantly at Alaric. "I could do her no more harm. I left her in the wood with money enough to buy a horse and clothes to make her look like an aging peasant woman. She was bound for Swaffham Bulbeck and would wait there until her brother and husband returned."

"I sent my riders to every nunnery in the country," Alaric protested.

Pierce shook his head. "They would have been sent away. Lady Edythe would not have returned to this place until she could be assured of Sir Conan's protection."

Alaric looked with hatred to his wife. "Your evil web so ensnared this hall that my own daughter feared to trust me!" he snarled. He turned back to Pierce. "And this message?" he questioned. "My wife does not speak. How does she know enough to send word to Tedric?"

"Milord," Pierce began, clearing his throat. "The lacemaker, Giselle, tells milady what she wants to know."

"So she *is* a sorceress!" Alaric shouted.

"Nay, milord. She does not play with spells, but sees the future through a crystal." He cast a worried glance toward

Udele and then straightened and went on resolutely. "There was little choice for the woman, Giselle, milord. Milady threatened her." He looked toward Udele again as if he could not bear the pain of what he was forced to do. "Beg forgiveness, milady," he said meekly. "I cannot give you aid when you plot against these children and murder —"

Udele looked at him coldly and then, in a measured action, spit at him. She lowered her eyes again, picking at her gown.

"Murder? Edythe lives —" Conan began.

"Your lady, sir knight," Pierce said, looking to the floor. "The fall was not an accident. That was Edythe's curse: she overheard milady admit to her hand in Edwina's death."

Udele gave a low moan of agony at the further discovery of her sins. She fell from her chair and lay upon the rushes, weeping and shaking.

Conan struggled with his rage, not understanding his mother's madness. He did not look at Pierce, but heard his voice.

"The money that Tedric gave to Medwin," Pierce was saying. "Milady gave him the sum —"

"Tedric knew!" Udele gasped. "Tedric knew before you were wed that you did not love your bride, but lusted after her younger sister! The disgrace would have made us seem a family of idiots!"

Conan would not look at his mother — he would not act as if he heard her excuses. "Where did she come by such a large sum?" he asked Pierce.

"Milady gave me jewels and other trinkets to take to the usurers to trade and borrow. When a larger sum was needed, Aaron, the Jew from the north, provided the sum."

"And by whose order did Tedric slay the Jew?" Conan asked.

"By no order, milord. But he begged more money to keep silent about the loan."

Conan turned now to his mother, looking down at her in disgust. "And this money that Tedric offers me now — this 'fair sum' to pay for the care and lodging of Edwina — did that come from your own purse?"

"I gave him nothing," Udele said in a hiss. "He could not betray me. He would have had to admit his part in killing the Jew!" Suddenly she began to laugh loudly. The laughter quickly melted into more despairing sobs.

"Take her from my sight," Conan ordered coldly. Pierce moved quickly.

"You would not consider a woman who could do you honor," Udele wept. "You would not hearken to my counsel and look abroad for a woman of wealth and name. These meagerly dowered wenches could not do you proud."

"Take her to her chamber and guard her there," Alaric ordered.

Pierce dragged Udele from the floor and could not, even under force, make her rise. Finally, desperately wishing to remove her and himself from the room quickly, he lifted her into his arms and carried her to the stair.

"I bore him and raised him," she whimpered to the servant. "He was to make this family prosper, allow me wealth and comfort in my retirement, and serve me . . ."

The ramblings drifted away and ended. In the quiet, Conan faced his father. "I leave her to you, my lord. I cannot deal with her, for she has cost me too much. Speak not her name to me again, and do what you will. Her madness will be well known in this land, and there is much to set aright."

"Will you ride on Tedric now?" Alaric asked.

"Yea, the time has come. Are you able to lend me aid?"

Alaric nodded and straightened his back.

"Galen?" he asked.

"Aye."

"Then prepare yourselves and my men. I have one small piece of work before we ride."

Sir Conan strode into the hamlet. He looked neither right nor left, and his strides were long and determined. Villagers paused in their doorways, watching him as he passed and wondering at his destination. When he stopped in front of the lacemaker's cottage, they withdrew into their homes and barred the doors behind them.

Conan raised one leg and applied a mighty kick to the door, forcing the wood to splinter and the leather hinges to give way under the blow. The room was glazed in a violet light, making the image of the old woman within hazy and dim.

He faced her angrily. "You helped Lady Udele to betray me," he accused.

Giselle was not frightened. "She held the difference between life and death over me. I saw the need to protect my life, sir knight. For now."

"Now?" he questioned. His eyes began to focus on the crystal before her. A sense of comfort began to replace his anger, and a vision swam before him. In his inner thoughts he could see Chandra.

"Come, Sir Conan, and listen to what I have to say," she invited him warmly.

He moved closer. "Sir Tedric will not keep his word.

Nor will he accept your treaty at Phalen Castle. It is his plan to await you within Phalen's walls and charm you with his promise of peace — and kill you when you are lulled into agreement."

"Chandra?" he asked.

"It is Tedric's plan to kill you first and then order her death. She is prisoner in her own keep where the guard is heavy, and the order is to kill her when Tedric sends word that you are dead."

"And the child?"

"Nay, the child is safe, though I cannot say where. Spend no worry on your son. Free the lady."

"Yea, and then I will fight Tedric."

"Nay, Conan, do not fight him. He cannot face your army nor can he attack you. Go to meet him, but do not enter Phalen's walls."

"He deserves to die," Conan snarled.

"Vengeance is for the weak and pompous," she said softly. "You are too strong. If you meet him and kill him, you will have sown the seeds for more war. Let Tedric be. He is too foolish and wicked to survive."

"Then you would have the bastard go free?" Conan asked incredulously.

"He will be justly punished. But you are not his judge. Do not plan to attack him, Sir Conan."

"And give him Phalen?"

"Bring your witnesses and call upon your friend and teacher, Theodoric, to stand and hear your charges. Take your evidence of Tedric's treachery to Phalen after the lady is free. Send a message to Tedric from Phalen's walls and ask him to answer to the charges. Order him to loose your lands from his hold."

"Theodoric supports his son," Conan argued.

"Theodoric yearns for peace, as Alaric does. Bring your father and Theodoric together. You are the only one who can mend the tear in their friendship."

"And if Tedric will not yield my lands? If he will not leave without a fight?" Conan asked.

"Your oath as a knight forces you to defend innocence. You must protect the lady, protect your friends and family — protect yourself. Defend and honor, Sir Conan. Defend and honor. Do not attack and destroy."

" 'Twill be difficult to meet Tedric on peaceful ground and —" Conan stopped abruptly. The crystal lost its glimmer and the room began to brighten. Before his eyes, the crystal became an ordinary rock and the woman aged, her skin wrinkling as he watched her, and her kindly gray eyes turning dull and small.

"Reach the lady quickly, Sir Conan," she implored, her voice sounding weaker and rougher.

Conan looked at her curiously. "You said you saw the need to protect your life for now — now, the day that you would show me the way to free the lady and liberate my lands?"

Giselle shrugged, feeling tired and weak. "I doubt that things could have been very different for you — until now. In truth, I could not ever foresee my purpose in this until you came to me. But I could see that there was a purpose. Without my urging, you would have ridden to Phalen, and the lady —" She looked up at him with tired eyes. "Lady Chandra, sir knight. Go quickly."

He looked at the rock. "And that?"

"It is done," she said softly.

Slightly over one hundred armored men stood about the courtyard at Anselm Keep. Shields bearing the blazon of

Sir Conan shone in the sun, and full battle gear hung from the ready steeds. Although Alaric's armor was old and had been retired for many years, it now shone like new. Galen, garbed in the fine mail that he kept perfect, stood beside his father. Conan's supplies and implements of battle were stacked neatly beside his horse, and two squires stood ready to help him don his heavy mail.

"Galen, you will ride with fifty men. Can you bear the command?"

"Yea, Sir Conan," he answered proudly.

"Surround Phalen Castle and allow no one to leave or enter. Do not fight except in defense of your life."

Conan turned to his father. "Take twenty mounted men and ride to Theodoric. Deliver him this message," he said, handing his father the rolled parchment. "He was the first to teach me justice and honor. Tell him I am prepared to meet Tedric and make any wrongs against him right. Ask Theodoric to stand as witness to this conference."

"Do you think it wise to stand before Tedric's father and accept the blame for the child?"

"Was this not Tedric's wish from the first?" Conan said. "Was it not his plan to oppose me long before marriage to Chandra was thought of? He wanted Phalen from the first — he did not love Edwina. Was it to place himself beside me and await the perfect moment to oppose me, not only setting himself against me, but our families against one another? And did he kill the Jew to free my mother of her debt, or in hopes that I would accuse him and stand shamed before my king? And Chandra — has he held her only because I would gladly have taken her? Has the child I sired become his victory?"

"And if Theodoric does not see his son's treachery?"

"Then we will war, but first Chandra will be free and Theodoric will hear Tedric's crimes aired."

"And where do you go?" Alaric asked.

"I will see the lady free without Tedric's consent. She is a prisoner in Cordell, not Phalen, as Tedric would have me believe."

Alaric did not question his son, though he did not know how Conan could have learned Chandra's whereabouts.

"We leave now in three troops. My lord." He bowed to Alaric. "North, to Theodoric. Sir knight." He bowed to Galen. "East with your men, to Phalen Castle. We come together there, and, God willing, this will be done."

The falcon flapped his wings. Conan stood before his destrier and allowed the squires to help him don his mail. He mounted his horse and took a moment to quiet its prancing. This mount, however new, was already accustomed to the firm hand that commanded him. Neither man nor beast, it seemed, was beyond his control. The banner of the Blue Falcon was raised high and the gate opened for the departing army.

"When this is done, my lord, you shall have your family at home," Conan told his father. Alaric thought of Edythe, Galen and a grandson he did not know was his before today. And his wife? He was not sure. There was sadness in his eyes as he nodded to Conan.

CHAPTER
25

LADY Udele was guarded in her chambers by men-at-arms as well as Pierce, his loyalty now doubted in the keep. Pierce sat on a stool near the door and leaned against the wall, dozing occasionally and then coming awake with a start to look in the direction of his pacing mistress. She would not meet his eyes. She would only hiss her anger and turn abruptly away.

Pierce looked with pity on his mistress now for he knew her to be mad. For so many years he had obeyed her every command, hoping for her happiness, but all that was for naught.

His head slumped again in slumber. He had been without sleep for two full days. He gave a loud snort and settled his back more comfortably against the wall. In spite of his efforts, he slept.

Udele looked suspiciously in his direction. A wry smile twisted her mouth. She crept toward the door and slowly pulled it open. At the bottom of the stair, she could see the guard talking to someone out of sight. Some matter had called him from his post just outside her door.

The keep was dark, but the risk of being seen was great. After closing the door to her chamber behind her, she tiptoed down the corridor. She was barely away when she heard the guard coming back up the stair. She listened as he settled himself on the stool in the hallway. With a snicker, Udele fled quietly to the back stair.

Only a few guards were posted about the dark streets. Other men, their positions high on the wall, did not notice the slight figure making her way into the hamlet behind huts and shops.

She reached her destination without incident and quietly opened the lacemaker's door. Giselle was awake and sitting on a stool across the room. The fire blazed on the hearth. On the table beside Giselle, the scarlet cloth was spread and on it rested an ordinary rock.

"You knew I was coming," Udele ground out.

"I did not know when," Giselle replied. "I knew you would come before very long."

Udele walked to the table and picked up the rock. "What is this?"

"My crystal. It is finished."

"And your sight?"

"Finished," she said wearily.

"As is your life," Udele said almost cheerfully. "My lord husband will have you cast from this earth."

"And you, madam?" the old woman asked. "What will he deal you?"

"He thinks me mad," she confided, a secretive smile playing on her lips. "He will do me no harm, for he thinks me mad. 'Tis a bad omen to kill someone crazed." A gleeful cackle escaped her, and she spun about in the little room. "But you see, even now he has little to say about whether I come or go. I was to be held prisoner, but I am here!"

"Your guard sleeps," Giselle said, moving from the stool to stand near the fire.

"I thought you could not see," Udele snapped. "You see as well as ever you did."

"Though I would have it otherwise, madam, I can still feel you rise and slumber. I feel your anger and your joy — and your madness. It is my curse, for I should have denied you long ago."

"You told me all this would have happened without your predictions," Udele chided.

"So it would have. But there are some things you must bear responsibility for. Lady Chandra's life would not be in danger now except for you. Edythe, poor child, would not have suffered so. And Tedric — I cannot see even now how you thought that aiding Sir Conan's enemy would give you more of him."

"This is your fault!" Udele raged. "You and your wretched stone, your predictions! If you had not been here with your lying promises, none of this would be happening to me now!"

"You are wrong, madam. Had you let charity and goodness guide you and sought only those rewards you deserved, you would have lived long and in comfort. By your wickedness you purchased your fate."

"My fate!"

"Your death," Giselle returned crisply, moving closer to Udele and facing her without fear.

"And whose hand will deal me death?" she questioned hotly.

"Your own hand, lady. Your own and no other."

"You are a witch," Udele spat. She whirled and picked up the rock and tossed it in her hand. "And your tricks will not work with me." She hurled the rock into the fireplace and the sparks flew as it settled into the embers.

Giselle stepped back from the flying sparks and pulled her shawl about her shoulders. "There is nothing I can do to help you now," she said calmly.

"Your help brought me nothing but pain," Udele snarled. She reached into the hearth and withdrew the heavy poker, and, holding it effortlessly, she raised it over her head as a weapon. The glowing red tip touched and ignited a piece of hanging lace. Giselle saw the tiny flame behind Udele and a glazed and peaceful look came into the lacemaker's eyes.

The first blow caused Giselle to fall, but Udele was beyond reason in her madness and struck her again and again, oblivious to what was happening behind her, not conscious of what her own murderous hand had wrought. The lace took light quickly, and like a torch the entire side of the room popped into blinding flames. With a scream of terror she dropped the poker and turned to see that her escape from the cottage was blocked by flames. They leapt out at her face and skirt, stinging her eyes and catching on her long hair as she whirled in terror.

Her screams melted into rending wails like those of a wounded beast. Her hair and gown were afire, and she felt her own death as if she stood apart from herself and watched.

Villagers awakened by the screams attempted to put out the fire, but were successful only in keeping it from taking the entire village. Not much time passed before the lacemaker's cottage was nothing but ash.

Pierce, who had come in search of his mistress, found her charred remains at daybreak. He wrapped her in his cloak and carried her toward the hall, looking straight ahead. In his mind he thought only of his mistress as she was at three and ten, a lass whose gaiety enchanted all who saw her smile.

Pierce approached the door to the hall. "She will not be welcome in the church," he said to the guard.

"Where do you take her?" the man asked.

"To her chamber where her women will shroud her," the old servant wearily replied. He accompanied his lady to her grand chamber for the last time.

Sir Conan turned off the road to Cordell before reaching Colchester. He sent his troop along the preferred road, flying his banner, while he took a path through the wood. When night fell, he hung his shield on his saddle and removed the mail he wore. His spurs were stacked with his other battle gear, and he kept only the broadsword at his belt. He knew the horse could serve him no longer. Only the dangers of gullies and pits in the forest kept him from walking through the night. He rested against a sturdy tree, dozing. Every sound aroused him, and when he did close his eyes he suffered through visions of Chandra and his child.

He feared that too much time had passed, that too many things stood between them. They had loved against the laws of God for so long that he did not imagine many blessings would be theirs. But he would take the pains with the pleasures, of that much he was sure. Even now if he could free her, she would not be able to come to him easily. There would be scandal and hardship.

The sun was high the next day when Conan found paths he recognized. He could sense the presence of men about him. And before long, a man stood before him, a knight garbed in rough leather tunic and chausses that showed the signs of many mendings. Mallory smiled and gave a small salute. "Your sister lives and is safe," he said.

"It was my own mother who would have had her slain," Conan replied.

"Yea, Edythe knows this. Now she cares for your son. She is with Wynne in a small room we provided in a little town near Anglesey."

"Then Tedric is holding my son for ransom when my son is not even there," Conan said. "Tedric makes it hard for me to think of sparing him."

"He has contacted you?"

"Aye. He will trade the lives of his wife and the child for free title to Phalen, and with that Cordell as well."

"We watched him ride out, but seeing that he did not take his lady, we waited here."

Thurwell stepped onto the path and smiled his greeting. "You tarried so long we thought we would have to finish your business for you," he said and chuckled.

Conan's smile was stiff and strained, but the sight of his friends brought him more comfort than he had had in some time. "Are you prepared to scale a seawall of slippery rock?" he asked.

Mallory whistled low and looked at Conan with some surprise.

"At night," Conan added.

"Tedric's army is small. Sir William's force could take them if they can be drawn out."

"And if Tedric's order is to kill the lady in the event of attack?" Conan asked. "She is in the custody of his guard. There will be no attack until she is safe."

"And so you must enter the keep by the cliffs," Thurwell concluded. "There is no other way."

"I have done so before," Conan confessed.

Mallory and Thurwell smiled at each other, both thinking like thoughts. "We reasoned that you had," Mallory said.

"There is naught to fear," Conan told them. "If you should slip, your pain would be short."

"That gives me great comfort," Mallory returned.

"We will enter the hall through Chandra's chamber at night. My troop of men will come to Cordell down the road, drawing out some of Tedric's forces. When that battle has begun, Sir William can take the hall and we will be ready to defend the lady. I think more than a few will be killed. I fear it cannot be avoided."

"And then the damsel will be yours," Thurwell remarked.

"I will free her from her imprisonment," Conan said casually.

Both men stared at Conan and noted the faraway look in his eyes. Now that fulfillment of his dream was at hand, would he let the moment pass?

"Conan," Mallory pressed. "Do not in a foolish moment allow the lady to think you do not want her."

Conan laughed ruefully. "I first wanted her when she came to my pavilion at Anselm, but there were other things on my mind and I did not realize that my life would be empty without her love. Years have passed since that time. After all that has held us apart, do you think it will be easy for her to forget and come to me in love? If I kill her husband, can she forgive?" Conan shook his head and looked at his friends. "Time will tell if there will be any reward for us after all the evil we have seen."

"You do the lady wrong, Sir Conan," Mallory said. "You lectured me on love and called me the fool if I did not find a way to take my heart's desires, in spite of difficulties. Now, will you be the fool?"

Chandra sat on the floor and stared into the fire. A fur pelt was the only buffer between her kirtle and the cold stone. She hugged her knees with her arms and wondered how many more of these long nights would pass before the door to her chamber came crashing open and Tedric's guards rushed in to finish their work and kill her. She had heard Tedric give that order, but she would not be an easy victim. She imagined, with great hope, her rescue.

Chandra had looked down the jagged rocks outside her bedroom terrace and remembered clearly the night that Conan had come to her via that dangerous climb. She considered making that journey herself, but could not summon the courage to risk her life in such an attempt. And a guard had been posted down and far to the left of the rocks to witness any such climb. Tedric had anticipated her desperation.

The door to her chamber opened and a young maid from the town entered, carrying a tray of cold meats and hard bread. Chandra moved quickly to meet her. She could not remember the maid's name. She took the tray and whispered, "Please, you can help me."

"Nay, lady, I fear —"

"Listen," Chandra pleaded. "My door. Watch my door, and when the guard moves away, tap lightly. I will flee —" The door, which had not closed behind the maid, squeaked as it was pushed farther open.

"Out!" the guard barked at the maid. The lass skittered fearfully from the room. "It will not work, lady," he said to her. "I do not leave this post."

Chandra's fingers tightened about the tray in anger.

"Why do you bother to feed me if it is your intention to murder me?" she asked tartly.

The guard chuckled. "Your husband would not have you starve," he taunted.

In a fit of temper she hurled the metal tray at the guard, but he used her door as a shield and the thing never came close to hitting him. When her food and drink were scattered about the floor, he opened the door again and smiled tolerantly at her. "Your dinner is wasted." He shrugged, closing the door behind him.

Fists clenched and face reddened with anger, she walked toward the door, looking down on the cold chicken that would have fed her. She thought to retrieve a piece but could only kick at it, scattering it farther, tears of frustration stinging in her eyes.

She sat again before the fire, hugging her knees to keep warm, her throat aching from holding back useless tears. Her ears caught a distant sound and she crept near the chamber door. There was no sound from the corridor. She listened another moment and heard the guard shift and grunt. She could not decide whether relief or disappointment would be in order. It did not sound as if they were coming to kill her now.

She settled again on the pelt, sighing in resignation. But again she heard the sound. She craned her neck to find the location. A soft scratching came to her ears. It came from the balcony and she went there swiftly, leaning her ears against the oaken door. A light tapping, so soft she could barely hear it, came from the other side. She tapped her fingernail against the thick oak and she was answered in kind: *tap, tap, tap.*

She leaned against the door and her mind raced. Conan!

It had to be Conan! She felt a rush of fear and relief at once. What was his plan? The bolt had been removed from her chamber door, and the sound of the balcony doors opening would bring the guard. Did he intend to stand against the entire force that occupied the hall?

She had no alternative but to open the terrace doors as quietly as she could. There stood the one she expected! No sooner did she behold him than the door to her chamber opened. Conan backed away from her quickly with a finger to his lips. He silently mounted the balustrade, and she saw his intention to jump to the twin terrace. Hoping to hide the sound of his landing, she turned abruptly to the guard entering her room.

"And am I not even allowed a breath of fresh air?" she questioned tartly.

The guard smiled lazily and came to where she stood, brushing past her and going to the balustrade to look over. A torch lit far below to the left silhouetted the guard who stood watch there. The sound of the water against the rocks was loud, but the first guard's whistle alerted the second to look up to where Chandra stood. The man below raised an arm to signal he was alert and keeping his post.

"Don't try to make my work easy for me, my lady," the guard said. "It would be most difficult to find your body on the rocks below."

"That would surely disappoint my lord husband," she snapped. "And it would no doubt disappoint you as well, since you are so anxious for your chore."

"You do me wrong, lady," he said in feigned hurt. "It will not be an easy task to take the life of one so lovely." He reached out to touch her soft cheek, but she jerked away from his hand. He laughed at her distaste.

The guard walked to the door of her bedchamber and turned once more in her direction. "Do not attempt the climb, lady. It is useless."

"I value my life more than you think," she returned. "I do not intend to make it easy for anyone to end it for me."

He chuckled again and left her. Her breath came out in a sigh and she turned to look across the space between the balconies. Two figures rose from a supine position on the deck and stood. She leaned against the door and closed her eyes until she heard the soft thump of one man's feet as he came safely across the space between the balconies. Conan stepped aside to make room for his companion's flight, but Mallory did not make the jump as skillfully. He did not clear the balustrade and he grappled desperately for something to hold. Conan's hands came out quickly to grab him, and Mallory found the lower ledge with his feet. He regained his balance and paused on the outside of the balustrade, his knuckles white and his arms stiff as he held on. He looked at Conan and whispered, "I am not going to do this again — for anyone."

Chandra gave an anxious look toward her chamber door and decided the slight noise of Mallory's slip had not reached the guard. When a moment had passed and they were all convinced the guard would not bother her again, Chandra turned to Conan. "How did you come around the guard below?" she whispered.

"We didn't," Conan returned, looking down. "It is Thurwell."

Conan and Mallory stealthily entered her bedchamber and blew out the candles that lit the room. Should the guard enter now they would at least have a chance at surprising him. Conan drew Chandra near the fire. "Enjoy the fire for now," he whispered, barely audible. "When that log is finished we will let it die."

She nodded her head, afraid to speak. But Conan had many things on his mind and risked discovery in whispering, "Why did you not tell me of my son?"

She looked up at him and tried to study his eyes, but the room was too dark. Tears gathered in her eyes. "I was afraid you would act too hastily," she murmured. "You were sore tired and needed rest before this battle."

"And you did not tell me how Tedric treats you," he said.

Her chin trembled and the tears came against her will. She had not cried since being shut in this chamber, but Conan's presence eased her fear enough so that old worries took precedence over courage. "My baby," she quavered.

"He is safe," Conan comforted. "Chandra, why did you not tell me of Tedric's abuse? I have learned from others that he has killed and stolen."

Her voice came in a pitiful squeak. "I could not burden you; you were only lately come from war!"

"Could it be you did not want me to be the one to free you?"

"Nay," she breathed. "But neither could I ask it of you."

"Chandra," he said softly, hurt in his voice. "I thought you would beg it of me."

"Beg?" she said. "Conan, my love, would I beg you to risk your life for me? Has my love not hurt you enough but that I would ask more of you?"

"Your love will never sting," he answered, "until you hold it back. When you cannot take what I offer, then there is pain."

She shook her head and the tears ran down her cheeks. "Conan, you have risked so much without my asking."

He just looked down at her, watching the golden light from the fire make a play of moving shadows on her face. There were tears in her eyes. "I did not want to hurt you," she said gently.

Conan did not speak again. He turned to see that Mallory had made a quiet corner for himself near Chandra's chamber door. Conan drew the long broadsword carefully from his belt and laid it on the floor. He then settled himself against the wall, his sword ready before him. With his arm he indicated she should sit beside him.

Chandra settled next to him and his arm brought her comfort. There were no more words between them even though there were many things each wanted to say to the other. Chandra stilled her tongue lest the sound of her voice would bring the guard, and Conan held silent in hopes there would come a better time to declare himself.

Chandra dozed against his shoulder, and every time she awakened she could feel the tension in his arm. He was alert through the night. She had no reckoning of their plan, but she learned it quickly, for the morning came with a near explosion. A shout from below caused Conan to bolt to his feet. Mallory and Conan stood ready, legs spread and swords drawn, just inside her chamber door.

Moments later, the door to her chamber was thrown open, and the first man entered and was slain before the look of surprise could fade from his face. His cry of pain brought two more guards. These two held up the fight longer, and Chandra backed away from the sight with a hand covering her mouth to still her own cries of fear. She wished to close her eyes but could not.

The noise in the hall below became greater, with shouting and the screams of those losing the battle. She covered her ears, for she could not guess the victors. It seemed an eternity before Tedric's men lay dead and Sir William stood in the frame of her chamber door.

"As easy as plucking an apple from a tree," Sir William beamed. "Cordell has fallen."

Thurwell appeared in the door. "Conan, some of Tedric's men have escaped. We must ride quickly."

Conan turned and looked at Chandra. She smiled. "Cordell is yours, sir knight. My men serve you now."

"Nay, my lady, it is yours as promised by your father. I only do my part to wrest it from Tedric's hands and free you from your imprisonment."

"And the lady of the hall?" she asked. "You lay no claim?"

"Nay, Chandra. You are not a prize of war. Your life is your own."

She looked at him closely. "Nay, Conan. My life is yours. It has been thus for a very long time."

"I must reach Phalen quickly before Tedric hears of this. Where do you wish to go? You would be safe here. Your son could be brought to you or you could go now to receive him. I will provide protection for you from now on."

"Take me with you, Conan."

Mallory had hurried out just behind Thurwell, and Conan stood alone with Chandra in her chamber.

"That could well be the most painful journey of your life," he warned.

She nodded. She might see her husband or the father of her child slain. Indeed, her own life would be in danger.

But she would see the battle through. She turned and grabbed her mantle from the peg near the door. She stood before Conan, ready, determination in her eyes.

"You've liberated me and provide my protection now," she said softly. "But you speak naught of love," she whispered.

Conan looked at her for a moment, and then, taking two large steps, he reached her. One hand reached around her and the other lifted her mouth to his lips. His lips covered hers hungrily, devouring her, silencing her doubts. Quickly he released her and his breath was warm in her mouth. "There are battles ahead, love. When those battles are won, we can talk more freely of what is to be."

"Tell me there is love," she whispered.

"Aye," he breathed. " 'Til the end of time."

That said, he turned on his heel and went quickly out of the room, leaving Chandra to follow him.

CHAPTER
26

THEY set out at once for Phalen Castle. Despite their haste, the journey could not be completed in one day. At nightfall they were forced to make a camp.

Conan helped Chandra make a pallet on the ground and he fashioned something akin to a tent by attaching a length of heavy linen to the limb of a tree.

"You need not fear to sleep, lady," he told her. "There will be guards posted through the night. It will not be comfortable, but it will be safe."

"Will you sleep, Conan?" she asked tenderly.

"Nay" was his simple answer.

She braved a smile for him. She wanted to lie beside him and feel the strength of his arms to comfort her through the night, but it would not be so. Conan was bent on the business of fighting and could not give his thoughts to gentler things. She could wait.

"I am not afraid, Conan," she said softly.

"Then rest," he returned. "And pray."

Conan settled himself on his own pallet and the familiar churning thoughts kept him from sleep. Mallory had warned him that Tedric would aim for his back and would one day have to be dealt with. Tedric was his determined enemy. Would things have worked out very differently if Conan had not taken Edwina to wife? Would Tedric have married her, acquiring Phalen Castle legally, and still have eventually found a way to come to blows with Conan?

He closed his eyes on what might have been and focused on what was. He hoped to avoid family wars, but if there was a battle, he would fight.

As they approached Phalen Castle, Conan could see where his brother had positioned his men. Galen had raised a tent a fair distance from the barbican so that he could easily see if any force came across the bridge. A fair number of men were there and others were patrolling the perimeter of the wall in twos and threes. They were sent to watch, not to fight.

On the bastion's wall and surrounding the keep were Tedric's men, many of whom had once sworn to serve and protect this keep for Medwin. Conan knew it would be only moments before Tedric learned that he had arrived.

Chandra was kept to the rear of Conan's troop, and on both sides of her his men rode. Beside Conan were Mallory and Thurwell, but as they approached Galen's pavilion, Conan went alone.

A few moments passed while Conan spoke to his brother and heard his report of what had been taking place. Soon they sighted forces of Alaric and Theodoric approaching. The two aging knights rode side by side, and behind them rode the four sons who had been with Conan on Crusade, with a large mounted troop behind them.

Conan stood in wait for them, and when they finally drew in rein he bowed low before them. Rising, he saw Theodoric's angry face.

"My lords," he greeted.

"Is this some new custom of war, to have enemies escort each other to battle?" Theodoric asked brittlely.

"It is my hope that you will leave here friends, my lord," Conan explained.

"You are prepared to battle my son, by the looks of your army," Theodoric boomed.

"My lord," Conan invited politely, "a few moments of your time is all I ask. This can be finished here and now."

"And why am I called to this conference?" he asked.

"You were delivered the message Tedric sent to me. You know that he invited me to come to Phalen without arms to gift him with this castle in return for his wife and the child. But look yonder, my lord," Conan said, indicating Chandra. "She was held prisoner at Cordell, the order left to slay her when Tedric's message arrived that I was already dead."

Theodoric and his four sons dismounted. Alaric responded in kind. Mallory and Thurwell came closer.

"You tread on thin ice, Conan," Theodoric said. "You have sinned against my son and yet bring me here to gain my support."

"I am prepared to make my sins right, my lord."

"You will yield him this castle?"

"What was his offer to me? He claims his right to Phalen through the money he gave Medwin and through the only heir to any of Medwin's daughters. First, the money that bought Chandra came from my mother. She borrowed from the Jew, Aaron, and when Richard is returned and the records surveyed again, we will see the proof of this. Tedric did slay the Jew and begged more money from my mother in return for her silence. And the child that is a wedge for the inheritance of this estate is mine. I will gladly return Tedric his own bargain; a sum to cover the cost of Chandra's keeping and to ease the insult of my sins against him."

"And you claim the lady?" Theodoric asked.

"Nay, my lord. I offer her protection and freedom from her husband. He has brutally abused her. He lately murdered the priest that tried to give her aid. You have seen how he treasures her; he offers her life in exchange for this keep, a promise he would not have kept. There are other crimes that Tedric will have to answer to when Richard is home, but I will not be the fool twice. My next charges will come with more proof. Take yon army and travel to Bury Saint Edmunds. Ask those who survived the massacre of Palm Sunday if your son was among those nobles who slew the Jews. Ask those in Cordell who stood and watched as the priest in that burgh was hung on a gibbet."

Theodoric's jaw was set and his face became red. He did not wish to believe Tedric capable of such horrors. "If not for my other sons, I would not be here."

"Regardless of what others say of me, ill or well, you have never had just cause to doubt me. I have been faithful. I present myself now as your enemy, if that is your wish."

"My wish," he sputtered. "You, of all people, would know that I feel as if two of my sons did battle against each other."

"Royal sons have battled, my lord," Conan said. "As with Richard and John. Even now John plots his brother's death — our king. And to his death, Henry fought for John; and when King Henry was slipping into death, John deserted him." Conan paused and looked closely at Theodoric. "But Richard saw his father properly buried."

"It is an old story —" Theodoric said, looking askance at Phalen's walls. The old knight felt a hand resting on his shoulder and turned to look into his eldest son's eyes. "Father, I have known Conan well. It is not his way to slay a man with words, but rather meet him on equal ground. He tells you this that you might see your son's worth should our families come to war. Tedric is not worthy of your support."

"And you desert him, too?" Theodoric huffed.

The man looked away in discomfort. He had never defied his father.

"Will you support your brother?" Theodoric insisted angrily.

With sadness in his eyes, he shook his head. Theodoric turned full circle to meet eyes with his other sons. Each one looked down and held silent.

Theodoric clenched his fists at his sides. It was not an easy thing to walk away from a son in need. "This day has been coming for a long time," Theodoric said to Alaric. "Have you any notion where this fight could end?"

"We can fight until the last wall has crumbled," Alaric returned. "Your sons have sons now — and they will have sons one day."

"There is another way," Theodoric said humbly. "We can let them have their day, your son and mine. I will give my oath not to avenge this day. Will you?"

"Yea, I will let this battle be the last. And I will not look upon it," Alaric replied.

The two old lords clasped hands and moved together to where their horses stood. They had led the troop of many horsed knights into this clearing before the barbican and their horses stood at the forefront of all the others. The knights mounted their steeds and prepared to ride away.

Chandra was helped down from her horse and ran to Conan. "What will happen?" she asked anxiously.

"It is between Tedric and me," Conan said quietly.

Tedric had watched from the high wall of the barbican as Theodoric walked away with Alaric. He would not have his father's support in a battle against Conan. And if his rage was not intense enough, he saw the small and slender form of a woman as she ran to Conan's side, a wisp of her blond hair falling from under her snood.

Tedric stood in muted rage. He whirled and looked to the men littering the courtyard below. No horses were ready to mount except those few he anticipated needing to send riders out. His plan was not to do battle but to see Conan quickly slain when he came to negotiate for Chandra's life. How could the Falcon have known she would not be here in Phalen's walls?

He was not prepared to do battle and, indeed, knew better than to put his forces against Conan's. He could hold off a sizable army for many days behind Phalen's stout walls, but never did he intend to fight the Falcon on equal ground.

Tedric shouted his anger from the high wall, but his father did not turn. How could his own father desert him now? When he needed him most! When Conan's final defeat was so close at hand. With the help of his father and brothers, he could have bested the mighty Conan!

He looked again at those outside the wall and saw only Conan, his men far behind him. The knight stood alone with his falcon on his shoulder — in wait.

"Lower the bridge," he bellowed. "Mount!"

Long strides took Tedric below to the courtyard where

the screeching and clanking of the bridge could be heard. He looked about and saw his army standing idle. "Mount! We fight the Falcon now!"

No move was made and he looked at the closest of his men-at-arms with an angry glare. The man shrugged. "You promised there would be no battle."

"And I was wrong! We fight Conan now!"

The man shook his head. "No one here will ride against the Blue Falcon. We would defend ourselves, and even then with little heart: he is strong."

"You defy me?"

The men inside Phalen turned from their privy lord. In a battle between Conan, whose reputation was well known, and Tedric, only a fool would ride against the Falcon.

Tedric stomped toward a ready horse and mounted just as the bridge came completely down. Enraged at his father's abandonment, he had no hope that Conan might still bargain — still yield him his life. He saw but one end to this day: his certain death should he fight Conan's forces with his own modest army.

Tedric spurred the charger, and the horse came bounding over the bridge. Conan stood midway between Theodoric's departing army and his brother's pavilion outside the barbican. Many of Conan's men scrambled for their horses as the rider from Phalen came into view, but Conan stood his ground afoot. He had no weapon to defend himself but a simple bow. In an unhurried manner, he readied it with an arrow.

With lance braced and head down, Tedric raced in the direction of his departing family. A cry of fury from the charging knight split the air. Tedric did not charge Conan.

He rode toward his father. Here, now, riding toward his own father with lance ready, a scream curling his lips, he showed how much he would betray for his own wants.

Theodoric heard the cry and turned. A look of pain and surprise showed on his face as he saw Tedric's horse racing toward him. He made no move for a weapon. In agony he watched his charging son.

Tedric threw up his head in shock as an arrow pierced his chest. The lance fell from his hands as he grasped the arrow. Blood stained his hands and gamberson. The horse slowed as Tedric looked in shock at his father and then, turning slowly, looked to the side where Conan stood with a bow in his hand. The charging knight gave an agonized moan and fell from his horse.

Theodoric looked past his son to Conan and saw the bow. Their eyes met over the distance, each standing as still as time, each knowing the other's thoughts. Armies behind Theodoric and Conan and all those looking from Phalen's walls held silent and still.

Theodoric's sons began to dismount and go to the body of their brother. There was no movement and the expression frozen on Tedric's face was one of fear and surprise. Conan walked toward Theodoric, the bow limp in his hand. Chandra rushed past Conan and stood above the body of her husband.

Conan stood before his friend and teacher. His hair blew around his face and his eyes were moist. The bow was still in his hand.

"I taught you to use the bow," Theodoric said quietly.

Conan nodded and looked up at the aging knight.

"I could not have thought I made your aim perfect for this."

"You taught me how to use the bow," Conan said. "You taught me how and when to kill."

"He would have —"

"I would not have let him slay you, my lord."

"You could have killed him long before now. You could have had your vengeance."

"Tedric would never have met me on equal ground, my lord. I could have killed him, but only in the same way he would have killed me, through trickery and lies. However profitable the victory, it means little if there is no honor."

Sir Tedric was taken to the northern lands to take his final rest on his father's lands. Chandra did not presume so much as to think herself welcome at that burial. Instead she went with Mallory and Thurwell to find her son.

Mallory felt the need to return Edythe quickly to her father and brother that all might see her well and content. Thurwell was left with the chore of escorting Chandra, Wynne and baby Hugh to Cordell. And in Cordell there was much to be done to see that village returned to the tidy and peaceful place it once had been. Thurwell's helpful hand was put to good use. He was invited to stay on for as long as he desired. Thurwell worked hard every day, closely with William. He seemed to thrive in the little burgh, but Chandra soon understood that there was more of a reason for him to stay. The presence of her woman, Wynne, seemed to remove a season from his years with every shy smile he earned from her.

June brought a green to the land that made every heart glad, and the planting was done with great optimism. All those living in Cordell felt the freedom and joy, and the spring weddings and celebrations were more festive than ever before.

Chandra took great pleasure in the contentment she saw all around her, but her heart fought to maintain hope. Word came from Anselm that the family had returned to find Lady Udele dead and much of that village destroyed by fire. With so much destruction in both Cordell and Anselm, Chandra did not wonder that she received no word from Conan. She struggled against doubt and decided that if she heard nothing from him for yet another fortnight she would send her own messenger to Anselm. She could not invite him to her bosom; he would have to come of his own free will. But she prayed that her missive would at least be answered in his own hand.

Late on a June night, as she sat on a stool near the hearth and brushed her hair, she heard a sound in the direction of the balcony. She smiled to herself as she remembered nights past when that same sound brought great changes. With soft, measured steps, she moved to her chamber door and threw the bolt — a lock replaced since the battle in her own bedchamber. When she turned again toward the terrace, Conan stood in the open door, his hands on his hips and a sly smile on his face. She frowned at his mischief, but shortly it melted into a grin.

"With all our troubles past, can you not beat your path to my front door and honorably ask for my hand?" she asked impishly.

"It seemed too easy." He shrugged. "I have become suspicious of a woman won easily."

"But, sir knight," she replied in feigned hurt, "you compromise my reputation. Surely my men know you have passed this way."

"Sir William is most helpful; but then he was the man

to tell me I have a son." He raised a brow and peered at her. "If it pleases you, I shall leave by yon cliffs and ride in through your guard in the morning and plead my case before witnesses."

She laughed softly and her eyes glowed. "I have seen that whatever we have shared, however innocent, has not been our secret. Indeed, your presence will be welcome here. And after all I have been through to have you, do you think I would allow you to climb those cliffs another time?"

"I have grown fond of the act," he said with a smile.

"And I have not slept a night through without hearing phantom footfalls on my porch."

He opened his arms and smiled. "Then come to me, lady. I have worked hard for this day. Show me some ease."

Epilogue

King Richard's release from Duke Leopold was a long time coming, and a bitter king returned to England. The English had been slow to pay his ransom and in fact had not raised the entire sum, forcing the king to leave behind several hostages to be held until the balance was paid. And if that insult was not enough, he returned to find his kingdom filled with strife and dissension: his brother, Count John, had planned to take possession of the throne.

Richard returned from the Crusade a hardened man. He was still the recklessly brave and hot-tempered knight who had led so many into battle, but this already sturdy man was further toughened by four years of privations and imprisonment. He was not likely to yield anything. And returning from a war in which precious few who fought for him were English, he did not greet the overfed lords and earls with much affection.

The king called a meeting of the great council in Nottingham, in the center of Count John's lands, and made his business short. He restrained his younger brother and demanded the balance of his ransom. His right to rule was quickly reestablished.

King Richard was roughened and unforgiving, but in

his heart there was still room for remembering loyalty and good service. When the council ended, there was time for paying courteous calls to his most ardent supporters: those who had fought for him without hesitation and who would support him now. Pleasure was not the order of the visits, but neither was he bent to business alone.

Anselm rested between Nottingham and London, and Richard sent word to the lord of Anselm that he would pass through and spend a few nights. Many scurried about the huge keep to set every detail into perfection, and castellans and family traveled from afar to be present for the royal visit.

When the grand day finally arrived, the April sun shone brightly in the year 1194. Flags and banners flew from the bastions and baileys, and soldiers in their finest dress strode along the wall. Within the outer wall a carpet, a royal path, was run from the gatehouse through the courtyard.

The king and his men rode across the bridge, and Lord Conan of Anselm was there to greet him. Conan fell to one knee before his sovereign, and when he rose he stood equal in height to his king. "Welcome, my liege," he said.

Richard extended his hand in friendship and Conan received it, grasping it in fondness.

Richard looked about the grand keep and noted the many visitors and spectators. He was not one to ignore blithely pageantry on his behalf, and he smiled in appreciation. Anselm was one of the largest and richest holdings in England.

"Yea, this is a fine place," Richard said. "I regret that I could not visit this holding while your father was alive."

Conan laughed softly, a sentimental light shining in his

eyes. "Though he is gone, Sire, I feel that he watches over this keep and guides my every move. He was your loyal servant to the end of his days."

"The de Corbneys have always been a strong family. I am certain they always shall be. And," he said, looking over Conan's shoulder and seeing those gathered near the door to the hall, "I see the family grows."

Conan nodded and gestured with his arm for his king to precede him down the length of linen meant for his passage. With long strides, Richard moved toward the group of nobles and ladies that greeted him. He paused before the first man for Conan's introduction.

"Sire, my brother, Sir Galen. Stoddard Keep is his and he guards it well for the crown and our family. That is where our finest horses have been bred for many years."

Galen fell to one knee before his king and Richard bade him rise, taking his hand in friendship.

"Sir Mallory," Conan said next.

Before Mallory could bow himself, Richard took his hand. "Greetings, friend," he said with warmth. Both knew instantly that reminiscences of the Crusade would fill the night.

"His wife, Lady Edythe, my sister."

Edythe curtsied low before the king and upon rising could not resist her own introduction. She moved aside slightly and pulled a serving woman holding a squalling infant from behind her. "Our daughter, Sire. Eleanor."

The king smiled in pleasure and ran a finger along the infant's face.

"Sir Mallory keeps Phalen Castle for the crown and our family," Conan said.

Before Conan could introduce Thurwell, Richard took

his hand in established camaraderie. "My wife, Sire. Lady Wynne," Thurwell finally said.

"Sir Thurwell serves the crown and our family by maintaining Cordell, a small but very important holding on our eastern coast."

The king nodded his approval and moved along to the end of this line of noble guests. Conan then presented to him a woman of rare beauty. "Lady Chandra, Sire." In spite of the heavy roundness of her belly, Chandra curtsied gracefully and found the king's hand outstretched to aid her in rising. The warm beauty in the lady's eyes melted Richard's cold heart, and the king saw that Conan had done well for himself. Beside Chandra was a lad of nearly four years. "Master Hugh, Sire. My son," Conan said.

In the blue of the boy's eyes and the darkness of his hair, Richard could plainly see that he was Conan's child. But the king knew that Conan had only just buried his wife before joining the Crusade. There was a twinkle in Richard's eye when he turned to his host. He reasoned rumor, this once at least, was accurate. "You had more to return to than you knew," the king said.

"Yea, Sire," Conan said proudly. "Much more than I knew."

Richard looked at the boy again and he could see promise. He would be as strong and powerful as his father. For the first time since returning to England, the king felt some pride in his subjects. With only a few he would hold together his realm, if those few had the skill and honor of Sir Conan.

"Come into my hall, Sire, and let us make you welcome."

The king gave a sigh of genuine appreciation and offered Conan's wife his arm. She lightly laid her hand atop his. "If my eye does not deceive me, I may be in residence for another grand event," he said, looking down at her swollen middle.

"It is indeed possible, Sire," she replied quietly.

"Chandra?" he queried. "The name is neither French nor English."

"Nay, Sire," she answered.

"I have heard the name in my travels. Do you know what it means?"

"I know the meaning, Sire," she replied somewhat shyly.

"It fits you well," he said. "Your beauty does shine brighter than the stars." He stopped and looked down at her for a moment. "If your loyalty to your lord is as bright as your eyes, he is a lucky man."

Chandra looked at her husband and then returned her gaze to her king. "If my eyes are bright, Sire, 'tis for his loyalty to me."

Robyn Carr was born in 1951 in Saint Paul, Minnesota, and lives with her husband and two children in Sacramento, California. She is the author of *Chelynne*.